Jacky Boy

Jacky Boy

Ken McCoy

PIATKUS

Copyright © 2004 by Ken Myers

First published in Great Britain in 2004 by
Judy Piatkus (Publishers) Ltd of
5 Windmill Street, London W1T 2JA
email: info@piatkus.co.uk

The moral right of the author has been asserted

A catalogue record for this book is available from the British Library

ISBN 0 7499 0693 6

Set in Times by
Phoenix Photosetting, Chatham, Kent

Printed and bound in Great Britain by
Clowes Ltd, Beccles, Suffolk

With grateful thanks to my old Geordie pal, Arthur Rowell, a former mining engineer who, in return for the odd several pints, was able to give me excellent first hand information about life down the pits in the 1950s. I therefore forgive him for allowing his head to get in the way of my golf ball that time, thus denying me a crucial treble bogie at the twelfth.

TO JACK

Chapter One

'Araaagabone! . . . Any old raags?'

A rag-and-bone man's cart, drawn by a skeletal horse, clattered along the cobbled back street. The ragman, from deep within a decaying army greatcoat glared up at the sky for signs of rain. His cry troubled the air of that noiseless, January afternoon like the screech of a crow. On the cart behind him was a broken mangle, a large recumbent guard dog, oddments of scrap metal and a pile of old woollens – and he had left his waterproof sheet at home. The rag merchants wouldn't thank him for taking a load of soaked woollens in. He'd have to dry them out before they weighed them. The devil take that.

Jacky looked up to see Willie O'Keefe's greasy-capped head beyond the back-yard wall as the old Irishman sawed at the reins and cursed the horse when it didn't stop immediately. Willie swivelled a shifty eye in the boy's direction; his other eye was covered by a piratical black patch which he thought might earn him sympathy but which, in fact, earned him ridicule as he could never make up his mind which was his blind eye.

'Anythin' today, boy? Any ole stuff ye'll nivver need again. Clothes . . . suchlike stuff?'

The boy stared at him for a second; realising what the old rogue was after and wondering at the cheek of the man who should know not to bother people, today of all days. There was a wreath hanging from the door behind him which gave the game away. The ragman's eye settled on it and glinted, greedily. Where there was a wreath there was a profit.

'Who's popped their clogs?' Willie's voice had a Gaelic lilt; but it was reedy and high pitched, as unattractive as the man himself.

1

'My dad.'

The boy's response was barely loud enough for the ragman to hear. Willie turned down the nearside collar of his coat and revealed a long, red ear to which he cupped a gloved hand and asked, 'Who?'

Jacky looked away.

'I said, who's popped their clogs?'

'My dad!'

'Will ye not shout at me, so? I only asked!'

The ragman took his hand from his ear and shaded his unpatched eye with it. He peered through the window at the assembled mourners and decided today was not the best day for doing business at this house. The fingers had been cut from his gloves and he poked one of them into his nose as he called out to Jacky, 'Maybe next week, eh? I'll pop back next week if ye want ter get some stuff ready. Tell ye mammy – she'll be glad ter get shut. They always are – once all the weeping an' wailin's done. Give her Willie O'Keefe's sincere condolences. Don't forget. Good boy. God bless.'

Jacky shrugged. Willie shouted, 'Araagabone!' Then he clicked his derelict animal into motion and moved off. For the first time Jacky wondered what bones had to do with his trade. A ragman didn't collect bones, did he? Bones were to do with dead people. Like his dad. It was the second time his dad had been dead. He'd been blown out of a troopship just after the war started, before Jacky was born. They'd told his mam he was dead, but that was a clerical error. This time a Leeds tram had succeeded where one of Hitler's mines had failed. This time his dad was definitely dead. There wasn't a spark of life in any of the three pieces the tram had divided him into.

The burial itself had been a sparsely attended affair; just two friends, three neighbours, one of Bert's workmates, his sister from Pontefract and the vicar. Bert had a brother who had emigrated to New Zealand just after the war – he was the one who had sent the wreath that hung on the back door. A lot more people turned up at the house to drink the tea and bottled beer, and eat the ham and pickle sandwiches. They all arrived with sombre faces, nice things to say about a man they hardly knew, and healthy appetites.

Jacky was sitting on the back step clutching a football and wondering why the people inside the house sounded so normal.

Not much more than an hour ago those who had taken the trouble had been watching with funereal faces as his dad's coffin was lowered into an oblong hole in Brierly Street Cemetery. Some, most of all his mam, had even been crying. And now everything was normal. Why was that? A week ago his dad had been sitting on this very step with him, showing him how to put dubbin on his football to make it waterproof.

A man Jacky had never seen before came out of Charlie Robinson's house next door and smiled at him. Frank McGovern swung his long legs over the low wall that divided the two back yards and said, 'I reckon you're the one they call Jacky boy.'

The boy nodded.

'And are you okay?'

Another nod, this one not quite as truthful as the first nod. Jacky was far from okay but he was too polite to burden a stranger with his troubles, even one with such a friendly smile. He was a tall man, whose luminous blue eyes were accentuated by the blackened eyelashes that identified him as a miner who had only managed a cursory wash after coming off a shift. Had Jacky been a girl he might have been impressed by the man's good looks.

'I'm Frank. I'm a friend of Charlie's.'

'Pleased to meet you, sir.'

'Sir? Blimey! You make me feel old. Try calling me Frank. I reckon your bum'll freeze if you sit on that step for much longer.'

Jacky smiled at his genial new friend; his first smile that day. He got to his feet. The man was right – his bum *was* a bit cold.

'Charlie's inside if you want him.'

Frank looked through the window at the crush of people inside. 'It looks a bit throng in there,' he said. 'Besides, I'd sooner talk to you. I'm very pleased to meet you, Jacky Gaskell.' He was holding out his hand for Jacky to shake. 'Very pleased indeed as a matter of fact.'

The boy stepped forward, tucked the ball under his right arm, and held out his left hand because he wasn't used to shaking hands with people. Frank took the boy's hand in between both of his. Something comforting and strong transferred itself from those hands to Jacky, who didn't know this man, but knew he liked him.

'I suppose you feel a bit fed up,' said Frank. 'I know I felt fed up when my mam died. I never met your dad but I've heard he was

3

a good bloke. "Good bloke that Bert Gaskell" – I've heard that said many a time.'

Jacky nodded again, removed his hand from Frank's gentle grip and stuck it in his pocket. He still had his best clothes on with a black tie that his mam had borrowed from Mr Fenwick from next door but one. His older brother, Brian, had worn their dad's black tie and army medals. Ellie had worn her navy-blue gabardine coat and a black ribbon in her hair. They had each been given a rose to drop on to the coffin and a clean hanky. Jacky had mistakenly dropped both the rose and his hanky. No one said anything but it didn't mean that they wouldn't be thinking things. When everyone left his mam had stayed by the graveside and Jacky had turned back to join her but had been checked by Ellie who told him their mam needed a little time on her own. Jacky knew he should have known that and wished he didn't behave like such a kid at times like this. He was ten.

'Did you cry?' Frank asked.

Jacky pressed his lips together and frowned away the surfacing tears as he shook his head.

'Neither did I,' said Frank, 'not in the cemetery anyway. I didn't want people to think I was soft – and I was a lot older than you. If you fancy having a cry now, I'll hold your ball. It's a well-known fact that you can't cry properly when you're holding a football – unless you play in goal for Castlethorpe Town. Then you've got something to cry about.'

Jacky needed no further encouragement. He handed Frank the ball and allowed the tears to flow. Frank crouched beside him, allowing the boy to weep on his hard-muscled shoulder. They stayed like that for several minutes with Jacky sobbing away in the secure arms of a man whom he had only just met, but for some reason trusted almost as much as he'd trusted his dad. A woman wearing a black hat decorated with a bunch of fake grapes came out of Jacky's house and hurried to the lavatory in the yard. The man and the weeping boy were deaf to the distinct sound of the woman relieving herself of the several bottles of milk stout she'd just drunk, followed by a rustling of paper, then a loud flushing. The woman emerged, slightly embarrassed, as she assumed the sound she made must have been overheard. She would have been even more embarrassed had she known her hat was now askew and that her skirt was tucked into the back of her knickers. Her

curiosity overcame her embarrassment and she seemed about to
ask what was going on, but Frank gave her a look that said: Please
do not disturb. The woman meandered back into the house
without saying a word. Not to them, anyway.

Jacky eventually stood back and tried to blink away his tears.

'Here, use this.' Frank produced a large, very clean handkerchief. Almost as if he'd come prepared for such an eventuality.
Jacky wondered if Frank knew about him dropping his own hanky
on his dad's coffin. But it didn't matter if he did.

'Thanks . . . Frank.' He wiped his eyes and handed the handkerchief back.

'You might want to do a bit more crying later on,' said Frank,
'so I should keep it. It's a real good hanky, that.'

'I dropped my hanky on my dad's coffin. I didn't mean to.'

'You do all sorts of things you don't mean to at times like this.
Feeling a bit better?'

'Yes thanks.'

'Good lad . . . It does you good to have a good weep. How are
you doing at school?'

Jacky shrugged at this unexpected question. 'Okay,' he said, 'I
suppose.'

'Okay? Never mind okay – I heard you were top of the class.'

'Sometimes.'

Frank gave him one of those smiles that forces you to smile
back. 'You don't take after me then. I was nine years old before I
got a tick.'

Jacky wondered why he should take after this man, then he
realised it was just a joke. 'I take my scholarship next year,' he said.

'I bet you don't pass.'

'What?'

'I said, I bet you don't pass.' There was a broad, challenging
grin on Frank's face. Jacky took up the challenge.

'Well as a matter of fact I bet I do.'

'Oh yeah – how much?'

'Much as you like.'

Frank's smile was still intact as he studied the boy. There was a
hint of darkness beneath Jacky's cobalt-blue eyes and a smudge of
freckles high up on his winter pale cheeks. His ears stuck out
slightly and gave him an impish look; but he was a fine-looking
lad for all that. It was a cheerful face in mourning.

The man took a gold pocket watch from his waistcoat pocket and swung it on its chain in front of the boy's eyes. It glinted brightly, even on that grey day.

'If you pass,' he said, 'you get this gold watch.'

'Pull the other leg, it's got bells on.'

'I mean it. Solid gold.'

Jacky's eyes lit up for a second. Of course there was a catch. He could see it now. 'What if I don't pass and you win?'

Frank rubbed his chin. 'Good point. What's the best thing you've got?'

The boy needed no time to answer this. 'That,' he said, pointing at the football Frank was still holding. 'It's a proper match ball like they use at Elland Road.'

Frank weighed the ball in his hands as if assessing its value against that of his watch. He put it to his nose. 'Hmm . . . well dubbinned.'

'My dad did it last week – same day as he got run over. I haven't played with it since.'

'Fair enough.' Frank said it quickly before Jacky's tears returned. 'It's a bet. If you fail, I get your football. Do you like football?' He gave the boy his ball back.

Jacky tucked it under his arm and said, 'I play for the juniors at school. Right-half mostly.'

'Maybe we should go to a match. Who do you support? Castlethorpe Town or Leeds United?'

Jacky didn't actively support anyone. He thought about saying Castlethorpe Town, but Frank might ask a simple question about them that he couldn't answer, and he'd feel a fool. He'd been caught out telling a pointless lie once before. So he just shrugged.

'We could go to Elland Road,' suggested Frank. 'In fact we can go on Saturday if you like. I'm sure they're playing at home. Have you ever seen John Charles, the Welsh Wizard? Nineteen years old and the best player in the country. That's what they're saying and I reckon they're right as well. They say he's earning fifteen quid a week. Fifteen quid for kickin' a ball around a field. Not bad work if you can get it.'

'I've got a picture of him,' Jacky said. 'My dad said he'd take me to see him when it fitted in with his shifts.'

'Your dad was a good bloke. The best, so I've heard. I bet he wouldn't mind if I took you.'

'I'll have to ask my mam.'

Frank's face clouded for a second, then he smiled again, like the sun coming out, Jacky thought. 'I should wait 'til Friday before you ask her. Your mam's got enough on her plate at the moment.'

Jacky tilted his head to one side and looked up at Frank, with the football still tucked under his arm. 'Do you know my mam?'

'I used to know her. She's a good woman is your mam, a very good woman. You look after your mam.'

Jacky's mother appeared at the door, alerted by the woman who had visited the lavatory. Maureen Gaskell's black dress only served to accentuate her startling beauty. Jacky turned and wondered whether to ask about the football match right now. He didn't notice the awkward pause as the two adults looked at one another; each wondering what to say. Frank broke the silence.

'Hello, Maureen. I didn't come to the funeral because I didn't think it was my place to—'

'It's been a long time, Frank.'

'Too long,' he said, 'But what choice did I have?'

'You didn't have a choice.'

Frank filled the ensuing silence by placing a hand on Jacky's shoulder and looking the boy up and down until Jacky felt uncomfortable.

'He's a grand lad,' Frank said. 'Bright as well, so I'm told. He must get that from you.'

'Bert was a clever enough man,' said Maureen, defensively. 'Had it not been for the war he'd have got on, would Bert.'

'Oh, I think Jacky's a lot brighter than his dad ever was,' said Frank.

Jacky didn't know whether to take this as a compliment to him or an insult to his late dad. He looked at his mother for her reaction. There was something in her eyes as she looked at Frank. Had Jacky been older and wiser he might have known what it was.

'Charlie tells me you've got a girlfriend.'

Frank gave a wide grin. He had a broken tooth but the rest were white and even. 'You know me, Maureen. I've always got a girlfriend. Can't settle down, that's my trouble.'

'Maybe you should look for one who hasn't got a husband.'

'Hmmm – I wonder where you got that from?'

'Mam,' asked Jacky. 'Frank says I can go to Elland Road with him on Saturday.'

'And I say you can't.' His mother gave the question no consideration at all. She didn't even take her eyes off Frank.

'But Mam, John Charles is playing. He's the best pla—'

'Jacky!' The composure his mother had held intact all day was cracking. She looked down at her son with narrowed, disapproving eyes and a slight shake of her head. 'We've just buried your dad and all you can talk about is football.'

'Sorry, Maureen,' Frank apologised. 'It was my fault.' He ruffled Jacky's hair. 'Maybe some other time, eh kid?' He looked up at the boy's mother. 'Trust me to put my big foot in it, on a day like today. I won't trouble you or the boy, Maureen – not if you don't want me to.' He added the last part with his eyes fixed on hers. She held his gaze for a second then looked at her son.

'I think you'd better come in, Jacky boy,' she said.

'Okay, Mam.'

'See you, Jacky boy,' smiled Frank.

'See you, Frank.'

Meeting this man had taken some of the gloom out of Jacky's day. It was only a brief meeting and, although he would never see Frank McGovern again, a bond had been formed that would stay with Jacky for the rest of his life.

Chapter Two

Friday, 16 February 1951

The cold night air amplified the thump of leather against brick and boot that echoed around Barr Road school playground. It was four days since Bert Gaskell's funeral and the events of that night would shape Jacky's future; even though he wasn't there.

A sliver of moon made an occasional appearance from behind slow clouds and added what illumination it could to the boys' game, which was mainly lit by a street gas lamp poking its flickering light above an adjacent wall. The boys were making too much noise to hear the man's whimpers of grief and horror and self pity. They probably wouldn't have been interested anyway.

They were kicking the ball against a wall. Both had short trousers, chapped legs and wellington boots; not the ideal footwear for such a game, but they made do. They shouldn't have been there but no one ever said anything to them; neither of them even went to the school. They went to the Catholic school almost a mile away. In a garden at the other side of the wall the man was pacing up and down with a look of shock etched on his face and a bloodied jackknife in his hand. The boys had runny noses, head colds and balaclavas; that, plus the noise they were making meant they didn't hear him talking to himself, 'It wasn't my fault. How can it be my fault? It was all his fault. He caused it. Oh God! I'm going to be hanged. Please don't let them hang me.'

The boys continued with their game, making more noise than ever as they began to play 'Shots In'.

The man moaned, pitifully: 'It was him. He's the one who should be hung . . . not me, not me.'

He looked down at the knife and recoiled with almost comical horror as though he'd never seen it before. Then he held it as far away from him as possible, not wanting to be anywhere near it. He turned his face away so he couldn't see it, drew his arm back like a discus thrower and, with a tormented howl that caused the boys to pause in their game, he hurled it high into the air, over the school wall.

As the knife disappeared into the night sky it seemed to relieve him of the appalling reality of the past few minutes. But he had also experienced something else, with an intensity that had shuddered through his slight body and left him breathless with shock and fear and ecstasy.

He turned and half walked, half stumbled back into his house; still talking to himself, but more rationally now. Shock had numbed the unacceptable part of his memory and left him with half a story, the half that suited him. He picked up the phone but had a problem inserting his trembling index finger into number nine on the dial.

The operator was saying 'Emergency, which service, please?' as he was shouting, 'There's been a murder!'

He gave her his address and put the phone down. Now he needed to think quickly. The police would blame him because he was covered in her blood but he was very much the injured party in all this; you'd have to be blind, deaf, dumb and stupid not to see that. It would be wrong to put the blame on him. He must also think clearly, find a story to fit the situation. Tears froze on his cheeks. Chilled rationality came to his aid. His eyes darted around in their sockets like well-greased ball bearings and his mouth edged into a thin smile as the story began to take shape. He kept nodding and grunting his approval of his own ideas as each phase of his plan slipped into place.

'That's right,' he babbled. 'Of course. That's exactly what happened. I wouldn't be here, would I? I wasn't the one who ran away. That proves it.'

Had he been *completely* rational he would have known that throwing the knife over the wall was a silly thing to have done. But shock is a funny thing.

Chapter Three

September 1951
According to the clock on the prison tower it was a quarter to nine when the sun came out from behind a cloud and shone down into the bleak cell, bathing the kneeling man in a shaft of dusty light. Its sudden warmth sent a shiver up the man's spine as though alerting him to some divine visitation. He turned his head and shouted towards heaven which lay somewhere beyond the barred window.

'Okay, God, you've got my full attention. What is it you want of me? You *know* the truth. I don't need to be telling this bloody priest all this.'

The priest continued murmuring Latin words of absolution; his hand rested on the condemned man's head. The morning sun drifted behind an endless-looking cloud taking its light and warmth with it and leaving the cell as grey and soulless as before, its occupant seemingly deserted by his Maker. The man got to his feet and walked over to the window, then he grasped the bars and pulled himself up on to his tiptoes. And called out, 'You know the bloody truth!'

A flurry of rain sent Jacky hurrying under the shelter of the chip shop doorway. He had his new trousers on and his mam would go mad if he got them wet and muddy like the pair he'd gone home in last night.

'You'll have to go to school in your best pair tomorrow, Jacky boy, and woe betide you if you get so much as a mark on them.'

Whatever woe betided Jacky it didn't come from his mother. There were others who gave him plenty of woe; Brian, his older

11

brother for one. But all older brothers were as bad, despite all this nonsense about brotherly love. Fozzie Symonite was striding up the other side of the street, oblivious to the rain. He was no one's older brother but he acted like one. Worse even.

Fozzie jeered at him. 'Hey up, Jug ears!'

Jacky was a bit self conscious about his ears, so he countered with 'Hey up, Squinty.'

Fozzie had a cast in one eye which didn't help his looks at all, and the fat boy's looks needed all the help they could get.

'I didn't think yer'd be goin' ter school today of all days,' Fozzie said, yobbishly, strolling over to Jacky.

'Why not?'

'I thought yer'd be off ter see yer old man strung up.'

'You wanna watch what you're sayin' about me dad.' Jacky was annoyed now.

'Why, what will yer do?'

'I'm not scared of you. You shouldn't talk about people's dads when they're dead.'

'Not yet he's not.' The fat boy pressed his fat face right into Jacky's. There was a mole just above his upper lip as big as a shirt button. 'Not for another ten minutes. That bloke what got sliced by that tram weren't yer real dad. They're hangin' yer real dad in about ten minutes. In ten minutes he'll be as dead as a nit, swingin' about like a leg o' lamb. Dint yer know?' Fozzie seemed delighted to be the teller of this macabre news.

'You're bloody barmy, you!' Jacky tried to push past him but Fozzie held on to his coat. 'Frank McGovern's not my dad. Anyroad, he didn't do it.'

'He'll be dancin' on th' end of a rope by t' time yer get ter school,' Fozzie was laughing, cruelly. 'Ha, ha. Swingin' about like a leg o' lamb. A great big leg o' lamb in prison clothes.'

Jacky had no words to counter this. He didn't understand the implication of Frank being his dad, and he put it down to Fozzie being as thick as two short planks. He couldn't make head nor tale of how Frank McGovern had come to be in so much trouble, and he certainly couldn't come to terms with the fact that Frank was to be hanged in a few minutes. His mother had never spoken to him about it except to warn him not to tell anyone that Charlie was a friend of Frank's.

'If that gets out there'll be reporters and God knows who around,' she had told him. 'Charlie can do without that.'

12

Charlie and his mother had been to court together every day, except the day of the sentencing when Maureen had gone on her own. She had come home that day and cried. Jacky had cried as well when she told him what had happened, although he wasn't sure why he should be crying for a man he'd met so briefly.

Fozzie was a good four inches taller, so when Jacky head-butted him his forehead burst Fozzie's nose and sent the bigger boy to his knees squealing with pain. Jacky ran away, not at all sure what it had all been about. He wasn't a violent boy but he had a low boiling point when it came to people insulting his family. And he knew how to fight.

Fozzie was a gormless lad who rarely said anything that made sense but there was no excuse for him to insult Jacky's dad . . . and his pal Frank. Jacky would have to stay clear of a Fozzie for a while in case the big dope decided to exact revenge.

The sky cleared and the sun lit up the damp, cobbled street. Women came out to see what damage the rain had done to their washing and discussed whether it was worth leaving it out on the lines.

'I wish it'd mek up its flamin' mind,' one grumbled, looking up at the undecided clouds.

'I think I'll get t' fire stoked up an' finish mine on t' clothes airer,' decided another, lowering the clothes prop and unpegging an assortment of shirts, sheets and underwear. 'Might as well get used to it. It's gettin' a bit back-endish ter be hangin' stuff out.' She wore a hairnet full of curlers and spoke without taking her cigarette from her mouth.

Jacky dodged under the clothes lines and spotted old Willie O'Keefe as he rounded a corner and clicked his scraggy animal alongside the boy, who suspected him to be the one who had stolen his mam's best tin bath from off the yard wall. The ragman wasn't beyond a bit of opportunistic thieving. It had gone missing just after his mother had given Willie an earful when he came round asking if she might have any man's clothes or suchlike that she might be interested in getting shut of.

'And can I take this opportunity to offer ye my condolences, missis?'

'You can take yourself out of my sight, you bloody grave robber!'

As the horse and cart clattered slowly past, Jacky realised he was on the same side as old Willie's black patch. He strode alongside to see what was on the cart.

Some rags stirred and the erstwhile recumbent guard dog poked its unruly head out to watch the boy pick up a heavy, flat iron. Jacky knew of the dog's reputation. Two pairs of eyes met, then the animal yawned, hugely, before disappearing beneath the comfort of the rags. Jacky grinned. He reckoned his mam would have a use for the iron. It might even cheer her up. She needed a bit of cheering up did his mam, especially today. Jacky's insides needed cheering up as well. He felt a heavy weight in the pit of his stomach; heavier then the flat iron he was now carrying.

Down the street, beyond the flapping washing he could just make out Fozzie going the other way with his hands to his face; he wouldn't be bothering Jacky today, thank heavens – and when you're ten tomorrow's a long way off. You don't have much foresight at that age either, or Jacky would have stolen something a bit lighter. He hid the iron behind the big bin in Milligans' coal yard, hoping it would still be there when he returned. As he approached the school a bell began to ring from the playground. He looked up at the clock on top of Backhouse Mill. Five to nine. Frank had just five minutes left to live and Jacky had just enough time to get a sherbet dip from Mrs Forbuoys' sweet shop. That might help cheer him up; a man's execution was a lot for a boy of ten to cope with.

Maureen Gaskell looked out through the front-room window with folded arms and moist eyes. She lit an unaccustomed cigarette and coughed out the smoke. It was a while since she'd had one but she felt the need right now. She believed him when he told her he was innocent. Frank McGovern was capable of many things but not murder. Victor Mumford, the murdered woman's husband had burst in and found them in bed. It was he who stabbed her, not Frank, who had foolishly run away. It wasn't cowardice that sent Frank fleeing, but horror. Horror that his promiscuous ways had led to a death. When Maureen asked him if he had loved the woman Frank looked into her eyes and said, with deep sincerity, 'Maureen, it's just not possible for me to love two women at the same time – not properly.'

He told her that although he hadn't actually *loved* the woman he liked her a lot and being the indirect cause of her death saddened him deeply.

Mumford had told the police and the court that Frank had attacked him and his wife as they were making love.

Victor Mumford was an insurance agent, a freemason and a pillar of the community with no criminal record. Frank was a miner with a chequered criminal history who had once spent three months in jail for assaulting the landlord of the Blissett Arms. Most people, including the police, knew the publican had deserved all he got but it didn't stop them locking Frank up. At the murder trial other husbands were called by the prosecution to testify how Frank had seduced their wives. Maureen's husband might well have been one of them. Had he lived.

Jacky was conceived while Bert Gaskell was in France with the British Expeditionary Force. He had survived Dunkirk to find his wife had become pregnant but he had forgiven her for the sake of the other two children; besides, she was too good a woman for him to let go just like that. He never asked who the father was and Maureen never told him, except to say it was a brief affair caused by grief, not love, and that Bert didn't know the man and was most unlikely ever to bump into him, even in the street.

'Does he know he made you pregnant?' Bert had asked.

'No,' Maureen lied. 'And he never will.'

Blotting out Frank's very existence simplified things; he had reluctantly agreed not to bother her again. Maureen always felt she could have tamed him if she'd had the opportunity. On the night of Bert's funeral she'd felt guilty about having such a burning desire for Frank. Imagining him lying with her in bed, making love to her. But he was involved with someone else. She knew it would only be a question of time before his latest affair came to an end; he always chose married women. Maureen suspected it was because he was afraid of commitment – but he would have to commit himself to her or she wouldn't have him. Then this happened.

She remembered his eyes when she visited him in prison. All the devil and spark had gone from them. He had taken her hand in his and told her, 'I didn't do it.'

'I know,' she said.

Every day in court she had seen the evidence piling up against him. His previous conviction for violence; his admitted affair with Mrs Mumford; her blood all over him, and paradoxically, the fact that the murder weapon was missing and only he could have got

15

rid of it so successfully. Mumford hadn't left his own garden. Footprints in the frost proved that.

Maureen had been there when the verdict was announced and she had seen the judge put on his black cap and sentence Frank to death. Although it was expected, the words had seared through her heart like a hot dagger and she knew, there and then, that he was the only man she had ever truly loved. She hadn't felt like this when the news of Bert's death came through. That day she'd felt shock and sadness and a sense of great loss. This time the pain was physical. It took her breath away. She had shouted 'No!' and fainted. By the time she came round Frank had been taken away. So she wasn't there to meet his eyes as he turned to look at her and she didn't hear him scream at the jury, 'I didn't kill her. You're hanging the wrong man!'

Months later, in prison, Maureen squeezed his hand and said, 'Mumford's got away with it, hasn't he?'

Frank had lost his appeal and the Home Secretary hadn't seen fit to commute his sentence to one of life imprisonment. He had a week and a day to live. Up until then he hadn't spoken to Maureen about the details of the murder except to assure her that he didn't do it. He gave a resigned nod.

'Looks like it. Maybe he thinks it's poetic justice. He caught us . . . I was in bed with her . . . sorry.' He added the last word when he thought he saw reproof in Maureen's eyes.

'I have no hold on you, Frank,' she pointed out. 'Who you go to bed with is your business.'

'I wish it had been you.'

'So do I.'

'Really?'

'Of course, *really*,' said Maureen. 'You wouldn't have been in all this trouble if it had been me.'

'I know my timing's not what it should be,' Frank said, regretfully, 'but I always loved you. Never loved anyone else.'

'I bet you say that to all the girls.'

He summoned up a grin. 'Most of them,' he said. 'But I never really meant it. Not like I mean it with you.'

Maureen believed him because Frank was a very believable man. It was a pity the jury didn't believe him, but they had been all male and therefore not susceptible to his ways.

'I've always loved you, Frank,' she told him.

They kissed as best they could under the eyes of the guards and Frank said, 'It's better you don't come any more.'

'You know the truth! You know the truth! You know the bloody truth!' Frank kept shouting through the window until he broke down in tears, let go of the bars and sank to the floor. The priest didn't have the words to cope with this. The condemned man's sobbing gradually subsided. He looked up into the priest's eyes; tears now streaked his prison-grey face.

'I was never very devout, Father. I admit that – but once a Catholic, always a Catholic – that's what they say, isn't it?'

'That's what they say, my son.'

'I never stopped believing.'

'That's good, Frank. Keep the faith to the very end and God will grant you eternal life.'

'You never stop believing in the sacraments, Father, no matter how much of a villain you are.'

'The Blessed Sacraments are the cornerstones of the faith, my son.'

'So, if I'd committed murder I'd be telling you now, wouldn't I?'

The priest, who could see this coming, remained silent. Noncommittal.

'Wouldn't I?' repeated Frank. His tone demanded an answer. The priest conceded the point by nodding, but this wasn't enough. Frank wanted to hear the words.

'WOULDN'T I?' He shouted at the priest, angrily.

'Not to confess a mortal sin at this stage would be the ultimate foolishness,' admitted the priest. 'A mortal sin causes spiritual death.'

'Do you think I'm a foolish man, Father?' Frank's burst of anger had drained him. He slumped against the wall and buried his head in his hands.

'No, Frank, I do not think you're a foolish man.'

'Father, I killed no one.'

His voice was strained and weak but there was deep sincerity there. It wasn't the first time the priest had heard a condemned man's confession. The others had all admitted their guilt and begged forgiveness during their final moments, even the ones who had hitherto protested their innocence. Frank had confessed many

17

sins of the flesh and an interesting assortment of other, more venial sins; but he hadn't confessed to murdering anyone.

'We live in an unjust world but there will be a place waiting for you in Heaven, my son,' said the priest, helplessly. It was all he could offer but it didn't seem enough. 'I'd like you to make a good act of contrition.'

Frank McGovern clasped his hands together and began to pray; then he stopped and asked, 'Will you tell my son I'm innocent, Father?'

'I didn't realise you had a son.'

Frank shook his head. 'He doesn't know he's got a father – not one that's alive, anyway. But he'll find out, and when he does I want him to be told the truth.'

'I cannot betray the secrets of the confessional.'

'I'm not asking you to, Father. I just want you to tell him that you heard my last confession and in your opinion I'm innocent. You do know I'm innocent, don't you?'

The priest looked into Frank's eyes. He saw beyond them, right down into the bareness of the condemned man's soul; and he saw the truth staring back at him as he'd never seen it before. The priest's heart sank and he felt dismal and helpless. All these years in the service of a God who hadn't given him the wherewithal to prevent the same miscarriage of justice that had once befallen His own son. 'I truly believe you to be innocent,' he said.

Frank let out a long sigh as if expelling all his anguish in one long breath. 'Thank you, Father. So, will you help me? Will you stop them from hanging me?'

In a house behind Barr Road School, a whey-faced man stared through his front-room window. His body twitched and his soulless eyes couldn't keep still, as if he was ready for someone to pounce on him but he didn't know where from. It would soon be over and then he would be okay.

Victor Mumford had got away with killing his wife and was now wreaking terrible vengeance on her lover. He knew it should have been him dropping through that trapdoor to hell and the thought sent a shudder of terror through him. Supposing they somehow discovered the truth? What then? Could they hang two men for the same crime?

Mumford tried to shake such thoughts from his mind. He would be half an hour late for work that day but he wanted to be on his own when the time came in case his thoughts somehow registered on his face and someone saw the truth of what had happened.

'Don't be so bloody stupid, Victor!'

He chastised himself and put on his coat. This was the end of it. Only he knew the truth and he would now put it right out of his mind. His wife had been well insured, his mortgage was now paid off, he had plenty of cash in the bank, and he was only thirty-six. But the uneasiness persisted. In a few minutes he would be responsible for two deaths.

'Victor, you've got everything to live for. Oh, bloody hell, stop it!'

Then the memory of the murder flashed across his mind and he didn't want it to go away. It was just too good a memory.

The priest shifted his gaze from the pleading in Frank's eyes. 'I'm truly, truly sorry, my son. But I can't help you.'

The glimmer of hope faded from Frank's face. He nodded, slowly, as he struggled to regain his dignity – which was all he had left. There was an awkward silence, broken eventually by Frank.

'Will you tell my boy you think I'm innocent?'

'I will.'

There was gratitude in the condemned man's eyes now; gratitude the priest felt he hadn't earned.

'I left him all my stuff, for what it's worth. There's a watch I said he could have if he passed his exam. He was going to give me his football if he failed. But there was never any chance of me ever getting that ball. He's such a bright lad, Father. Such a lovely kid. He doesn't deserve having a dad who was hanged. That's no life for a kid. You will tell him I didn't do it, won't you?'

'I will, Frank.'

'My lawyer will tell you who he is . . . he's done bugger all else to earn his money.'

The priest nodded, then asked, tentatively, 'Do you want me to be with you . . .?'

His voice tailed off but Frank knew what he meant. It was the priest's job to be there at the end if the condemned person requested it. Most did. In this case, more than any other, the priest was dreading it.

'No, thank you, Father. It's not a thing I'd wish on to any of my friends.'

19

The priest barely knew him but he felt an unaccountable flush of pride to be counted among this man's friends and saw no reason not to tell him so. 'I'm proud you regard me as a friend, Frank. I will say a Mass for you, that you will be granted a plenary indulgence.'

'Thank you, Father.'

'You know, it's rarely a man gets to be granted complete absolution so near to the end.'

'Are you telling me I should think myself lucky, Father?'

The priest almost smiled at the gallows humour in Frank's voice. 'I'm just saying I hope God gives me the same opportunity for eternal salvation that He's giving you.'

'You *will* tell my son that you think I'm innocent.'

'I'll tell him I'm *sure* you're innocent.'

'Thank you, Father.'

The memory persisted in Victor's mind and he couldn't block it out. He had suspected his wife was having it off with Frank McGovern, so that night, instead of attending a Lodge meeting, he'd walked the streets to give her lover-boy enough time to make himself at home, then he'd sneaked in through the kitchen door with the intention of catching them in the act. He had felt a certain sexual frisson at the thought. Seeing his wife *doing it* with another man. The knife wasn't planned. It was a jackknife he'd had for years and had left on the kitchen table. He opened the blade, thinking perhaps he might scare them with it.

As he stood outside the bedroom door he could hear them. She had never moaned like that when they'd done it. Her lovemaking with him had always been more that of a dutiful wife than a passionate lover. His hand gripped the knife tighter as he slowly turned the handle on the door and, very slowly, pushed it open.

They were naked on the bed, not even under the sheets. She was gasping with pleasure and thrusting herself up at her lover. Neither of them saw him at first; they were far too pre-occupied. Then his wife saw him for the last few moments of her life as he suddenly hurled himself at her and stabbed her, repeatedly through her breasts, screaming at her, 'You dirty bloody bitch!'

Eventually, Frank pulled him away from her and knocked him to the floor where Victor lay bleeding at the mouth. When he staggered to his feet and looked around Frank had gone. His wife's blood-soaked body lay on the bed, the dripping knife was still in his hand and he was a murderer!

Bile surged into his throat as he looked at the gore before his eyes. But beneath the bile and horror there was something else. Something stimulating.

In a trance he had stumbled out of the house. He only had a vague memory of throwing the knife away. It was stupid act that could have got him hanged, but the knife was never found. Why? He could only guess.

During the five minutes it took the police to get to his house Victor had cooked up his story. It was too simple to be a lie. His confusion and obvious shock and tears all reinforced his story. He had found out about his wife's affair with Frank McGovern and confronted her. They had decided to give their marriage another go. She had told Frank she didn't want to see him any more and he had refused to accept it. Frank had come into the house while Victor and his wife were making love and Frank had stabbed her in a rage before running away. Victor was covered in blood because he was right next to his wife as she was being stabbed and he could do nothing about it. He should have able to protect her, he wept, but McGovern was just too strong.

A constable had been left to look after him while the other police seached the house and the general area. Looking for Frank and the murder weapon.

'You did all you could, sir,' the constable had said. 'It's lucky he didn't go for you.'

'I thought he was going to. He hit me and I thought I was going to die.'

The policeman took his helmet off to reveal a badly scarred forehead. Mumford recoiled slightly at the sight of it. The policeman saw this and replaced his helmet, thinking that the man had probably seen enough physical disfigurement for one day, although this didn't endear him to Mumford. There was some- thing not normal about the way he was reacting. More *self*-pity than pity for his murdered wife.

'We'll get a doctor to check you over, sir.'

'Don't worry about me. Get him to check my wife. Are you sure she's . . .?'

'I'm afraid so, sir.' The policeman felt like adding: *Do you really care?*

Two women had seen Frank running away. One said she thought he had a knife in his hand, the other told of the frenzied look on his face. A look that had sent a shiver down her spine.

Then Victor had to endure the agony of the police searching for the knife. They searched between his house and Frank's. Every street, garden, yard, back alley, outside lavatory, dustbin, roof, drain, parked vehicle; but the knife was not to be found. They searched the school playground at the back of his house but didn't spend too long there as Frank hadn't gone that way. Victor was sure they'd find it, covered with his fingerprints and none of Frank's. How would his story stand up in the face of such evidence? It wouldn't, simple as that.

He broke down at this stage and a doctor had to give him sedation. But the knife was never found. After the police finished he went out to the school yard look for it himself, but it wasn't there. Then he remembered the children's voices coming from over the wall. So that was it. One of the little buggers had stolen his knife; hopefully wiped the blood off without realising what it was in the dark. Yeah, kids were like that; thieving little buggers who never thought of others. Good job he and his wife hadn't had kids. He wouldn't want a thieving little bugger who never thought of others. The knife would never turn up now and even if it did his fingerprints would be long gone.

But it would be nice to know for sure.

The clock on Maureen's mantelpiece said one minute to nine and she allowed the tears to flow. It would soon be over. Thank God the kids weren't there. The tears would have been difficult to explain. But there'd be explanations to make, she knew that for certain. She knew about the newspaper reporter who had been sniffing round, asking questions. Neighbours had been bribed into voicing suspicions that had hitherto been old news and no longer worth gossiping about. But many ten shilling notes loosened many tongues and the reporter had a good story. A story worth selling to the nationals.

The murderer Frank McGovern had a bastard son.

Jacky ran through the gates as a teacher on playground duty blew her nose and herded the stragglers through the school door. 'Hurry up, Gaskell,' she called out, irritably, coughing into her handkerchief. 'Last again. You'll be late for your own funeral, you. Mine's not far off, the way I feel.'

'Hey, miss. It's not the cough that carries you off, it's the coffin they carry you off in.'

There was an engaging insolence about Jacky that left her undecided whether to ruffle his hair or give him a clip round the ears. She settled for a pretend kick at his backside. He was laughing but there were tears in his eyes which she couldn't understand. Maybe the boy had a cold too.

Footsteps sounded outside. A key rattled in the lock. Frank knew there were only fourteen paces from the door to the rope and that there would be no time wasted. Once out of the door, in less than one hundred seconds he would be dead. He got to his feet, squeezed his eyes tightly shut and felt hands forcing his arms behind his back and binding his wrists together. People were talking but he couldn't hear; he was too busy emptying his mind. They were making him walk now.

Starting at one hundred, he began to count backwards.

As he walked his lips moved silently, as if in prayer.

He only got down to seventeen.

Chapter Four

The man in the trilby gave Maureen's door the cheerful knock of a milkman collecting his weekly money. He had a Tommy Trinder chin, an automatic smile and obvious false teeth. Everyone opened the door to his milkman's knock. Maureen instantly saw him for what he was. There was a camera in its case hanging around his neck. All he lacked was a ticket saying 'Press' sticking out of his hatband.

'Yes?'

He spoke through his smile. 'Rodney Tripp – West Riding Press Agency.' There was no such agency but he had a business card to prove there was. He showed it to her then put it back in his pocket. 'I was wondering if you would care to make a statement about your youngest son's father being hanged this morning?'

'My husband was killed last year.'

'Please accept my sincere condolences, Mrs Gaskell. But I understand he wasn't the boy's father.'

'Yes, he was.'

She slammed the door in Tripp's face. He switched his smile off rather than waste it on a closed door, then he raised his hand to knock again; persistency always bears fruit in the end. A loud slamming of a bolt from inside followed by an unladylike curse had him changing his mind. He looked at his watch – ten to four – and thought there were more ways than one to skin a cat. Rodney Tripp was more of a photographer than a reporter but he was loathe to share this story with anyone else. A nice exclusive like this would earn him the down-payment on the Ford Popular he had his eye on. His wife would tidy up his copy if necessary. You don't have to be Shakespeare to write up a good story like this.

24

Maureen watched through the net curtains as he walked out of her gate and she knew this was only the beginning. Why the hell hadn't she told Jacky the truth before now? Between Bert dying and Frank being hanged it had been her duty to put the boy straight before someone else did.

Ten years ago there had been local suspicions but no one voiced them to her. Few of her female neighbours would give her the time of day. Mavis Fenwick was okay. She often came in for a cup of tea and a natter about her worthless husband, who had been marked down as 'unfit for combat' during the War and was unfit for anything else according to her; and Mrs White from across the road whose husband had been killed in Germany during the last week of the War – so Maureen was no threat to *her* family life.

The men liked her just a bit too much. She didn't do anything to encourage them, apart from setting their pulses racing every time she walked down the street. Women like Maureen Gaskell were a rarity, especially in Yorkshire mining towns. She was a tall, physical woman with a raw, natural beauty to her. She wore little make-up and had no need of permed hair. Hers was dark and glossy and hung over her shoulders like wild mink. Jacky, on the other hand was fair. Just like Frank McGovern.

As a girl she'd been a local swimming champion with a potential that required more dedication than she was prepared to give. It would have meant endless training and she had a life to get on with. Maureen sat down at the table and wondered what life was that? How her life had come to this. Her girlhood dreams and ambitions had been forestalled at every turn. All her misfortune led back to one name. Morgan Pettifer. What sort of a life would she have had if she hadn't met him? It would be better than this, surely. A rented pit-house with no inside toilet; and since the tin bath had been stolen from the yard wall they'd had to shower at the public swimming baths. She could have bought another tin bath, but it was all so awkward, what with her family growing up so quickly. Still, she was on the council house waiting list and it shouldn't be long now.

Rodney Tripp, smile at the ready, was standing at the end of the street as Jacky came home from school. Jacky smiled back at him and said, 'Hello, mister.'

'Are you Jacky Gaskell?'

Jacky's eyes went from side to side, suspiciously. What was this about? He was carrying the flat iron he'd just retrieved from Milligan's yard. Could this be it? Had old Willie somehow spotted him that morning and reported him to the police? Was this man a detective? Jacky's imagination searched for innocent reasons why he should be in possession of a stolen flat iron. In the meantime he settled for 'I might be.'

'It's okay, lad. I just wondered if I could take your picture.' The man was taking a camera from the case hanging around his neck.

'Why?'

'Why? Because you're a likely looking lad and I'm a reporter who's doing a story about kids. I'll give you half a crown and you'll get your picture in the paper. Now, I can't say fairer than that, can I?'

'What paper?' Jacky asked, excited now. Fame and half a crown were not things to be sneezed at.

Whatever paper offers me the most money, thought Rodney. He picked a name at random. 'Daily er, Herald. Just stand where you are, I want to get your street in the background.'

'What, *this* street?'

Jacky turned round and wondered what was so special about Gaythorne Street. It was long and repetitious. Forty-eight grimy, brick, terraced houses, twenty-five one side, twenty-three and Barraclough's chip shop on the other; each house had a front garden not much bigger than a window box. The houses were divided at intervals by ginnels which gave access to the back streets where the toilets and coal sheds were. Coal was something no one went short of. The street climbed upwards towards the pit, the top end being some twenty feet higher than the end where Jacky now stood. In the distance the pithills and winding wheels of Castlethorpe Colliery stood in grim silhouette against the pale sky line, and below flapped lines of washing, strung across the street in a dozen or more rows, ascending the cobbled hill and billowing outwards like the sails of a great ship o' the line – or so Jacky had often imagined. On washing day he would narrow his eyes and conjure up an image of a great galleon bearing down upon him, firing broadsides at the lines of dirty Frenchies on either side, especially Mr Higgins at number thirty-seven, who had confiscated Jacky's football when it went through his window. Old man Higgins could well have been French, Jacky thought. With his black beret, impenetrable Geordie accent (that might

26

well have been French) and squeaky bike that always had a shopping bag dangling from its handlebars containing, Jacky assumed, onions.

Maureen had retrieved the ball at no little expense and was currently deducting the price of the window from Jacky's pocket money. The only other sign of life was the spark from a knife sharpener's wheel as he ground the blade on someone's best kitchen knife; that and a shameless tomcat in the middle of the pavement, scrutinising its reproductive organs. None of the other kids were home from school yet. Soon it would be a hive of activity when the street games started up. Jacky turned back to the reporter. Half a crown, eh? He'd never had half a crown before. He put the iron on the ground and gave the reporter his broadest smile.

'No, don't smile. Look as if you've lost a shilling and found a penny.'

Jacky obliged and the camera clicked. His sister, Ellie, rounded the corner and weighed up the situation in an instant.

'Jacky, what are you doing?'

'This bloke said he'll give me half a dollar if he can take me photo,' Jacky grinned. 'That's nearly three weeks' pocket money. It'll pay off old Higgins's window.'

Ellie grabbed him by his arm and hurried him down the street. 'Don't you know what he is?' she hissed into her brother's ear.

'He's a reporter,' Jacky protested. 'Leave off! I haven't got me half crown yet.' He tried to escape her clutches but she held on to him even firmer. By the time he broke free Rodney Tripp had gone, his valuable photograph safely locked in the camera and half a crown saved. Jacky ran to the end of the street just as the reporter was mounting his bicycle.

'Hey, Mister!'

But Rodney Tripp ignored him and cycled away at a speed which indicated that Jacky could whistle for his money. The boy turned, picked up the iron and walked back to where his sister was standing. He was angry with her.

'What did you do that for?'

'You'll find out soon enough. Where'd you get that iron?'

'Found it.'

'Pinched it, more like.'

The rumour had reached her school that morning. She'd been denying it all day with diminishing conviction. Ellie was fourteen

27

and at an age when the news of her mother having once had an affair both disgusted and thrilled her. Frank McGovern's picture had been in the papers and all the girls at school agreed that for a murderer he was a very handsome man. Ellie scrutinised her brother's features, looking for some similarity. Her brother might scrub up to look almost human but she couldn't see any of the handsome murderer scowling back at her. Just a blue-eyed, cheeky-faced kid with sticky out ears.

'What're you lookin' at me like that for?'

'Nothing. We'd best go in. I think Mam might have something to tell us.'

Maureen wasn't ready for such a confrontation. To be faced by two of the three people she loved most in the world and to have to tell them the truth. To tell them she'd been a wicked woman and gone to bed with someone who wasn't their dad. At the time it hadn't seemed wicked to her – at the time she'd thought she was a widow. Frank had excited her more than any man she'd known and now, more than ever, she regretted doing the noble thing – giving him up for the sake of the family. He would still be alive and she would have a man who fulfilled her. She could see in Ellie's eyes that her daughter knew the truth. Jacky looked more annoyed than disgusted. Maureen took a deep breath.

Mostly she ducked her parental responsibilities. Her idea of bringing up kids was to smother them with love and let providence do the rest. After Bert died it was usually Ellie who took care of things. Brian wasn't interested and Jacky more of a liability than a help. So Ellie did the cooking and cleaning with minimal help from the others.

Maureen's ambition had been to become a fashion designer but her hopes had been dashed by a certain student at Leeds College of Art. Since Bert's death she had been supplementing her meagre widow's pension by earning a living as an outworker for Lipscombe and Lile – a menswear tailoring firm, the major employer of Castlethorpe women. Every Friday someone would call round from the factory with the the pre-cut cloth, ready for Maureen to turn into coats, waistcoats and trousers. She was good and fast and earned enough to keep the wolf from the door.

'Eleanor . . . Jacky.' Her eyes went from daughter to son and back again. 'You'd better tell me what you know.'

28

'I don't think Jacky knows anything,' said Ellie. 'I just saw a reporter taking a photo of him in the street.'

'He were gonna give me half a crown,' said Jacky. He jabbed an elbow into Ellie's side. 'Cos of her I ended up with nowt.' He put the heavy iron on the dining table. 'I found this,' he said.

'Thank you, Jacky.'

'I think he might have pinched it, Mam,' Ellie warned.

Maureen ruffled Jacky's hair and sat on the arm of the settee so her eyes were at his level. 'Jacky boy,' she said, gravely. 'You're my son. Always will be and I'll always love you.'

Jacky put his arms around her. He was scared, but didn't know why. She hugged him, then pushed him away so she could hold him at arms length and look into those luminous blue eyes that reminded her so much of Frank.

'Frank McGovern was hanged today, Jacky love. He was hanged for a murder he didn't commit.'

Jacky nodded. He didn't know what to say.

'How do you know that?' asked Ellie, accusingly. 'How do you know he didn't do it? He was found guilty.'

Apart from her tears on the day of sentencing Maureen had never spoken to any of them about the murder trial. They had all wondered why she'd been so affected by it; but asking her seemed the wrong thing to do.

'I know because I knew him a lot better than most,' said Maureen, holding on to Jacky and looking up at Ellie. 'Believe me, I know for sure he didn't do it.' She looked at her son. 'And it's important you know that as well, Jacky boy.'

'I do know, Mam. I thought he was a smashing bloke. He was going to take me to Elland Road. Did you ever meet him, Ellie?'

'No,' said his older sister, glancing accusingly at her mother. 'Unlike some I don't think I ever had the pleasure of Mr McGovern.'

Maureen ignored the innuendo. 'Jacky's right,' she told her daughter, without taking her eyes off her son. 'He was a good man.' She held Jacky in her gaze until she thought he was ready to receive her news. But she knew he'd never be ready. No one was ever ready to receive news such as this. She had thought of various ways of how to tell him. The long, drawn-out version, where his conception would come as a natural conclusion to the months of trauma she'd suffered at the hands of the bunglers at the

War Office. How she hadn't actually been unfaithful to Bert just
. . . misinformed? No. That all sounded as if Jacky had been a
mistake and shouldn't be here at all. Jacky *was* here. He was
Frank McGovern's son, and if the truth be told she wouldn't have
had it any other way.

'Frank McGovern was your real father,' she said, nervously.

'How d'you mean?'

She hugged him to her again. 'Oh, Jacky. I wish there was an
easy way to say this. I'm so sorry. I'm not a very good woman.'

'Course you are, Mam,' said Jacky. 'I don't know what you're
on about, that's all.'

'She had it off with Frank McGovern while our . . . *my* dad was
away in the Army,' explained Ellie, half helping her mother, half
condemning her. 'He *was* my dad, wasn't he?'

'What?' said Maureen. 'Oh, of course he was your dad. He was
Jacky's dad as well, only—'

'Only what, Mam?' Jacky asked. Procreation wasn't a subject
he was well up on.

Maureen sighed, heavily. It was time for the birds and the bees,
an awkward subject at the best of times. It was one of the few
parental duties she'd felt obliged to carry out. Ellie and Brian had
both been Jacky's age when she told them in her own un-
conventional way; but she hadn't told Jacky yet because he was
her baby and she didn't want him to grow up too quickly. Maybe
he'd worked it out for himself.

'Jacky, do you know how babies are made?' she asked, tentatively.

'I think so.' Jacky was blushing.

'A man puts his . . .' Maureen searched for an appropriate word

'Willy?' suggested Ellie, helpfully.

'. . . inside a woman,' continued Maureen.

'I knew that,' Jacky said, uncertainly. 'Everybody knows that.'

'Then why didn't you flipping say so?' grumbled Ellie.

'Never mind,' said their mother, whose heart was going ten to
the dozen. 'The thing is, Jacky boy . . . me and Frank McGovern
. . . did it.'

'Oh heck!' said Jacky, who was more confused than upset.
'Why?'

'Why indeed?' remarked Ellie.

Maureen chose not to answer. She cleared her throat, nervously, and said, 'What it means is that Frank McGovern is . . . was . . . your real father.'

There was a complete lack of comprehension in Jacky's eyes. He looked from his mother to his sister. Ellie looked away. Her mother was definitely on her own in this. Maureen held her son in her gaze.

'Jacky, it doesn't mean that Bert wasn't your father as well,' she said, gently. 'In fact, he was your *proper* father. He was the dad who loved you and helped bring you up and fed you and clothed you and he was there when you took your first steps and he played football with you and taught you how to ride a bike and—'

Jacky stopped her in mid-sentence. 'But he wasn't my real dad?'

Maureen stroked his hair. 'Not in the strictest sense of the word, love. I'm so sorry.'

'Did Dad know?' asked Ellie. 'I mean *my* dad?'

'Yes and no, love.'

'Yes and no? What sort of an answer's that?'

'He knew he wasn't Jacky's dad, but he didn't know who was and didn't want to know. He stayed with me for the sake of you and Brian. When Jacky was born Bert loved him like he would his own son. Treated him no differently. He was a very good man.'

Jacky broke away from her and ran outside. Ellie made to go after him but Maureen took her daughter's arm.

'Leave him be, love,' she said. Then she got to her feet and walked into the other room where she had a pile of men's coats still to finish. She could pretty much do them in her sleep. It would be something to do as she cried.

Jacky shared a double bed with his elder brother, Brian, who had just started work at Castlethorpe Colliery, much against his mother's better judgement. Brian was a big, awkward lad, with too many elbows according to his mother, but he was ideally suited to be a miner and at an age where his mother held little authority over him. Jacky was sitting on the bed, staring out of the window when his brother came home from work. The luxury of the pithead bath hadn't arrived at Castlethorpe yet and Brian's face was caked in coal dust when he popped his head round the bedroom door and sniggered at Jacky.

31

'I've just heard the good news, Jacky boy. Allus thought yer were a bastard. Now I know. A murderer's bastard at that.'

Maureen's angry voice came from below. 'Brian! I heard that. Get yourself down here this minute.'

Brian gave a grimace that had Jacky smiling to himself. When push came to shove their mother always had the upper hand. He heard his brother clattering down the stairs and his mother's raised voiced as she berated Brian for saying *that* to Jacky.

'I were only kidding,' Brian protested.

But Jacky knew he wasn't. He knew there'd be others as well. He could imagine the reception he'd get at school. There were plenty of kids who had it in for him. Although he was only ten he didn't suffer fools gladly and there were plenty of fools at Barr Road Primary. Why couldn't he be Bert Gaskell's son like the other two? It wasn't fair. He hated Frank McGovern – no he didn't – he hated his mother and his brother and he hated his dad for not being his dad. He had no right not to be his dad. Why had he lied to him, called him 'Son' – let Jacky call him 'Dad' when he knew he wasn't?

He began crying again and wished he could stop doing it. He looked round for his football. Frank's words had come back to him. 'It's a well-known fact that you can't cry properly when you're holding a football.' Jacky picked it up and hugged it to his chest but it didn't work because Frank had been joking. He must have known Jacky was his son so what right had he to make daft jokes about footballs instead of telling Jacky who he really was?

Ellie came to the bedroom door and watched as her brother's shoulders heaved up and down in time to his sobbing. She walked in and put her arm around him.

'It'll be all right, Jacky boy,' she assured him. 'It'll be all right, just you wait and see.'

'It won't though, will it?' muttered Jacky. 'How can it be all right, ever again?'

Chapter Five

Jacky had always felt assured in school. When the tests came at the end of each term he was always placed in the top three of a class of over forty. He liked his aged desk in Standard Four with its chipped inkwell and its lid scarred with the initials of former pupils. It had once been the desk of Reg Osbaldison who was currently opening the batting for Yorkshire. Under the lid the great man had carved his name: R H OSBALDISON 1938. Jacky had added YORKSHIRE AND ENGLAND 1951, then he carved his own name underneath.

He liked the soft sound of chalk on blackboard and the massive, arched, classroom windows, through which he could see Barr Road conducting its business. School dinners weren't up to much, especially pom (dehydrated potatoes) and frog spawn (sago pudding). But he liked the daily gill of milk and spoonful of malt which ensured the kids had a balanced diet despite the food rationing that hadn't ended with the War. He liked Monica Nuttall who sat at the desk next to him and who laughed at his jokes, and said she'd go out with him but not until he was at least eleven and old enough. Whatever that meant. He enjoyed Friday afternoons when Miss Evershed would read them *Tom Sawyer*, which quickly became Jack's favourite book. Normally a strict teacher who brooked no nonsense, she relaxed for an hour and did great American accents, especially Aunt Polly and Huck Finn, which always made the children laugh. Jacky would go to America one day and hear all those accents first hand. He liked looking at the faraway places on the huge Mercator Projection stretched out on the back wall showing a flattened version of the circular Earth, and at the blank faces of the other kids when Miss Evershed fired out one of her random arithmetic questions.

'What is the square root of one hundred and sixty-nine plus six minus one?' She would give the baffled faces five seconds then say, 'Tell them, Gaskell.'

'Eighteen, Miss.'

He would give the answer casually, without a trace of conceit and none of the kids ever took exception to him. Bert had taught him that, back in the days when he was Jacky's dad.

'The best way ter show off, lad, is *not* ter show off. No one likes a smart Alec. Let the others do yer showin' off for yer.'

But the time had arrived when Jacky liked Barr Road School more than Barr Road School liked him. Mr Booth, the headmaster, had taken a dislike to him since the revelation about his father being a hanged murderer. The headmaster felt that the school could do without such notoriety. Over the ensuing weeks Jacky defended his family honour on numerous occasions, often coming off worst. His biggest disappointment was that Miss Evershed turned against him. Prompted by Mr Booth, she put his frequent fights down to him having a hitherto unnoticed violent streak. She said as much to him in class when he came in from the playground with a bruised face and grazed knuckles. A boy from Senior One had been pushing him around in the dinner queue. Jacky had retaliated, but had come off worst.

'Like father, like son, eh, Gaskell?'

It prompted a sullen scowl from Jacky, who had just about had enough that day. Miss Evershed took a bamboo cane from out of her desk.

'Don't you scowl at me, Gaskell. Come over here and hold out your hand.'

She gave him three strokes, all delivered with vigour. Jacky felt like going home there and then, but he didn't dare. It would only make things worse. Roy had told him to 'ride it out', but Roy wasn't the one taking a hammering. It was Roy who told Jacky's mother what was happening to her son.

Maureen had threatened to go to the school to sort everyone out but Jacky insisted she would only make things worse. Ellie agreed with him. She'd had problems at her school but nothing like Jacky's.

Brian seemed to revel in his family's notoriety and took every opportunity to torment his younger brother. It was Jacky's scholarship year and he was expected to walk it into grammar

34

school, unlike Brian who had always been jealous of his younger brother's good marks. One night Jacky was at the table doing his homework when Brian sat down opposite him and asked, unpleasantly, 'What're yer doin', Jacky boy, writin' yer will?'

'It's called reading. You wouldn't understand.'

Ellie was at a friend's and their mother was out. Brian's arm swept across the table, knocking all Jacky's books to the floor. 'Don't you be cheeky ter me, yer little shit!' he snarled. 'Just because a murderer's left yer some stuff in his will. Anyroad, it should be shared out, fair an' square. Mam takes most of me wages off me.'

'He wasn't a murderer,' argued Jacky, stoutly. 'Why don't you tell Mam you think he's a murderer? I'll tell you why, because you daren't, that's why.'

Brian rounded the table, took hold of Jacky by the scruff of his neck and pulled him up from the chair. 'Daren't? Yer sayin' I daren't?'

Jacky kicked his brother on the shin and sent him hopping with pain. As Jacky bent down to pick up the books Brian swung a heavy punch that landed on the side of his younger brother's nose, knocking him to the floor with blood pouring down his face. Then Brian picked up the books, threw them on the fire, and stood there, warming his hands and laughing.

Jacky burst into tears of pain and anger. What sort of brother would do this to him – and for nothing? He picked up a dining chair and hit Brian over the back with it. His brother stumbled to the floor and banged his head on the hearth, knocking himself clean out. Still full of anger, Jacky lifted the chair above his head, intending to take advantage of the situation and give his brother a good belt. Then he thought better of it. Brian wasn't looking too good. He was thus poised when Ellie came in with her friend and shouted to him in horror.

'No, Jacky!' she shouted. 'Don't.'

He lowered the chair to the floor. Ellie's friend took in the scene: Jacky, with his face covered in blood, Brian lying on the floor – dead for all she knew – with Jacky about to make sure with a chair. The friend screamed and ran out of the house. The rumour about Jacky having bad blood in him was about to gather strength.

'I wasn't going to hit him,' Jacky muttered, wiping his eyes. 'He deserves it though. He threw my books on the fire and he hit me.'

35

'Looks like you got your own back.'

'He banged his head. I didn't do that to him.'

Brian was stirring. Ellie knelt down beside him. 'Are you okay, Brian?'

Her older brother shook his head, disorientated for a moment. Jacky's grip tightened on the chair, just in case. Brian pushed himself up into a sitting position and felt at the lump rising on his forehead. He threw Jacky a look of undiluted hatred. 'I'll get yer back fer this, yer little shit!'

Jacky was still angry and unmoved by the threat. 'Oh yeah – you and whose army?'

Brian made a sudden lunge than stopped as Jacky jabbed the chair at him, legs first, like a lion tamer holding the beast at bay. Ellie placed herself between the two of them and screamed, 'Stop it! Just look at the state of you both. You're supposed to be brothers.'

'He's no brother o' mine,' Brian said, viciously. 'He's a murderer's bastard. He dunt belong in this house. You'll have ter watch yerself, our lass. He'll be tryin' ter kill you next.'

'I never will!' protested Jacky, appalled at such an accusation.

Brian sneered. 'He's gorrit in him. He's a murderer's bastard and it's like father like son. You ask anyone. Like father like son. Keep yer wits about yer, Ellie. It's in his blood.'

It was the look of uncertainty on Ellie's face that shocked Jacky. Not her as well. This house was a bad place to live in. His sister didn't try to stop him as he ran out into the street, in tears again. She just sat down in the chair and tried to block out all the venom pouring from Brian's mouth.

Jacky roamed the streets, muttering to himself and wishing he'd put a coat on. He'd half a mind to run away like Tom Sawyer had. If only he had a couple of like-minded pals. Tom Sawyer had Huckleberry Finn and Joe Harper. They had an island in the Mississippi to go to, and warm American weather. All Jacky had was Roy Barnwell, the Castlethorpe canal, and a Yorkshire winter. He could leave his shoes by the side of the canal and disappear. They would think he'd drowned and been washed out to sea through all the open locks between here and the river. It would be good to go to his own funeral service, like Tom Sawyer had. Watch them all crying and praying and wishing they'd treated him better. Ellie, Boothie, Mrs Evershed, Brian – well, Ellie definitely.

It wouldn't be fair on his mam, though. She hadn't done anything wrong. Won't bother then.

He knocked on Roy Barnwell's door. Roy answered, looked over his shoulder furtively, then back at Jacky.

'What happened ter yer face?'

'Our kid hit me,' said Jacky, then he grinned. 'So I hit him with a chair. Knocked the daft bugger out.'

Roy laughed out loud, then suppressed it with his hand as a voice from inside asked who it was.

'It's only Barry, Mam.'

'Well ask him ter come in or go out. I'm fair nithered, sat sittin' here in this bloody draught.'

Jacky made to go in, not quite sure why Roy had called him Barry. He could have done with a bit of a warm.

'It's all right, he's got ter be in by seven,' called out Roy.

Jacky frowned. 'I haven't'

Roy whispered to him 'Loads of us have been told not ter play wi' yer. They say yer a bad influence.'

'What, *me* a bad influence on you? That's a laugh. Anyroad, you played with me today.'

'I know, but I'm not supposed ter. I'll see yer at school tomorrow, shall I?'

'Okay,' said Jacky.

He was at a loss what to do now. Running away was out of the question. His face ached where Brian had hit him and the cold was beginning to get to him. Not much point knocking on anyone else's door, not if he was a bad influence. He turned and headed for home with the intention of sitting in the outside lavvie until Mam got back. Then he decided to call in on Charlie Robinson next door. He was all right was Charlie and it'd be warm as well. He tapped on the door and opened it a few inches.

'Are you in, Charlie?'

'Come through, lad,'

It was the cheerful and friendly voice of a man who always had time for Jacky and could have belonged to someone thirty years younger. Charlie was sixty-six. The boy went in and sat in one of the two old easy chairs in Charlie's back room. Charlie was in the other, enveloped in pipe smoke. Jacky intended smoking a pipe when the time came, which would be after he'd gone through the cigarette phase. Charlie gave his old meerchaum a few vigorous sucks then leaned over and switched off the wireless that was playing brass-band music.

'Brighouse and Rastrick,' he said. 'I personally favour t' Black Dyke, but that's only me.'

Jacky, who knew nothing about brass bands, nodded his approval of the Black Dyke.

'What can I do fer yer, Jacky boy?'

'I just thought I'd come to see you. Nothing wrong with that, is there?'

'No, lad. I'm right glad yer did. No particular reason, then?'

Jacky shrugged and shook his head, innocently. Charlie puffed away and said, 'It's just that I thought it might have summat ter do wi' all that blood on yer face an' you runnin' out o' the house scrikin' like a baby just half an hour ago.'

Jacky was too embarrassed to say anything. People seeing him crying was nothing to be proud of.

'Walked into a door, did yer, Jacky boy?'

'It was our kid. He never leaves us alone.'

'I thought it might have been summat like that.' Charlie offered no solution to Jacky's domestic problems other than 'I'll teem a drop o' water in t' kettle an' mek us a cuppa tea, shall I?'

'Thanks, Charlie.'

It was an hour before Jacky heard his mother come home; a few minutes later Brian went out, slammed the door behind him, pushed his bike through the gate and pedalled off in anger.

'I think I'll be off, then,' said Jacky.

'I'll allus be here, lad. If ever yer need a daft owd bugger ter talk ter.'

Maureen had her coat on and was setting off to look for him when he emerged from Charlie's door. He climbed over the wall and allowed his mother to hug him.

'Thank God you're safe, Jacky boy,' she said, relieved. Then to Charlie, 'Thanks for looking after him, Charlie. Him and his brother don't seem to be . . .' her voice tailed off and she left the rest of the sentence unfinished.

Charlie examined his pipe bowl and said, without looking up, 'Can't be easy, lass.'

When Jacky told his mother about the burnt books she looked totally confused and at a loss what to do.

38

'I'll have another word with Brian.' She was glad her eldest son wasn't there to complicate things. 'He's got a lump the size of an egg on his head. He says you hit him with a chair.'

'I didn't do that to him, he fell.'

'I reckon it was six of one, half a dozen of the other,' said Ellie.

'You weren't there to see it,' Jacky said. 'I was doing my homework and he wouldn't leave me alone. He's a right bully is our Brian. He wants to pick on someone his own size.'

'Just ignore him next time.'

Maureen knew it was poor advice but she couldn't side with one son against the other and Brian was beyond listening to reason; she'd tried but he'd gone storming out of the house leaving her with the words 'Murderer's bastard' ringing in her ears. Whatever grip she'd had on Brian was well and truly slipping.

Maureen's female neighbours were frustrated at not being able to snub her due to her ignoring them anyway. It was well over a month since the hanging and they still talked about her behind her back but none of it got to her ears, although she knew it was going on. A sudden turn of a head or a mouth shielded behind a hand as she passed by, followed by a disingenuous smile. Gossiping women were not her favourite species. In fact, apart from Ellie, she wasn't too struck on women in general, especially with Miss Evershed caning Jacky for nothing.

'Is it possible for a woman to be a misogynist?' she said to Charlie. 'Because I think I might be one.'

The two of them often chatted across the back-yard wall, but they had much more in common than just a wall. A watery sun took some of the chill off the early November afternoon and they were enjoying cups of tea Charlie had made for them both.

'What's one o' them?'

'Not you, for a start.'

'No? Well it dunt sound something I'd be.'

'It's a woman hater.'

'Ah, well yer right about me not being one.'

'I know that, Charlie. I used to see women coming and going through your back door at all hours.'

'Not lately, you haven't,' he said, sadly. 'I think I'm losing me sex appeal. Mind you, that Betty Barraclough at t' chip shop's been givin' me the glad-eye. I think I might be in with a chance there.'

'Her husband'll be battering more than cod if he catches you,' Maureen warned, tongue in cheek. Then she became suddenly serious. 'I've never said anything, Charlie, but it must have been hard for you.'

A look passed between them. Charlie lowered his eyes and frowned. 'Hard as the devil, lass.' He glanced up at her. 'But we each have us own way of coping.'

'At least no one's gossiping about you. I try and ignore it, but I know it's going on. Women mainly.'

'Hey, it's nobbut good old-fashioned jealousy, lass. That's why the women don't like yer. There's not a man round here wouldn't leave his wife fer you. Not one in 'is right mind, anyroad.'

This brought a smile to Maureen's face. 'Charlie, it does buck me up talking to you.'

'Anytime, lass. How's young Jacky boy bearin' up?'

'Not good.'

'I reckon young Brian knocks him about a fair bit.'

She gave him a look that asked him what business it was of his but Charlie held her gaze, defiantly. They both knew it *was* his business.

'It wouldn't so bad,' she said, 'if Jacky wasn't so damn cheeky to him. If he kept his mouth shut our Brian wouldn't be nearly so rotten to him.'

'He's a spirited lad is Jacky. Yer don't want ter knock that out of him.'

'I doubt if anyone could do that.'

'It's not my place ter say but Bert'd have nipped it in the bud,' said Charlie. 'It needs stoppin' before summat bad happens.'

He was right, she thought. The boys had never got on but Brian had had too much respect for his father to bully Bert's other son. However, now he knew Jacky *wasn't* Bert's other son it was a different kettle of fish altogether. But Jacky was still *her* son, so why couldn't Brian respect that?

'Oh, Charlie, it's probably all my fault,' she said, despondently. 'I shouldn't be letting Jacky suffer for something that's my fault. Having them both under one roof's becoming almost impossible. Brian's bringing in a wage now, so I can't treat him like a kid – even though he acts like one. I honestly don't know what's wrong with him. Jacky's a lovely lad.'

40

Charlie finished off his tea, swished the dregs around in the bottom of his cup, then stared at them, engrossed, as if the answer to her problems lay in the leaves.

'Am I going to meet a tall, dark stranger who'll sweep me off my feet?' she asked him, joking.

'What? Oh aye, see what yer mean.' He grinned and placed the cup on top of the wall. 'Ee, I wish it were that simple.'

'My needs *are* simple, Charlie,' she said. 'I just need to make things right for Jacky.'

'We all know how yer feel about Jacky, lass,' he sympathised. 'It's been as plain as the nose on yer face since the day he were born. I've watched him grow like I've watched the others, and I've seen how you are with him.'

'How I am with him? How do you mean, Charlie?'

'Well lass, he's special ter yer, there's nowt no surer than that. More special than the other two. Yer a good mother, Maureen, a good mother to all three. But Jacky's allus been a bit special ter yer. An' I reckon young Brian knows it.'

The old man took his time to light a pipe as Maureen digested what he'd told her. He was right of course. Maybe she'd tried to compensate for any resentment Bert might feel towards the boy. Ellie had been Bert's favourite. Poor Brian had been no one's favourite.

'Why don't yer let him stop wi' me for a bit?' Charlie suggested, as casually as he could.

'What? . . . who?'

'Jacky boy.'

She considered it for a while. Jacky got on well with Charlie. In fact Jacky had got on well with everyone until this business had reared its ugly head.

'I'll ask him,' she decided.

'In that case I'll make a bed up,' said Charlie, confidently. 'I'll treat him like me own grandson.'

There was a long pause before their eyes met and Maureen said, 'Actually, that shouldn't be too difficult, should it?'

'No, lass. I don't expect it'll be difficult at all.'

'On account of the fact that he *is* your grandson.'

She knew he knew, but it was the first time she'd aired the subject. Charlie's pipe-puffing quickened, then he took it out of his mouth and stared into the bowl, as if seeking further inspiration. He cleared his throat, noisily.

41

'Aye, I reckon he is, lass,' he said. 'I reckon I've known all along.'

'Thanks for not saying anything.'

'Nay, I could hardly say owt lass, without gettin' meself into bother. I reckon my Bessie might have been a bit curious as to how I'd come by a son and a grandson without her bein' involved. She knew about Frank takin' you out but she never mentioned owt about him probably bein' Jacky's dad. None of her business, yer see. And it wouldn't have done your Bert any good knowing, neither. He were a good pal ter me were Bert.'

'I told Bert it was someone he didn't know and would never see,' Maureen said.

'That were near enough the truth.'

'Didn't Frank say anything?'

'No. Our Frank were never very forthcoming about it, but as yer know he never came round here after t' lad were born, I allus had ter visit him. That told its own story ter me. That an' the fact that Jacky's got his granddad's good looks.'

Maureen smiled. 'Does *anyone* know you're Frank's dad?'

'Not as far as I know, lass. Only you and his mam, an' she's long gone. My Bessie never knew, God bless her. She'd have been mortified, what with her not bein' able to have kids of her own.'

'We've led complicated lives, Charlie, you and I.'

'Too bloody complicated, lass.' He took a few contemplative puffs of his pipe and said, 'Yer know, lass, in a daft sort of a way this is all my fault fer livin' next door ter yer. If I'd not come ter live here our Frank'd never have come ter visit and he'd never have met you. My Bessie thought he were just a pal from work. D'yer know, in all his life he never once called me dad, even after my Bessie passed on. He allus called me Charlie.'

'Have you got over what happened to him?'

'No lass. Nor never will until it's all cleared up. I'd take a knife and fettle that bastard Mumford meself if I thought it'd clear my Frank's name. I hope yer told Jacky his dad didn't do it.'

'I did.'

Maureen thought long and hard before telling Charlie, 'A priest came round and told Jacky the same. He came round especially to tell him he was sure Frank was innocent. He'd heard Frank's last confession but he couldn't tell us any more. He told us in the strictest confidence.'

42

'Thanks fer tellin' me, lass. I didn't need no priest ter tell me what I already knew, but it were good of him. Frank's mam were a Catholic. She brought Frank up the same, which were hard under the circumstances.'

'I imagine it was. She must have been a special woman.'

Charlie smiled at a distant memory. 'Well, ter be honest she was, lass. I did wrong by her but she never blamed me. "It takes two ter tango," she'd say.'

It occurred to Maureen that Frank's mother sounded a bit too forgiving – naive even. Charlie's smile faded and his eyes misted over. His pipe-sucking became audible as he tried to control his emotions.

'By God, lass, I miss my Frank. I know he were born on t'wrong side o' t' blanket and he were a devil at times but he were cheerful as a lark and he were very good ter me – so were his mam. She never let on I were his dad, yer know. Never once. That were for my Bessie's sake. She never asked for nowt – never asked for a brass farthing – that's not ter say I didn't help out when I could.' He breathed out a mixture of smoke and emotions. 'She worshipped that lad . . . then she died. Her and my Bessie, both within six months.'

'His mother going before Frank was a blessing in a way,' said Maureen. 'If that happened to any of mine I don't know what I'd do.' She finished off her tea and handed the cup back to Charlie. 'Frank left Jacky all his things in his will,' she told him. 'They're at the solicitor's. I haven't been to pick them up yet. If there's anything there that you want, to remind you of him, I'm sure—'

Charlie refused her offer away with a shake of his head and a smile. 'Nay, I don't think he had much, love.'

'If Jacky comes to stay, don't tell him you're his granddad, not just yet, anyway. His life's confused enough.'

'We'll have to tell him sometime.'

'I know, Charlie. Leave it 'til he's twelve eh?'

It seemed a long enough time for her to think of a way to break such news.

Chapter Six

Although she saw Jacky every day she missed him desperately and felt as though she had betrayed him. There were nights when Maureen would put her head to the bedroom wall to see if she could hear her son breathing in his new bed just a few feet away from her. During the day the smiles he gave her didn't seem as bright and the hugs not as tight and she didn't blame him. If anyone was to blame it was Brian, but the only way to right this injustice would be to kick her eldest son out of the house. And where would he go? One thing was certain, Charlie wouldn't swap Brian for Jacky.

It was mid-November by the time Maureen summoned the enthusiasm to go to Frank's solicitor to find out what had been left to Jacky. He went with her because she insisted.

As the two of them sat in the chair opposite the man reading out Frank's will Maureen could hear the distaste in the solicitor's voice. It was hurried, nasal and monotone and contained no compassion or interest in the will's contents. He was reading out the will of a murderer. It displeased him to have to do it and he didn't care who knew it. Maureen interrupted him.

'Did you work on Mr McGovern's case?'

'I did some of the work, yes,' he replied, astringently. 'Of courses, Mr McGovern was represented in court by a barrister.'

'Well, you and your barrister friend managed to send an innocent man to the gallows.' She felt like telling him he had a mouth like a dog's bum but that wouldn't have helped matters.

'Victor Mumford's the man they should have hanged,' added Jacky. 'He stabbed his wife and blamed it on my dad. He caught 'em at it.'

44

Maureen glared at her son for making such a distasteful remark, then she transferred her glare to the solicitor. 'No doubt Mumford thought it was poetic justice,' she said, remembering Frank's words. 'But it doesn't alter the fact that a murderer's running around free because you legal experts couldn't get things right. I'd like you to start from the beginning and keep this in mind when you're reading Mr McGovern's will, if you don't mind. Show the man some respect.'

The solicitor blushed, violently. Jacky smiled. He loved it when his mam brought people down a peg or two. He would learn to do this himself. The solicitor cleared his throat and began again.

It transpired that apart from a weeks' wages due to him, Frank's most valuable possession was his gold pocket watch. On the back was engraved:

Frank McGovern
Bravest man we know
Wilf, Eric, Stan

Jacky picked it up and remembered the last time he'd seen it. He showed it to his mother.

'We had a bet,' he told her. 'He bet me I wouldn't pass my scholarship. If I passed I won this watch, if I didn't I had to give him my football.'

'He was a genius at backing losers,' smiled his mother. 'They used to say the best way to stop a runaway horse is for Frank McGovern to put ten bob on it.'

'What's this mean?' Jacky was looking at the inscription.

Maureen examined it carefully and suddenly her eyes flooded with tears. 'I've never actually seen it,' she said. 'But I heard he saved some men's lives down the pit.' She looked at her son and smiled. 'I'll tell you what, Jacky, he must have thought a lot about you to want to give you something like this. It seems it's the most precious thing he had. The pit owners presented it to him. Small price to pay for what he did.'

'I only talked to him for a few minutes,' remembered Jacky. Then he added, almost guiltily, 'I cried mostly. He held my football while I cried. He said it's a well-known fact that you can't cry when you're holding a football – it's not true, actually.'

'Maybe not, but it sounds like something Frank would say.' Maureen ruffled her son's hair and looked up at the solicitor.

'Jacky's father was a hero,' she told. 'As big a hero as anyone who was in the war. And they hanged him for something he didn't do. What do you make of that?'

The solicitor wasn't able to make anything of it.

Charlie still hadn't admitted to Jacky that he was his grandfather, and wouldn't until Maureen gave him the go-ahead. But he made a point of telling him what a good bloke Frank was. No way in the world could he ever commit a murder.

'Who do you think did it, then?' Jacky asked. It was the first time he'd discussed the murder with Charlie. 'I think it was Mumford.'

'Think? I don't *think*, Jacky boy, I know. Victor Mumford killed his own wife because Frank were havin' it off with her. That's how Frank said it happened and it makes sense ter me.'

'And Mumford caught 'em at it so he stabbed her.'

'Nail on the head, lad.'

It would have made more sense to Jacky if Mumford had stabbed Frank, but grown-ups have their own way of doing things. Why would Frank be having it off with Mrs Mumford? Jacky knew there was a logical answer to this and he should know without asking. So he didn't ask. He changed the subject.

'Mam says he was a hero for rescuing them blokes down the pit.'

'Some say that,' said Charlie. 'I say he were foolhardy. He'd no business goin' back ter them men. The whole bloody roof could've caved in, an' him underneath it.'

'But he saved their lives, didn't he?'

'As it happens he did, lad. Nine times outa ten he wouldn't have got out alive. He must've dug like a bloody mole ter get at 'em. Pulled 'em all out one by one.'

'Don't you think that was brave?'

Charlie remembered that night. How he'd waited at the pithead for news; and how he'd cursed when someone told him that Frank had gone back through the seam despite being told not to be such a bloody idiot by the deputy. Four men died that night. Charlie had watched their bodies being brought out, one by one. He still remembered the frightened silence which accompanied each body as it was stretchered out of the cage. Wives and mothers of missing men would push forward and wait for the face to be

46

uncovered for identification. Most would turn away in relief – but not all of them. As the dead man's name was murmured, sadly, through the crowd the bereaved loved ones would be supported by family and friends as they accompanied the body to the waiting ambulance. Word came that there was little hope for the men still trapped down there. And that night Charlie remembered how it felt to lose a son.

Then they brought Frank up, along with the men who owed him their lives. Those who knew what he'd done offered muted congratulations but Frank waved them away. This was no night for glory. This was a sad night. Charlie had wept with joy when he shook the hand of the man no one knew to be his son, and such was his relief that he felt like telling the world the truth and to hell with the consequences.

And now Charlie wished he'd lost him there and then – a hero – instead of how he finally went.

'Aye, lad. He were brave all right. Brave as a lion – daft as a brush. Most brave people are, yer know. Daft as brushes. You show me a hero and I'll show you a man who's as daft as a brush.' He looked at Jacky with the same fondness he'd felt for Frank. 'Yer know, lad,' he said. 'Yer can't blame him fer lovin' yer mam. He were only human. You love her, don't yer?'

'Well, yes . . .'

'There yer go then. If Bert hadn't turned up, Frank'd have married yer mam like a shot.'

'How d'yer mean, if Bert hadn't turned up?' Jacky asked. 'Me mam was married to him . . . wasn't she?'

He added the last two words after a long pause. There was too much he didn't know about his mother. Charlie took out his pipe and tapped the bowl on his cupped palm as he thought. A thimbleful of burnt tobacco fell out, which he threw into the fire, causing a brief sparkle amid the glowing embers. It was nearly bed time and they were both having a mug of cocoa. Jacky enjoyed these times. Charlie had often regaled him with tales of his days at sea before he got married and went down the pit.

'It's happen not my place ter tell yer, lad.'

Jacky watched as he lit his pipe. There was something comforting about it. The gentle sucking and the smell of tobacco wafting past his nose. As soon as he was old enough Jacky would smoke a pipe, never mind cigarettes. He'd tried Charlie's once or twice when the old man wasn't looking, but it made him cough; nevertheless it seemed a skill worth mastering. Charlie was nodding to himself, as if he was granting approval to what he had to say next.

'But if it makes yer feel better towards yer mam,' he said. 'I reckon I see no harm in it.'

Jacky remained silent. He sipped at his cocoa and stared into the fire. Charlie spoke.

'The thing is, Jacky boy, yer mam thought Bert were dead. She'd got a telegram sayin' he were missin'. He'd been on his way ter France an' his ship hit a mine in t' Channel. Sank like a stone. There were only half a dozen survivors, includin' Bert. They got picked up an' transferred to another ship an' got sent on their way.'

'He told me about that,' Jacky recalled. 'He told me he'd been blown clear by the explosion. He had a life jacket on because he couldn't swim and he were scared o' drowning.'

Charlie gave a quiet laugh. 'Bein' scared saved many a life in that war.' His pipe-sucking became more vigorous. His eyes narrowed and his head nodded as he marshalled his thoughts. Jacky knew this meant he was coming to the crux of his story.

'Trouble was, them pen pushers at t' War Office got everyone's names mixed up. There were over two hundred killed an' six survivors. One o' them killed were called Arthur Gaskell. He were from Leeds, eighteen year old, nobbut a lad. Anyroad, with Bert bein' called Albert they mixed t' names up and sent yer mam a telegram sayin' Bert were missin' presumed dead. I remember that day like it were yesterday. She came round to us because she had no one else – an' we'd only been living here a few months. She showed me t' telegram an' asked if there might be a chance it were wrong.'

Charlie shook his head, as if still remonstrating with himself, even after all these years. 'I told her they didn't get things like that wrong.' He looked at Jacky, as if for forgiveness. 'I didn't want her ter get her hopes up an' be let down again. I were certain he were dead.'

Jacky nodded because it seemed the right thing to do. He had never heard the actual details of the story.

'There was a lot o' bad stuff goin' on in France back then. Nobody reckoned them Frenchies'd keel over as quick as they did,' Charlie went on. 'Letters weren't gerrin' back home as fast as they ought. It were nearly two months afore she heard he were still alive.'

The old man got up and walked to the window. 'Yer mam were a beautiful woman back then.' He pushed the curtains to one side and stared out to identify some noise he thought he'd heard. Then he let them go and turned back to Jacky. 'Still is. My Fran . . .' Charlie stopped himself just short of revealing who he really was, then he cleared his throat, noisily. 'Frank came round ter visit one night an' yer mam were here, talkin' ter my Bessie. Next thing I know Frank's asked her out ter t' pictures.'

'Pictures?' said Jacky, for want of something better to add to the conversation. 'What did they go and see?'

'Hey? . . . no idea. I tell a lie. It were a Bob Hope picture. Yer mam likes Bob Hope.'

'Does she?' said Jacky. 'I never knew that.'

'So, that were it, really,' said Charlie. 'They started goin' out regular. Frank were right taken with her and yer mam needed cheerin' up . . . and I suppose one thing led to another.'

'I suppose,' said Jacky, who understood this part.

'Then yer mam got a letter from Bert. She brought it round ter me asking if it were right. I said it must be, but I felt a fool because I'd already told her they don't make mistakes. We went down ter t' police station ter see if they could help – an' I have ter say they were very good. A few months later Bert came home from Dunkirk. By which time yer mam were pregnant wi' you.'

'Meaning Frank was my dad,' concluded Jacky, who had learned a lot about procreation recently.

'I reckon so, lad. Nowt were never said, not even ter me nor my Bessie.'

'But Frank will have known he was me dad.'

'He will – but it was up ter yer mam what were done about it, lad. It's mams what have the last word at times like that. Fellers have ter tek a back seat an' do as they're told. A few tongues wagged but I put it about that Bert had been home on embarkation leave round about the time . . .' He searched for a suitable way to put it.

Jacky helped him out. 'Me mam and Frank had it off.'

'Aye, lad. Some believed it, others didn't. Yer mam an' Bert made the best of a bad job.'

'What about Frank?'

'He never came round here again, lad. Best way, really. I'll tell yer what, though. Frank thought the world of yer mam. It were just one o' them things what happens in war.'

'So, that's what I am?' Jacky said. 'Just one o' them things what happens in war.'

'There's good an' bad in everything,' Charlie said, running his hands through his grandson's hair. 'You're one of the good things.'

Chapter Seven

January 1952

Brian had been given a job on the pit bottom. Up until then he'd been working on the screens at the pithead. He would be earning an extra fourpence an hour, bringing his take-home pay up to three pounds five shillings after deductions, from which Maureen would take two pounds five shillings board. Out of his own money Brian had an outlay of five shillings a week for a bicycle he'd bought on tick.

On his first day he parked his bike in the bike shed, collected his cap lamp and token from the lamp cabin and made his way, with the other men on the shift, past the winding engine house. One man, walking immediately behind Brian, pointed at his back and stuck up his thumb at Joe, the engineman, who was watching the passing group from behind his grimy window. The engineman, who controlled the cage which took the shift to the pit bottom, winked. Some of the other walking men grinned in anticipation as the group walked up to the shaft gates. The banksman did a check of the men for contraband, such as matches and any other ignition materials, then lifted up the gates for the first of the men to fill up the bottom deck of the two-deck cage. Brian's pulse quickened as he stepped inside, his brass token still clutched in his hand. This was an exciting moment for him. First time down the pit, well, as a worker anyway. He'd been down once before, in his first week there. 'To get the feel of the place,' the manager said.

Beside him was a man with a canary in a cage, still the most effective means of gas detection. The banksman withdrew the keps to allow the cage to drop the few feet required for the top

51

deck to move into position, and after loading the rest of the men, he ensured the cage gates were down and the shaftgate cleared before rapping the 'Man riding – lower' signal to the winding engineman. Safety procedure is paramount down a mine.

There were nudges and looks of expectation on the faces of the men around Brian. All of them were hanging on to the side handrail. Some were making comments.

'I hope that bloody wire dunt snap. It looked a bit dodgy ter me. Did you notice it, Les?'

'I bloody did. It'll be a quick trip down if it snaps.'

'They reckon yer fallin' at two hundred mile an hour when yer hit t' bott—'

'Bloody Jesuuuus!' screamed Brian.

The cage dropped a hundred feet in less than five seconds, leaving Brian's stomach at the top and a scream frozen on his lips as the floor seemed to drop from under him. Then the cage slowed and he felt the floor under his feet again. The men laughed at the terror on his face. The boy opened his fingers to reveal blood where he'd gripped his identity token and he smiled, diffidently, at the smirking men around him.

'Bloody 'ell,' he said. 'What 'appened there?'

'Nowt ter worry about. T'engine man must've thought it were just materials goin' down, not valuable human cargo,' said one of the men, casually, as if nothing much had happened. 'He's a deaf owd bugger is Joe.'

Brian was too gullible to immediately see through the broad grins of his new workmates. His younger brother would have seen through it in an instant, but Brian was slower.

The cage descended almost a thousand feet then it came to a gentle halt against the keps. Sid, the onsetter, standing outside with a face like thunder, made no move to pull up the cage doors.

'I reckon somebody's been playin' silly buggers. Worrisit? New lad on t' bloody shift?' He looked directly at Brian, who was beginning to realise he'd had a joke played on him.

'Hurry up, Sid,' grumbled one of the men. 'Arnold's farted and t' canary's just fell off it's perch.'

'Has tha never bloody heard o' bloody safety,' complained Sid, pulling the gate open. 'Riskin' bloody lives just ter scare the shit out of a young lad. I'll bloody report that bloody Joe.'

'Report him fer what?' said one of the men.

'Tha knows very well what. I can tell what's goin' on up there by what's bloody goin' on down here.'

'Nowt happened,' said Brian. 'Honest, mister.'

The onsetter looked at Brian. 'Who might thee be, lad?'

'Brian Gaskell.'

'Well sithee, lad, tha'll be workin' wi' me. An' I shall be keepin' an eye on thee. I hope tha's not bloody accident prone.'

'I'm not so sure about that, mister,' grinned Brian. 'I think I might have already had one. Where's t' shit'ouse?'

There was roar of laughter from the passing men, some of whom slapped him on his back as they made their way to the paddy train which would be pulled by a locomotive half a mile to the coal face. He grinned at them, happy to have made a good start.

The pit bottom was a huge chamber, 30 feet wide, 200 feet long and 10 feet high, hewn out of the ground at the turn of the century. At the centre was the downcast shaft, one of only two ways up to the outside world, the other being the upcast shaft which was situated at the far side of an airlocked door in another chamber about a hundred yards away.

Brian felt a shudder of claustrophobia as he wondered what would happen if ever the shaft became blocked. That's how men died. One of the many ways men died down the pit. His mother hadn't wanted him to go down there; she'd wanted him to work in a local engineering factory – sod that. Brian's heart and imagination raced as he tried to shrug off his fears. It was normal, he'd been told; like a sailor being seasick on his first voyage. It'd wear off. When he came out of the primitive lavatory his fears had gone.

The roof of the chamber was supported by rolled steel joists, and at each end were roadways, 8 feet high by 12 feet wide, that led to the coal faces. From the downcast shaft ran two narrow-gauge railway lines that joined at a set of points and went into the roadways. A third track ran around the side of the cages and joined the other line at each end of the chamber. It was on these tracks that Brian, with the help of the ponies, would be pushing and pulling tubs of coal into the cage, ready for dispatch to the surface.

The lighting was fluorescent and would have been much brighter but for the muck on the tubes. It was a cold and dirty light that added no colour to this black and grey subterranean world. Brian stood by the doorway of the onsetter's cabin, like a spare part, for a while, awaiting someone to tell him what to do. He listened to the sounds of the pit bottom – the clanking of tub wheels, of couplings and gates, the onsetter rapping his instructions, ponies farting, echoing voices, and the low, distant hum of a fan that swept a draught of cold air gently past, causing him to shiver. To his left a couple of tethered ponies stood with resigned patience, their eyes reflecting the light from his cap lamp.

'It's warmer up at t' face.'

An oldish man appeared from seemingly nowhere. He introduced himself with a gnarled outstretched hand. 'Cedric,' he said. 'But everyone calls me Ced. Yer'll be workin' wi' me.'

'Brian . . . Brian Gaskell.'

He noticed Ced was wearing a scarf; he'd bring one on his next shift. Within half an hour Ced had told him just about all he'd ever need to know about the work. Brian found it straightforward and put his back into it.

'Pace yersen, lad,' advised Ced. 'If yer pace yersen yer'll be able ter move these tubs round all day without breakin' sweat. There'll be time enough fer breakin' sweat when they put yer on t' coal face.'

'That's where t' money is, though,' said Brian.

The man laughed. His shiny, false teeth seemed out of place in a face criss-crossed with deep lines, all ingrained with pit dust that no scrubbing would ever remove.

'Money?' he grunted. 'There's no money down t' pit, lad. There's back breakin' bloody work an' dust an' shit, but I've never seen no money. See that, lad?' He held out his right hand and stuck two fingers up.

'If yer want me ter go away, Ced, yer've only to ask.'

The man cackled and examined the fingers himself. They looked stiff and drained of colour. 'White finger,' he said. 'Useless, both of 'em.'

'White finger? How d'yer get that?'

'Workin' t' drills all day long, lad. All that vibration knackers yer fingers. Me lungs are shot ter bits, I've got piles, dermatitis, and a knackered ankle what I broke when I got hit by a bleedin' locomotive. I'm half blind in one eye, I'm deaf in one ear and I've got athlete's foot. If things get any worse I might have ter give up playin' centre forward fer Castlethorpe Town.'

'Eh?'

'It were a joke, lad.'

'Oh, right.'

'Yer need a sense of humour down here. I like a good laugh. Are you any good at jokes?'

'I can never remember 'em,' Brian said.

Cedric peered at him, intuitively. 'No, lad. I don't suppose yer can. Anyroad, it's because of t' state I'm in that I'm seein' me time out on t' tubs. I retire in seven months. I don't reckon I'll cost t' buggers much in pension.'

'I'll not be doin' it fer long,' said Brian, confidently. 'Just long enough ter get some brass together so's I can get outa this dump of a town.'

'Now where have I heard that before? If that's t' way yer thinkin' I'd get in that cage right now an' bugger off out of it while yer can. Once they get yer down here they've got yer fer good.'

'Not me.'

'That's what they all say.' The old miner pushed his helmet back and tapped his temple with one of his good fingers. 'Education, that's what yer want. Get yersen off ter night school, lad. Get some education.'

'Nah.' Brian grimaced and heaved at a tub. 'I hated school. Waste o' bloody time. Couldn't wait ter leave.'

'Pity. Yer can make more money from stickin' at yer books than yer'll ever earn wedged in a two-foot seam, drillin' bloody house coal.'

Books. Brian thought of Jacky for the first time that day. He wouldn't be able to stand it if Jacky did better than him with his life. The little sod had always got the best of things. Their mother had a different look in her eye when she looked at Jacky. Brian wanted her to look at him like that. He'd once mentioned it to Ellie and she'd noticed it as well. At least she'd been the apple of their dad's eye; Brian had never been the apple of anyone's eye. Even now that Jacky was living next door it was as though he was still there. The number of times his mother, without thinking, had set three places at the table and called him for his tea. And the distance in her eyes that told Brian she was thinking about her

55

favourite son. As he pushed the tubs he rekindled his hatred of his brother; which set his adrenaline surging.

'Nay, lad,' Ced cautioned him. 'Pace yersen, like I said. Yer'll not get no thanks for all this rushin' and pushin'.'

'I don't want no thanks,' muttered Brian. 'I just want me dues, that's all.'

Chapter Eight

Jacky was leaving school at hometime when he saw Fozzie Symonite chalking on the wall:

Wats Jacky Gaskells favoret game?
Hangman

A group of children were laughing, some at Fozzie's joke, others at his spelling. Mr Hepton, the caretaker, was glaring at the smirking youth.

'Hey! I hope yer gonna rub that out, young man, because I'm damn well not!'

Fozzie told him to get stuffed. The caretaker commanded little respect among the children – or teachers for that matter. 'I'd tan yer arse if it were up ter me,' he grumbled. 'That's what wrong wi' kids today. Not enough arses get tanned.'

'You've spelt it wrong,' Jacky taunted Fozzie, after the disgruntled caretaker had shuffled off. 'You spell worse than a two year old. I don't know why you bother comin' to school.'

Fozzie stuck two fingers up at him. 'Yer know what that means, Gaskell?'

'Yeah,' Jacky said. 'It's the biggest number you can count up to.'

Some of the children laughed. Fozzie frowned, then glared at Jacky.

'Don't think I won't get yer back for what yer did the day they hanged yer dad.' He pulled at an imaginary noose around his neck and lolled out his tongue as if he was choking to death.

Jacky saw red. Insults against himself he could take because he knew he had the wit to more than hold his own. But insults against

57

his family were another matter altogether. He walked up to Fozzie and, without warning, hit him hard on the end of his nose. The bigger boy howled with pain as blood poured down his shirt. He swung a scything punch, which Jacky ducked beneath and jabbed his fist into Fozzie's face.

A shout of 'Fight' went up and the combatants soon found themselves encircled by hooting fight fans, only a few of whom were shouting for the beleaguered Fozzie. Jacky occupied the centre of the human fight ring where least energy is needed, easily in control of the situation. Many battles with his older brother had taught him how to handle bullies like Symonite. Fozzie was darting and stumbling all around the edge of the ring, panting and bleeding; then rushing at Jacky with flailings arms, only to be rewarded with a painfully accurate jab or two as Jacky moved easily out of his path and allowed Fozzie to stumble into the spectators who would push him back to face more punishment. Eventually the bigger boy sank to his knees. Exhausted and beaten.

Neither of the fighters noticed the expectant hush that had descended on the crowd. Jacky felt a hand grabbing his collar. Without turning he recognised the headmaster's voice.

'It's nowt ter do wi' me, sir,' Fozzie called out. 'He started it, sir. He just came up and hit me, sir. I didn't do nowt, sir. He started it.'

'I didn't sir,' protested Jacky.

'I saw who struck the first blow, Gaskell. I saw the whole thing from start to finish. That was an unprovoked attack.'

Jacky would normally have kept quiet about who started it, but Fozzie's squealing annoyed him. 'He was writin' stuff on the wall about me, sir.' He pointed to the wall to prove his argument. 'Mr Hepton told him to rub it out, but he told Mr Hepton to get stuffed, sir.'

The headmaster gave Fozzie's misspelt handiwork a dismissive glance. 'Then you should report it to the school,' he said, 'not take matters into your own hands.'

Booth knew that such an action would make Jacky an outcast among his fellow pupils but it wasn't his position to say so.

The head's study window was crammed with watching faces as Jacky received six vigorous strokes of the cane. 'You're a bad lot, Gaskell,' Booth told him, loud enough for all the spectators to hear. 'A thoroughly bad lot. Any more behaviour like this and I'll expel you without a second thought.'

One face watching was that of Rodney Tripp. Satisfied with what he'd seen and heard he went to the school gates where Fozzie was waiting for him. He took the camera from its case as the boy made to wipe the blood off his face with his sleeve.

'No, lad, don't do that. I want to see as much blood as I can. I never thought young Gaskell was as tough as that. Turned up trumps did young Jacky boy.'

'Hey! I let him beat me, mister, like yer said.'

'Aye, lad. I'm sure you did. By heck! I reckon you'll have two proper shiners tomorrow.'

'Do I get me half a crown, now mister?'

The reporter handed the boy a coin. 'Here you are, lad.' He studied Fozzie's battered face and rubbed his chin, thoughtfully. 'Tell you what, lad. See me here at half past eight in the morning. Don't wash any of that blood off – and if you've got a pair of half decent shiners for me to photograph there's another couple of bob in it for you. I can't say fairer than that.'

Fozzie trudged home, not absolutely certain that he'd done well out of the arrangement. Rodney went on his way well satisfied. His earlier investigations had made him aware that Jacky would give as good as he got in a fight and it was but a simple matter to find out the boy most willing to provoke him – for a small fee. The story was bought by a Sunday tabloid. Half the front page was taken up by a photograph of Fozzie's bruised and bleeding face below the caption:

MURDERER'S SON ACCUSED OF TERRORISING SCHOOL

This is the face of twelve-year-old Foster Symonite after he was allegedly assaulted by Jacky Gaskell, the illegitimate son of Frank McGovern, the man hanged for the murder of his lover last September.

It went on to say how the reporter had been told by one of the teachers that the headmaster, Mr Booth, was most unhappy at having such a young thug in the school. He had, with great reluctance, had to punish the boy most severely. The unnamed teacher went on to quote Mr Booth as having said, 'Our job is to educate, not to reform.'

*

Among his fellow pupils, who all knew the true story, Jacky earned a certain kudos from the article. The headmaster was fuming and held an unsuccessful investigation to find out who the blabbermouth teacher was. He wasn't to know that the teacher in question was but a figment of Rodney Tripp's imagination – albeit a very useful figment. The sight of Booth administering the beating to Jacky, whilst not punishing Fozzie, who had provoked the fight (at Tripp's instigation) had given the reporter a fair insight into the headmaster's mind. Booth was an unjust bully and maybe one day there might be a story here. Unjust bullies tend to come unstuck and when they did it was Tripp's duty as a concerned citizen to write about it.

And sell it for a nice price.

Chapter Nine

Bill Scanlon walked down Gaythorne Street and wondered for the thousandth time if he'd done the right thing. He didn't love his wife. He'd liked her well enough when they were both too young to know any better. In fact he'd liked her well enough to go out with her for four years, since they were both at school. She said she loved him but he wasn't sure about that. The only thing he knew for sure was that it was his fault she was in that wheelchair. They had been fooling around on the dance floor; he had picked her up and put her over his shoulder, then he had slipped. It was drunken horseplay but it had ended up with a severed nerve in Pam's spinal column. They had both been only nineteen.

The heels of his boots clicked, rhythmically, against the stone-flagged footpath as he proceeded at his usual, measured pace. A curtain twitched and a woman's face appeared in the window, wondering who he was going to see. He passed a small boy, who glanced at him over his shoulder and instantly tried to look as if he was doing something other than peeing against the wall. More twitching curtains which he scarcely noticed. He was used to it in his job.

Prior to the accident it had been generally accepted that they would one day go the way of all their friends: engaged, married, house and kids. But Bill hadn't wanted this. He had been going to tell her that night at the dance, only he didn't quite know how. He had met Kathy McAlister, the girl he was going to ditch Pamela for. She was bright and pretty and made him laugh and as far as he could tell he loved her. It was time to move on. Then this. And it had been his fault. He'd been drinking to give him Dutch courage, only it hadn't given him courage, it had made him act daft. Pam had been acting just as daft. She'd told him later that it had been the best evening of her life . . . until she broke her back.

So he'd made the sacrifice. He didn't know whether he'd made it out of decency or cowardice. I mean, how would it have looked if he'd turned his back on her the minute he realised she'd never walk again? He'd never be able to hold his head up again.

Bill took a deep breath and tried to put it from his mind as he knocked on the door. Fourteen years married to a woman he didn't love. Married for all the wrong reasons. Last week he had told her just that during the latest of their increasingly frequent arguments. She had forced it out of him; challenged him to deny that he'd had only married her out of sympathy.

'Don't lie to me, Bill.'

'If you think that, why did you go through with the wedding?' he had asked.

'Well, I was hardly going to let you cripple me for life and then go running to that cow Kathy McAlister.'

'She wasn't a co –! Here, how did you know about Kathy McAlister?'

'Bill, I didn't mean that. It came out all wrong.'

'You knew?' he said, trying to make sense of what this meant.

'Bill, I'm sorry. I didn't mean it—'

'You knew about me and Kathy McAlister? I didn't know you knew.'

There was a rattling of a bolt on the inside of the rarely used front door. Bill cleared his mind of marital problems and straightened his helmet. He had never met Maureen Gaskell before and the unexpected sight of such a beautiful woman brought a smile to his face.

Maureen, who knew why he'd come, didn't return his smile. She looked beyond him at the twitching curtains, of which there were now several sets. He introduced himself.

'PC Scanlon, Featherstone Road Police. Are you Mrs Gaskell, Jacky Gaskell's mother?'

'Yes, you'd better come in.'

Bill removed his helmet to reveal a badly scarred forehead which held Maureen's gaze a little longer than was polite.

'Got it during the war.'

He didn't normally explain, but she looked like someone worth the bother. Pam had recently blurted out that she had welcomed his disfigurement as she thought it made him almost as unattractive to the opposite sex as she was. An outburst for which she had instantly apologised.

'Sorry,' Maureen said. 'It was rude of me to stare.'

There was nothing wrong with the rest of him. He had a nice face, which might have been even nicer had he not worn a moustache; Morgan Pettifer had put her off those for life.

'No need to apologise,' he smiled. 'I reckon you probably get stared at more than me.' He didn't mean to come out with such a clumsy compliment and he winced the instant he said it. 'I've er, I've come about the incident at school. It's just a courtesy visit really. No complaint's been made.'

'And why do you think that is?' Maureen asked.

'Well, the headmaster says he dealt with it himself. It's just that the papers got hold of it and some of the senior officers started asking questions down at the station. I've been asked to make a report.'

'Do you want to see my son?'

'I suppose I ought to. Is he about?'

'He lives next door.'

'Next door?'

'It's a long story – but it's not Jacky's fault.'

'I see.'

'Jacky's had a hard time since his father was wrongly hanged.'

'Yes, I can well imagine he has.'

Maureen's face softened. The constable hadn't questioned her opinion. In fact he sounded as though he sympathised with her. Did he know something? No harm in asking. She invited him to sit down. He took out a packet of Players Weights and offered her one.

'No thanks. Not one of my vices.'

He glanced up at her as he lit his cigarette, wondering what vices she *did* have. She didn't have a husband; he knew that for sure.

'Tell me, constable,' she said. 'Did you think Frank McGovern did it?'

'I'm afraid I'm not allowed to go round voicing my opinions, madam. If it gets back to my sergeant he might start voicing opinions about me.'

'Your opinion won't go beyond these four walls.'

'Then I shall have to hope that my sergeant never comes within these four walls.' Bill's smile was as broad and genuine as that of Frank McGovern's. There was a reassuring strength behind it. Then it faded away and he became serious. 'In my private opinion,' he told her, 'there was too much doubt. They never found the murder weapon and the judiciary was under a lot of pressure to keep the murder rate under control. I think they hanged him more as a deterrent than as a punishment.'

'Victor Mumford did it.' Maureen said it with conviction.

'You and plenty of others think that, Mrs Gaskell.'

'That's because it's the truth.'

'You can't go throwing accusations like that around without proof.'

'Why not?'

'Because he can sue you.'

'I know he can. But you and I know he won't. He just wants it all to go away.'

Bill conceded her point with a nod and a smile. 'I can't argue with that.'

'You came to talk to me about Jacky?'

'Er, yes . . . Look, I don't need to see the lad. You just tell me what happened and I'll put it in my report.'

'Right,' she began. 'Well, the boy he's supposed to have assaulted is a bully called Fozzie Symonite. I imagine he's known to you.'

'He is,' Bill confirmed.

'He's a year older than Jacky and a good deal bigger. I won't deny that Jacky's quite handy with his fists, but that's what comes of having an older brother . . . sibling rivalry and all that.'

'So, what happened exactly?'

'Well, Jacky admits to throwing the first punch—'

'Sometimes it's best to get the first one in.' Bill found himself helping her.

'Er, yes, I suppose it is. Fozzie was chalking something on the wall about hanging. I'm not sure what, but it was designed to upset Jacky . . . a fight started, Jacky got the better of it, the headmaster chose to punish Jacky and let the other boy get off scot-free

'. . . and that's about it, really. Next thing I know it's blown up out of all proportion in a Sunday rag.'

'How do you think the newspapers got hold of it?'

'Well, certainly not through me,' said Maureen, emphatically. 'I suggest you ask the school. Apparently some teacher gave an interview. Probably made money out of it. Would you like a cup of tea?'

Normally Bill made it a rule to refuse all offers of liquid refreshment. There was only one public toilet on his beat and it wasn't very fragrant. 'That would be very nice, thanks,' he said.

As he watched her busying herself an adulterous thought crossed his mind. He'd been having quite a few such thoughts recently, but none quite so adulterous as this. Then the thought of Pam sitting in her wheelchair returned to chastise him. Her attitude recently was probably understandable. Life in a wheelchair was bound to make a person tetchy, especially when confronted daily by the person who put you there. Still, there was nothing wrong with having a pleasant conversation with a nice-looking woman who could see beyond the ugly scar on his head. Each of them had a personal life which they didn't want to share with a casual stranger, so they talked about what was on the radio and how they had both enjoyed Horatio Hornblower at the pictures. Gregory Peck was Maureen's favourite actor and Bill wasn't exactly averse to Virginia Mayo, his co-star in the film. Oh, what different lives those film actors led, Maureen said. All that money and glamour.

'All you're missing is the money,' Bill commented. Another clumsy compliment. He got to his feet. 'I think I'd better go before I get accused of making a pass at you.'

Maureen held out her hand for him to shake. 'Maybe we'll meet again, under better circumstances.'

He grunted, awkwardly, not knowing whether to take this as an invitation to ask her out sometime – or was she just being nice? Probably nice, he told himself, reluctantly. She was a nice lady was Maureen Gaskell, a very nice lady.

Jacky's pocket watch had become famous. Everyone in the school had seen it because Jacky never hesitated to show the inscription off with pride and tell the story of how Frank McGovern had saved three men from death down the mine. Jacky rarely referred to Frank as his dad. Somehow it didn't seem fair on the man he had always loved and known as his parent. It was also too confusing. One of the men whom Frank had saved had a son at the school, who confirmed Jacky's story.

'They hanged an innocent man,' Jacky told anyone who would listen. 'One day I'll prove it.'

The murder had taken place just over the school wall and it became a game to guess the identity of the real murderer. As there were only two suspects and one of them was unquestionably an innocent victim of the gallows, it was a short game. Having a local killer on the loose was far more interesting than Frank McGovern being actually guilty.

The girls especially saw romance in the story of Frank being wrongly hanged as a result of loving another man's wife. One of them had kept his photograph from the newspaper, which she brought to school. Close examination of this left no one in any doubt that handsome Frank McGovern had been the victim of a miscarriage of justice. It was a story worthy of a skipping song. All it needed was a composer.

It was now almost a year since Mumford killed his wife. A respectable period of mourning, he thought. Time now to move on. He considered himself to be of average appearance. Average height, average build, brown hair and neither ugly nor handsome. In an attempt to give character to his average face he had grown what he thought was a Chaplinesque moustache. His bathroom mirror should have told him he looked more like Hitler than Charlie Chaplin but he was a master of self-delusion. In other people's eyes he was a physically awkward, pallid-faced, slightly built, unthreatening-looking, emotionally adolescent man. The last was a quality some women found challenging. But he had a quick mind and had built himself a nice business as an insurance agent – and he was much more comfortably off than most men. A quality some women found quite attractive.

Most men, however, looked upon him as a bit of a weed. Boys had picked on him when he was at school. Called him Clumsy Mumsy. How he hated that. They often stole from him and bullied him. He would lie in his bed at night dreaming of the revenge he would one day take on his tormentors; these people who took things from him, such as his dinner money and his dignity.

Marion Halliwell was a customer he'd had occasion to visit regarding a life insurance policy. She was locked in an unhappy marriage to a penniless wastrel and was susceptible to Mumford's generosity and amused by his gauche wooing. His late wife had also fallen for it, and had unwisely allowed herself to be drawn into a marriage with a man about whose sanity she began to have grave doubts.

With her husband away on business, Marion had gone on a secret date with Victor – and had ended up at his house. She had certain misgivings at being there but it wasn't to do with Victor – more the house and its violent history.

'I honestly don't know how you can go on living here, Victor,' she said. 'Knowing what happened.'

'I shut it all from my mind.'

Nothing was further from the truth. He had been in a state of fearful limbo right up to Frank being hanged; after which he had experienced a sense of euphoria. He had wreaked terrible revenge on an unfaithful wife and her lover, and he still cherished the ultimate erotic memory of her. One minute she was in the throes of ecstasy, thrusting her beautiful naked body up at her lover, and then she was screaming with terror and pain as Victor plunged his knife into her breasts.

Getting away with it had been part of the thrill – a major part – as was still living in the same house and sleeping in the same bed. He didn't want these memories to go away. The house and the bed kept it all alive and fresh in his mind. He'd had the sheets and mattress cleaned rather than throw them away. They were all part of this precious image he kept locked in his mind.

He and Marion made love in that same bed, with Marion inwardly comparing him to her husband – unfavourably. Her husband was a pig in many ways but he knew his way around the bedroom. Victor was a clumsy, unimaginative and selfish lover. It was six in the morning when she woke up and wondered what the hell was she doing there. He'd wined and dined her and maybe she'd dropped her guard just a little too much to end up in bed with him. Whatever charm he'd displayed last night somehow didn't manifest itself in that sleeping weed beside her. She saw a skinny, pale-skinned version of Adolf Hitler, lying with his mouth open, snoring; with a thin line of drool making its way down a thin chin that was in need of a razor blade.

She grimaced and swung her legs out of the bed, catching a glimpse of her naked self in the dressing-table mirror. What she had was far too good for the likes of Victor Mumford. He woke up and asked her the time.

'Time I was going.'

'What? Why? Your old man's not due back, is he?'

'Not 'til tomorrow.'

'Can't we have another before you go? Look at this – we can't let this go to waste.'

He threw the bedclothes back to reveal an unhealthy-looking early morning erection. It matched the rest of him, she thought. All it lacked was the moustache.

'I don't think so, Victor.'

She got to her feet and stretched the sleep from her body. Victor had two views of it. One from behind and one in the mirror. He leaned out of bed and pulled her back in.

'Just one more. You can't leave me like this.' For all his skinny apearance he was quite strong – stronger than she was.

'Victor! I said no. We had a nice time last night and I want to leave it at that. I am married, remember.'

His voice turned petulant. 'Why – wasn't I up to scratch? Is that it? Am I not as good as your husband?'

He pushed her back down on the bed and knelt over her, with a leg either side. She struggled violently, freeing a hand and slapping him hard across his face.

'You're nowhere near as good him,' she sneered.

'I'll tell him that, shall I?'

'You wouldn't dare. He'd kill you if he knew what you'd done. He's twice the man you are, even if he is a pig to me.'

'I can be a pig if you like.'

He grunted like a pig and lowered himself on to her, thrusting but getting nowhere as she tried to wriggle away from him.

'Get off me! I don't want you anywhere near me!'

She slapped him again and he punched her, hard, in the mouth, Shouting at her, 'Behave! Or you'll get more of the same.'

He thrust a clenched fist in her face, saw fear in her eyes and liked what he saw. Marion dropped her arms in surrender. He now had complete control over her. She was his for the taking. The stimulation in his loins was almost unbearable.

'Tell me you love me,' he commanded, shrilly. There was an

unhinged look in his eyes that scared her. 'Tell me I can do whatever I want with you.'

'What?'

'Tell me!'

'Okay, okay . . . I love you.'

He hit her again. 'Liar! Better than me, is he? This pig you're married to?'

'Victor, I don't know what's happening.'

He slapped her face several times. She was now subdued to the point of terror. It seemed to Marion that there was only one way out of this. Lie back and think of England.

'Victor,' she said, as calmly as she could. 'Do whatever you want to me. Just don't hurt me any more.'

But Victor's mind had drifted back to the night he killed his wife. That glorious night. This was that night all over again, except it was morning and this time there wasn't a witness. No one knew she was here. Blood was trickling from her nose and mouth, and her breasts were heaving with fear. He hit her again for the pure pleasure of it, but it wasn't enough. Nowhere near enough. Beside the bed was a heavy lamp; he grabbed it, yanked the cable free of the plug and held it upside down like a club.

'Oh, no, Victor. Please don't hur—'

His first blow cut short her plea. Then he moved his ear close to her mouth and listened for a sign of life; head to one side, poised, like a hungry cat that had just heard a bird twittering in a nearby tree. When she twitched he gave a scream of rage and bludgeoned her to death. Then he stood and allowed his heavy breathing to subside as he surveyed what he had done, his head on one side again, committing this precious vision to his memory.

That day he didn't go to work. He was ill, he told them – gippy tummy. Be all right tomorrow. He spent the morning digging a grave in his garden, which was secluded and overlooked by no one; not even the kids from the school could see in. He threw the blood-stained bedclothes in the bottom of the hole, splashed them with paraffin and threw a match in. Then he burnt the mattress the same way – he had no valid excuse for having the blood cleaned off this time. Marion weighed little more than eight stone so it wasn't much of a problem lugging her body out of the house and dropping it down the hole. By lunchtime the job was done; the grave was filled in and disguised with stones from his rockery. It was as if she'd never existed – and the beauty of it was that no one knew of his association with her. She had taken great pains to keep their brief affair a secret. Good old Marion. Such a thoughtful woman.

As he stood over the grave a song started up at the other side of the school wall. It was being sung by several kids at once, both boys and girls, to the beat of a skipping rope slapping on the ground and the off-beat of a dozen thudding feet:

'Frank loved Victor Mumford's wife,
So Victor stabbed her with a knife.
Frank McGovern got the blame,
But we all know the killer's name.'

The singing became a shout, as the line of skipping children spelled out his name, letter by letter, in between jumps:

'M . . . U . . . M . . . F . . . O . . . R . . . D
MUMFORD!'

Mumford felt his courage and excitement draining away as the implication of this skipping song hit him. Would the kids somehow find out about Marion the same way they had found out about his wife? He must put a stop to this before it went any further.

'Stop it!' he screamed. 'Just . . . stop it!'

Jacky had dared the kids to do it right under Mumford's wall and they'd taken up the dare because it was common knowledge that Mumford was never in during the day. What they didn't know was that ten minutes earlier Jacky had heard someone working in Mumford's garden – hopefully Mumford himself. The wall was over six feet high so he couldn't see over it, but it was worth giving it a go.

When they heard Mumford's angry shout the children had all paused with their hands over their mouths, looking at each other with hunched shoulders and guilty grins creeping across their faces, delighted that they'd hit a nerve. As they ran away, laughing, they all agreed that Mumford was definitely the killer.

Half an hour later, when Jacky was summoned to Mr Booth's study, Victor Mumford had been and gone. The headmaster had assured the obviously distressed man that he would have no further need for complaint. The problem would be dealt with quickly and severely. Jacky looked at him, warily. The headmaster's face was almost as grey as the unruly garlands of hair that decorated each side of his otherwise bald head. His bloodless lips curved down like a scimitar; sharp and sneering. His eyes were as cold as the Castlethorpe canal and about the same colour.

'Have you been spreading malicious rumours, Gaskell?'

'No, sir.'

'You're lying, boy. Do you know how I can tell you're lying?'

'No, sir.'

'Because your lips move, Gaskell.'

Booth smirked, briefly, at his own joke, then his mouth curved back into its natural scowl. 'I promised I would expel you if you gave me further trouble.'

'But I haven't done anything, sir.'

'Are you trying to tell me that you haven't been going round telling lies about your father being innocent?'

'They're not lies, sir.'

'And haven't you been going round telling every one that a decent and well-respected local man is the real murderer.'

'No sir,' said Jacky, truthfully. He'd never said anything about Mumford being decent and well respected. Booth knew he hadn't the power to expel Jacky on hearsay, but he pressed on, nevertheless.

'I imagine it was you who made up this childish verse.'

'Oh no, sir. If there's one thing I can't do it's make up verses, sir. You ask Mrs Evershed. She once asked us to make up a poem about a donkey, an' mine were useless, sir. She gave me one out of ten, sir. And she says I only got that because I spelled me name right, s—'

'Silence, boy!' roared Booth. 'Hold out your hand.'

Jacky held out his hand and received yet another six strokes, each delivered with venom. He looked up at the headteacher with more hurt in his eyes than in his hands and walked out of the study. With each passing day he had more and more reason to prove Frank innocent and to make fools of everyone who said otherwise. He warmed his hands on a radiator to ease the pain, then grinned to himself at the knowledge that the new skipping

71

song was very popular at his sister's school – being as it was Ellie who had made it up. It was her version of poetic justice. Soon it would be all round Castlethorpe. And they couldn't blame Jacky Gaskell for that.

Chapter Ten

Maureen was having a bad day. The sort of bad day that arrived regularly each month. There had been a couple of times in her life when that day hadn't arrived and she'd wished it had, but this wasn't one of them. That morning she'd decided to harness her foul temper and take it down to the housing office to check on her position on the council housing list. Things had all gone quiet since Bert died, and a larger bedroom for the two boys would make it a bit easier for Jacky to come home. She was confronted by a junior assistant housing officer, not much older than Brian.

'I'm afraid you're not on the current year's list, madam.'

'But I must be. When my husband came down just before he died, which was eighteen months ago now, you told him we would be rehoused inside twelve months.'

'Ah . . . that could be the reason, madam.'

'What could be the reason?'

'That fact that your husband has, er . . . sadly died.'

'Have I become less of a priority since he died?'

The young man looked inside a file, then at Maureen, who was twisting her head to see. 'It, er, it seems your present accommodation is adequate, madam.'

'Adequate? I don't want to be adequate, I want to be comfortable. I want a bathroom and a garden and a proper kitchen. Do you realise what you're saying?'

'Madam?'

'You're telling me I've not only lost my husband but I've also lost a house with a bathroom and garden and a proper kitchen. Do you know how that makes me feel?'

'I, er . . . in view of the housing shortage we have to give priority to people living in overcrowded homes.'

'I see. So, my husband dying has solved my overcrowding problem, has it? Tell you what, sonny, instead of building houses why don't you just go round bumping people off. It'd be a lot cheaper.'

'Madam?'

'Could I have your name please?'

The young man gave her a worried stare, then glanced at the door to the side of him as if planning an avenue of escape.

'Question too difficult?' asked Maureen, caustically. 'I need a name. I'm complaining to my local councillor about you people taking advantage of me because of my husband's death. I assume you have a name, do you? Or hasn't your mother registered you yet? You scarcely look old enough for your birth to have been registered.'

There was too much rising heat in her voice for the young man to cope with. He backed away through the door. 'I'll get my superior, madam.'

The superior arrived in the form of a woman who made an attempt at a patronising smile, but Maureen didn't look up, which annoyed the woman. 'How can I help you, madam?' she asked, brusquely.

Maureen had her diary out and was poised with a pencil. 'I asked your assistant for his name but the question seemed too difficult for him. I don't suppose you know his name, do you?'

'What is it about, madam?'

Maureen looked up now, meeting the woman's eyes. 'I thought I explained everything to your assistant. Are you not in communication with your staff? If you want to know what it's about ask him. All I want is a name to take to my councillor. I would have thought that taking advantage of a bereavement is a sackable offence. It would certainly make a good story in the *Yorkshire Post*.'

The door opened and the previous young man's head popped out. He gave Maureen a brief smile of recognition and said, 'Mrs Elliot, there's a phone call for you when you've got a minute.'

'Mrs Elliot,' said Maureen. 'That'll do. I assume that's two Ls.' She began to write. 'Mrs Elliot. Doesn't communicate with her staff. My husband dies and the council sees it as a convenient ploy

74

to take me off the housing list.' She looked up, gave the woman a dismissive smile and put the diary in her bag. 'Thank you, Mrs Elliot. You can take your phone call now.'

Mrs Elliot tried to call her back but Maureen strode out of the building. Sometimes leaving people to stew in their own juice was better than becoming involved in a long, protracted argument which would have left Maureen feeling murderous and no further up the housing list. Men's heads still turned as she strode past. This set her thinking. Going to see her councillor might not be such a bad idea. He was a man, after all. If she could harness her bad temper to take a council official down a peg or two she might as well take advantage of her other assets. By the time she was descending the council office steps she had thought better of it. Experience had taught her that her *other* assets were best reserved for one man alone. If he ever turned up in her life. Maybe he already had.

In the meantime, Jacky's living next door was getting her down. It wasn't right, but she couldn't see an alternative, other than kicking Brian out. Was she being mercenary? Her eldest son's money came in handy, no doubt about that; and Brian always paid up without grumbling. Maybe if she invited Jacky round for tea that night the brothers might just bury the hatchet. Maureen was nothing if not an optimist.

A large saucepan full of water was bubbling on the hob, in readiness for when Brian came in from work and needed a wash in the sink. Since the theft of the tin bath from the yard wall the whole family took a shower once a week at Jack Street public swimming baths, where Maureen would swim fifty lengths of the 25-yard pool while Jacky and Ellie generally fooled around off the diving board and Brian sat on the balcony, eating crisps and eyeing up the girls.

On the mantelpiece above the black-leaded Yorkshire Range fireplace was a clock, a pair of ornamental clogs that Bert had brought back from wartime Holland and a photograph of him in his army uniform. He wore a forage cap set at a jaunty angle which, to Maureen, always seemed at odds with his personality. Bert had been a decent man, but never jaunty. Jacky was sitting in Bert's favourite chair, reading the *Yorkshire Evening News* when Brian walked in and asked his mother, 'What's he doin' here?'

75

He was referring to Jacky, who answered Brian's question without troubling to look up from the paper. 'I'm reading about a woman who's gone missing,' he said. 'I don't suppose you fancy going missing, do you. You'll get your name in the paper – and your photo. Look.' He gave Brian a benign smile and showed him Marion Halliwell's photograph. 'This could be you, our kid, if you play your cards right. All you've got to do is clear off and never come back. It's got to be worth a try.'

Brian took Jacky by his collar and yanked from his chair.

'Just stop that!' shouted Maureen, despairingly. 'Brian, he's your brother.' Her hatchet-burying hopes collapsed. 'I asked him to come for tea.'

Brian let go of Jacky and glared at his mother. 'I haven't got a brother.'

'You haven't got a brain, that's your problem,' said Jacky, blithely. 'I reckon they're training you up to do the same job as a pit pony. They've got their work cut out.'

'You little sh—'

'Stop it!' said Maureen, fiercely. 'I've had a very bad day today.'

'Why's that?' asked Jacky, genuinely concerned for his mam.

'We've been taken off the council housing list because your dad's dead and we're apparently not overcrowded anymore.'

'That's awful,' Ellie said. 'Can't we do anything?'

Maureen shrugged and said, hopelessly, 'We could kick up a stink, I suppose, for what good it'll do. There's just too much going on in my life at the moment. Living on top of one another in this hen-hutch isn't doing us any good. Jacky can't live at Charlie's forever.'

'I'm okay at Charlie's,' Jacky said. He went across and put his arm around her. 'We get on okay, me and Charlie. It's not like being with you but it's the next best thing and you're just next door.'

She squeezed his hand in appreciation. Brian saw this and said, 'Well, yer'll get no trouble from me. It's been nice and peaceful livin' in this house since Big Ears left.'

'Tell you what, Mam,' said Jacky, innocently, going back to his chair. 'Our kid's reading's coming on if he's on to Enid Blyton books.'

'Piss off!'

76

'Watch your language, Brian!' said Maureen, sharply.

Jacky chipped in with: 'Ooo, wash your mouth out Brian Gaskell. Since you started work down that mine with all those nasty men you've got a mouth like a sewer. Are the other pit ponies as foul-mouthed as you?'

Maureen glared at them both. 'If you two have got any respect for me you'll behave yourselves. If not you can get out of this house and don't come back until you've seen sense – and that goes for you as well, Brian. You're old enough to know better. It's because of your stupidity that Jacky's having to live with his gr ... with Charlie.'

She almost bit her tongue off but none of her children had picked up on her slip.

'Sorry,' Jacky said.

Today was definitely not a good day for Maureen. On top of everything else, Frank's death was just beginning to have a serious effect on her. It was as if she'd been numbed by the gross injustice of his trial and execution and the pain and reality was just beginning to seep through. A sudden picture of him came to her mind as Brian glowered at her and muttered, 'I'm not so stupid that you won't take most of me money off me.'

Jacky kept quiet; happy in the knowledge that Brian was digging his own grave.

'If you like, Brian,' Maureen said, pushing Frank's image to one side. 'I won't take *any* money off you. Not a penny. Just as long as you don't expect to live here.'

'I've every right to live here. I'm me father's son.'

'Mam, I can't stand this,' said Ellie. 'You'll have to make the tea, I'm going upstairs.'

'Don't blame yer, our lass,' sniffed Brian. 'Yer never safe while Jacky boy's around. Slit yer throat as soon as look at yer.'

Maureen hurled a cup in blind anger. It hit the photo of Bert; both cup and photo shattered into pieces and fell into the hearth.

'Now look what you've made me do!'

The three children stared at her as she picked up the broken frame and looked at her late husband's image, smiling at her in his army uniform. Jauntily. What the hell was happening to her? She'd been thinking of Frank and had smashed Bert's photo. Placing the broken frame face down on the mantelpiece, she returned her displeasure to Brian. Ellie changed her mind about going upstairs; her mother might struggle to cope with this situation on her own. Maureen was breathing heavily. Brian had squared up to her; ready to face her down once and for all; to show her who was master in this house. His mother was doing her best not to lose control of the situation.

'Your father would be ashamed if he could see the way you're behaving,' she said, flushed with anger.

'Whose father are yer talkin' about – mine or the murderer's bastard?' taunted Brian.

'Jacky's dad wasn't a murderer!' she shouted, out of control again.

'Oh yeah. Why did they hang him then?' Brian was confident that he had got the better of his mother for the first time in his life. 'He were a murderer and he's a murderer's bastard.' He jabbed his finger in his younger brother's direction. Jacky was halfway out of the chair with fists clenched when Maureen suddenly screamed, 'Better a murderer's bastard than a rapist's bastard – and that's what you are, the son of a rapist!'

Her mouth fell open and she slowly brought a hand up to it in the classic manner of someone closing the stable door after the horse has bolted. Then she sat down in the chair, her three children stunned into silence. After a while Ellie put an arm around her mother's shoulder. Maureen's hand was still over her mouth. Brian went over to the hob and picked up the bubbling pan. He hadn't seen this coming. In a few shocking words she'd managed to knock all the fight out of him. The stunned silence in the room was disturbed only by the sound of him pouring the hot water from the pan into the sink and running the cold tap until the water temperature was right. He then stripped off to the waist, picked up a bar of soap and began to wash himself, slowly. It was all he could think to do. He was hoping his mother had just flown off the handle and had said it to get the better of him. But he knew she would never say anything as hurtful as that to him, not if it wasn't true. A rage was building up inside him and he didn't know who to take it out on.

Jacky stared into the fire trying to make sense of everything. He was sure his mother was telling the truth. She was crying now and Ellie was trying to comfort her. Jacky felt like taking a pan and hitting Brian over the head with it. This was all his doing. If he *was* the son of a rapist it was no better than he deserved. At least Jacky had a father he was proud of. Even if he had been hanged.

Brian dried himself off very slowly. Then he put a clean shirt on and walked across to his mother's chair, where he stood with his arms folded. Challenging her. Maureen looked up at him. Her face was ashen with guilt.

'What were that yer said, Mam? Yer know – that thing about me bein' the son of a rapist.'

She wiped away a tear with the heel of her hand. 'Brian, I never meant to tell you this, I'm so sor—'

He didn't let her finish. 'It's true then?'

'Yes.'

'So, what you're saying is, somebody raped you . . . and here I am,' Brian summarised. 'Me dad wasn't . . . me dad?'

His mother spoke very quietly as if she didn't want to hear her own words. 'I was raped nine months before you were born. I told the police and they arrested the person who did it but he told them I'd been willing. It was my word against his. We were both students at art college. He was a year older than me but he had an influential father. I didn't even have a father. Then I found out I was pregnant.'

'What did he do when you told him?' Ellie asked, as gently as she could.

'Tell him? Why would I tell him? Why would I want to have anything to do with a rapist? He subjected me to the most degrading experience of my life. I never wanted to see him again.' She took Ellie's hand. 'I'd been friends with your father since we were kids. He found out I was pregnant and . . . well, he sort of took care of me, I suppose. I told him what had happened and he was the only person who believ—'

Brian interrupted her. 'So, that's how yer think of me, is it? The result of the most degrading experience of yer life.'

'It was never like that, Brian. When Bert and I got married we looked upon you as our own child.'

Brian dismissed this with a shake of his head. 'I often wondered why you married him. I'd have thought you'd have gone for someone a bit more—'

'A bit more what?' his mother asked, quietly; daring him to insult Bert.

Brian didn't pursue it but everyone knew what he meant. Their mother was a beautiful, intelligent woman and Bert was no better than ordinary.

'I married him because he loved me and he was the kindest man I'd ever met.'

'Mam,' said Brian. 'Yer married him because yer were pregnant.'

Ellie deflected this dangerous line of argument with 'Did you love him?'

'I grew to love him, Ellie. When he died it was like having my heart ripped out. And before you ask, yes, he was your real father.'

Maureen looked up at Brian, whose eyes were now damp. Even Jacky felt sorry for him. He vowed he would never call his brother son of a rapist, no matter what Brian called him.

'Where is he now?' Brian asked her. His voice was hoarse with emotion. 'This bloke who . . . this new father o' mine?'

'America, I imagine,' replied his mother. 'His name was Pettifer . . . Morgan Pettifer. He was American. His father had some high-flying job over here and took his family back home just before the war started.'

'Morgan Pettifer,' repeated Ellie. 'What sort of name's Morgan Pettifer?'

'Blimey, he even *sounds* like a rapist,' commented Jacky.

Brian glared at him but said nothing. He needed to take his rage out on someone and he had decided who.

'I'm off out,' he muttered.

'Okay,' said his mother. 'Handle it your own way, Brian. Just remember, Bert was a real father to you, the same as he was to Jacky.'

Brian corrected her. 'Actually,' he said, 'that's not true. He preferred our Ellie ter me, the same as you preferred Jacky. At least I know why now. I always thought it were summat ter do wi' me bein' thick an' ugly.' He looked in a mirror and pulled a face. 'He must have been an ugly bastard, this Morgan Pettifer.'

'Brian,' protested Maureen. 'No one thinks you're thick and you're definitely not ugly—'

She was cut off by the sound of the door slamming behind her departing son. Brian rode his bike up the street and looked at the watch in his hand; the one he'd just taken from Jacky's coat which had been hanging on the same hook as his. His immediate intention was to throw it away, depriving Jacky of his most prized possession. Then he had a better idea.

An hour later he returned home. The house was still quiet. Maureen, Jacky and Ellie were still sitting at the table although the meal was long since finished. They glanced up at Brian, apprehensively. He gave a broad grin as he hung his coat up.

'Have yer left owt fer me?' he asked.

'I can rustle you something up, love,' Maureen said, getting to her feet. She stood beside him. 'Are you okay, love?'

'Right as rain, Mam,' he assured her. 'Right as rain.'

Jacky got to his feet and retrieved his coat from under his brother's. As he put it on he automatically tapped the pocket in which he kept his precious watch.

'My watch has gone,' he said, puzzled. He looked on the floor to see if he might have dropped it when he unhooked his coat.

'Don't look at me,' said Brian, holding up his hands. 'I haven't got yer rotten watch.'

'No one says you have, Brian,' said Maureen. 'Jacky, have you looked through every pocket?'

He made a thorough search of his coat, shaking his head as he came to the last pocket.

'Maybe it's at Charlie's,' suggested Ellie.

'Could be,' Jacky conceded. 'In fact that's where it'll prob'ly be – on the table in my bedroom. I'll nip and get it, then I'm off out to play with Roy.'

'I should leave it where it is,' Maureen advised. 'It worries me you taking it with you all the time. It's worth something you know. Solid gold.'

'It's worth more than solid gold to me,' Jacky said. 'It's like carryin' Frank's Victoria Cross around.'

'Well, you leave it where you know it's safe.'

'All right, Mam. Thanks for me tea.'

He was halfway out of the door when Brian called after him. 'An' don't you be getting' into any mischief, Jacky boy. I've heard all about the trouble yer ger yerself into.'

'Well, you've heard wrong then!' retorted Jacky. 'I'm a little angel, me.'

*

The little angel had his wings clipped when he was summoned into the head's study the following morning. PC Bill Scanlon was there, standing by Mr Booth, whose normally pallid face was faintly flushed with anger. The room was in a mess. The floor was littered with books pulled from a bookcase, the desk was on its side and the contents strewn all over the floor, someone had scored the surface of the desk with a knife and carved in it, BOOTHY IS A BASTAD. Ink had been splashed on every wall and over all the books and papers littering the floor; the window had been smashed, as had Booth's chair. The headmaster came straight to the point. 'This is your work, isn't it, Gaskell?'

'No, sir.'

'Don't lie to me boy—'

Jacky pointed to the message carved into the desk. 'Sir, if it'd been me I'd have spelt it right.'

'Don't be so damned insol—'

The policeman intervened. 'I'll handle this, Mr Booth.' He took Jacky by the shoulder and led him to the broken window. 'Whoever did this got in through this window,' he said. 'And when they climbed through they dropped that.' He pointed to the floor, where Jacky's watch lay amid shards of broken glass. 'Would that be your watch, lad?'

It took Jacky only an instant to weigh up what had happened. This was Brian's work. He'd taken the watch from his pocket. Jacky had suspected Brian when the watch didn't turn up at Charlie's. His own brother had set him up for this.

'I think so, mister. But I don't know how it got there. I didn't do this. Somebody framed me, mister.'

'Framed you?' said Bill, raising an eyebrow. 'I think you've been watching too many gangster pictures, son. How do you get in to watch them at your age?'

'Because he's a deceitful boy, an habitual liar and a thoroughly bad lot,' growled Booth.

'I didn't do it, mister,' Jacky protested.

'Wait outside,' snapped Booth.

'Can I have my watch back, sir. It was my da—'

'Get out!'

Jacky trudged into the corridor as Booth and the policeman decided what to do.

'This isn't the first time you and I have spoken about this

boy,' said Booth. 'The last time was when he assaulted another pupil.'

'I'm aware of that, Mr Booth,' said Bill, 'and I was never able to work out why no one pressed charges. On top of which the boy he's supposed to have assaulted is well known to us – quite a lot bigger than Jacky Gaskell, I'd say. Assault seems an odd word to use.'

'What are you getting at, constable?'

'The truth, Mr Booth. I always try and get at the truth.' Bill took out his notebook. 'I assume you'll want to press charges on this occasion.'

'Of course I do.'

'Right,' Bill began, 'Apart from the watch – which he says was stolen from him and dropped here to incriminate him – so we can't use that; what else have we got to connect the boy with the vandalism?'

'What else?' Booth bridled. 'How do you mean, what else. Isn't the watch enough?'

Bill tried to hide the distaste in his eyes and wondered if the headmaster recognised him. No, it had been nearly twenty years since he'd been a pupil there. Had it not been Booth and Jacky he was dealing with, he'd have taken the watch as sound evidence, but Booth wasn't to know that. It was to be hoped this didn't get back to his sergeant.

'You need to discredit his story, Mr Booth. Prove conclusively that he was here.'

'I thought that was your job.'

'The only evidence I have is what I see around me – one watch – which may or may not have been stolen from the boy by the real culprit. A court would need much more than this.'

'Can't you take fingerprints or something?'

'It would be inconclusive, Mr Booth. The boy would have to have no reason ever to have left prints in your office. Does he ever come in this office? Perhaps for a caning?'

'Occasionally,' Booth admitted.

I bet that means frequently, Bill thought.

'Look, officer,' said Booth. 'All I know is that he's constantly in trouble at school. It wouldn't surprise me if it was the one who tried to strip the lead off the roof last winter. That's another crime you failed to solve. You know who his father is, don't you?'

'Yes, Mr Booth. I am aware of who he is. But if the lad's denying he did it—'

'He's lying.'

'If he's denying it,' continued the constable patiently, 'we've only got the watch to go on. It's not beyond the bounds of possibility that he's telling the truth.'

'He's lying!' snarled Booth. 'Couldn't you see it in his face?'

'No, Mr Booth,' Bill said, calmly. 'As a matter of fact I couldn't. I've seen plenty of delinquent kids in my time and they didn't look anything like Jacky Gaskell.' The policeman was enjoying himself at Booth's expense. Whether or not it was a form of revenge for the treatment Booth had meted out to him as a boy or because Jacky was *her* son, he didn't know. 'Tell you what, I'll take him down to the station and question him, sir.'

'Take him where the hell you like. Just don't bring him back here. As far as I'm concerned he's expelled!' Booth went to the door where Jacky was listening, intently. 'Did you hear that, boy? You're expelled!'

Jacky went pale. This was unfair. 'I didn't do anythin', sir. Honest, it wasn't me.'

'Get out of this school and take your lies and your vandalism with you,' screamed Booth. 'How the hell I'm supposed to impose discipline in this school with the son of a murderer as a pupil, God only knows.'

'Can I have my watch back, sir,' asked Jacky, in tears now.

'Just get out of my sight, boy.'

'You'll get your watch back soon enough, lad,' Bill assured him. He guided Jacky away from Booth's wrath, then turned and said to the headmaster, 'I'll let you know what our decision is, sir.'

'I'm not interested in your decision, constable. I just want rid of that detestable boy. Look at the state of my study!'

'I think you might be better off at another school, lad,' said Bill to Jacky, loud enough for Booth to hear.

'But I take me scholarship tomorrow, mister.'

'Not from this school, you don't!' snarled Booth. 'I'm withdrawing your entry as of today.'

'That seems very unfair, sir,' said Bill, turning round to face the irate headmaster. 'Very unfair indeed.'

'Unfair, unfair?' Booth swept a theatrical hand across the devastation in his study. 'This is unfair. How can I, in all conscience, send a delinquent pupil to a grammar school, even to take an examination. As of right now he is no longer a pupil of this school. I will report the matter to my governors but I am confident of their full backing in this.'

Bill was seething at the obvious injustice of all this. 'In that case I think I'd better take the watch, Mr Booth. I don't want to have to come back and investigate another crime now do I?'

'What other crime?'

'Well if the watch goes missing I'll be investigating a theft. I hope you're within your rights expelling the boy for something that he quite possibly didn't do.'

'Let me worry about that, constable.'

Most of the governors had already expressed dismay over having the son of a murderer at their school. Jacky's expulsion wouldn't be questioned. Booth watched the policeman take Jacky out of school and breathed a sigh of relief. A vandalised study was a small price to pay for getting rid of that troublesome boy. He wasn't sure what right he had to cancel Jacky's exam entry but he could put a big enough spanner in the works to ensure the boy didn't take it tomorrow. That made him feel better.

Chapter Eleven

The following day, 6 February 1952, the king died, but Jacky's mind was preoccupied with thoughts of revenge on Brian. If there was bad blood in this family it wasn't flowing through Jacky's veins. Frank McGovern was a hero. Now a rapist – that was another matter altogether. His conscience told him that Brian wasn't responsible for who his rapist father was – but he *was* responsible for ruining Jacky's life.

He was sitting with Charlie, who had instantly taken his side in this. Jacky hadn't told him about his older brother's violent conception, so Charlie couldn't understand where Brian got his bad ways from. Maureen was down at the police station trying to sort things out. On the wall was a poster of Marion Halliwell, the missing woman, which only served to remind Maureen of the enmity between her sons. That was how it had started – Jacky showing Brian that photograph and recommending he went missing as well. In a way she could appreciate Jacky's thinking. She knew it could have been Brian who had wrecked Booth's office just for spite. He was capable of such a thing, and the timing was right. In fact he was the hot favourite. No, she wouldn't let herself believe such a thing of him. He was a handful at times but never *that* bad.

'I do hope you had nothing to do with this, Brian,' was all she said.

'Me?' He feigned affront. 'Would I do such a thing to my baby brother?'

The smirk on his face almost had her striking him for the first time in his life, and just for an awful instant she saw Morgan Pettifer there. Smirking.

*

It had started out as an innocent date. Morgan Pettifer sat next to her in still-life class at Leeds College of Art. It was Maureen's least favourite subject but it was part of the course, so she had no option. Her ambition was to be a designer in one of the major fashion houses such as Norman Hartnell. Maybe even own her own fashion house one day.

He had a handsome face with an Errol Flynn type moustache; and he was American, which set him apart from most of Maureen's friends who were from West Yorkshire and spoke northern nondescript, whereas Morgan had an attractive transatlantic twang to his voice. Maybe it was that which persuaded her to let him take her out that night.

His dad had lent him his car, which was a treat for Maureen; no young man she'd ever been out with had had ownership of, or even access to a car. She had lived with her mother in Castlethorpe, her dad having died in France before she was born. His only two brothers had died in the same war, as had her mother's only brother. It had been a useless sacrifice that had left Maureen embittered and had given her a resentment of any kind of authority. Because of the callous stupidity of the generals and politicians, sitting on their backsides behind their safe desks, she and her mother had been left without a family.

Morgan had taken her to several pubs in Leeds and had suggested going back to his house for a coffee. Maureen had accepted because she assumed his parents would be there and anyway she was quite attracted to him. She was only nineteen and still a virgin.

It transpired that his parents were away for the weekend. As soon as they got through the door, Morgan pulled her to him quite roughly and forced his mouth against hers. Rather than be thought a prude she responded as best she could, then had to pull away to catch her breath.

'Steady on,' she said. 'Didn't you say something about coffee?'

Placing his hands on her breasts he gave the smirk that would remain in her memory. 'Afterwards,' he said. 'I can't wait, sorry.'

He forced his mouth onto hers again, this time fumbling with the buttons at the back of her dress. She pushed him away, shouting at him now. Needing to stamp her authority on the situation.

'Stop it. I don't want this!'

'Liar! You want it as much as I do.'

Morgan was panting like a dog on heat and she felt him hard against her as he thrust his body into hers and gripped her tightly. Hurting her. She screamed at him.

'I don't want to do this. Stop it!'

He hit her and knocked her to the floor, then pounced on her with a wild grin on his face, pulling at her clothes. 'This is how you like it, eh? Suits me, slut. Suits me just fine.'

'Please Morgan . . . No!'

Her dress was off now; her bra came with it, exposing her breasts, which inflamed him even more. Within a few seconds he had her stripped naked and was pulling down his trousers as Maureen lay, terrified, beneath him. A man in this uncontrolled frame of mind was capable of anything. Maybe rape was the least of her worries.

'Please don't hurt me, Morgan!'

He forced himself inside her thrusting with brutal ferocity; one hand over her mouth to suppress any screams. The pain was unimaginable. She felt nothing but fear, pain and loathing. No way for a girl to lose her virginity.

After he had finished he lay on her until he had recovered his breath then he calmly got to his feet, adjusted his clothing and went into the kitchen to make coffee as if this was an everyday occurrence. Maureen had covered up her nakedness as best she could with her dress and was curled up in a ball, still sobbing when he got back with two steaming cups.

'I'll take them through,' he said, cheerfully. 'Join me when you're ready.'

Maureen didn't say anything. She was racked with pain, blood was trickling down her legs and she desperately needed to go to his bathroom, but her need to get out of this place was even greater. She managed to get dressed and left the house, not knowing what to do or where to go. A passing car driver noticed her obvious distress and stopped for her. She backed away, fearfully, as he called out through his window.

'Are you all right, love?'

A woman in the passenger seat leaned forward and looked at her. 'She's *not* all right,' Maureen heard her say. 'Can we give you a lift anywhere, love?'

She got in the car without daring to speak lest she broke down in tears.

'Where do you want to go, love?' asked the man. 'Home? Police station? Has someone . . . done something to you?'

There was a long pause as Maureen considered his question. The man opened his mouth to repeat it but was nudged into silence by his wife, who smiled at Maureen and said, 'Take your time, love. It was a man, wasn't it?'

Maureen nodded and said, 'Police station, please,' in a voice that was almost inaudible.

'I damn well thought it was something like that,' the woman said to her husband. 'Some men. They want it bloody chopping off!'

The police took her complaint seriously but could have been more sympathetic. Maureen didn't even know where Morgan's house was. Had it not been for the couple in the car pointing them in the right direction they wouldn't have able to arrest Pettifer that night. He arrived, loudly protesting his innocence and insisting that his father's solicitor be called before he made any statement. Maureen was in an adjacent room and could hear him shouting at the top of his voice, calling her a slut and telling the police how she'd gone willingly to his house and wanted it as much as he had. A policewoman sitting with her had offered her a well-intentioned piece of advice.

'If it's your word against his love it's a very thin case. The jury has to be very sure – sure enough to send him down for seven years.'

'I'd hardly have come here if it hadn't happened,' Maureen said. Her voice was tired.

'You know that, and I know that,' said the policewoman, sympathetically. 'But if it goes to court you'll be put through a lot worse than he's put you through tonight.'

'Oh, really? And you'd know that, would you?' There was a bitter edge to Maureen's voice.

'Yes, I would, as a matter of fact,' said the WPC, her gaze steady.

Maureen's eyes asked the question, the WPC nodded. 'About four years ago. The court case lasted two weeks. He got away with it. It's one of the reasons why I joined the police.'

'I don't follow.'

'It gives me power over men,' explained the WPC. 'Well, some men anyway. Gives me back something of what I lost.'

'Oh.' Maureen managed a brief smile. 'That's just about the strangest thinking I've ever heard. I think I understand, though. I was nothing back there. Just a piece of meat for him to use as he wanted. What happened to the man who raped you? Did you ever see him again?'

The policewoman hesitated then said, 'Oh yes. He's serving six years for a crime he didn't commit. Which is a lot worse than doing time for something you did do. Especially with him thinking I fitted him up for it.'

'And did you?'

The WPC gave her an old-fashioned look that said, 'Work that one out for yourself.'

'Well I'm not joining the police just to get back at Morgan bloody Pettifer,' Maureen said. 'Just saying his name makes me want to throw up.'

'I could have a word with the lads and tell 'em you think it's a waste of time pressing charges and you might drop them tomorrow.'

'What good will that do me?'

'Well, if you don't drop the charges 'til tomorrow, our lads can give him a very rough time tonight. He can't get hold of his solicitor so we'll have to keep him here. We might even charge him for resisting arrest. It's not much, but it's the best we can do.'

'Why would they do that for me?'

'My husband's on the next shift. He knows how I feel about rapists. If I tell him I think you're telling the truth it'll be good enough for him and his mates.'

'How do *you* know I'm telling the truth?'

'Because you look like I felt when it happened to me – you couldn't fake that in a million years. Trouble is, it won't help you in court. Believe me, I've been there.'

Maureen shook her head. 'I'm not sure about this,' she said. 'Are you saying if it went to court he'd probably be found not guilty?'

'If it's only your word against his, yes. It's a minefield is rape. The best we can guarantee is to make him think twice before he tries it on with another girl.'

'Won't you get into trouble?'

'Listen love, between you and me the lads'll frighten the living daylights out of him – I've seen them do it before. When they've

90

finished with him, if he gets a whisper that there's a chance you might drop the charges, he'll shoot out of here like a rat up a drainpipe while his solicitor's still eating his cornflakes.'

'Is that the best thing to do?'

'Well,' said the WPC, 'the correct thing to do is to press charges. I'm just giving you my advice. If you want to go through with it you'll find you're pretty much on your own. It's a man's world out there – us girls have got to do what we can.'

'Okay,' conceded Maureen. The prospect of prolonging the agony didn't appeal to her. 'I'll do what you say.'

'Good girl. Right, I'm going to take you to Leeds Infirmary to have you checked over, if that's all right with you?'

'Please.'

That night Morgan Pettifer was charged with resisting police arrest on a serious matter. It was through the grapevine that Maureen heard that all charges had been dropped and that Pettifer was back at the art school, covered in unexplained bruises. Unflattering rumours abounded, such was his reputation. He left after a few days. Maureen never went back.

She knocked on Charlie's door and went straight in. With her son living there she felt entitled. Jacky got up from his chair and asked, 'What did they say?'

'Well, the school has agreed not to press charges just as long as you don't expect to go back there.'

'That's not flippin' fair,' muttered Jacky. 'I didn't do it.'

'Beats me how your watch got there.'

'Doesn't beat me. Ask our Brian. See if he can shed any light on it.'

'Brian had nothing to do with it. He wouldn't do an awful thing like that to you.'

Jacky gave her a look that said *of course he would.* 'Whoever did it stopped me taking my scholarship,' he grumbled. 'What do I do now?'

'There are other schools,' said his mother. 'And you can take your scholarship another time.'

'When?' asked Jacky.

But his mother didn't know. This, plus the Morgan Pettifer smirk on Brian's face had left her hating her eldest son. And she hated herself for hating him. What kind of mother was she?

*

Jacky got the idea when he saw Brian's bike leaning against a wall in the backyard. Under cover of darkness he slipped out of Charlie's back door, wheeled the bicycle out of the yard and rode off on it, his destination Blissett Road about two miles away. In the Blissetts dwelt a sub-strata of society. It was a district of squalor, nightly brawls, drunkenness, violence, theft – and the occasional domestic murder. It was a place where dogs and cats were mostly without tails, windows mostly without glass and adults mostly without teeth. The police only patrolled the Blissetts when there was something specific to go there for, which, as it happened, was all too frequent.

A group of mean-eyed boys with knife-and-fork haircuts, mostly older than Jacky, spotted him cycling through their territory on a brand-new bike and gave chase on foot like a pack of wild dogs. They shouted threats and foul obscenities, insisting he stopped or they'd kick his head in. Jacky kept his nerve and rode just in front of them, allowing them to stay within sight of him. Ordinarily he would have stood on the pedals and lost them; but not that night. To his left a window scraped open and a harridan called out to her young in a voice heavily punctuated by expletives. Jacky was glad his mam wasn't like that. Another window scraped open and a second harridan chastised the first for being so foul-mouthed in the street. A window-to-window argument ensued with both women now freely exchanging the foulest of language, which eventually intermingled with the equally foul language of the chasing youths. It faded away as Jacky rode around a corner and headed for the Blisset Arms, famous for its excellent beer and the three murders that had been committed on the premises since the war. It was an area that lacked charm.

Outside the pub was a street lamp that didn't work – very little worked in the Blissetts. Jacky dismounted from the bike, leaned it against the lamp and ran off down a side street before the chasing pack arrived. He knew they'd soon be fighting over the bike like hungry wolves and not worried about him. He was back in Charlie's house when Brian banged on the door and shouted, 'Where's me bloody bike?'

Jacky's reply came from inside the house, 'How do I know where your rotten bike is?'

'Well it's not where it should be. If I find out it's you what stole it, I'll . . .'

Maureen was at her back door now. Jacky opened Charlie's door and called across to her.

'He's lost his bike and guess who he's blamin' it on? That's nice, that is. He blames me for everything.'

'And was it you?'

'Not you as well, Mam.'

She held him in her gaze, still questioning him. He didn't like lying to his mother so he just said, 'What am I supposed to have done with it, Mam, hidden it up my jumper?' Then, to his brother he added, 'I didn't pinch your bike just like you didn't mess up Boothie's office.'

Brian and Maureen looked at him – hate in one pair of eyes, exasperation in the other.

'It's a right bugger is this, Mam,' grumbled Brian. 'If I don't get it back I'll be payin' five bob a week wi' nowt ter show fer it.'

'Jacky,' said his mother. 'If you know anything about it just tell me. Please love. Do it for me.'

She could be irresistible when she wanted to be, especially to Jacky. But this time he felt a conflicting mixture of guilt and resentment. She hadn't subjected Brian to the same moral pressure when she asked him about the vandalism to Booth's office. Probably because she knew it wouldn't work on him, or maybe because she didn't want to know the truth.

'Mam, I honestly don't know where Brian's bike is.' Jacky was fairly certain he was telling the truth. The bike would have been stolen within a minute of him leaving it.

'Would you tell me if you knew?'

'Prob'ly not, Mam. Not after what he did to me.'

'Jacky, Brian didn't do anything to you.'

'Hear that?' Brian grabbed him by the scruff of his neck and dragged him out into the yard. 'I didn't do anything to you.'

'Stop that!' Maureen shouted.

Brian hesitated long enough for Charlie to come out and place himself between the brothers. 'That'll do, lads,' he said before lighting his pipe, an action that had an oddly calming effect on the brothers. 'Tell yer what, Brian, why don't you an' me go look fer yer bike. Somebody might've taken it fer a laugh. Yer know what daft beggars they are round here.'

'Good idea,' said Maureen, grateful to Charlie for his help in

93

diffusing a situation she was about to lose control of. 'I should put your coat on, Brian. You don't want to catch your death.'

Brian paused as he considered the viability of Charlie's offer. It was possible that some kids had taken it for a laugh and it might be leaning against a wall somewhere. Unlikely though.

'Okay,' he said, gruffly. 'But if I find out you've taken it, Jacky boy, I'll get yer for it.'

'Oh yeah, and what will you do?' Jacky taunted. 'Hit me with your handbag. Look, my knees are knocking.'

He knocked his knees together and Maureen shouted at him, 'That's enough, Jacky. Brian, come and put your coat on ... Thanks Charlie.'

Charlie gave her a wink and followed Jacky back into his house. As he put his coat on he said, as much to himself as to Jacky, 'Are we likely ter find this 'ere bike?'

'I wouldn't bet on it,' said Jacky. 'I reckon some o' them kids from the Blissets took it.'

'Yer seem very sure o' that.'

Jacky didn't answer and Charlie sucked on his pipe. 'Well, I'm not going anywhere near there,' he said. 'We'll just have a poke round, see what we can see. Maybe I'll try an' knock some sense into that brother o' yours.'

'He's not my brother,' said Jacky. 'If you don't believe me, ask him.'

Chapter Twelve

'What's up, Charlie?'

'Nowt's up, lad.'

'Well, I reckon there is.'

Jacky knew Charlie had something on his mind because of the volume of smoke puffing from his pipe. When deep in thought the pipe got up a better head of steam than the Flying Scotsman.

'I'm just doin' a bit o' courting, that's all.'

'Oh yes – who's the lucky lady?'

'Never you mind.'

It was mid-August and Jacky was getting ready to go down to Clugston Road Rec to play football with Roy Barnwell and a few of his other pals. Jacky was no longer the outcast he once was. In some people's eyes he was a martyr. The now ubiquitous skipping song had subliminally revised many people's opinions of Frank McGovern's guilt. It was discussed at length in pubs, barber's shops, over backyard walls and was a constant topic of conversation in Barraclough's Chip Shop where Jacky was often given a free bag of scraps and a fishcake – and a pat on the head. Jacky, Maureen, Ellie and Charlie were always ready with their opinion, which was eagerly sought by the gossip-hungry populace of Castlethorpe.

Fartown Secondary Modern had been selected for Jacky by the Castlethorpe Education Committee. Inevitably it went by the nickname Fart Town School – especially with the Blissetts being within its catchment area. Jacky, the bastard son of a hanged man, was not quite so much of an oddity at this school. The Victor Mumford skipping song had been banned at Barr Road School, which was a surefire way of promoting its popularity among the kids of Castlethorpe and surrounding districts.

95

Mumford had decided to ride it out. Many others would have left town but the thrill of living in *that* house and sleeping in *that* bed were too much for him to give up for the sake of a stupid skipping song. He'd heard that a local folk group had made it into a folk song and had consulted his solicitor with regard for suing for slander, but had been advised that as folk singers generally didn't have two ha'pennies to rub together it wouldn't do much good.

'Blimey, Charlie. Somebody'll be ringin' the Fire Brigade if they see all the smoke in here.' Jacky went to open a window to allow some of the fumes out.

'I'm thinkin', lad. It helps me think.'

'I hope you haven't got her into trouble, Charlie.'

'Hey? What do you know about gerrin' women into trouble? I'm sixty-seven. How can I get anyone into trouble at sixty-seven?'

'It's all to do with sex,' explained Jacky, cheekily. 'You do remember what sex is, don't you Charlie?'

'Aye lad. It's what yer coal comes in when yer posh.' Charlie continued puffing away. The lad had a been a great source of companionship. Frank would have been like this when he was a lad, but Charlie had seen very little of him.

'No, It's nothin' to do with coal,' Jacky went on. 'I've read all about it. Roy Barnwell's mam's got a book about medical stuff and it's got a chapter on something called sexual copulation. There's diagrams and all sorts of stuff. Roy reckons it's his favourite book – that and Billy Bunter.'

'Well, I wouldn't know about that at my age.'

'Give over. Roy Barnwell reckons his granddad's having sexual copulation at eighty-four. Mind you, his grandma's not so suited.'

'Why not?'

'They live at eighty-two.'

'Gerron, yer cheeky young beggar! Tek yer football with yer. I'll not have an eleven-year-old kid tell me how to conduct me love life.'

'I'll be back at tea-time,' said Jacky. 'So if there's anything you need to know about sexual copulation it'll have to wait 'til then.'

There was a smile on Charlie's face as he watched his grandson run out of the yard and down the street. He hadn't expected him to stay this long but Brian had been very awkward every time Maureen had broached the subject of Jacky going back. The lad was doing okay at his new school and Charlie would be happy to have him forever. He'd given the old man a new lease of life. Charlie looked at the clock – quarter past twelve – he was due at the bowls club at half past two. So was Enid Wharmby, his doubles partner. Do no harm to call on her. See if she fancied a drink of two to calm her nerves before the big match. She liked a drink did Enid – not too much – but she knew how to enjoy herself. Shame about her husband dying last year but to be fair he had been a miserable sod. She was five years younger than Charlie and looked a good five years younger than that. Looked after herself had Enid. Still had all her own teeth – good ones too, which was a rarity. Charlie spun his own teeth around in his mouth as he thought of her. Then he looked at himself in the mirror and decided a shave wouldn't go amiss – and maybe a dab of that men's cologne that Frank had bought him the Christmas before last. It'd be brilliant if someone could prove Frank innocent. The weight Charlie carried around on his old shoulders might go away if that happened.

He was sitting on a bench next to Enid, smoking his pipe and watching another bowls match when Jacky and Roy Barnwell passed behind them; Jacky had a finger to his lips, shushing his pal into silence. There was a privet hedge between the boys and the courting couple, who were holding hands behind their backs so the bowlers couldn't see them. It was a warm, sunny afternoon and Charlie was wearing a gleaming white cap to complement his grey flannels and white pumps. Enid's all-white outfit was topped by a straw boater with a red band around it. Her hair was still dark and her figure slim. From behind she could have been any age, from thirty to seventy. The drink had played a large part in the defeat they'd just suffered, but neither of them cared overmuch. It gave them a chance to sit together and watch the proceedings.

The green was at its best, with two sets of players bowling diagonally to each other, and twenty or so spectators standing or sitting on benches and deckchairs, a rural scene set amidst a grim, urban sprawl. There had been a bowling green at the back of the Clugston Arms since the turn of the century. On one side of the green were the allotments and on the other side was the Clugston Road recreation ground where the boys had been play-ing soccer.

'I think it were that last pint,' Charlie was saying. 'Can't bowl with too much inside me. It knocks me timing off.'

'Last pint?' Enid replied. 'What about the other three pints?'

'Hey, you matched me drink for drink. I reckon if we'd been match fit we could have bowled the pants off this lot.'

'Well, I enjoyed it, anyway,' smiled Enid. 'I must say, I do enjoy your company, Charlie.'

'Me an' all . . . Did Walter never bother? With bowls, I mean?'

'My Walter never bothered with anything but his pigeons. I swear he'd have rather slept with his pigeons than with me.'

'Finger ball, Billy!' Charlie called out to one of the bowlers.

'I bloody know that!' berated Billy, after his aim had been spoiled by Charlie's untimely shout. Billy's doubles partner reprimanded him for using bad language on the green. Billy was pointing out that it was Charlie's fault as Charlie smiled, innocently.

'To be honest, Charlie,' Enid confided, 'I know it's wrong to speak ill of the dead but Walter was a miserable sod. He could bore the arse off wooden horse, could Walter.'

'So, it wasn't a marriage made in heaven then?'

Enid sighed and shook her head. 'Charlie, I was married to him for forty-two years and I never loved him. When he died I didn't shed a single tear. Gettin' married was the biggest mistake I ever made. I'd have enjoyed my life a lot more if I'd stayed single and never got married at all. If I was to have my time over again wild horses couldn't drag me up that aisle.'

'So, I take it yer've got over him, then?'

'You know what they say,' she said, playfully, digging him in the ribs with her elbow. 'The best way to get over someone is to get under someone.'

'Well, yer fast cat!'

'At our age there's no point in hanging around,' she said.

'No point at all. Fine-lookin' woman like you and your Walter preferred his pigeons eh? I'd sooner have you lyin' at the side of me than any old racin' pigeon.'

Jacky and Roy were nodding their approval of Charlie's seduction technique. Enid inched closer to Charlie, who slid his hand around her waist.

'It can be arranged, Charlie,' she said, 'very easily. I'm a woman with needs and my needs never involved homing pigeons.

In fact, my Walter had one particular pigeon that didn't find its way home for the last three years of his life. God rest his miserable soul.'

'Ah, yer mean the lesser-spotted trouser pigeon. A rare breed, so I understand.'

Enid had a girlish giggle. Roy Barnwell had trouble not laughing out loud as Jacky threatened him with a silent fist.

'Three years eh?' Charlie said. 'Happen it forgot how to get itsen aloft.'

'It never did get aloft much,' remembered Enid. 'In fact it were more of a budgie than a pigeon.'

Charlie grinned. 'Budgie, eh? Now there's a novelty. Could it whistle? I wish I had one that could whistle. Make a fortune in Billy Smart's Circus.'

Enid burst out laughing at this and earned herself and Charlie a fierce stare from one of the bowlers. Someone muttered something about them being drunk, but they didn't care. Charlie was hugging Enid close to him. It was obvious from behind that they were giggling like naughty schoolkids.

'Happen if yer'd given it some budgie seed it might have whistled a bit more,' Charlie remarked.

More heaving of shoulders. The boys were as amused as the old couple.

'Well, it's whistled its last tune, now,' said Enid. 'I assume yours has got a whistle or two left in him.'

'Less of yer whistle, woman – more yer slide trombone. It's like going to bed wi' Glen Miller.'

Enid screeched with laughter, as did the boys. The players on the green glared at the disruptive pair, with arms akimbo. Charlie spun round in his seat, just in time to catch Jacky and Roy ducking behind the hedge.

'Who is it?' inquired Enid.

'Just some kids,' said Charlie, wondering just how long Jacky had been there. Then he smiled to himself. What the hell? Do no harm for the lad to know his granddad's got a bit of life left in him.

By the time the winter of 1952 arrived Jacky had proved himself to be far and away the most able pupil in his year. His teacher, Mr Overend, had recommended that when the time came he could sit the 13-plus examination, designed for children whom the net had missed the first time around. This was good news for Jacky, almost as good as the news he'd got on his twelfth birthday when Maureen brought his present round to him – a pair of roller skates.

'I've got him a present meself,' said Charlie. 'I hope yer don't mind, lass.'

'Why should I mind?'

'Well, yer might when yer see it.'

He went into the back yard and wheeled Jacky's present into the house – a brand-new bike. Drop handlebars, ten gears, racing saddle – Jacky's eyes almost popped out of his head. He'd started building his own bike from odd bits he'd scrounged but he had only got as far as a frame, handlebars, one wheel and a bell. The boy let out a yell of delight as Charlie handed it to him.

'Puts my present into the shade,' said Maureen, dryly. 'And God knows what Brian will say. For the past nine months he's been paying five bob a week for fresh air.'

'I'm sorry, lass, but I thought I'd buy him summat decent to soften the blow, like.'

'Soften what blow?'

'He's twelve, lass. Yer said we should tell him when he's twelve.'

'Can I go out on it?' asked Jacky, spinning the pedals round. He hadn't heard a word of their conversation.

'What . . . oh, right,' said Maureen, realising what Charlie was talking about. 'Er, no, Jacky. Not just yet.'

'When then?' He was jumping up and down in frustration.

'In a minute,' she said. 'We've got something to tell you.'

Jacky climbed on to the bike; his toes just reached the floor. He had dreamed of a bike like this.

'Jacky boy,' said Maureen. 'I'd like you to listen to this and then you can go out and play.'

'Okay, Mam.'

She looked at Charlie as if to say *The ball's now in your court.* He nodded and fiddled with his pipe.

'It's about yer father, Jacky,' he said. 'I mean Frank McGovern.'

Charlie had Jacky's attention now. 'What about him? Have they found out he didn't do it?'

'Not yet, lad. There's summat about him I haven't told yer. I would have told yer before but it wasn't the right time.' Charlie looked at Maureen as if hoping for her to help him out. But she

100

was looking at her son with love dripping from her eyes and the old man realised how difficult it must be for her to have to live apart from him like this – for the sake of a son she loved less.

'What is it, then?'

'Well, I'm blessed if I know how ter say this, other than come straight out with it an' see what yer make of it.'

'Come straight out with what, Charlie?' Jacky asked.

Charlie screwed up his face, looked at his pipe, then at Jacky, then at Maureen, then at the floor.

'He's trying to tell you that Frank was his son,' said Maureen, quietly.

'Aye, lad,' said Charlie. 'That's about the size of it. Frank were my lad . . . I were his da—'

The old man suddenly began crying. It was the first time he'd admitted this to anyone and the very words saddened him so much. Maureen put her arm around him as Jacky tried to make sense of it all. Charlie tried to smile at the boy through his tears.

'My Bessie never knew, bless her. Yer see, I've been a bit of a . . . a ladies' man in me time, Jacky boy. I've always liked the ladies and they've liked me. Can't be helped, you are what you are. Anyway, Frank was the result. Never regretted bein' his dad, mind. Never for one minute. The circumstances weren't ideal, what with one thing and another, but by heck he were a grand lad. His mam died a while back. She'd have been yer grandma. Yer'd have liked her. By God she were a belter when she were young.' Maureen gave him a look that recommended he didn't pursue this line.

'Does this mean . . . you're my granddad?' Jacky asked.

'Aye, lad . . . I'm yer granddad.'

Jacky looked at his mother who gave him an uncertain smile, then when he looked back at Charlie a broad grin lit up the boy's face.

'Honest?' he said.

'Honest,' said Charlie. 'Well, Jacky boy, what do yer think?'

'I think I'm very pleased to have you as my granddad.'

Charlie wiped his eyes. 'Did you hear that, Maureen. He's very pleased.'

'Very pleased indeed,' said Jacky, remembering how Frank had once said that to him. Such had been the poignancy of his few minutes with his father that he remembered every word Frank had said.

'That'll do for me,' said Charlie.

'It's better than a bike,' said Jacky, happily. 'Having you as my granddad is better than a bike.'

'Maybe Charlie should take the bike back, then,' teased Maureen. 'We don't want to spoil you. A new bike *and* a new granddad.'

'*And* a pair of roller skates,' Jacky reminded her. 'They're my favourites.'

'What?' said Maureen, almost smugly. 'Even better than a new bike and a new granddad?'

'Loads better,' said Jacky, taking his mother's outstretched hand. 'Because you bought me them.'

'By God, he'll charm the birds off the trees, will that one,' laughed Charlie. 'He'll wed a princess one day – an' she'll think she's married above herself.'

Maureen flung her arms around her son and almost hugged the breath out of him. She felt guilty that she had never felt like this about her other two children, but neither of them had Frank McGovern for a dad. She understood Charlie's tears and unsuccessfully fought back some of her own. Her damp eyes met Charlie's.

He nodded at her as if to say, 'I know, love. I wish he were here as well.'

Chapter Thirteen

The idea of applying psychological pressure on Mumford was Ellie's brainchild. She'd given it a lot of thought and was as sure as Jacky that Frank McGovern wasn't a murderer. And Ellie was coming up to that rebellious age where she felt the need to set right all the wrongs of the world. It did cross her mind that her own father wouldn't be offering her too much encouragement were he still alive but she explained her reasons to him when she visited his grave with Jacky.

'We know you probably don't think much of him, Dad – but to be fair, him and Mam did think you were dead. So it wasn't really their fault. You can't really blame him for falling for Mam. I mean, you've only got to look at her . . .'

'And if it hadn't been for him, I wouldn't be here,' Jacky added, persuasively. 'And me and you loved each other, didn't we, Dad?'

Ellie nudged him into reluctant silence, not absolutely sure that he was helping. 'Anyway,' she said. 'It turns out that Frank McGovern, who's Jacky's dad, was Charlie's son, which makes Charlie Jacky's granddad – and you always got on with Charlie.'

'So, if my other dad could be anybody,' said Jacky, 'I bet you'd prefer it was Charlie's son. I don't call him dad, by the way. I always call you dad, always will. I call my other dad Frank. He was okay, actually. He told me you were a good bloke. Not that I needed him to tell me that.'

Ellie dug him in his ribs again because he was waffling and Bert never liked a waffler. It was something he used to say. Thus convinced that they'd squared things with Bert they headed for home, with Ellie thinking of ways to apply psychological pressure on Mumford. It was coming up to Christmas. That evening the two of them went out carol singing.

They had been concentrating on rows of terraced houses which had no gardens or yards and which opened directly on to the street. Here they could sing outside two adjacent doors, with one of them knocking on a door each after reciting the traditional closing rhyme of the carol singer:

Christmas is coming,
The goose is getting fat,
Please put a penny in the old man's hat.
If you haven't got a penny,
A ha'penny will do,
If you haven't got a ha'penny,
God bless you.

As they walked between houses a thought occurred to Ellie. 'I reckon my skipping song must be getting to Mumford,' she said. 'All the kids are singing it.'

'Maybe we should go and sing it outside his door?' suggested Jacky, joking. 'We could do "Silent Night", "Away in a Manger" and "Victor Mumford Stabbed His Wife". Hey, he might give us a tanner each if we sing it nicely.'

'Why not?'

'Eh?'

Jacky stared at his sister. Sometimes he didn't know if she was joking or not. She shrugged and said, 'Let's get some of the other kids together. What can he do?'

'Apart from murder us, you mean?'

She gave his suggestion some consideration, then dismissed it with a shake of her head. 'Doubt it. Not with a load of kids around.'

'We could sing it at his gate and clear off when he comes to the door,' Jacky suggested, half joking.

'Let's do it,' decided Ellie.

'Eh?'

'It's the only way. We've got to make him crack up.'

'I s'pose so.'

They had pretty much run out of houses on their patch and when they met up with other carol singers who were also done for the evening they put the proposition to them. Most of them thought singing outside Mumford's house would be a great laugh and within minutes they had seven volunteers. All of them knew Victor Mumford as a man whose demeanor didn't match his reputation. He seemed strange, almost timid – definitely ripe for having a cruel trick played on him. But to Ellie it wasn't a trick; it was all part of a long-term wearing down process. One day he would crack.

Victor smiled as he heard them start off with a somewhat discordant 'Silent Night'. Maybe this was where the kids forgot about him. Season of goodwill and all that. He took a handful of change from his pocket and counted it as they sang. Three and sevenpence – most people gave threepence. The carol changed to 'Away in a Manger' and he decided to give them the lot. That would change their opinion of him; stop them singing that stupid song. Maybe they'd make up another song about how generous Victor Mumford was. He tapped his foot and hummed along as they sang. They weren't the best carol singers in Castlethorpe by a long way, but to him they were a heavenly choir. He peeped through the drawn curtains and saw them moving back down the path to his gate. Surely they weren't going without collecting their money. He froze when the skipping song began, sung with far more gusto than either of their carols. Loud enough for all the street to hear. Victor put his hands to his ears to shut it out and screamed for them to stop. Then he ran to the door and flung it open just in time to see them scatter and run away, still singing, still taunting him. He saw the boy standing there – McGovern's bastard son, so he'd learned. The boy was staring at him, fiercely. There was a girl as well. Both were standing their ground and Victor didn't know what to do.

'Bloody murderer!' shouted Jacky.

Ellie shouted too. 'Murderer!'

The other carol singers had stopped, emboldened by Jacky's and Ellie's defiance of the man. A door opened at the other side of the street, and another. Confident now that Mumford wasn't going to do anything to them, Jacky and Ellie started a chant of, 'Murderer, murderer, murderer . . .'

By now the other kids had rejoined them, shouting as well. Mumford screamed for them to stop or he'd call the police, but their voices drowned his. More doors opened; windows too as neighbours watched this spectacle, then, led by Jacky, the kids began to sing the skipping song again:

'Frank loved Victor Mumford's wife,
So Victor stabbed her with a knife.
Frank McGovern got the blame,
But we all know the killer's name . . .'

Mumford ran at them in a rage. The kids scattered but were still laughing, Jacky and Ellie with them; happy that they had done damage to him. Damage that Mumford wouldn't be able to repair.

'Do you know what would be really good,' said Ellie, as they walked home. Their spirits were high with the success of their adventure. She answered her own question, as Jacky knew she would. 'It would be good if Frank's ghost came to haunt him.'

'Is this psychological pressure again?'

'Course it is. If we put enough psychological pressure on him he'll crack and confess his crime, then Frank will get a free pardon.'

'S'posing there aren't any such thing as ghosts,' said Jacky. 'What then?'

'Well, of course there aren't any such things as ghosts, you daft ha'porth. We'll have to make our own.'

Jacky's face split into a broad grin. 'How do we do that?'

'Simple. Someone gets dressed up as Frank's ghost and scares the shit out of Mumford.'

'Scares the what out of him?'

'You heard.'

'Wow! I didn't know you swore,' said Jacky with great admiration. Hardly any of the girls he knew used bad language.

'I don't,' she said. 'But I couldn't think of any other way to put it. If there's no other way to put things it's okay to swear.'

'What about fart?'

'Break wind's much politer,' she said. 'Polite people break wind.'

'I didn't think polite people farted at all.'

She ignored him. 'You've got some of Frank's clothes, haven't you?'

'Yeah,' said Jacky. 'Mam wanted me to throw them away but I haven't got round to it. They're all in a suitcase in my bedroom.'

'That's it then,' she said, decisively. 'We'll get dressed up as

106

Frank and scare the shit out of Mumford. You get on my shoulders.'

Jacky laughed out loud at this great idea; so did Ellie. The more they talked about it and planned it, the better the idea became.

'When shall we do it?' Jacky asked. He was eager to get on with it. The danger aspect hadn't occurred to him yet.

'These things need careful planning,' said Ellie. 'We'll leave it 'til after Christmas.'

Christmas Day 1952 didn't go terribly well for the Gaskell family, with Brian protesting about Charlie being invited there for dinner. Maureen had explained that, as he was now officially Jacky's granddad they should forget any silly disagreements they might have. She and Ellie served up the meal, Christmas crackers were pulled, paper hats donned and a toast proposed by Maureen to welcome Charlie, officially, into the family. Brian could stand it no longer. He sat back, sullenly, with arms folded.

'He's not *my* granddad; he's not Ellie's granddad – he's nobody's granddad but the murderer's bastard's.'

'Hey! Just watch yer tongue, lad!' growled Charlie. 'My boy's no more a murderer than you are.'

'Oh, yeah, why did they hang him then? They don't hang people for fun, you know.'

'The law sometimes gets the wrong man,' said Charlie, grim faced. 'Sometimes the real villain gets away scot free.'

'It happens all the time to rapists,' Jacky added, blithely. 'More often than not rapists get away scot free.' He was sorely tempted to call Brian a rapist's bastard, but his granddad didn't know about this and it would hurt his mother, so he didn't. Brian glared at him, venomously, and mouthed that he'd get him later. Jacky grinned and placed a finger on either side of his nose in an insolent V sign that snapped his brother's temper.

'Aye, an' you can fuck off an' all!'

'Brian!' exploded Maureen. 'Don't you dare use that sort of language in this house!'

Brian got to his feet, kicked over his chair and stormed out of the house, slamming the door hard enough to dislodge the coats that were hanging on the back of it.

Jacky said, 'I think I might be stayin' with you for a while longer, Granddad.' In front of the family he had called Charlie that from the day he found out; as much to annoy his brother as anything else.

'Aye, Jacky boy,' acknowledged Charlie. 'I reckon yer will.'

It wasn't what Maureen wanted to hear. Once again she'd harboured hopes of bringing her family together and once again it wasn't to be. Perhaps with a disjointed family such as hers it was too much to hope for. Despondently, she looked around at the faces remaining at the table and realised there was more than one missing. She desperately needed a man to share her troubles, the rent, her hopes . . . and her bed with.

Chapter Fourteen

Both of their hearts were palpitating wildly as Jacky and Ellie sneaked around the side of Mumford's house. During their 'casing of the joint', as Jacky put it, they had established that Mumford's kitchen window didn't lock properly and that it was easy to open it if you knew how. They also knew that he slept in the front bedroom and that he went to bed around half past eleven; it had taken several late-night recces by Jacky to ascertain the latter. Once inside they would dress up in Frank's clothes – Jacky in the jacket and cap, Ellie in the trousers pulled up beneath her armpits. Then they would climb the stairs, Jacky would get on to Ellie's shoulders and they would silently creep into Mumford's bedroom and stand at the bottom of his bed making ghostly sounds until he woke up. Then Ellie, in a ghostly voice, would say, 'Own up to your crime, Victor.'

'What if he gets out of bed and comes after us?' Jacky had asked. Ellie dismissed this as highly unlikely.

'He'll be so petrified he'll hide under the bedclothes. Then, when he looks out again we'll be gone. Disappeared into the night.'

'Like a ghost.'

'Like a ghost,' confirmed Ellie.

'What if he doesn't believe in ghosts?'

'It's all very well not believing in ghosts if you haven't actually seen one,' Ellie told him. 'It's up to us to make Mumford a believer.'

Jacky thought this was sound thinking. Hiding under the bedclothes was exactly what he would do under such circumstances. 'Maybe he'll think it was all a dream,' he said, 'then we'll have wasted our time.'

'Not if I ring him up a few days later at exactly the same time as he saw the ghost and I say the same thing in the same voice. "Own up to your crime, Victor".'

'Yes!' Jacky saw the brilliant simplicity in his sister's plan. 'That's brilliant. We haunt him once and then make as many phone calls as we like. He'll soon crack.'

Their initial date had to be postponed due to a fall of snow which would leave incriminating, unghostly, footprints. It took a week before a lengthy spell of rain washed it all away. Jacky and his sister met in their adjacent backyards at midnight. Jacky carried a shopping bag with his father's clothes inside – it had felt odd unpacking them. In the lapel of a jacket was a National Union of Mineworkers badge. Jacky made a note to remove it once this night's work was over.

'Have you got everything?' Ellie asked him.

'Yeah.'

The clothes still smelled of the mothballs they had been packed in and Ellie wrinkled her nose when he opened the bag and showed them to her. Their eyes met under the glow of a street lamp, both full of trepidation but neither wanting to display weakness in front of the other.

'You're not scared, are you?' Ellie said.

'Course I'm not,' lied Jacky.

Ellie had hoped he'd say yes, thus putting him in the same boat as her. 'Good,' she said. 'Let's go.'

It was cold, damp and dark as they made their way along the route they'd both travelled hundreds of times on their way to school. They wore gaberdine raincoats, Ellie's was a bit too small. It had been too big when it was new nearly two years ago and her mother was hoping it would 'see this winter out', then she could swap the buttons over and Jacky could get some wear out of it. But he wouldn't need it now; his granddad had bought him a new one. They dodged into a doorway as a policeman crossed the road a hundred yards in front of them.

'Actually, I think I *am* a bit scared,' Jacky admitted.

'Don't be,' said Ellie, happy now that she wasn't the only one.

With the policeman gone they continued on their way, talking to each other as if to bolster each other's spirits.

'Ellie,' said Jacky. 'Why are you doing this?'

110

'How do you mean?'

'I mean, *I'm* doing it because he was my dad . . . but he's not your dad. You never even met him.'

Ellie gathered her thoughts before she answered. It had been a question that had been puzzling her. Why should she be so concerned about a man she'd never met?

'Well, him being your father makes him part of our family,' she began. 'And like I told Dad when we went to see him, Mam and Frank thought Dad was dead when they . . . you know . . .'

'Made me?'

'If you want to put it like that . . . and Mam must have loved him – so that's another reason.'

'Good job you didn't mention that to Dad,' Jacky said.

'I'm not that insensitive. You still call him Dad, don't you?'

'He *was* my dad. Can't think of him any other way. So you're doing this because Mam loved Frank?'

'The main reason,' Ellie said, 'is that Frank was unjustly hanged and someone should do something about it.'

She could have added that she had somehow fallen in love with his memory. The photograph in the paper was a studio photograph that had Frank looking like a matinée idol.

'Anyway,' she said. 'Let's not talk about that. Let's concentrate on what we've got to do.'

They had gone over the plan many times until it was etched into their brains. They must leave Mumford's house without a trace of them ever having been there: leave nothing behind; close the kitchen window; don't knock anything over; disappear silently into the night like the ghosts they were supposed to be. Jacky had loved the plan, but its execution was beginning to scare him. Too many 'what ifs' were coming to his mind, the main one being 'what if we get caught?' But Ellie looked so determined he didn't like voicing his concerns. If the plan worked it would be great – and Ellie was doing this for a man who wasn't even her dad.

Then it occurred to him for the thousandth time that the man they were trying to scare was a murderer. What if he murdered them? What then? Without Ellie's knowledge he had left a note in his bedroom telling of what they intended doing that night and if they disappeared or were found dead it would be Mumford's doing. Without Jacky's knowledge Ellie had left a similar note.

111

They had now reached Mumford's gate. All the house lights were out and Ellie walked down the path without hesitation, with Jacky hard on her heels. Both of them wore rubber-soled pumps for stealth, and the cold ground was beginning to strike through.

'I think I've got frostbite in my toes,' Jacky whispered, stamping his feet to get some circulation going.

'Shhh! Stop doing that.'

'Sorry.'

'We've got to be quiet.'

'I said I'm sorry.'

They were beside the kitchen window. It wasn't the first time they'd paid this window a midnight visit; they knew it well enough to be able to ease the top sash away from the bottom one and push the broken catch up with an inserted penknife. The window opened without much effort or noise. Ellie gave Jacky a leg up then followed him in, leaving the window open for an easy getaway.

This was uncharted territory. The kitchen was dimly lit via the window and they daren't switch a light on. Jacky found the door to the hall and opened it, slowly, grimacing when it made what, to him, sounded like a deafening creak.

'Shhh!' said Ellie.

'It wasn't my fault – I didn't know it flippin' creaked.'

'All right . . . just shhh.'

They tiptoed up the hall where the the only light came from a stained-glass transom over the door. Jacky walked straight into a small table, knocking it over along with something heavy that fell to the linoleum floor with a bang, but didn't break. The two of them froze. Jacky could sense Ellie looking daggers at him; he thought it would be a good idea to get out, but she was standing her ground. What he didn't know was that she was wondering why *he* hadn't run away. She would have followed him for sure.

They tried to control their breathing as they listened for sounds from above. Nothing. Ellie bent down to pick up the table and the cut-glass vase that had fallen on the floor. She replaced them without a sound. Jacky felt his heart racing as he held on to the bag of clothes. This plan had been all right in theory but how many other pitfalls hadn't they anticipated? Ellie left it a full ten minutes before she decided it was safe to continue. If they *had* woken Mumford up he would have listened for a while then decided it was his imagination or a cat outside or something. By now he should be asleep again; and it was safe to proceed.

Ellie led the way up the stairs, hoping against hope that none of them creaked, testing each one before putting her full weight on it. One gave a suspicious squeak. She took her foot off it and tried the next one up; this one was okay. Turning to Jacky, whom she could hardly see, she was forced to whisper to him, 'Miss the next step.'

'What?'

'Don't tread on the next step – it squeaks.'

'I know – I wasn't going to.'

'For once in your life can you not be so flipping argumentative?'

'I wasn't—'

'Shhh!'

They were now on the landing and both their hearts were thumping wildly. This was where it got serious. There was just enough light for them to see by. Ellie pointed to a door to identify Mumford's room, Jacky nodded his understanding. He took the trousers out of the bag and gave them to her. They had tried them on before and figured out the best way to make it all work. Ellie pulled them up to her armpits and fastened them with a belt. Jacky put the coat on over his raincoat, did up all four buttons and folded the lapels across his chest. He put on the cap which had been packed with newspaper to make fit better. Between cap and coat his face was mainly in shadow, which was how they wanted it. Ellie now dropped to her knees and Jacky climbed on to her shoulders. He helped her to get upright by pushing down on the balustrade, as practised at Charlie's house. Frank's coat just covered Ellie's head and shoulders. It the dim light they looked like a tall, oddly shaped man. They were now ready.

Ellie, peering through the coat, took two unsteady steps towards the front-bedroom door and turned the handle. The door opened easily at first, then caught the carpet. It made a brushing sound as she pushed it fully open, enough to make Mumford stir in his sleep. Jacky banged his head on the top of the door frame and would have fallen off had Ellie not stopped and taken a step back as he wavered on her shoulders. Mumford stirred again. The children could only make him out as a vague lump in the bed. They waited with hammering hearts as his breathing settled down again. Jacky leaned forward so his mouth was close to where his sister's ear should be, and whispered, 'You nearly knocked my flippin' head off then.'

'Shhh, let's get into position.'

There was a gap in the curtains which allowed in a thin strip of light from the streetlamp outside. Ellie positioned the two of them in its slim illumination – enough to identify a shadowy ghost in a flat cap. Jacky thought the pounding of his heart might knock him off balance and he was glad it was Ellie who had to make the ghost noise and not he; all he'd be able to manage was a frightened squeak.

'Ooooo.'

Ellie's low moan was more a product of fear than anything else. Jacky's nose twitched. There was a strong smell of something in here. He'd smelt it sometimes when his granddad came in from the club. Charlie would give Jacky a bob to go to the first house at the Rialto Cinema with his pals while he went to the Castlethorpe Miner's Welfare Club. Stale beer, that was the smell. Only this was a lot stronger than his granddad ever smelled. Mumford turned over, muttered something and began to snore.

'Ellie,' whispered Jacky.

'What?'

'I think he's drunk.'

'So do I.'

'Moan a bit louder.'

'Oooooooo!' went Ellie. 'Own up to your crime, Victor.'

Mumford snored on, mumbled something in his sleep, then gave a rumbling burst of flatulence.

'Did you hear that?' Jacky whispered. 'One of them snores was a fart.'

'I know,' said Ellie, 'I heard . . . Ooooo! I am the ghost of Frank McGovern. Own up to your crime, Victor.'

More snoring. More flatulence. Jacky whispered, 'Ellie, he's farting again.'

'I know,' whispered Ellie, irritated. 'I'm not flippin' deaf.'

Mumford's nocturnal noises continued to alternate and Ellie sensed that Jacky was laughing, noiselessly. It infected her. She could never keep a straight face when someone was laughing, no matter what the circumstances. Unfortunately Mumford hadn't finished releasing his trapped wind. A few snores later it all came out in a musically ascending burst that had the two children

114

heaving with out-of-control silent giggling. Jacky felt himself sliding backwards and let out a yell of alarm. Mumford sat bolt upright in his bed and gave a loud, unintelligible, shout which made Ellie jump with fright. Jacky fell off her shoulders and landed on a dressing table with a loud crash, enough to shock Mumford to his senses, and make him pee himself. The game was up.

'Scram!' shouted Ellie.

She turned and ran from the room, assuming that Jacky would be close behind. When she got to the kitchen he wasn't with her. There was someone stumbling down the stairs. Out of the gloom she saw her brother hopping towards her. He still wore the cap but had divested himself of Frank's coat.

'Hurry up,' she whispered, urgently.

'I can't. I've hurt my flippin' ankle.'

Mumford was ringing the police from his bedroom as Jacky sank to the kitchen floor in agony. 'I can't go any further,' he moaned. I think I've broke it.'

'I'll carry you.'

'Okay.'

Ellie tried to help him out of the window but she was doing his ankle more harm than good. He cried out in pain. Any minute now they expected Mumford to come downstairs and attack them.

'You'd better go, Ellie,' said Jacky. 'I'll be okay.'

'I'm not leaving you with a flipping murderer.'

This came as something of a relief to him, but when he heard the wail of a police siren he urged her, 'Just clear off. Scarper over the school wall. No point us both gettin' caught.'

He made sense but she was reluctant to let her brother carry the can for all this.

'I'm not going to leave you.'

'What good's it going to do if we both get caught?' he argued. 'We were only playin' a trick on him. We haven't done anything really bad.'

'Are you sure? I'll stay if you want. I'll make sure he doesn't harm you.'

'Give over. The cops won't let him do anything.'

'I don't like—'

'Go!'

'Okay,' she said, reluctantly. 'I'll wait outside the window right up to when the cops come.'

Jacky tried to give her a smile but the pain stopped him. 'I think I might have to go to hospital,' he said. 'I'll give the cops Mam's address. I don't want to involve Granddad in this. You'd better be in bed when they get there . . . ouch!'

The siren grew louder as the police car turned into the street. Ellie was outside the window now. Hating what she was about to do.

'Clear off!' shouted Jacky to her. 'Don't be so daft.'

A car door slammed and heavy footsteps clattered across the footpath. Ellie gave her brother an apologetic smile, ran into the back garden and clambered over the wall. The drop at the far side was unexpectedly high and, just for a second, she thought she'd got a damaged ankle as well. A shout of 'Stop!' from the other side of the wall soon put it to the test and it came through with flying colours. By the time the police arrived at her house she was in bed.

Jacky was sitting with his back against a kitchen cupboard when the police constable switched on the light. Mumford was peering at him from over the officer's shoulder. The sight of him took away any apprehension Jacky was feeling and replaced it with hatred. This was the man who had killed his dad.

A sergeant pushed past the two men and knelt beside Jacky. 'Right, lad,' he said. 'What's all this about?'

'I've broke my ankle,' said Jacky.

The sergeant looked around his colleague. 'Better get an ambulance, Les,' he said. Then to Jacky, 'What are you doing in this house?'

'I came to give that murderer a fright.' Jacky pointed to Mumford. 'Everybody knows he killed his wife. They hanged my dad for it. But he did it. He told the pol—'

'All right, lad.' The sergeant, who knew the story and didn't need chapter and verse, turned to look at Mumford, to gauge his reaction to such an accusation. Mumford looked from one to the other. He was wearing striped pyjamas with an unwholesome-looking damp patch around the crotch area which caused the sergeant to grimace.

'What are you looking at me for?' Mumford whined. 'Arrest him.'

'All in good time, sir. Now then, lad. Let's take a look at that leg.'

'Ouch!' went Jacky, as the sergeant ran his hand along his ankle.

'Best stay where you are, lad. While we're waiting for an ambulance would you like to give me your name and address?'

Mumford was in a rage. This Gaskell kid was beginning to plague him. He went upstairs to get dressed and, as he went into his bedroom he saw Frank's coat on the landing. Grinning to himself, he picked up his wallet from the bedside table and stuck it into one of the pockets. Then he opened the dressing table drawer and took out his late wife's jewellery box. He selected her engagement ring and a gold bracelet and put them in another pocket; then he placed the box, upside down on the floor and arranged the rest of the jewellery in a manner that suggested it had been thrown there. That done he shouted down the stairs.

'Officer, could you search the boy? There's all sorts of things missing up here.'

'Hey, I never took anything,' protested Jacky.

'In that case you won't mind if I have a look in your pockets,' said the sergeant. He had taken to Jacky, partly because he knew of the Mumford case, and had his own own doubts about Frank's guilt.

'There's nothing on the lad,' he called out. 'It could have been the other one. We saw one climbing over the back wall.'

Mumford appeared at the kitchen door. 'My wallet's gone,' he said. 'And they've been in my wife's jewellery box.'

'You smell as if you might have been drinking, sir,' said the sergeant, who hadn't taken to Mumford one bit. 'Are you sure you've been robbed?'

'How do you mean, am I sure? Of course I'm sure.'

'We never took nothing,' said Jacky.

'We?' said the sergeant. 'Who's we?'

'I never split on my mates,' Jacky said. 'But we never took nothing. We only came to scare him.'

The sergeant suppressed a grin. 'Scare him? How did you propose to scare him?'

'Well ...' It all sounded so stupid to Jacky now. 'We got dressed up in some of my dad's clothes—'

117

'Sarge.'

The constable's voice came from the top of the stairs, interrupting Jacky's explanation. Mumford suppressed a smirk.

'I think you'd better take a look at this.'

The sergeant left Mumford in the kitchen with Jacky as he went to see what his constable wanted him for.

'They'll lock you away for this,' gloated Mumford.

'Give over,' retorted Jacky, defiantly. 'You're potty you. Everybody knows you murdered your wife. One day they'll hang you for it.'

'You little bastard!'

Mumford hit Jacky across the face with the flat of his hand, causing the boy to yell out loud in pain. The policemen came clattering down the stairs to find Jacky lying on his side holding his cheek.

'What the bloody hell have you done to the boy?' shouted the sergeant.

'What you should have done,' snarled Mumford. 'I've given him something for his insolence.'

'I've a good mind to arrest you for assaulting him. You can't go round hitting people while they're in our custody.'

'Never mind that. What are you going to do about my wallet?'

The constable stepped forward, holding Frank's jacket.

'Is this your jacket, son?' he asked.

'It was Frank McGovern's,' said Jacky. He pointed at Mumford. 'The one who was hanged for something *he* did. Frank was my real dad.'

The policeman took a wallet from the pocket. Mumford covered his smirk with his hand.

'Can you explain how this wallet got in the pocket?'

Jacky looked totally bemused at first, then the answer dawned on him. 'He must have put it there when he went back upstairs just now.'

'Don't be so damn ridiculous!' snorted Mumford. 'I didn't even notice the blasted jacket. Where was it?'

'It was on the landing, sir,' said the constable, suspiciously. 'You must have walked past it when you went upstairs. There was some jewellery in the pocket as well.' He showed Mumford the ring and the bracelet.

'They belonged to my late wife, constable. They're very precious to me.'

118

'Hmmm. Odd you didn't notice the jacket yourself, sir,' commented the sergeant, dryly.

'Well, I'm very sorry I didn't notice it, sergeant. But I had other things on my mind. Do you honestly believe this boy's cock and bull story? The fact is that he and someone else broke into my house in the middle of the night when I was asleep in my bed. You find my wallet and my wife's jewellery in his pocket and you question me about it? Would you mind if I come down to the station with you so that I can discuss your conduct with a senior officer?'

'That's up to you, sir.' The sergeant looked down at Jacky. 'If you took this stuff you'd better own up now, lad.'

'I didn't take it,' grumbled Jacky. 'He's lying. Just like he lied about Frank McGovern.'

'Well,' said the sergeant, 'you were doing stuff you shouldn't, lad. There's no doubt about that.'

'So was Frank. But they shouldn't have hanged him for it.'

'There might be other things missing as well,' said Mumford, sensing a profitable insurance claim here. 'I'd better go and have another look. You've only recovered what this boy had on him. His accomplice might have got away with something as well.'

The constable went to the front door and called back, 'I think the ambulance is here, Sarge.'

'He's lying if he says anything's missing,' protested a dejected Jacky. 'He's a liar and a murderer.'

'That's enough of that, lad,' said the sergeant. 'I reckon your mouth gets you into a lot of trouble, one way or another.'

'There's nothin' wrong in tellin' the truth,' Jacky proclaimed, stoutly. 'And the truth is that Victor Mumford's a murderer and a liar.'

The ambulancemen came in with a stretcher. 'Go steady with him, lads,' said the sergeant. 'He's had a nasty knock tonight.' He gave Mumford a sharp glance. 'In fact he's had a couple of nasty knocks.'

As Jacky was being carried to the ambulance he began singing the skipping song.

'Blow me, not you an' all, lad,' grinned one of the ambulancemen. 'The kids sing nowt else down our street.'

Jacky stopped singing and pointed back to Mumford, who was

standing at the door. 'That's Victor Mumford,' he told them. 'He's the one in the song. He's a liar and a murderer . . . and he farts in his sleep.'

'That's not all he does,' murmured the sergeant, eyeing Mumford's pyjamas with distaste.

Chapter Fifteen

'I thought they'd have had a cop guarding yer. Girt big desperado like you.'

Brian strode into the ward and plonked himself down in the chair beside the bed where Jacky lay with his leg elevated and encased in plaster.

'I'm hardly going to run away, am I?' Jacky said, scornfully. 'Anyway, why have you come? We don't like each other, me and you.'

'That's right. I think yer a stupid little pillock.'

'There's only two pillocks in our family,' countered Jacky, 'and you're both of 'em.'

Brian chose not to pursue the exchange. 'If it hadn't been for our lass,' he said, 'I wouldn't have bothered comin'. Yer want ter keep her out of yer stupid bloody pranks.'

'Is that what she told you?' Jacky said. 'That it was my idea?'

'I don't need to ask whose idea it was. I know full well it were yours. An' if yer've got our lass into bother yer'll have me to answer to.'

'Ooh! I'm scared now.'

The X-rays had shown Jacky to have a spiral fracture of his lower fibula. He would be in hospital for two weeks before being released into the custody of the police; whether he was allowed home after that would be up to the magistrates.

'Our Ellie's talking about owning up to bein' the second person,' Brian said, ignoring his brother's taunts.

'She can't do that.'

'I know. This Mumford's bloke's saying he's been robbed of all sorts o' stuff. They'll be layin' all that on her.'

121

'She didn't take anything,' Jacky said. 'Neither of us did.'

'Well that bastard reckons he's lost stuff worth hundreds o' quid – fancy watch an' all sorts. If she owns up to bein' there, they'll lock her up for sure. You'll probably gerroff wi' a bollockin'. They don't lock little pillocks like you up for first offences; but they'd lock our lass up for sure.'

'Why would they lock her up and not me?'

'Because she's old enough ter know better. You're just a brainless little pillock.'

'Does Mam know she was with me?'

'Not yet. Our lass wouldn't have told me, but I heard her sneak in just before t' bobbies came knockin'. Talkin' o' bobbies – have yer said owt to 'em?'

'Don't talk soft. I've told 'em it were a lad who calls himself Fizz, but I don't know his real name nor where he lives. They asked me to describe him. I said he were tall with a spotty face and a bit gormless. I think I must have been thinkin' about you.'

Brian's face stiffened but he let it go. 'Just as long as yer keep our Ellie's name out of it,' he said. 'Otherwise I'll come an' break yer other leg.'

'Oh aye, you an' whose army? Just tell Ellie not to say anything. Tell her to come and see me. I'll talk her out of it.'

'Make sure yer do, Jacky boy,' said Brian. 'I wouldn't want yer draggin' our lass down ter your level. By the way, me mam gave me some bananas ter give yer. I ate 'em on t' bus. They were very nice, thanks. I left yer all t' skins, though.' He dropped a brown paper bag on Jacky's bed.

'Bugger off, Brian.'

'See yer, Jacky boy.'

Booth screwed a letter from the education committee into a ball and threw it across his office. It heavily criticised his behaviour in expelling Jacky from school, thus stopping such a promising boy taking his scholarship examination. The boy's mother had been down in person to complain. She had referred them to the police, who said they could offer no evidence to charge the boy with any of the offences Booth said he was guilty of, and to top it all a teacher at the boy's new school had nothing but praise for his behaviour and his ability. The boy's mother had accused the school of picking on the boy simply for being the son of a criminal. If this was the case it would reflect badly on Booth's career prospects.

'Damn and blast that bloody boy!'

He had applied for the headship of Abbey House, a school in a much more affluent part of the town. It was more money and would have him dealing with a better class of pupils and parents; a job like that would see him comfortably into his retirement. Up until receiving this letter he had been very confident of getting the job. The interviews were to be held in two weeks' time. If he couldn't come up with a plausible reason for having expelled Jacky before then he could forget it. The phone rang. He picked it up and said, irritably, 'Booth.'

'Mr Booth, this is Victor Mumford.'

'Mr Mumford.' Booth knew exactly who he was. 'How can I help you?'

'I think we can help each other, Mr Booth. I understand you might have a few problems with a job you've just applied for. I assume you've had a letter from the education committee.'

'How the hell do you know that? I've only just read the letter this second.'

'I have a valued customer on the committee who is also a governor of Abbey House. He's been keeping me appraised of your situation.'

'My situation? . . . I see.'

'I believe we have a mutual antagonist, Mr Booth – a certain Jacky Gaskell?'

'Bane of my life, Mr Mumford.'

'And of mine, Mr Booth, as you well know.'

'You mean the song? . . . I banned it from my school.'

'And I thank you for that, Mr Booth, but it's being sung all over the town. The boy is a constant thorn in my side.'

'Well, I expelled the boy from this school over a year ago, so I doubt if I can help you.'

'Oh, but you can, Mr Booth.' His voice was treacly, but his words were persuasive. 'Did you know that he's up in court next week for breaking and entering my house . . . and stealing goods worth several hundred pounds?'

Booth's spirits soared. 'Several hundred, you say?'

'Including a fairly new Rolex watch. A present from my late wife.'

'Really?' said Booth. 'Well, I'm sorry for the trouble he's caused you, but I have to say this is good news.'

'Music to your ears, I should have thought, Mr Booth,' oozed Mumford. 'But I need to make sure the little pest doesn't get away with it. He's claiming it was little more than a boyish prank.'

'And you need my help in this?'

'I need you in court to blacken his character.'

'Just tell me when.'

'The day before your interview. A conviction would completely vindicate every action you've taken against the boy, would it not? Would it be too inconvenient to meet me down at Featherstone Road police station at ten o'clock on Wednesday morning?'

'Not at all.'

'Then I shall look forward to seeing you, Mr Booth.'

This time Bill Scanlon went to the back door as it wasn't an official visit. He hadn't liked what he'd heard that morning about young Jacky's court case. At least that was the excuse he'd given himself for being there. Maureen opened the door and looked instantly uneasy.

'What is it?' she said. 'Jacky's down at the hospital. His gran . . . er, my neighbour's taken him.'

'What? Oh, no. I, er . . .'

She gave a quick sigh of relief. 'Would you like to come in, constable? We've met before, haven't we? When you came round to—'

'I came round last year to talk to you about a scrap your son had with another boy.'

'That's right. I'm sorry I can't remember your name.'

'Scanlon, Bill Scanlon . . . as in the Old Bill – but not so much of the old.'

As he brushed past her he felt his senses quicken and wondered if she felt the same. Of course she didn't. She scarcely remembered him. Was he here just on a pretext to see her again, or was he genuinely concerned about the boy?

'This is not an official call, Mrs Gaskell. In fact it's strictly unofficial. My sergeant would play pop if he knew I was here.'

'Why *are* you here?' Maureen followed him through to the front room, where he stood, awkwardly. 'Won't you sit down, PC Scanlon?'

124

He sat down and removed his helmet. This time Maureen made a conscious effort not to look at his scar.

'I heard something I didn't like at the station and I thought you should know,' he told her. 'Only I would appreciate it if you didn't say you'd got it from me.'

'I assume it's to do with Jacky?'

He nodded. 'He could be in more trouble than you think. Another witness has come forward to speak against him.'

'What other witness?'

'The headmaster of Barr Road School. If you remember I went to see him about the business between Jacky and the Symonite boy.'

'You mean Booth?'

'Yes. He expelled Jacky from his school for vandalism.'

'I'm well aware of that, constable,' she said, sharply. 'He had no proof it was Jacky.'

Bill inwardly winced at having annoyed her by telling her what she already knew. He tried to make up by saying, 'I agree with you, Mrs Gaskell. But he's coming as a character witness and he's going to pull your son to bits . . . I heard them talking.'

'They?'

'Him and Mumford. I actually know this Booth bloke of old. He taught me when I was at Barr Road.'

'I see. What did you think of him?'

'The man was a bully. Preferred hitting kids to teaching them. I got more than my fair share and I wasn't a bad kid. He came down to the station to make a statement, Mumford was with him. Mumford seems to have a real grudge against your boy.' He took out his cigarettes and made to offer her one.

'I don't, thanks.'

'Sorry, I should have remembered.'

'I don't see why you should,' she said. 'We hardly know each other. So Booth's still got it in for Jacky, has he? I wonder if it's got anything to do with a complaint I made to the education department about him. It was supposed to have been brought up at a committee meeting, but I never heard anything. That was months ago.'

'The wheels of bureacracy turn fairly slowly,' explained Bill. 'It seems it was brought up at last month's meeting. The education committee asked for a report on your son. It was passed to me. I gave him a clean sheet. Don't suppose that did Booth much good.'

'Oh, God! I hope I haven't made things worse for Jacky.' She looked intently at Bill and he felt himself wishing that she was looking at him with something else in her eyes, other than concern for her son. 'What do you think?' she asked him, dismally. 'Have I done something that might make things worse?'

'To be honest, I don't know, Mrs Gaskell,' he said, lowering his eyes from her unnerving gaze. Perhaps uncomfortable that she might see what was going on inside his head.

'And I'm er, . . . I'm not sure what you can do about it . . . but I thought you should know.'

'Thank you. I gather you were there when he was expelled.' Her eyes glanced momentarily at his scar. Jacky had mentioned it. Bill didn't need to ask how she knew it was him.

'I was,' he confirmed.

'Constable, Jacky's due in court next week. What will happen to him?'

'I don't know, Mrs Gaskell . . . sorry.'

'All he did was try and scare the man who got his father hanged; is that so great a crime? Wouldn't you bear a grudge against a man who had done that to your father, constable?'

'More than just a grudge, I think. My name's Bill, by the way. If you like, I'll call back if I hear anything else.'

'I'd appreciate that, constable.'

'Bill.'

She forced out a smile, 'Bill,' she said.

He left her knowing neither he nor she would be able to do anything to alter the course of Jacky's future. But she might be able to alter the course of *his* future.

'If I was to pick one word which described this boy it would be heinous.' Booth pronounced the word wrongly.

'Highness?' inquired one confused magistrate of his colleagues.

'I believe it's pronounced heinous,' said the chairman, pronouncing the word correctly.

'Well, why didn't he say heinous?' The confused magistrate looked up at Booth. 'What did you say your profession was?'

'Headmaster of Barr Road School, your worship,' replied Booth, reddening and wishing he'd chosen a word he knew how to pronounce.

'Hmmm,' said the magistrate, glaring at the teacher and writing something uncomplimentary down.

Maureen, who had come to speak up for Jacky, couldn't help but voice her opinion. 'He's hardly fit to be a headmaster if he can't pronounce everyday words,' she said.

The chairman glared at her, biliously. 'The word heinous might be commonplace in your household, madam,' he said. 'But it certainly isn't an everyday word.'

Booth grinned at Mumford. Thanks to that tart's big mouth he'd come out on top. She'd alienated the chairman of the bench even before she got the chance to speak for her son. Jacky looked at his mam and wished she'd keep her mouth shut. Things didn't seem to be going too well. Mumford had already accused him and his unidentified cohort of stealing an expensive gold watch, a pair of diamond earrings and an assortment of jewellery to the value of over nearly three hundred pounds. Not revealing Ellie's identity wasn't doing him any good either.

'In what way is the boy er . . . heinous?' inquired the chairman, pausing before he said the final word, as if it wasn't one he'd have chosen himself.

'He's a bully, your worship. Constantly attacking boys smaller than himself. He even brought disgrace upon the school when a picture of one of his many victims was splashed across the front page of a Sunday newspaper.'

'It was a fair fight!' protested Jacky. 'And he's loads bigger than me.'

He could actually walk with a stick but his mother had advised him to use a crutch to play on the magistrate's sympathy.

'Be quiet, young man,' said the clerk, sternly.

'He's telling lies,' muttered Jacky, unhappy.

'You were told to be quiet,' snapped the chairman. 'Now do as you're told, young man.'

Jacky looked at his mother for help but she could offer none. These men were about to take her son away, just as they'd taken Frank from her. And there was nothing she could do about it.

'I understand he was expelled from your school,' said the chairman. 'Why was that?'

'Because he broke into my office and wrecked it, your worship.'

'I didn't,' said Jacky. 'He's lying again.'

127

'Young man. If you persist in interrupting these proceedings I will have you removed from this court,' said the chairman, haughtily. He looked up at Booth. 'Go on, Mr Booth. Was this vandalism reported to the police?'

'Yes, sir. But I didn't press charges because I run a school. If I pressed charges every time a pupil did something wrong I wouldn't have time to do my job, nor the police theirs.'

'Quite,' the chairman agreed. 'Thank heavens we allow teachers the right to discipline pupils themselves. I suspect our teachers keep more pupils on the straight and narrow than any amount of police or magistrates.'

Booth inclined his head, taking this compliment gracefully. 'Thank you, your worship. We do our best. Unfortunately some pupils are beyond our control.'

Mumford had fixed Jacky in his gloating gaze. This would teach the little shit to mess with him. Making up stupid songs, spreading vicious stories and breaking into his house. He'd left none of this out when he'd been called to give his version of events. Booth's character assassination should get the boy out of his hair for a year or two, hopefully in some suitably spartan reform school many miles away. Jacky's only independent character witness was Mr Overend from Fartown School, and he hadn't turned up yet. Maureen's eyes were continually on the door, wondering where he was. Mumford spotted this and smirked to himself. The teacher wouldn't be coming, his friend on the education committee had seen to that for him. A word in the right ear and Overend had received a very firm instruction from his head not to get involved. If Jacky was freed on his recommendation and subsequently caused them problems they would be held responsible; and Fartown had enough problems with pupils without adding to them. Maureen addressed the bench on her son's behalf.

'What he did was naughty but understandable,' she began, choosing her words carefully. 'You see he's convinced, as many people are, that his father was hanged for a crime he did not commit. That's why he went into Mumford's house, to try and scare the truth out of him.'

'I don't follow,' said the magistrate, who had been confused by Mumford's pronunciation.

'Mumford was there,' Maureen explained, 'when the murder was committed. Jacky is convinced that his father didn't do it.'

128

'And who does he think did it?'

The confused magistrate's two colleagues turned to him in amazement. 'I think the answer to that is fairly obvious,' said the chairman.

'He thinks Mumford is the murderer,' clarified Maureen. 'So do I as a matter of fact.'

Mumford sprang to his feet. 'I must protest, your worship!'

The magistrate waved him down and looked, sombrely, at Maureen. 'Madam,' he droned, 'if you wish to slander anyone I suggest you do it outside this court.'

'I'm sorry, sir,' said Maureen. 'Jacky had this brainless idea that if he scared Mumford into thinking he was being haunted by his father's ghost he might crack and confess. So if my son is guilty of anything it's of acting in a childish manner. He didn't steal anything. And as far as the school is concerned my son is the one who was being bullied. All he did was defend himself – something his teachers should have been doing for him. He was expelled for wrecking the headmaster's study; but Mr Booth hadn't a scrap of evidence to say he did it – that's the reason my son was never charged. The man is a bully and a liar and he's not fit to teach children. My son is a good . . . b . . .'

Her words were choked by a flood of tears. The chairman cleared his throat and waited for her to regain her composure.

'Mrs Gaskell, your spirited defence of your son is understandable. But when all is said and done he is your son and we would expect no less; it would be a poor mother who wouldn't defend her son with every means at her disposal. Paradoxically, however, the fact that you are such a loving mother weakens the credibility of your defence of him. Some mothers would defend their sons of the foulest of crimes. That's what being a mother is. We have seen it so often before in this court and no doubt will again.'

The chairman looked down at his notes, and back again at Maureen. Then he removed his glasses and rubbed his eyes as if trying to arrive at some decision. He continued in a lower voice than before.

'Mrs Gaskell. I'm afraid the fact that your son's father wasn't your husband does little to help your credibility as a character witness.'

Maureen went pale with anger at his insinuation. 'I wasn't unfaithful to my husband,' she seethed. 'I had been told by the

129

authorities that my husband was dead. Can you imagine what that's like? Being told your husband is dead.'

No one on the bench offered a comment so Maureen told them, 'My father and my uncles were all killed after being made to fight in the First World War – the most ridiculous of all wars. Then my husband goes off to fight in the next war and I'm told he's dead. It makes you act strangely. You seek comfort where you can. You have no right to judge the way I behaved after I had been wrongly told that my husband was dead.'

The three men on the bench shuffled in embarrassment as Maureen continued, 'You see, gentlemen, the authorities frequently make mistakes. They made a mistake when they hanged Frank McGovern for a murder committed by Victor Mumford.'

'Madam,' said the chairman, relieved to have been given back the moral high ground, 'if you persist in this slander I will find you in contempt of court.'

Maureen met the chairman's censorial gaze with one of her own. 'Sir,' she said. 'My son is in this court because of what the authorities did to his father. He was expelled from school because the school did not want to be associated with him. My son is a victim of other people's errors and vindictiveness. Please do not wreck his future by adding yourself to this list of stupid people.'

Even as she said it she wished she'd said 'mistaken' instead of 'stupid'. It obviously annoyed all three men on the bench. The ones on either side leaned inwards and all three conversed in low voices. Then they resumed their positions and the chairman spoke to her.

'Mrs Gaskell. Whether or not your son's father was guilty of the crime for which he was executed is not a matter for this court. We do not visit the sins of the fathers upon the sons.' He consulted his colleagues before adding, 'If no one has anything else to add we will rise and consider our verdict.'

Maureen was still in her seat ten minutes after the verdict had been given and the court had emptied for lunch. *Two years.* They were taking her boy away from her for two years. And for what?

Bill Scanlon was in the doorway watching her; wondering whether to interrupt her grief. She suddenly turned and summoned up a smile for him.

'That was wrong,' he said.

His voice echoed across the empty court room.

'I seem to live in a world of injustice, constable.'

He went over to her; a bit put out that she hadn't called him by his name. She looked so bereft he felt like putting his arm around her and hugging her to him. Then she looked at his scarred forehead and asked, 'How exactly did you get that?'

He instinctively touched it. 'It's my lucky charm,' he said. 'A German shell killed two of my mates and all I got was a bit of a burn.'

Maureen ran her fingers lightly across it. 'Do you think it'll bring me luck?'

'I'm not sure it actually works,' he smiled. 'It never brought me much luck with the ladies.'

'They weren't proper ladies, then. You seem a good man, Bill Scanlon. Is it possible for me to see my son before they take him away from me?'

'I'll see what I can do.'

As they walked along a deserted corridor a door in front of them opened and Booth emerged from the toilet, adjusting his tie and smoothing back what hair he had. A brief look of concern crossed his face when he recognised Maureen. He stood back, allowing the two of them to pass, intending to go the other way, thus avoiding an unpleasant confrontation. Before Bill could stop her, Maureen, without a word of warning, walloped Booth right on the end of his nose and sent him to his knees with pain. Blood gushed on to his clothes, staining his white shirt bright red. He looked up at the policeman.

'Well, what are you thtanding there for? Arresth the bloody woman.' His voice was distorted by the damage to his nose.

Bill whispered into Maureen's ear for her to make herself scarce, then he knelt down beside Booth and hissed in his ear, 'Do you remember me, you sadistic bastard?'

Booth looked at him in amazement and no little fear. 'No,' he said. 'I've never theen you before.'

'You taught me,' growled Bill. 'You were the worst bloody teacher I've ever come across in my life. You're a bully and a useless shit – so don't involve me in any of your lies about Mrs Gaskell attacking you. You tried to get away from her and you walked into the door.'

'But the woman athaulted m—!'

'I'll assault you myself if you carry on lying like this. Then I'll arrest you for being a useless, lying bastard!'

Maureen was waiting in the entrance, half expecting Bill to come and arrest her for assault. It wouldn't have bothered her unduly; it had been worth it – apart from her bruised knuckles and aching wrist.

'I think he might have broken his nose on that door he walked into,' Bill said when he caught her up. 'Came out with this cock and bull story about you hitting him – as if anyone would believe that. He obviously didn't realise I'd seen the whole thing. What a liar that man is!'

'Thanks, Bill. Can I see my boy now?'

'Wait there. If a man with a swollen nose comes out, try not to hit him.'

'It won't be easy.'

'Do your best.'

Chapter Sixteen

When Brian came in from work, Maureen was nowhere to be seen. Ellie was frying bacon. Brian sniffed, appreciatively.

'By, heck, Ellie, that smells good. I'm fair clemmed. I could eat a scabby donkey. Where's Mam?'

'Upstairs, moping,' said his sister. 'Our Jacky's been locked up for two years. If I wasn't so hungry I'd be up there with her. It's partly my fault he's been locked up. Partly my fault, but I reckon it was mainly your fault.'

'My fault? What's it got to do wi' me? It was you an' him who broke into Mumford's house.'

'It was that louse Booth that did for him,' Ellie said. 'He stood up and told the court how Jacky had been expelled for wrecking his office.' She looked at her brother, gravely, and shook her head. 'Brian, you did that, didn't you? You ruined his chances of going to grammar school and now you've got him locked up.'

She had caught him off guard. Ordinarily he'd have denied it but he knew it wouldn't have done any good. Ellie was no fool.

'What if I did?' he retorted, churlishly. 'The little sod deserved it.'

'I'd like you to leave this house!'

Brian spun round. Maureen was standing at the bottom of the stairs.

'What?' he said.

'I don't want you to live with us any more.' His mother spoke in a voice that told him arguing was useless. 'You've done your best to destroy your brother's life and you've succeeded. Pack a suitcase. I want you to go tonight.'

'Hey? . . . but where will I go?'

'There's a lodging house on Morton Road. They'll be able to take you.'

Her face was drained from crying. Bill had taken her to see Jacky who had looked absolutely lost. He wasn't crying – more bemused and frightened. Wearing short trousers, although he had just started wearing long ones before this trouble arose. Maureen had thought short ones might make him look more innocent. He was leaning on his crutch with one foot still encased in plaster which was due to come off next week. How cruel to take him away from her in this state. God, he was just a baby and yet he'd gone through so much in the past year or so.

'Mam, I haven't done anything.'

'I know you haven't, Jacky boy.'

'It was Brian who smashed up Boothie's office.'

'You don't know that, Jacky.'

'Mam. I think we both know it was him.'

He hadn't pressed the point before because it wouldn't do any good and he knew how much such a thing would upset his mother. But things had gone a bit far now. Maybe his mother could put things right if she would just accept the truth. He hadn't expected Booth to say all these things about him in court.

'Mam,' Ellie turned the gas right down to stop the bacon frying to a frazzle. 'Supposing our Brian went to the police and admitted wrecking Boothie's office . . . trying to put the blame on Jacky?'

'Hey!' protested Brian. 'Supposing *you* go to the coppers and tell them you were the other one who broke into Mumford's house? It was her, y'know, Mam. She was the one with our Jacky.'

'I know,' said Maureen, doing her best to hold the firm line she had taken with her son. 'She told me. But she didn't do it out of badness. And if she owned up she could be locked up along with her brother. But you've been deliberately trying to harm Jacky and that's why you're going.'

'But Mam—!'

'No buts, Brian. Jacky's my son. I've asked you to respect that and you've gone against me. So now I'm going against you.'

Brian pushed past her and clumped up the stairs, muttering things about favouritism and how she'd never liked him. Maureen ignored him and sat down, oddly calm now that she'd dispensed a bit of justice.

'I'll make us a cup of tea,' said Ellie.

'Actually, I wouldn't mind a bacon sandwich.'

'Coming up. What about our Brian? Shall I—?'

'Our Brian looks after himself from now on, Ellie. He can get fish and chips. He doesn't live here any more.'

She felt cold towards her eldest son. It wasn't right that she should feel this way about one of her children but under the circumstances there was no other way she could feel. It didn't seem right that one son should be locked away because of an older son who was being looked after by her. If she couldn't have Jacky she didn't want Brian. Maybe time would allow her to get things into perspective. In the meantime Brian had to go.

Bill knocked on the door. 'Is Mrs Gaskell in?' he asked Ellie. He wasn't in uniform.

'Who is it?' said Maureen.

'Bill Scanlon,' he called out, over Ellie's shoulder.

It made her feel better. She hadn't been as pleased to see a man since . . . since Frank, if she was honest with herself. Bert had just been, well, there. Part of the furniture. A good man who had done his best for her, and she missed him like she'd miss a beloved brother. The emptiness inside her was caused by Frank's awful death. When he was still alive he had occupied a large but secret place in her heart and somehow she always knew that if she ever dared take the plunge she could have him back. But now that chance was gone.

'Don't keep him standing there, let him in.'

Ellie stood back to let Bill past. She smiled at him as he took his hat off; momentarily her eyes were drawn to his scar. Maureen saw this.

'That's his badge of honour,' she said. 'The Germans did that to him.'

'What? Oh, I didn't notice.'

Brian came clumping back down the stairs carrying a suitcase. He paused when he saw Bill.

'Is that why yer kickin' me out?' he said to his mother. 'So yer can move yer fancy man in.'

Maureen fumed. 'This is PC Scanlon,' she told him. 'Have you got something to tell him about how Mr Booth's office was wrecked?'

Bill looked from mother to son, not having a clue what all this was about; but he knew enough not to join in. Brian went out of

135

the house without a word, slamming the door behind him. His mother went to the window and watched him walk out of the back gate and disappear into the night. Then she stood there, looking at the empty street and wondered what the hell was happening to her life. Was it all her fault?

Bill opened his mouth to say something but Ellie put her finger to her lips. The room was silent as the three of them stood as still as statues, only two of them knowing why. Then Maureen released a long sigh and turned to Bill.

'That was Brian, my eldest boy,' she said, quietly. 'I've just kicked him out.'

'I see.'

'No, you don't.' Maureen gave a despondent smile and rubbed her forehead with her fingertips, as if massaging a pain. 'I'm not sure if I see myself.'

'You did the right thing, Mam,' Ellie assured her. 'It's not the end of the world for Brian. It might make him face up to his responsibilities.'

'This is my daughter, Eleanor,' said Maureen. 'We call her Ellie. She's the one who doesn't cause me any trouble.'

'Pleased to meet you, Ellie.'

'Why are you here?' Ellie inquired, bluntly.

'Ellie!'

Ellie ignored her mother. It was obvious to her that this wasn't official police business. Bill was interested in her mother; which meant that Ellie had a vested in interest in Bill.

'I just called to see if your mother was okay.'

There was an element of truth in this but it wasn't the whole reason, as Ellie suspected. 'Mam says you're a nice policeman,' she said. 'It's good to know there are *some* nice policemen about.'

'I'm not sure your brother will share your opinion,' Bill replied. 'If the police hadn't caught him he'd be home with you now.'

'It could have been worse,' Ellie said, provocatively. 'They could have caught me as well. Only they were a bit slow. Perhaps *you'd* have caught me if you'd been there. You look as though you're a bit quick off the mark.'

'Ellie!' admonished Maureen. 'Don't make jokes like that.'

'I'm not joking,' said Ellie. 'I'm just testing him to see how nice he is.'

'Ellie, you're compromising him.'

136

'No, she's not,' Bill smiled. 'I know a joke when I hear one.'

'It's not a j—'

'Ellie! Don't push your luck,' warned her mother.

Bill sniffed the air and changed the subject. 'I think your bacon's burning.'

'Bang goes my bacon sandwich,' groaned Maureen.

'I imagine you'll be getting something a bit more substantial than a bacon sandwich when you get home,' said Ellie to Bill. 'Is your wife a good cook?'

She assumed she was fishing in barren waters, but it did no harm to test him out. Maureen was about to rebuke her daughter once again but was stopped when Bill said, 'She does cook – but she's a bit limited.'

'Oh?' said Maureen.

'With her being in a wheelchair,' he explained. 'She can't walk, you see.'

'Oh,' said Maureen again. 'I'm sorry to hear that.' But she was more disappointed than sorry.

Ellie felt guilty at having misjudged him.

But her judgement wasn't that far out.

Jacky spent that night in the four-bed hospital annexe to Westhill Boys' Home in York, some 30 miles way from Castlethorpe. In the only other occupied bed was a thin boy who cried a lot. Jacky had made up his mind not to cry while he was in there. If he felt like crying he would count backwards from a hundred – his granddad had taught him that. Charlie said it was something he had taught Frank when he was a boy. And Frank was no cry-baby.

'Have you had mumps?' inquired a middle-aged woman who had a scrubbed face, a long, navy-blue uniform and an odd hat. Jacky couldn't make up his mind whether she was a nurse or a nun.

'I think so.'

'You only think so? I make no wonder you end up in here if you don't know if you've had mumps or not.'

'I've definitely had them,' Jacky assured her, deciding she was probably not a nun with an attitude like that. It seemed a good idea to get on the right side of this intimidating woman. 'Why is that boy crying?' he asked her, amiably.

'Because he's got mumps, which is what you'd get if you hadn't already had 'em.'

'Oh,' said Jacky, wondering if he should revert to not being certain about having had mumps. From the distress it was causing the boy it didn't look like a good thing to have. Surely he would have remembered having something as obviously painful as that.

'You probably had it when you were little,' the woman said, as if reading his thoughts. 'Doesn't affect you as much when you're little.'

This relieved Jacky somewhat. He thought he remembered his mother telling him he'd had mumps. He definitely remembered having measles – so he'd probably had mumps as well. Thus reassured by his own logic he got into the next bed to the weeping boy and tried to talk to him.

'My name's Jacky,' he said. 'I'm in here for something I didn't do, so I won't be here long. What's it like, this mumps? I told that woman I'd had it but I'm not sure, to tell the truth.'

The boy turned his back to him and snivelled on. This worried Jacky. Was this thin kid crying just because he had mumps or was there some other, more sinister reason? What sort of place *was* this?

In a cupboard beside Jacky's bed was a Biggles book. He picked it up and began to read, thinking this place couldn't be all that bad if they gave you Biggles books to read. As soon as he got his pot off he would set about proving his innocence. His mam would help, so would Ellie. As far as Jacky Gaskell was concerned his situation was only temporary.

In the middle of the night, when Jacky was sound asleep, the thin kid in the next bed stopped snivelling and started thinking. He got out of bed, took off the bed sheet and twisted it into a rope, in which he tied a noose. He then took a chair to the barred window, climbed on it and tied the twisted sheet to the middle bar and placed the noose around his neck. He stood there in the gloom, listening to Jacky's breathing and he felt sorry for this poor new kid who would have to endure this awful place. As for him, he was leaving.

Daylight streaming through the window woke Jacky up. He half opened his eyes and in that twilight of consciousness between being asleep and awake he saw Frank McGovern being hanged. He shut this awful vision away and turned over, knowing that was all it was, a dreadful hallucination. He'd had stuff like this happen to him before. When your dad's been wrongfully hanged it's only natural.

But he could sense it behind him and a shudder ran through his body. The crying kid in the next bed was no longer there. Slowly Jacky looked round again and allowed his eyes to focus on the awful sight. The petrified expression on the hanging boy's blood-less face was now but a frozen echo of his last, frantic moment of life. His thin body hung as limp and as empty as a wet shirt on a washing line on a windless day. Dead eyes stared down at nothing. Jacky's own eyes went wide with shock and he tried to shout out. But no sound would come. He heard footsteps in the corridor outside and tried again.

'M . . . m . . . m . . . Missis!'

'What?' boomed a stentorian voice from beyond the door. It opened. She looked at him and then beyond him to the dead boy.

'Oh, no! Oh my God!'

She rushed past him to try and lift the boy clear of the noose. Jacky blanched at the sight of the woman lowering the body to the floor and listening at his mouth. She looked up at Jacky and said, accusingly, 'This boy's dead. Did you have anything to do with it?'

The very suggestion shocked Jacky. 'No, missis,' he said.

'Oh, Jesus bloody Christ!' cursed the woman, who was definitely not a nun, but a matron. 'This is all I bloody need. Wait outside, I'll have to get someone to sort this out . . . QUICKLY!'

Her urgent shout jolted Jacky into action. He swung out of bed, picked up his stick and hobbled out into the corridor. Within minutes people were rushing in and out of the room, totally ignoring him. It occurred to him that he could probably walk straight out of this place and make his way home if he knew where home was; but wherever it was he didn't fancy hobbling there in his pyjamas. The image of the hanged boy was burning itself into his memory where it would stay forever. This was how Frank must have looked after they'd hanged him.

A week later his pot came off and he would have been made to leave the hospital wing had he not got mumps. 'I got it off that kid who hanged himself,' he told his mother.

'Did anyone ask if you'd had mumps?'

'The matron did . . . I said I wasn't sure.'

'You weren't sure?'

'Then she got all mad at me for not knowing, so I said I'd definitely had it—'

His mother was gone before he had finished telling her. Maureen had already crossed swords with the matron after hearing about her asking Jacky if he had anything to do with the boy's death. The woman showed little sign of being a member of the caring profession. Maureen took her by the collar and forced her up against her office wall.

'What sort of a bloody institution is this where my boy has to witness a suicide and catch mumps off a dead boy?'

'Take your hands off me, Mrs Gaskell or I'll—'

'Or you'll what? Maybe I'll go to the papers and maybe you'll be out of a job before this day's out. From now on you treat my boy with kid gloves or I'll really come gunning for you.'

There was too much determination in Maureen's eyes for the matron to argue with her.

'I'm really sorry, Mrs Gaskell. I did ask him if he'd had mumps and he said he had.'

'He said he wasn't sure. He only changed his mind when you got mad at him for not knowing. Jacky's a kid. Don't you know anything about kids? It's bullies like you that put most of them in here. My Jacky's different. He's in here because of a couple of liars. God knows what you put that other poor boy through for him to hang himself.'

'Now look here, Mrs Gaskell—!'

'I'll be watching you sadists like a bloody hawk. They've put my boy in here for something he didn't do and when the truth comes out, woe betide anyone who's added to his problems . . . and that includes you . . . *matron*.' She spat out the last word with withering scorn.

Jacky wilted like an untended flower in the confines of the boy's home. The boys were looked upon as a lower form of life, not as good as the rest of society. Many deserved this label, some didn't care; Jacky deeply resented it because he was as good as anyone. They were allowed out of the school grounds during certain hours but they had to wear an easily identifiable uniform of brown shirt, brown jumper and brown trousers. It was as if all the colour had

140

been removed from their lives for the duration. The 'brown boys' were personae non gratae around the Westhill area and were accused of every crime committed within a mile radius of the home. Sometimes with good reason.

The regime was oppressive but not brutal. Stories abounded of homosexual abuse but mercifully Jacky saw none. He had a reputation for speaking up for himself and was unlikely to keep quiet about any would-be abuser. He had, in his mother, a doughty champion – unlike most of the residents who, like the hanged boy, had no one.

His mother, Ellie and Charlie visited him as often as they were allowed. Rarely a visit went by without Maureen demanding to see Mr Mullen, the governor, to complain about the inhumane treatment being meted out to her boy.

'He's treated no better, no worse than any other boy,' she was constantly told. 'Please remember that this is a reform school, Mrs Gaskell.'

'You're not reforming these boys, you're turning them into full-blown criminals,' she grumbled. 'Shouldn't your people be leading by example? It seems to me you use the, Do as I say, not as I do, method.'

'We do our best under difficult circumstances.'

'And I've heard rumours of abuse.'

'There will always be rumours in a place like this,' said the governor. 'But that's all they are – rumours.'

'Let's hope for your sake they are. If anyone lays a finger on my boy, you won't know what hit you. He's in here for stealing stuff that never existed – except in the mind of a thieving murderer.'

'I assume you're talking about Victor Mumford.' Mullen knew Jacky's history better than that of most of the boys.

'I am,' Maureen confirmed, bitterly. 'Everyone knows he killed his wife and Jacky's dad was hanged for it. Now the lad's having to serve time so that Mumford can make a fat insurance claim.'

'I think you'll find Mr Mumford would have had to prove ownership of the stolen items,' said the governor.

'Mumford's an insurance agent. He'll have found a way round all that,' said Maureen. 'He's also an expert liar.'

'Then you'd be better employed proving it rather than bothering me all the time.' There was a sharpness in his tone, but Maureen saw beyond it. Her voice became reasonable.

'How do I do that?' she asked.

Mullen sighed, wondering what he'd let himself in for. He got to his feet and walked to the window so that his back was to her. Her beauty was having an effect on him. It was making him help her and he had enough on his plate without helping parents prove their son's innocence. He knew the regime in this place wasn't perfect, but governors came and went too quickly for any of them to stamp their authority on it. He was thinking of going back to teaching in an ordinary school. A man need a proper vocation to do this job – and he just didn't have that sort of vocation. Not many did. Having one of the boys commit suicide was an awful thing to live with. The boy shouldn't have been sent here; he had mental problems that were beyond the scope of his staff. Mental problems and mumps. It proved to be a suicidal combination. How was he to know that?

He turned and looked down at Maureen and decided to help her. Maybe it would ease his conscience if he could make a genuine difference to just one boy's life. He collected his thoughts and brought a packet of cigarettes out of his pocket.

'Do you smoke?' he asked her.

'Only in times of stress.'

He offered her the packet. She hesitated before taking one. Mullen remained deep in thought well after he had lit both cigarettes.

'Mrs Gaskell,' he said, eventually. 'As it happens I worked in insurance for a while before I came into teaching.'

'I'd appreciate any advice you can give me.'

'Well,' he said. 'All insurance companies have what's called a duty of care to their investors. Paying out on bogus insurance claims puts up premiums and affects share prices. If Mr Mumford's claim wasn't properly looked at then it should be. If the assessor didn't do his job properly it would have serious repercussions. Especially in this instance.'

'Why in this instance?'

'Because, indirectly, the insurance company also has a duty of care to your son. If their assessment is the only proof that the theft took place and their assessment wasn't done thoroughly it would throw a whole different light on his conviction.'

'What should I do?'

The governor drew on his cigarette and blew out a chain of

smoke rings. It seemed such an ungovernorlike act that it made Maureen smile. He rubbed his chin and sat on the edge of his desk. 'Insurance fraud's a difficult thing to prove,' he said, 'even for the professionals. Mumford will know that this is a relatively minor claim, and wouldn't justify a fraud investigation even if it did look a bit suspicious. It would help if you knew someone in the insurance company – or perhaps hired a private detective who could do some digging.'

'I know a policeman. He believes Jacky didn't take the stuff. In fact most of the police believe the same.'

Mullen smiled. He almost believed it himself. But then again he was willing to believe anything this extraordinary woman told him. 'Having the police on your side is no bad thing,' he said.

Maureen's mind was racing with ideas of her own. 'Or I could just walk into the insurance offices and kick up a stink. Accuse them of being party to a fraud that ended up with my son being wrongfully convicted of theft. It should make someone sit up and take notice.'

'Or cover up their tracks if they are in cahoots with Mr Mumford,' pointed out the governor.

'Well, it's an option,' she said.

Mullen held out his hand for her to shake. 'I wish you well, Mrs Gaskell, and I'll make sure no harm comes to your boy. If I can help you in any way, I will.'

'Let's hope you already have.'

143

Chapter Seventeen

The ages of the boys ranged from twelve to fifteen. By virtue of his mother's influence on the governor Jacky was soon placed in a class of fourteen year olds. Even among boys of that age he could easily hold his own – academically at least. But it soon became apparent to him that he would need a friend and protector if he was to survive among these bigger boys, many of whom would have stricken fear even into the heart of a kid from the Blissetts.

Aaron Johnstone was in for car theft. It was his ambition to be a racing driver when he grew up and he needed the practice. His dad, who had brought his family to England from the Caribbean aboard HMS *Windrush*, couldn't afford to buy his son a racing car so Aaron took his destiny into his own hands. He also took several cars into his own hands and drove them around Leeds with a natural expertise which boded well if he could only stay out of jail long enough to pursue his ambition via a legal route. The trouble was that Aaron looked upon the law as an obstacle to be overcome at all costs. He took a liking to Jacky, which was handy as Aaron was a big lad and quite hard when the occasion arose.

The school was on the fringe of a newly built council estate and many of the residents took exception to having a reformatory on their doorstep despite the fact that the school had been there for thirty years. Jacky had been coping tolerably well with life at the home until one Saturday morning in June when he and Aaron were heading for a parade of shops on the estate.

'What're you in for?' Jacky inquired. He hadn't asked any of the boys this question before but Aaron seemed such an unlikely inmate. There was a decency about him that said he didn't belong in this place.

'Touching the dog's arse.'

'What?'

'TDA – Taking and driving away. The coppers call it touching the dog's arse.'

'Wh—? Oh, I see,' Jacky grinned. 'You must have touched a lot of dogs arses to get sent here.'

'Thirty-seven in two years. It got to be a bit of a habit. What about you?'

'Burglary,' said Jacky, kicking at a stone. 'Only I didn't do it.'

Aaron looked at him, keenly, then said, 'I believe yer.'

'Honest?'

Aaron shrugged. 'Course, honest. No point lyin' ter me is there?'

'No, I don't s'pose there is. Did you know that kid who killed himself?'

'Willie Wilmot?'

'Yeah,' said Jacky. 'I never knew him, but I was the last person he saw. He didn't talk to me. He just cried.'

'He cried a lot, did Willie. Weepin' Willie we used ter call him.'

'I often think about him,' Jacky said. 'It scared me when I saw him hanging there. Why do you think he did it?'

'He wasn't all there.' Aaron tapped his temple. 'There was something wrong with him . . . up here. Weird kid. Shouldn't have been in here. It's a load o' crap is this place. They call it an approved school. Who approves of it? The people who live round here don't approve of it. I don't approve of it. Do you approve of it?'

Before Jacky could answer and, as if to prove Aaron's point, there came a harridan's screech.

'Hey! Brown boys. Don't come down our street with yer thievin' ways.' The insult was hurled at them from one of the gardens. 'They should keep you thievin' pillocks locked up.'

Jacky stopped in his tracks. It was the first time he'd been subjected to this. Aaron, being black, was used to it, brown boy or not. He walked on a few paces then turned round and called back to Jacky. 'Leave it. She's just a silly owd cowbag.'

'Less o' yer bloody cheek. There's allus stuff goin' missin' from these houses,' shouted the sour-faced woman. 'An' we're not so daft as not ter know who's bloody tekkin' it!'

'Well it's not us, missis,' retorted Jacky. 'Anyroad, I reckon

145

you've nothin' worth stealin' round here. You don't look as if you've got a tanner ter scratch your fat arse with.'

The woman shook her fist at him. 'Clear off where yer belong, yer cheeky little bleeder an' tek yer bleedin' nigger pal with yer!'

'Hey, missis!' called out Jacky, cheerfully. 'Are you from Norway?'

'What sort of a daft question's that?' snorted the woman.

'I thought you might be, that's all. You've got a face like a Norse!'

The boys howled with laughter, as did a man in the next garden. The woman fumed and threatened to tell the police. Jacky and Aaron ran off, laughing.

'Hey, that were a good un, Jacky,' chortled Aaron. 'Face like a Norse. Good un, that. Must remember that. Face like a Norse, eh?'

They had been doing the Scandinavian countries in geography or Aaron might not have picked up on the joke. He wasn't the sharpest kid in the class but Jacky liked him. Despite his predilection for driving other people's cars Aaron had his own set of values which included an honesty of spirit and Jacky trusted him.

'That's them!'

The sour-faced woman was standing in Mr Mullen's office to which Jacky and Aaron had been summoned within minutes of them returning from the shops. She looked at Aaron and smirked triumphantly. 'Thought yer'd gorraway wi' it, didn't yer?'

'Gorraway wi' what?' inquired Aaron, whose patois was much more West Riding than West Indian.

'Mrs Pickersgill says you went into her house and stole a diamond ring,' said Mullen, gravely. 'She also says you swore at her and insulted her.'

'Jacky just asked her if she was from Norway, sir,' grinned Aaron. 'Because she's got a face like a Norse . . . Do yer get it, sir? Norway . . . they call people who come from Nor—'

'Quiet, boy!'

'She started it, sir,' said Jacky. 'She started shouting at us in the street. Calling us names.'

'You little liar!' seethed Mrs Pickersgill. 'I were mindin' me own business when yer started insultin' me. I've never heard such foul language. Next thing I know me diamond ring's gone missin'.'

146

'She called me a bleedin' nigger,' said Aaron.

'That's what you are, int it?' argued the woman. 'Just cos yer talks like us dunt stop yer from bein' one. You are what you are.'

The governor ordered them to turn out their pockets. Aaron had a sixpence and eight Woodbines left from a packet of ten – he and Jacky had smoked one each on the way back from the shops. Jacky had three toffees, fourpence and a letter from his mother which the governor began to read until Jacky said,

'It's private, sir.'

'There's no such thing as privacy in here, Gaskell,' sighed Mullen.

'Quite right too,' sneered Mrs Pickersgill. 'I don't know why yer allow the thievin' little beggars out on the street, ruinin' things fer decent people such as me.'

'There doesn't appear to be a ring,' said Mullen, relieved.

'Well I didn't expect them ter still 'ave it on 'em,' she sniffed. 'They'll have hid it somewhere, crafty little bleeders.'

'Did you actually see them taking the ring, Mrs Pickersgill?'

'Course I bleedin' did. I wouldn't be here if I hadn't seen 'em.'

'You're a flippin' liar!' shouted Jacky. 'Just like all the rest of them. It's you who should be locked up in here, not us.'

'Please be quiet, Gaskell!' The governor sounded more agitated than angry. He wasn't at all sure about this woman. It wasn't the first time a boy from the home had been wrongly accused. The trouble was, it wasn't the first time one of his boys had been rightly accused. Which one was it this time?

'I'll have to ring the police,' he decided, resignedly. 'Let them sort it out.'

'Can't yer just give 'em a good hiding?' suggested the woman. 'It seems a shame ter be botherin' t' bobbies. They've got enough ter worry about.'

'It's a police matter, Mrs Pickersgill. It's not up to me.'

The desk sergeant at Featherstone Road police station didn't look up as Maureen rang the bell. He never looked up straight away when people rang the bell because that would make the bell ringer more important than he was – and that would never do.

'Shop,' said Maureen.

The sergeant looked up, intending to say, 'I'll be with you in a minute', but the sight of Maureen knocked him off guard. And he

147

couldn't have been more stunned if Gina Lollobrigida had walked in. He cleared his throat and adjusted his tie.

'Yes, madam?'

'I was wondering if I could have a word with Bill Scanlon.'

'PC Scanlon?'

'Yes. It is a police matter, but PC Scanlon knows some of the background so I thought it would save time if I spoke to him.'

'What sort of police matter . . . er?'

'Maureen Gaskell. It concerns my son, Jacky Gaskell. I assume you've heard of him.'

'Actually, no, madam.'

This pleased Maureen. It was good that her son wasn't known to every officer at the station. The sergeant studied her and asked no further questions. As much as he would have liked to deal with this woman it seemed as if she'd come about a trivial, juvenile matter; far too trivial for him to bother with. He turned to a constable sitting at a table behind him.

'Give Bill Scanlon a shout will you?'

The constable disappeared and came back with Bill, whose face lit up when he saw her.

'Maur . . . Mrs Gaskell.'

'I was wondering if I could have a word with you about Jacky.' Two other people arrived at the desk – fortuitously for Maureen for it gave her the excuse to add, 'In private?'

'Sure,' said Bill. 'Come through here.'

He led her into a small room. Maureen glanced at the sparse furnishings, just a table and four chairs. 'Is this where you grill the mobsters?'

Bill grinned. 'Just sit down there, madam, while I get a light to shine in your eyes.'

They sat down at opposite sides of the table and for some reason Maureen asked him how his wife was. She didn't know why.

'She's okay.'

'Do you have any children?'

'No.'

'Oh.'

'I understand you've come about Jacky?'

'Yes,' she said. Her thoughts had wandered off on a dangerous tangent. Bill was obviously a decent man and it would be wrong

148

for her to corrupt him. Although she sensed he wouldn't take much corrupting. 'I think there might be a way to prove him innocent,' she said, 'but I don't know how to go about it.'

'If I can help, I will.' His tone was more that of a friend than a policeman.

'You see,' said Maureen, 'I've been thinking . . . both Ellie and Jacky swear they didn't steal anything from Mumford and I believe them, but I understand that he claimed on his insurance for all sorts of things. How could he do that if nothing was stolen?'

'By lying to us for a start,' Bill said. 'Claiming stuff was stolen that wasn't. All we can say is that there had been a break-in. We'll have been asked to confirm to the insurance company that a crime had been committed.' He shrugged. 'After that, I suppose it's up to the assessor.'

'Wouldn't the assessor need some sort of proof that he owned the stuff he said was stolen?'

'Theoretically, yes.'

'How do you mean, theoretically?'

'I mean, Mumford's an insurance agent,' explained Bill. 'No doubt he puts a lot of the business the insurance company's way. Could be that they didn't look into his claim too deeply. Especially if he kept his claim below a certain figure. He'll know what that figure is.'

'Do you have a list of the things he claims were stolen?'

'Yes, we will.' He could see where she was headed. 'I'll take a look at it.'

'You see,' explained Maureen, 'Mumford's lies have not only defrauded the insurance company, but they've got my son locked up. Not to mention what happened to Frank.'

'Mrs Gaskell—'

'Maureen.'

He smiled, happy she'd insisted on that. 'Maureen . . . It was the court that sent Jacky away, not the insurance company. They believed Mumford, the same as the insurance company seem to have.'

'But if we could prove Mumford was lying it would make the court think again, surely?'

Her eyes were on him, mesmerising him. He looked down at his hands, slightly embarrassed that she would see how much he was taken with her. 'I'll ask the insurance assessor to show us what-

149

ever receipts they have for the stolen items. Trouble is,' he mused, 'if they took him on trust I'm not sure what we can do.'

'You could tell them you've good reason to believe his claim was completely fraudulent,' suggested Maureen. 'If the insurance company finds out the assessor didn't get any receipts, surely it should raise a few eyebrows.'

Bill smiled at her and she smiled back. '*You* should be doing my job with a mind like yours,' he said. 'I'll do whatever I can.'

'Thanks. You're my best chance, Bill.'

He couldn't help but place a wishful interpretation on these words. Their eyes met and there was a mutual need that neither would dare admit to.

Jacky sat on a wall with his head between his hands. 'I'm right fed up of this,' he muttered. 'Fed up to the back flippin' teeth.'

'Me an' all,' agreed Aaron. 'They'll take her side, yer know that, don't yer? The owd cowbag. If it's our word against hers they'll take her side. Me bein' a black kid doesn't help. No one ever takes yer side if yer a black kid.'

'Never really thought about it,' said Jacky, 'you're the first black kid I've ever really known.'

'Would you like it if people went round callin' you a nigger?' asked Aaron.

'Well, it's only a nickname, but it flippin' sounded bad the way that old bat said it.'

'It's the way they say it that counts,' Aaron grumbled. 'Like yer summat they've jus' scraped off their shoe.'

'Like bein' a brown boy, you mean?'

'Sort of. Only when you get out of here you'll stop bein' a brown boy, – I'll allus be a brown boy.' Then Aaron flashed him a mouthful of dazzling white teeth and added, 'It's a good job I'm a handsome devil.'

'Handsome, you?' laughed Jacky. 'Give over. You've got a face like a tram smash.'

'Hey! Me mammy says I'm a handsome boy and that's good enough for me. You'd like me mammy. She's not as strict as me dad. Very strict man, me dad. Yer've never met anyone as God-fearin' as me dad. God-fearin' as buggery.'

'I wish my mam were here,' said Jacky. 'She'd kick up a right stink about this would my mam.'

'Me dad'll blame me,' grumbled Aaron. 'He's allus blamed me. Jus' because I never liked school as much as me brothers and me sister. I even used ter knock off goin' ter Sunday School. I can't do with all that bible stuff. It's bad enough bein' called Aaron.'

'I've got a pal called Billy Mycock,' said Jacky. 'They should have called him Aaron.'

'Why?' asked Aaron.

'Aaron Mycock.'

'What? . . . oh yeah.' Aaron laughed. 'Hey that's good that is. Aaron Mycock . . . I'll remember that. Next time somebody asks me what me name is I'll say Aaron Mycock. I'd like ter see their face when I say that.'

'You're a right case you are, Aaron,' laughed Jacky. 'A proper nutcase.' He couldn't remember liking any friend as much as he liked Aaron. Daft as he was.

Aaron wrinkled his nose and said, 'Me dad reckons I'm the black sheep of the family.' He then laughed and Jacky joined in because he got the joke without his pal having to explain it, although Aaron took no chances. 'Black sheep,' he said. 'Get it?'

'Course I get it. I'm not stupid.'

'Not like me yer mean?'

'Give over . . . you're not stupid,' said Jacky. 'You're just barmy.'

'Is barmy better than stupid?' Aaron asked.

'Loads better,' Jacky assured him. 'Trouble is you get into trouble when you're barmy. I think Frank McGovern was a bit barmy . . . and they hanged him.'

Aaron could think of no comment to make about this. His situation wasn't good but he wouldn't swap it for Jacky's. His dad was very strict but at least he was alive and the thought of him ending up like Frank McGovern made Aaron shudder. 'Why do you allus call him Frank?' he asked. 'I thought he was yer dad.'

'You can only really have one dad,' Jacky explained. 'Your dad's the bloke who looks after you when you're a kid. Frank never did that. Mebbe it wasn't his fault, but it wasn't my dad's fault that he wasn't my *real* dad either.'

It took Aaron a while to unravel the confusion of Jacky's explanation. 'It must be a bugger that they both died,' he said.

'It was,' agreed Jacky. 'A proper bugger.'

151

There was a long silence as both boys contemplated the unfairness of their lives.

'Do you know the first thing I did when I met Frank?' Jacky said, eventually.

'No idea.'

'Guess.'

'I hate it when people do that. Ask yer ter guess at something what's impossible ter—'

'I cried,' said Jacky. 'Just like Weeping Willie Wilmot. It was my dad's funeral and Frank told me it was all right to cry. He held me in his arms and I cried.' Jacky hugged himself and rocked backwards and forwards on the wall, remembering that day. 'He seemed a real good bloke to me. I felt . . .' He paused, trying to remember *how* he had felt. 'I felt loads better when he put his arms round me. And when I'd stopped crying I felt as if everything was going to be . . . you know, okay. I cried like a baby . . . and then I felt okay.'

'It doesn't mean yer a baby if yer cry,' Aaron said. 'Jesus wept . . . it's in the bible. Yer can cry now if yer want.'

He put an arm around Jacky's shoulder and Jacky leaned in to him. Tears were near the surface but he held them at bay and pulled himself together. Aaron was a good pal, but he was no Frank McGovern.

'I wish my mam was here,' he said.

'Why don't yer ring her?' Aaron suggested. 'I'd ring me dad but it won't do any good.'

'We're not on the phone,' said Jacky. 'Neither is my granddad. I'd have to write.'

'I reckon owd Mullen'll be doin' that fer yer. There'll be a letter on it's way ter yer mam right now. One ter me dad an' all. That should make his day. He'll have everybody prayin' for me.'

'Praying? What sort of praying?'

Aaron jumped down from the wall and clasped his hands together in prayer; then he rolled his eyes heavenwards, dropped to his knees and howled in a pure West Indian patois.

'Hallelujah! Save me poor boy from de fires of hell, dear Lord. Keep him from sinnin' and doin' bad tings . . . like playin' wid his willy when de lights is out.'

Jacky howled with laughter. 'Give over, yer flippin' nutcase. You'll get struck by a bolt o' flippin' lightning if you carry on like this.'

152

'Lordy, me won't never get ter heaven now.' Aaron was still in West Indian mode. 'Anyways, me don't want ter go to heaven when me dies. Me want ter be with me friends.'

Jacky was still laughing when Aaron got back on the wall and took out his cigarettes. He gave one to Jacky who was very much a beginner as far as smoking was concerned. The boys lit up and fell into deep thought once again.

'What d'yer think'll happen to us?' Jacky said, after a while.

Aaron shrugged. 'Keep us here fer a bit longer, mebbe.'

Jacky grimaced at the injustice of it all. 'I bet there's loads of kids locked up cos grown-ups are liars,' he said.

'Mebbe,' said Aaron. 'Mind you, they didn't have ter tell lies about *me*. I'm here cos I'm trainin' ter be a racin' driver. Which in my case involves nickin' cars.'

'Do you know how to start a car without a key?'

'Course I do. Blimey! Anyone can do that.'

'Could you start that one?' Jacky pointed to a Rover parked by the roadside. The owner had left it to go into a nearby house. 'I don't think he locked it,' Jacky added.

The recent injustice had seriously affected their judgement. Common sense went out of the window as they headed for the car. It was in the back of both their minds that if they were to be punished they were entitled to do something to deserve it. Aaron had the car started within a minute. Jacky was impressed.

It was over two hours before the theft was reported to the police; by this time the two boys were fifty miles away, out of petrol and well and truly lost.

Chapter Eighteen

A sudden flurry of rain hammered against Mumford's shop window as he paused in his work and looked at his watch. He felt a great satisfaction at the way things had once again fallen into place for him. He'd bought himself the gold Rolex at Christmas as a present from his late wife; it was the least she could do to pay for her infidelity. Her life insurance would have bought him many such watches.

When he claimed for it on his insurance he'd been able to produce the receipt. It was enough to convince the assessor of the honesty of the rest of his claim, for which he could produce no receipts – on account of the claim being bogus. Altogether he'd been paid close on three hundred pounds – six months wages for the average man. A claim of over three hundred would have attracted much closer scrutiny. But the magnitude of the crime was still sufficient to get that Gaskell pest locked away where he could no further damage. The skipping song hadn't gone away though – there was little he could do about that.

Enough time had passed for him to wear the watch once again. After all, the sole purpose of the insurance payout was for him to replace the stolen items. Who would know it wasn't a new one? His secretary tapped on his office door and popped her head round.

'There's a policeman to see you, Mr Mumford.'

He frowned. Policemen weren't his favourite people. He hadn't liked their attitude all the way through the burglary case. They acted as though they hadn't believed a word he'd said. If it hadn't been for Booth throwing in his two penn'orth the boy might have got away with it.

'Send him through,' he said, curtly.

Bill came in with his helmet in his hands, a soaked rain cape over his shoulders and cycle clips on his trousers. Mumford's eyes went immediately to Bill's scarred forehead and he tried to remember where he'd seen it before. Bill's eyes went to the watch gleaming on Mumford's wrist and wondered if ...? No, it couldn't possibly be. No one could be *that* brazen.

'It's just a follow-up visit, Mr Mumford,' he said, amiably. 'Following the burglary. Standard procedure, more or less. More a courtesy visit than anything else. I usually save my courtesy visits for when its raining, to tell the truth. Wish it'd make up its mind, this weather. Half an hour ago I was thinking of going round in shirt-sleeve order.'

Mumford sat back in his chair and smiled. 'Would you like a cup of coffee or anything, constable?'

'A cup of coffee'd go down very nicely, thank you.' Bill made to take his cape off, then paused and looked at Mumford. 'Do you mind?'

'Be my guest. How do you like your coffee?'

'Strong and black with two spoons of sugar.'

'Take a seat, constable.'

Mumford took the cape from Bill and hung it on a coatstand. He called through the door for someone to make the coffee, then he went back to his chair and flicked open a gold cigarette case which he offered to the policeman. Bill took one and admired the case.

'Very nice,' he said, impressed. 'Proper gold, is it?'

'Nine carat. Present from my late wife.' He showed Bill the Rolex. 'As was this watch ... although she bought me this posthumously.'

'Really?' said Bill, puzzled. 'And how did she do that?'

'Well, I just wanted something special to remember her by so I used some of her life insurance money to buy myself a Christmas present from her. I know it's silly but I miss her so much.'

'I imagine you do,' Bill sympathised. 'Didn't you have a watch stolen in the burglary, sir?'

Mumford's eyes gave nothing away. He was enjoying this game. Dicing with danger – only he knew there was no danger.

'This very watch,' he said.

Bill raised an eyebrow. Mumford gave a laugh.

155

'Or should I say the watch this one replaced. I bought an identical one with the money.'

'From the same shop, sir? I bet you're a valued customer.'

Mumford didn't *think* Bill suspected anything, but he was enjoying the game anyway. 'Actually, no. I got this from a chap I know who deals in imported watches. I got this twenty per cent cheaper than the other one.'

'So, you made a bit of a profit on the insurance claim?'

'Yes, I did. Fortunately there's nothing illegal about it.'

'I never suggested there was,' Bill assured him 'Do you mind if I try it on. I've always wondered what it felt like to wear a really expensive watch.'

'Certainly.'

Mumford slid the watch off his wrist and handed it to Bill, who put it on at the side of his own watch.

'Makes my H Samuel look a bit sick,' he said. Then he took it off and examined the back. 'Waterproof, shockproof – pity they're not thiefproof.' He took out his pocket book and wrote something down.

'Is everything all right, constable?'

'Right as rain, sir.' Bill handed the watch back to Mumford. 'Do you have a receipt for this watch, sir?' The policeman spotted a brief flicker of apprehension in Mumford's eyes. 'Just in case this one gets stolen as well,' he explained. 'Best to be on the safe side, I always say.'

'Oh yes . . . not sure where it is I must admit, but I've certainly got one.'

'I should keep it somewhere safe, sir. You never know. Young Gaskell's not the only thief in this district.'

'Perhaps not, but I suspect he may come to the same sticky end as his father.'

'I understand he's very much like his father, sir – in many respects.'

'I'm glad we see eye to eye on the subject of young Gaskell,' said Mumford. 'I got the impression that some of your colleagues had a bit too much sympathy for the boy.'

'Oh I should take no notice of them, sir. Some of them don't know their arse from their elbow as far as villains are concerned.'

Mumford sat back in his chair, relieved to be talking to a policeman who saw things as they should be seen. 'Bane of my life, that boy,' he said. 'If there's one thing I hate in a person it's dishonesty. I've always been an honest man, constable – wouldn't last two minutes in my profession if I wasn't squeaky clean.'

'You and me both, sir.'

The coffee arrived and they chatted about things in general until Bill got up to go.

'Oh, by the way, sir,' he said, as though it were an afterthought, 'just so you know. The thing I wrote down just now – it was the serial number on the back of your new watch.'

Mumford's eyes widened enough for Bill to know he'd touched a nerve. He stuck his knife in a bit deeper.

'I understand there's a serial number on the receipt for the stolen watch, sir, so when I go to the assessors I'll be able to compare the two numbers. Just to cancel out any suspicion, you understand, sir. It's as much for your benefit in the long run, sir – you know how people talk.'

The blood drained from Mumford's face. 'For my benefit? In what way?'

'Well, if people look at your watch, which is a bit conspicuous if you don't mind me saying, and they ask how come you're wearing a watch that's supposed to have been stolen, all you have to do is say it's a different watch, and if they don't believe you, the police have checked it out.'

'I . . . I see.'

Bill twisted the knife. 'It's a good job you're an honest man, Mr Mumford, because if you weren't and these two numbers were the same I imagine you'd be looking at quite long custodial sentence.'

'Custodial?' gasped Mumford. 'How do you mean, custodial?'

'I mean banged up behind bars. Not just for theft but for perjury which is a worse crime, especially where it gets an innocent boy locked up for something he didn't do. These judges can get very funny with people who tell lies in court. If they had their way they'd make it a hanging offence. Very full of their own importance are judges, sir.'

Mumford was gulping now; his brain raced to find a way out of it. 'Constable . . . as it happens, the er, the numbers actually *will* match.'

'Will they, sir, will they indeed? And why would that be if they're two different watches?'

'Because they're not. I mean I, er, I actually found the watch afterwards. I honestly thought it had been stolen, but I found it . . . and I didn't want to look a fool – finding something that I'd reported stolen. Imagine how foolish I'd have looked.'

'I see. You found it and you chose not to tell anyone. That's not very honest, is it, sir?'

Mumford gave a toadying smile that Bill felt like wiping off his face with his fist.

'Well I don't suppose so, constable, but no harm done, eh? Tell you what, the money I got for the watch, you can have it. No questions asked, eh? Insurance companies pay out all the time for things that turn up later. They hate it when that happens, so much messing about and paperwork. Believe me, constable, insurance companies would much rather not know about it if something turns up afterwards.'

'Ah – you kept quiet to do the insurance company a favour, did you, sir? That was good of you.'

'I can let you have it in cash if you like. A hundred and eighty pounds. Call it two hundred between friends. No questions asked, eh?'

'What about the boy who was locked up for stealing it, sir? Should we leave him there to rot for something he didn't do?'

'Oh, he stole all the other stuff, constable. You have my word on that. Tell you what, make it two hundred and fifty, a nice round number. What do you say, shall we shake on it?' Mumford held out his right hand.

'Two hundred and fifty, eh? Well, that's too tempting for me to refuse. Tell you what, can I see the watch again, sir. No need to take it off. I just want to admire it.'

A smirk of triumph lit Mumford's face as he held out his left arm and displayed the watch to Bill. Within a second he had both of Mumford's hands handcuffed together, trapping the incriminating watch on his wrist.

'What are you doing?' wailed Mumford. 'You can't do this to me. I thought we had a deal.'

'Sorry. You must have caught me on a bad day,' apologised Bill. 'I'm a bit like that. Always having bad days. You don't mind if I use your phone to ring the station for a car, do you, sir? I'd take you down on the back of my bike but there's a spring sticking out

158

of the saddle, and it's giving my bottom some gip, I can tell you. About time they gave us all motor bikes. I'll read you your rights now, sir, if you don't mind. I always like to get the petty details out of the way so that I can get on with the job I'm paid to do, which is locking villains up.'

Chapter Nineteen

'It looks a right mucky 'ole does this place. Any idea where we are?'

'Well, according to all the signs we've been passing,' said Jacky, 'I think we're in Sheffield.'

Aaron nodded. His idea had been to get to the seaside. The car was parked by the roadside in an area dense with industry. It was late afternoon and the weather was still warm, but the sunshine wasn't bright enough to liven up the dullness of this part of town. There was an oily aroma in the air which disappointed Aaron, who could have sworn they had been headed towards the sea. He sniffed the air, seeking out the smell of salt or fish or candyfloss.

'I thought we lived on an island,' he said.

'We do,' Jacky confirmed.

'Well, if we live on an island and we keep driving, we should reach the sea eventually. Is Sheffield near the sea?'

'Don't think so.'

'Bugger!' said Aaron. 'I could have sworn it were near the sea. Are yer sure?'

'Fairly,' said Jacky. Then, as if to ease his pal's disappointment, he added, 'You're a pretty good driver. Do you think you could teach me?'

'Not without petrol. Once we've got some petrol I'll give you a lesson.'

'How can we buy petrol?' Jacky asked. 'We haven't got any money.'

Aaron grinned broadly, which made Jacky smile. It always did. 'Watch and learn, Jacky boy.'

'How do you know they call me Jacky boy?'

Aaron shrugged and said, 'I didn't – but I do now.'

'It'll be that daft song we sing at school,' Jacky decided. 'Among the leaves so green-oh – and all that.'

'Mebbe,' said Aaron, mysteriously. 'Mebbe I've got supernatural powers.'

'I hope you have. We could do with some supernatural powers to get this car going.'

'Who said anything about *this* car? I've been thinkin' about changing cars for quite some time now.'

'Oh yes, and what are you thinking of getting next – a Rolls Royce?'

'Mebbe,' said Aaron, getting out. 'Mebbe not.'

As they walked down the road their brown clothing attracted the occasional curious glance; nothing as disapproving as the glances they got in the streets around Westhill Boys' Home, but disquieting all the same.

'Do you feel a bit of a prat dressed like we are?' Jacky asked. 'We'll not get far dressed like this. As soon as a copper sees us he'll be askin' questions.'

They were walking past the end of a street of terraced houses with rows of washing lines hanging from one side of the street to the other, each one festooned with drying garments. Apart from two small girls playing a skipping game with one end of the rope attached to a lamp post, there were no people about.

'Can you see anything your size?' grinned Aaron, turning up the street.

Jacky balked at this idea. He'd nicked an occasional apple from outside the greengrocers and wasn't beyond taking a bottle of milk from a doorstep on his way to school or the odd item from Willie O'Keefe's cart, but this was real stealing – the sort of stealing he'd been locked up for, and it was different from stealing a car; this was personal belongings.

'We can't go nickin' people's stuff,' he said.

'Couple o' jumpers, that's all we need,' said Aaron. 'Or mebbe a shirt that's not brown. Look, over there.' He inclined his head towards the far side of the street. 'Yellow jumper, just your size. Look nice with a brown shirt. I'll get the prop.'

Aaron took a couple of steps into the middle of the street and eased back the clothes prop so that Jacky could unpeg the jumper before haring up the street with it under his arm. Aaron calmly replaced the prop and walked on, casting a discerning eye over the flapping shirts, pausing and rubbing his chin now and then, like a customer choosing just the right one in a gentleman's outfitters. Further up the street the skipping was in full swing with the small girls completely absorbed in their game, one of them spinning the rope as the other one skipped and sang.

'I'm a little girl-guide dressed in blue,
These are the things that I must do,
Salute to the Captain,
Curtsy to the Queen,
Show my knickers to the dirty submarine.'

In sequence to her song she saluted, curtsied, then turned around and lifted her dress to display her navy-blue knickers in the direction of Aaron, who laughed out loud. The skipping girl looked around at him, then, followed by her friend, ran away in acute embarrassment.

When Aaron saw a shirt he liked it was off the line in a flash and folded neatly under his arm. Jacky was waiting for him around the corner, now wearing his newly acquired jumper, which pretty much smothered him. Aaron stood back, gave his pal a look of appraisal and said, 'You'll grow into it in a couple of years.'

Jacky pulled a face and muttered, 'I wasn't planning being on the run that long.'

Aaron tried on the shirt which was far too small, so they swapped garments and, reasonably satisfied that they didn't look stupid, they walked on.

'A lot of people are still looking at us,' remarked Jacky after a while.

'It's me they're looking at,' said Aaron. 'Everybody looks at yer when yer black. It's just that I've got used to it. Me dad says there's loads o' black people in London and people don't look at you so much down there.'

'Why did you come to live in Yorkshire, then?'

'Me dad says they're supposed ter be more friendly in Yorkshire. Can't say I've noticed meself. Mind you, I don't know no different.'

'Have you thought about what we should do next?' asked Jacky.

'Keep our eyes and ears open.'

Jacky tried this out for a minute, then asked, 'What for?'

'For whatever comes along. You must be alert at all times.'

162

'I don't want to be alert. I don't like lerts.'

Aaron howled with laughter. 'Yer a funny boy, you, Jacky boy. I mus' remember that. I don't like lerts. It's a good one is that.'

'Where are are we going to sleep tonight?' Jacky asked. 'And what are we going to do tomorrow?'

'You know your trouble, Jacky boy?'

'What?' asked Jacky.

'Yer try and plan things too far ahead. People what do that worry themselves into an early grave. Tell yer what – we'll nick another car, then we'll drive to Liverpool and stow away on a boat to America.'

'What will we do then?'

'Yer beginnin' ter get on my nerves, Jacky boy.'

'I shall have to tell my mam,' said Jacky. 'I can't go swannin' off to America without telling her. Shall we go to Hollywood?'

'Is it near New York?'

'I think so.'

'Right,' Aaron decided. 'We'll go to New York then we'll get the last tram to Hollywood.'

'Why the last tram? Why not the first tram?'

Aaron sighed at the unworldliness of his companion. 'When yer get on the last tram the conductor's allus doin' his cash so he can get straight off home. You allus get a free ride on the last tram. Yer do where I live anyroad.'

'Why don't we just nick a car?' Jacky asked.

'Because cops have guns in America, an' if they see yer nickin' a car they shoot yer up the arse an' ask questions later. When we get to America we'll go straight.'

'Why do they shoot you up the arse?'

'Blimey! Don't yer know nowt, Jacky boy? It's 'cos Americans have great big arses which makes it an easy target. Yer better off catchin' a tram than gerrin' shot up the arse. They have smashin' trams in America. I've seen 'em on t' pictures. Judy Garland – she were in one with a tram.'

'I liked *The Wizard of Oz*,' Jacky said. 'That was my favourite picture.'

'We're off ter see the Wizard,' sang Aaron, and Jacky joined in with 'The Wonderful Wizard of Oz.'

Singing the song, which both of them knew all the way through, they linked arms and danced down the road, attracting glances and smiles from amused passers-by, some of whom laughed when the boys tripped over and fell in a heap on the ground. Aaron got to his feet, but Jacky stayed where he was.

'Gerrup yer daft ha'porth,' laughed Aaron.

'I can't,' Jacky groaned. 'I've done my ankle in again.'

'Oh 'eck! That's all we need.'

'How d'yer mean, that's all we need? I didn't flippin' do it on purpose. It really hurts if you must know.' Jacky rubbed his ankle and grimaced at the pain.

'Can yer gerrup?' asked Aaron.

'I'll try.'

Aaron helped him to his feet and, with one arm around his pal's shoulder, Jacky limped painfully on until they came to a low wall.

'I'll have to sit on this wall,' Jacky said. 'It's killing me is this.'

'Do yer think yer've broke it again?'

'Don't think so. It's not as bad as last time but it still kills.'

'Mebbe yer've just sprained it,' suggested Aaron, hopefully.

'Mebbe,' said Jacky.

He was first to spot the car. The black bodywork gleamed in the late afternoon sun and the engine noise was scarcely audible as it purred into a filling station on the other side of the road.

Aaron identified it accurately. 'Nineteen-fifty-one Humber Super Snipe. They cost about a thousand quid.'

A man in a black suit got out and leaned against the bonnet, chatting to the garage attendant who was filling the car with petrol. Both men went into the filling station office, presumably to settle the bill, leaving the car unattended. Without a word to Jacky, Aaron ran across to the car and got in. As he was starting the engine the man in the suit came out and ran towards his car but Aaron was already pulling away. He drove into the road, straight past Jacky, without sparing his pal so much as a glance, and sped away.

'Well, that's flippin' nice, that is!' grumbled Jacky to himself. 'What am I supposed to do now?'

The man, who had now been joined by the pump attendant, stood with arms akimbo glaring in the direction of his fast-disappearing car, then he looked at Jacky and shouted, 'Oy – you!'

Jacky would have run away had he been able, but under the circumstances all he could do was reply, with as much innocence as he could muster, 'What?'

'Did you see a car drive away from here.'

'Yes,' said Jacky. It would have been daft to deny it.

The man in the suit walked towards him. 'Did you see who took it?' He sounded extremely agitated.

Jacky shrugged. 'I wasn't taking all that much notice,' he said. 'I was sitting here. I've hurt my ankle.'

The man had no interest at all in Jacky's ankle.

'I think I might have broken it.' Still no interest from the man. Jacky knew his game was up. All he wanted now as to get to someone who could make his ankle better. This man wasn't helping much. Two can play at that game. Despite Aaron's treachery, he said, 'I think it was two white fellers.'

The man frowned momentarily at Jacky bothering to describe the thieves as white. Non-whites were few and far between in Sheffield.

'Right,' said the man. Then to himself he muttered, 'Jesus, I'm in trouble for this. It's me own flamin' fault, tryin' ter cut bloody corners. If I'd known it were nearly out o' petrol I wouldn't have taken a chance.'

Jacky hadn't a clue what the man was talking about. 'Is it your car, mister?' he asked.

'Do I look as if I own a car like that?' said the man irritably.

Jacky shrugged. He had no way of knowing what Humber Super Snipe owners looked like. The man looked a lot less out of place behind the wheel than Aaron did. He was pacing frantically up and down – like a wasp in a window, Charlie would have said.

'This is my job up the spout an' no bloody mistake.'

Jacky felt sorry that the man was going to lose his job over something Aaron had done. He felt like telling him he'd get his car back in a day or so without a scratch on it.

'You'd best wait here while I ring the police,' said the man, dismally. He seemed totally unaware that Jacky had hurt his ankle.

'I can't do much else, mister. I've bust my ankle. It really hurts.'

The man made no comment on Jacky's bust ankle and went back into the filling station, presumably to ring the police. Jacky sat there, pondering his immediate future. Should he tell the police about Aaron or should he say nothing and let them work things out for themselves? The man's attitude towards his injured ankle hadn't impressed the boy. He'd wait until he saw how helpful the

165

police were before he made any decision. Aaron would be caught eventually. Maybe the sooner the better. Serve him right for deserting a pal in his hour of need. Jacky wouldn't have done it to Aaron, he thought. Not in a million years. He decided to take his shoe off to ease the pain caused by the swelling. He was undoing the laces when Aaron drove on to the pavement, barely a yard away from him, and pushed open the passenger door.

'Hop in, Jacky boy.'

Jacky's delight in realising his pal hadn't deserted him after all helped him overcome the pain of getting into the car. The man in the black suit had seen the car arrive and was out of the filling station and halfway across the road, yelling at them to stop, just as Jacky was slamming the door.

Aaron watched the man in his rear-view mirror as the car sped away for the second time. 'He doesn't seem so pleased,' he said.

'It's not his car,' explained Jacky. 'He'll lose his job for this. Mind you, he didn't seem too worried about my ankle.'

'Serves him right then.'

'Mebbe. It's a bit rough about his job, though.' Jacky looked at Aaron. 'I thought you'd gone and left me. I couldn't believe it when you drove off without me.'

'Give over. I wouldn't desert me best pal.'

Jacky's first job was to take off his shoe and sock. Aaron looked down at his foot.

'Blimey!' he said. 'It's come up like a football. How's it feel?'

'I'm hoping it's only sprained,' said Jacky. 'But I'll have to rest it for a bit before I can walk again.'

'Right,' said Aaron. He drove on for a while before asking, 'Do you know which side of England Liverpool's on?'

'Middle left,' said Jacky, after some thought. 'Near Blackpool.'

'Is that east or west?'

'West,' said Jacky. 'I reckon Liverpool's west of here.'

'And the sun goes down in the west,' said Aaron. 'So if we head to where the sun's going down we should finish up in Liverpool.'

'More or less,' concluded Jacky after some thought. 'We should see a Liverpool sign somewhere. We once went on a day trip from Castlethorpe and it took about three hours. It might take longer from Sheffield . . . or it might not be as far.'

'Right,' decided Aaron. 'We'll drive for a bit then we'll get some kip. You can get in the back and put yer feet up.'

166

Jacky swung round painfully to take a look at the back seat and check on the comfort it would provide a lad with a poorly leg. For a while he didn't speak.

'Well?' said Aaron. 'What d'yer think? Was it worth nickin' or not?'

Jacky sat back down in his seat and stared forwards through the windscreen with widened eyes and mouth frozen open in shock. He spoke in a croaky voice without moving his head.

'Aaron.'

'What?'

'There's . . . there's an old woman sitting in the back.'

'How d'yer mean an old woman?'

'I'm not kiddin', Aaron. There's an old woman sitting in the back seat.' Jacky's voice was hoarse with alarm.

'Oh heck!' said Aaron. 'That's just what we need.' He adjusted the rear-view mirror so that he could see their back-seat passenger, who was quite small. 'Are you all right, missis?' he said, smiling at her. 'There's no need to worry, we'll see yer come ter no harm.'

Their passenger didn't reply.

'She's very quiet,' Aaron peered at the mirror. 'Is she asleep?'

'I don't think so.'

'She looks asleep ter me.'

'I think she might be dead,' said Jacky.

Maureen opened the door to Bill's knock. He smiled, removed his helmet and announced, 'I've got good news and bad news.'

'Right, I suppose you'd better come in, then.'

She stepped aside to let him through. Ellie, who was at the table doing her homework, glanced up and smiled at him.

'Hello, Bill. How's your wife?'

'Still in a wheelchair. Thank you for asking.'

Maureen glared at her and Ellie decided not to pursue this line of enquiry against a married man whom her mother obviously fancied like mad. It was up to her mother now.

'Take a pew,' Maureen said. 'I think the bad news can wait. Let's have the good news first.'

Bill sat down and took out his cigarettes. It seemed to Maureen that these two actions always went together with him. 'If I were your wife,' she said. 'I'd tell you you smoke too much.'

167

Ellie thought her mother deserved a glare herself, but she pretended to concentrate on her homework.

'If you were my wife you'd be in a wheelchair and you'd smoke more than me,' Bill said, lighting up. He saw Maureen's face drop in response to what must have sounded like a rebuke. 'Sorry,' he said, quickly. 'I meant nothing by it.'

Maureen shrugged off Bill's apology. 'You were about to give me some good news?'

He looked at her, wondering whether his good news would outweigh the bad. 'Er, yes. I called in to see Mumford at his work. No particular reason; I just wanted to see what he had to say for himself. Test the water, so to speak.'

'Rather you than me, he gives me the creeps,' said Maureen. 'What *did* he have to say?'

'Oh, we had a nice chat, and he very kindly showed me the watch he'd bought as a replacement for the one Jacky stole from him.'

'But Jacky didn't steal a watch from him, or anything else for that matter,' Ellie pointed out.

'You know, Ellie, that very thought crossed my mind when I looked at his watch,' Bill said. 'So I wrote down the serial number and told him I'd check it against the serial number of the one that had been stolen. I was actually being a bit naughty there, because I'd already been to the assessors and there wasn't a serial number on the receipt for the so-called stolen watch. The jewellers who sold him it weren't much help either – bit slack if you ask me. I'm amazed Mumford didn't know about it. Good job he panicked as it turned out. Silly sod tried to bribe me into keeping my mouth shut when I actually had nothing on him.'

'Bribe you?'

'Two hundred and fifty quid.'

'Wow,' said Ellie. 'I bet you were tempted.'

'Ellie!' scolded Maureen.

'If it had been anyone else I might have been,' said Bill. 'Anyway I arrested him for fraud. Honestly, you should have heard the weird and wonderful stories he started telling us down at the station. My sergeant told him that every lie he told us at this stage would add a year to his sentence.'

'Is that true?' Ellie asked.

Bill gave a short laugh, 'No,' he said. 'It's just something we try to scare people with.'

'Did the creep fall for it?'

'Oh yes, love – hook line and sinker,' grinned Bill. 'We ended up with the truth the whole truth and nothing but the truth.'

Maureen asked, 'What do you think will happen to him?'

'Well, if we get perjury added to his charge I reckon he'll be looking at a nice stretch inside.'

'How will this affect my boy?'

'Ah.' The grin fell from Bill's face. 'I'm afraid that's the bad news.'

'What bad news? Is he all right? He hasn't had an accident has he? If anything's happened to him I'll—'

Bill placed a calming hand on her shoulder. 'He ran away from the home this afternoon.'

Maureen was relieved. Running away was better than him being in an accident, or beaten up or whatever else had just flashed through her mind. 'Run away?' she said. 'The daft lad. Do we know why?'

'Apparently,' Bill told her, 'a local woman accused Jacky and another lad of stealing a diamond ring from her. The governor didn't seem convinced the lads had done it, but absconding hasn't helped their cause.'

'I think *I* might have absconded if people kept accusing me of doing things I hadn't done,' Ellie said.

'I'll see what I can do to help when he turns up,' Bill assured them. 'I reckon you've had a tough time, what with one thing and another. I'm sure Jacky won't have got far and when he turns up you should be able to get him home with Mumford confessing to fraud and perjury.'

'He's probably having a great time,' said Ellie. 'You know what our Jacky's like.'

'I do,' said Maureen. 'He's a one-off is Jacky boy.' She looked up at Bill and smiled. 'At least we've got Mumford for *something*.'

'Tell you what,' Bill grinned. 'I'd like to see his face when he finds out I didn't have a scrap of evidence against him. He ended up singing like a canary, silly sod.'

'I'd like to see his face when he's found guilty of his wife's murder,' said Ellie. 'That's what I'd like to see.'

'I'm not sure we could manage that at this stage,' Bill warned. 'And I suggest you stay clear of him after what happened last

169

time.' His mind went back to the day of the murder and how he took an instant dislike to Mumford. There had been something eerily unnatural about the man.

'Answer me honestly. Do you think Frank did it?' Ellie asked him.

He took time over his reply. 'Off the record, no. I was with Mumford just after it happened and he was weird. Can't put my finger on it.'

'I think the word's creepy?' suggested Ellie.

Bill nodded. 'That pretty much sums him up in my book. What always baffled me was what happened to the knife. He was like a jelly when I got there. He certainly didn't look as if he'd have the presence of mind to get rid of it so we couldn't find it. That takes some doing.'

'He could have buried it,' said Maureen.

Bill shook his head. 'Not in his garden, he didn't. It was frosty that night. He'd been in the garden all right, but we could see every footprint he'd made. If he'd buried it we'd have found it. No, he'd have had to throw it away somewhere, but even then we'd have found it.'

'Maybe someone took it?'

'That's one explanation, but it's a bit unlikely. We were at the scene within five minutes, and we offered a five pound reward to anyone who found it. It would have been a lot easier for Frank to get rid of it, and that's what did for him. The court only had his word for the route he took that night. He could have gone anywhere. It was not finding the knife near Mumford's house that went a long way to condemning Frank.'

'So if, by some miracle, we found the knife near Mumford's house we could clear Frank's name?' Maureen said.

Bill shrugged. 'Miracle's right. But I suppose it's a possibility,' he said. 'That knife had to be somewhere and if it's still around . . . and with Mumford's fingerprints on it . . . who knows?'

'Would his fingerprints still be on it after all this time?' Maureen asked him.

'If they haven't been wiped off. They've lifted fingerprints off Egyptian tombs before now.'

'I don't suppose there's much chance of them not being wiped off after all this time,' Ellie said. 'Still, finding the knife would be a start. We'll do it. We'll get Mumford one day.'

170

There was a determination about Ellie that made Bill puzzled as to why she had taken it so personally to bring Mumford to justice. Maureen read his thoughts and put an arm around her daughter's shoulder.

'I think it's all part of adolescence,' she explained to him. 'It's her way of rebelling against the stupidity of all adults.'

Ellie said nothing. She just thought her mother was being stupid.

'When I was not much older than Ellie,' said Maureen. 'I joined an anti-war group. Then Adolf came along and I realised that some wars were justified.'

'Just like I'm justified in wanting see Mumford hanged?' Ellie said, with a challenge in her voice.

'I doubt if you want to see him hanged half as much as I do, Ellie. It's just that I have to be realistic and get on with my life.' Maureen paused and gave her daughter's shoulder an extra squeeze. 'Having said that, if I ever see a way to get him, I'll be on to it like a shot.'

'So long as it doesn't involve ghosts and broken ankles,' warned Bill.

Maureen gave him a smile that set his heart racing. On balance the news was good, and she had something to smile about. Knowing Jacky he'd somehow get in touch and she'd tell him the good news about Mumford.

'You've done a lot for us, Bill.' Her eyes told him what she thought of him.

It's just a pity you're married, Ellie thought.

I wish I wasn't married, thought Bill. I knew it would come to this one day. What the hell should I do? I can't let Pam down . . . or can I? God, Maureen's beautiful.

I think I'll go and have a word with this woman who's accused my boy of stealing her ring, thought Maureen. It'd be unfair to ask Bill to come with me – he's done enough. I wonder what his wife's like. He doesn't like to talk about her. Why's that?

Aaron pulled in to the side of the road and was out in a flash, looking at the dead woman through the window. Jacky made no move to get out.

'C'mon, Jacky boy,' pleaded Aaron. 'We've got to get away.'

'How?' asked Jacky. His voice quivering with shock. 'I can't flippin' walk.'

171

'Well, I'm not drivin' no car with a dead woman in the back.'

'What shall we do, then?' said Jacky. 'I can't walk a flippin' inch.'

Aaron paced up and down the pavement, deep in thought. A man approached and he leaned against the car window, shielding the dead woman from the man's view. Jacky wound his window down.

'I think we might have to give ourselves up, Aaron. We're in a right fix if you ask me.'

'Never. You an' me are goin' to America, an' we're not gonna let some owd body stop us. Tell yer what we'll drive somewhere quiet and take her out.'

'You what? We can't go round dumping dead bodies all over the place.'

'There's only one body,' Aaron pointed out. 'And she's only little.' He looked through the car window. The body didn't seem so threatening or scary now. 'I could pick her up meself, no trouble. Hey! Have yer seen this?' He was standing at the back of the car reading some lettering painted in gold on the back window — HARVEY AND SON. UNDERTAKERS.

'It's an undertaker's car,' he called out to Jacky. 'That'll be why there's a body in the back.'

'I didn't think they just stuck bodies in back seats,' said Jacky.

'I *know* they don't,' said Aaron. 'When me Granny Clarice died some fellers came with a coffin. Yer s'posed ter cart bodies round in coffins, I know that fer a fact. First thing yer do when someone dies is ter put 'em in a coffin.'

'No wonder he thinks he's gonna get the sack,' deduced Jacky, talking through the window to Aaron. 'Fancy sticking someone in the back seat with her hat on and dressed up like a dog's dinner.'

'She most prob'ly died like that,' concluded Aaron, studying the body more closely now. 'She looks as though she were knockin' on a bit. My Granny Clarice were seventy odd and she didn't look as old as her.'

'I think it puts a few years on you when you're dead,' said Jacky, choosing not to turn round to check on the body's approximate age. 'Anyroad, what're we going to do with her? We can't just leave her anywhere, it's not right.'

'Tell yer what,' decided Aaron. 'I'll drive for a bit 'til we see

172

somewhere right – like a nice seat or summat. Then we can leave her there. It's nice weather, she'll come to no harm.'

The boys drove on, following the setting sun until they found themselves on a lonely road in the High Peaks of North Derbyshire. They came to a bus shelter built in stone with a seat inside which would shelter their dead companion until a bus came. Despite his youthful strength and her fragility Aaron found it a struggle to get her out of the car and on to the seat. She had been frozen by rigor mortis into a permanent sitting position and the only way Aaron could carry her was over his shoulders with a fireman's lift. As he did so her teeth fell out on to the ground.

'Her teeth have come out,' Jacky called out.

Aaron set the lady down on the seat and stared back at her teeth with distaste. 'I'm not puttin' them in,' he said.

'You can't leave her with no teeth in,' argued Jacky.

'I flippin' well can.'

'Aw, come on, Aaron. If she'd known she'd end her life sitting at a bus stop, stone dead, I bet she'd have wanted her teeth in. I know I'd want my teeth in.'

'Jacky, you haven't got false teeth.'

'I were speakin' hypothetically.'

'Speakin' what?'

Aaron was impressed at such a long word. There was no point arguing with someone who knew such words. Jacky pressed his advantage home. 'My grandad reckons he wouldn't be seen dead with no teeth in. Fair's fair.'

'Okay, okay – I'm doing it.' Aaron grimaced at the teeth and picked them up. He wiped them on his sleeve and, with acute distaste, he pushed them into the old lady's mouth; then he turned to Jacky for his approval.

'How's that?'

The top set were protruding which, considering the general state of the woman's health, gave her a grotesque appearance.

'Her top set need pushing in properly.'

'I wish you could walk,' grumbled Aaron, pushing the projecting teeth into place with two reluctant fingers. 'How's that?'

Jacky nodded his approval. She was leaning against the side wall with her hat tilted rakishly over one closed eye and her lips frozen into an elderly smile.

'She just looks as if she's asleep,' he said. 'Do you think she'll have minded coming with us?'

'She looks the type of lady who'd have been glad ter help us,' said Aaron. 'Old ladies like to help young kids out and I don't suppose she's any different. Hey up! There's a bus coming.'

Jacky adjusted the driver's mirror to see the approaching bus. It was two hills and a good mile away. 'I think we should hang about to make sure she's all right,' he said.

'All right, Jacky boy? But she's not all right – she's dead.'

'You know what I mean. Just drive forwards a bit so we can see what's happening.'

'Yer'll be the death o' me, Jacky boy.'

Aaron drove to a lay-by about a quarter of a mile up the road, where they waited for the approaching bus to come and solve their problem for them.

The South Yorkshire bus went straight past at first, much to the boys' chagrin. Then it stopped. The conductor got off, went round to the driver's cab and pointed back at the shelter. The boys breathed a sigh of relief when they saw the bus reverse, following the conductor who walked back and went inside.

'Wait for it,' said Aaron.

He and Jacky saw the conductor reappear. He took off his peaked cap, as if by way of respect, then he went around to the talk to the driver once again. There was an animated discussion. A curious passenger got off, went inside the shelter, then joined the conductor and the driver. One by one four other passengers alighted, each one visiting the shelter before joining the group who were obviously discussing the best course of action. Eventually the driver and conductor went in and emerged carrying the dead woman, still frozen in the seated position like half a swastika. They placed her in a front seat. The boys watched the vehicle drive past them, with their erstwhile travelling companion leaning against the window, as if watching the world go by for the last time. All the other passengers were crowded into the rear seats.

'I think we can safely be on our way,' said Aaron, starting up the car.

'Okay,' agreed Jacky, satisfied that the dead woman was now in safe hands. He suddenly forgot about his injured ankle and all the problems life had thrown at him. It was as if he'd remembered he was a boy and allowed to act like one, letting out a Wild West yell. 'Yeeeeah! Git this wagon rollin' pardner. I'm headin' west till muh hat floats.'

Aaron let out a similar shout and drove the car on to the road. The sun was in their eyes. It was still a long time from setting, but it was plain to the boys at which point on the horizon it would eventually make its exit – and that was where they were headed. Liverpool, New York, and the last tram to Hollywood.

The police sergeant stared, balefully, at the man in the black suit. They were in a room in the police station where the man had been taken to make a statement.

'Is this the normal way you people carry on?' asked the policeman, reading through the statement. 'Carting corpses around in the back seats of cars. I always thought it was a bit more dignified than that.'

'Of course it's not . . . I mean, it *is* more dignified than that usually . . . it's just that, it was more convenient on the day just to take her down to the funeral parlour in the car. We were short staffed, I was on my own and she was already dressed for going out. If she'd been in her night clothes I wouldn't have dreamt of doing it.'

'Dressed for going out, was she, sir? That was very thoughtful of her. Where was she going, exactly?'

'Apparently she was going to the pictures with her neighbour, only when it was time to go she didn't get up from the chair, on account of her having passed away.'

'I don't believe I'd have got up myself, sir, under similar circumstances.'

'Anyway, her neighbour rang us and I was the only one in, so I nipped round in the only car available. Her neighbour left me to it – she didn't want to miss the beginning of the film.'

'Good film was it, sir?'

'*Julius Caesar* – with Marlon Brando, apparently. I gathered the neighbour's something of a fan of Marlon Brando.'

'Must be, sir, to abandon her deceased friend like that. You didn't give the neighbour a lift, did you, sir? Dropped her off at the flicks on the way to the morgue?'

'No, I didn't, sergeant. Look, I know I should have organised for the hearse to pick her up, but she's only a small woman and it seemed a bit of a waste of time.'

'Pity you had to go and lose her, sir. Probably ruined her day.'

'You're being sarcastic, sergeant.'

'It might appear that way to you, sir, but from my point of view things look very different, very different indeed.'

'I'd love to be able to see things from your point of view, sergeant, but I can't get my head that far up my arse.'

'Now you're being sarcastic, sir. And I wouldn't have thought you were in a position to be sarcastic, with you just having lost a cadaver through your own negligence.'

'As a matter of fact she's not the only thing I've lost today,' said the man in the black suit. 'I've just lost my job. So if you've finished with your stupid jokes I'm off down the Labour Exchange. I'll have to take what crappy job I can get. If all else fails I might have to resort to taking a job where you get paid from the neck down – like a police sergeant.'

'Do you know what allus gets me, in cowboy pictures?' said Aaron. He was well used to the car by now and was driving it with ease.

'What?' asked Jacky.

'When they have gunfights and they run out of bullets and they throw their guns away. I wouldn't throw my gun away, would you?'

'I wouldn't,' Jacky agreed. 'Johnnie Mack Brown never throws his gun away. He was my favourite, was Johnnie Mack Brown.'

'I used to like Hopalong Cassidy.'

'Oh yeah. Hopalong Cassidy was great as well. If I was a cowboy I'd have been Hopalong Cassidy or Johnnie Mack Brown.'

'Never liked Roy Rogers,' said Aaron.

'Too much singing,' said Jacky. 'Not enough shootin' – I liked Trigger though.'

'Oh yeah. Trigger were great. Watch out! I think this is a cop car.'

A police car approached. The two occupants stared closely at the boys in the big Humber and spun the car round in the width of the road.

'Oh heck!' said Jacky, looking over his shoulder. 'I think we've had it.'

'Not yet we haven't,' said Aaron. 'This car's faster than theirs any day of the week.'

'Don't be daft, Aaron. I'd stop if I were you.'

'Yer not me though, are yer?' Aaron said. There was a manic excitement in his voice that Jacky hadn't noticed before. 'This is the moment I've been waitin' for, Jacky boy – to outrun a cop car.'

Jacky looked at the speedo which had crept up to sixty, despite the tortuous roads they were navigating. He looked round at the pursuing car which had already dropped away.

'See,' said Aaron, gleefully. 'I told yer I were faster. Stick wi' me, Jacky boy. I'll get yer to Hollywood. Mebbe I can be a stunt driver in one o' them gangster pictures.'

An oncoming car had to swerve out of their way. It sounded its horn angrily as the police car reappeared from around the last bend.

'They're still behind us,' said Jacky with panic in his voice. 'I wish you'd stop, Aaron. It's scarin' me is this.'

'Nowt ter be scared of, Jacky boy. I can beat 'em any day of the week.'

The police car was right up behind them now, siren howling, flashing its lights, telling them to stop. But Aaron put his foot down harder and drove the big car around the twisting roads with the expertise of a rally driver. Jacky would have been impressed under other circumstances, but not then. They were high in the hills, with miles of beautiful countryside stretching out into the distance. Down to their left was a reservoir, glinting in the evening sun, towards which they were still headed, at speeds of up to seventy miles an hour.

'Yeeehah!' yelled Aaron.

Jacky was choking with fear. Not of the police, but for his life. They were cornering at impossible speeds, with steep drops on one side and high banks on the other.

'Slow down, Aaron!'

'We're winning, Jacky boy! We've got the buggers beaten!'

The police car had indeed dropped back and was out of sight around the last bend. Another car approached. Aaron swerved to avoid it and his front wheel slipped over the edge of the road, tipping the whole car sideways. He put his foot down to regain some sort of purchase but the wheels just spun round and the car tipped even further over. The police car arrived and screeched to a halt. Two constables got out and ran to the Humber. But they were too late. It was rolling sideways down the hill, with a tank almost full to the brim with petrol and fire coming from under the bonnet.

The car came to a halt at the bottom of the ravine, over a hundred feet below and exploded with a huge blast which made the shocked policemen take a step back to avoid the heat.

'Oh, Jesus Christ!' said one. 'They were only kids. What the hell have we done?'

Unsure of what sort of reception he'd receive, Brian knocked on the door rather than barge straight in. His mother answered it. Her eyes made him welcome but her words were guarded.

'Brian.'

'Hello, Mam.' There was an awkward pause. 'I saw that copper as I came down t' street. Are yer seein' him regular like?'

'I'm not seeing him at all, Brian. He came to tell us something about Jacky.'

Brian nodded. His mother still hadn't invited him in. This slightly annoyed him; after all this was his rightful home. He held his annoyance in check.

'In a way that's what I came ter see you about,' he said.

'About Jacky? What about him?'

'Well, not actually about him. I mean . . .' he was trying to choose his words carefully. 'I mean it's daft, isn't it?'

'What's daft?'

'Jacky not living here and me not living here neither, that's what's daft. Now that he's gone I'd have thought yer'd be glad to have me back.'

'Is that what you thought?'

'Well, it makes sense. I can afford ter pay more board. I'm not on bad money now.'

'Brian, the policeman came to tell us there's a good chance of Jacky coming home very soon. How would that suit you? Would you be prepared to stop hating your brother and live under the same roof without making my life a misery?'

Brian stared at her for what seemed like an age. It wasn't the reply he'd been expecting. His mother's eyes were pleading with him to say yes. He gave a long sigh, turned around and walked away. Brian wanted to come home but the price was too high. Tears came to Maureen's eyes. She went back into the

house and got on with her work. It was all she had for the time
being.

The second the front wheel left the road Jacky's hand, already on
the door handle, pushed it open. He was on the low side of the car;
the door swung violently forward and banged against the front
wing. Aaron was wrestling with the wheel but still found the time
to shout, 'Jump, Jacky boy!'

Jacky needed no second bidding. He flung himself from the car
and plummetted down the hill, rolling, spinning, cartwheeling,
completely unaware of where the vehicle was in relation to him.
Halfway down he shot over a vertical bank and came to a sudden
halt against a tree growing out of a ledge some six feet below, just
as the car bounced right over the top of him with flames streaming
from under the bonnet. The boy watched in horror as the Humber
rolled and bumped and bounced all the way down to the bottom,
landing on its roof. There was a split second before the explosion
came. Jacky could feel the heat searing against his head. He could
only hope his pal had got clear as well.

After a while he tried to sit up, but couldn't move. His left leg
was twisted beneath him and hurt like hell; blood was running
down his face and into his eyes. Then he remembered the police
car and hoped it had been close enough to see what had happened.
Right now he needed the police – never mind what they did to him
afterwards. He clung to the tree and craned his neck to look for
any sign of Aaron who must surely have jumped clear the same
time as he had. Someone was shouting from the top of the hill.
Aaron maybe. Jacky tried to shout back but his voice came out in
a croak and he lost consciousness. When he came to his senses a
man was standing over him, leaning down and asking if he was all
right.

'I don't think so, mister,' Jacky managed to say, recognising the
man as a policeman.

'I'm going to stay with you, lad, while my colleague takes a
look at the car. Were there just the two of you?'

Jacky nodded as the policeman crouched beside him on the
ledge, with one arm around him to stop him falling further down
the hill. The other policeman was at the bottom, trying to peer into
the burning wreckage. As the flames subsided he turned, looked
up at his colleague, and pointed inside the car.

'Someone in there,' he shouted helplessly, and waved his arms to indicate there was nothing he could do, no matter how much he wanted to.

The policeman guarding Jacky waved his understanding and looked down at the sole survivor, who was unconscious again. 'I'm afraid your pal's dead, lad,' he said, knowing the boy couldn't hear, but he felt he had to tell him anyway. No one could have survived the conflagration at the bottom of the hill.

Chapter Twenty

Charlie Robinson peered at the number on the door to make sure he had the right house. It was a new house on a new council estate and Charlie wouldn't have minded a house like this himself. He'd always wanted a garden and an inside toilet.

The news about his grandson had hit him hard and he felt he needed to *do* something. There had been nothing he could do to help Frank and he'd felt useless at having to stand by and let Jacky be sent away for something he hadn't done. Right now his grandson was lying in hospital with a broken back and his life possibly in ruins. All because of lies. He'd lied himself once. Lived a lie in fact. But it had been a good lie. Stopped Bessie being hurt. At least that's what he told himself.

Maureen had dashed down to Sheffield with her daughter, but not before asking Charlie if he'd go to York and tell that lying woman just what she'd done. Charlie had been given Mrs Pickersgill's address by Mr Mullen, who felt some responsibility for Aaron's death.

'No point blamin' yerself, lad,' Charlie had told him. 'It were a daft lad's trick. But our Jacky reckons there were no real badness in him. Just daftness. It's such as that woman what accused 'em of stealin' when she knew full well they hadn't – that's proper badness.'

'I'd be obliged if you didn't tell her I gave you her address,' Mullen said. 'I'd like to give her a roasting myself but my hands are tied by my position here.'

'I understand, lad,' said Charlie. 'It's just that my grandson could be lying on a slab as well as his mate – an' all because o' that woman's lies.'

He knocked on the brightly painted blue door, loudly enough to elicit a complaint from within.

'All right – I'm not bloody deaf!'

Mrs Pickersgill came to the door with her head festooned in curlers and a cigarette in her mouth.

'Yes?' she said. 'What do yer want?'

A man's voice came from behind her, asking who it was. 'Never you bloody mind!' she shouted, over her shoulder. Then to Charlie, she asked, belligerently, 'Who are yer?'

'Me name's Charles Robinson. Me grandson's lyin' in hospital with a broken back as a direct cause of your lies. His friend's dead.'

'What?' The cigarette somehow clung to her bottom lip as her mouth dropped open.

'Yer lied about my grandson and his friend stealin' a ring from y—'

'I did no such bloody thing.'

'I'm not arguing with yer,' said Charlie. 'I don't argue wi' liars.'

Her husband appeared behind her, unshaven, wearing a soiled vest. 'What's he want, Ethel?' he asked.

'He's standin' on my step calling me a liar,' said the woman. 'Says I lied about that ring goin' missing.'

Charlie corrected her. 'I'm saying yer lied about seeing the lads stealin' it,' he said. 'And I just wanted to see what you had to say for yerself before the police come to arrest yer.'

'Arrest me? What the bloody hell for?' blazed the woman. 'Keep talkin' like that, mister an' I'll kick yer arse all t' way up this street.'

The shouting had caused a few doors to open. Curious heads were looking to see what the commotion was all about. Charlie took a couple of steps back and addressed her with a much louder voice. One everyone could hear.

'Yer lied about the lads stealing a ring from yer. They panicked and ran away. Because of you one of 'em's dead an' our Jacky might never walk again. Twelve years old and might never walk again – and all because of yer bloody lies.'

There was a murmur of disapproval from the watching crowd which was growing by the minute. Mrs Pickersgill's husband scratched his balding head and said, loud enough for Charlie to hear, 'Is he on about that ring what I pawned? I told yer about that.'

'Not 'til it were too late, yer didn't,' she hissed. 'I thought it had been stole.'

'So,' shouted Charlie at the top of his voice, 'it hadn't been stolen – you'd pawned it.'

'*I* never pawned it!' yelled the woman. '*He* bloody pawned it without me knowing.' She jabbed an accusing thumb at her husband. 'How were I ter know he'd pawned the bloody ring?'

Loud mutters of condemnation greeted her admission that the ring hadn't been stolen after all.

'Yer told the governor at the home that yer'd seen the boys steal it,' shouted Charlie. He had a lot to get off his chest and he was happy with an audience. 'Yer a bloody liar, missis. It were a liar such as you that got my grandson sent to that home in the first place, only they've found that liar out now and he's locked up. He's the same liar as got my son hanged.'

There was a murmur from the crowd, some of them muttering the word 'hanged?' to each other. This was all very interesting. Who was this man whose son had been hanged for a murder he apparently didn't commit?

'There's not only murderers kill people. Liars kill as well,' Charlie continued, pugnaciously. 'It's you, another bloody liar, that's landed my Jacky in hospital; and his mate dead – fifteen years old an' dead because of your lies. What have yer got ter say for yerself?'

People were moving towards her gate. Mrs Pickersgill was not a popular member of the community and the crowd believed every word Charlie was saying.

'Yer want lockin' up, yer lyin' owd bat,' shouted someone.

'Yer a liar and a bloody killer,' called out Charlie. 'A liar and a bloody killer!'

Mr Pickersgill had disappeared back into the house, not wishing to be associated with all this. His wife was ashen faced. Her trembling mouth formed into a protest but the words wouldn't come out. She slammed the door in Charlie's face but he'd done what he came to do; in fact more, because he'd ascertained, in front of witnesses, that Jacky hadn't stolen the woman's ring. He turned to face the curious crowd.

'My lad died because of a liar,' he said, with tears forming in his eyes. 'A feller goes an' kills his wife and they hanged my lad for it. Now this.'

'Was your lad Frank McGovern?' inquired a woman's voice. The crowd had been guessing at Charlie's identity and she had come up with an answer she wanted verifying.

Charlie was surprised to know his son's notoriety had travelled as far as York. 'Aye, love,' he said, 'It was. Feller called Mumford murdered his wife an' told the police my lad had done it. He were the same liar what got my grandson locked up, only they've caught him out this time an' he's locked up now.'

'Will they be hanging Victor Mumford, mister?' inquired a small boy. 'We know a song about him.'

'Not for this, they won't,' said Charlie. 'More's the pity. It'd not bring my lad back even if they did.'

Mrs Pickersgill's next-door neighbour came down his path and leaned against the gate. 'I'll tell yer why she did it ter the lad,' he told Charlie. 'She'll deny it, but it tickled me.' The neighbour now had the attention of Charlie and the whole crowd.

'Oh aye, an' why *did* she do it?' Charlie asked.

'Well,' said the neighbour. 'The lad asked her if she was Norwegian . . . cos she had a face like a Norse.' There were some chuckles from the crowd. Charlie smiled.

'That sounds like our Jacky,' he said. 'Never short of a wise-crack my grandson.'

'I mentioned it to a few people and they've started callin' her Trigger,' the neighbour went on.

As he moved through the crowd Charlie felt a couple of slaps on his back and heard voices saying good luck and we hope they hang the bastard. All in all his visit to York had been satis-factory. It was the first time he'd done anything to help restore his son's good name. He smiled to himself at the thought of Ellie's skipping song being sung as far away as York. He must tell her that.

'How is he?' Charlie asked, dreading the answer.

They were in the corridor outside Jacky's ward, where Ellie was at his bedside. Maureen gave Charlie a reassuring smile and took his hand.

'The doctor's had a look at the x-rays and they reckon it

184

sounds much worse than it is. I've been told not to worry too much. His leg's broken ... among other things. He'll be plastered up like an Egyptian mummy for a few weeks, maybe months. I've told him about the police arresting Mumford. That cheered him up no end.'

Charlie heaved out a great sigh. 'Oh, thank God fer that. Me heart's been thumping ten ter the dozen all the way down here.'

'So, said Maureen, 'did you speak to that bloody woman?'

'I did, love. I told her what she'd done and what I thought – and I think she got the message.'

Charlie related the story of his confrontation with Mrs Pickersgill, ending with the news he'd got from Mullen that the charge of stealing the ring had been officially dropped, and that there'd be no action taken against Jacky for the car theft. Under the circumstances the police thought he'd been punished enough and the undertakers, whose car had been stolen, wanted as little fuss as possible made of the whole business. The South Yorkshire Bus Company had given them enough grief for the time being – threatening to sue for loss of revenue after having been made to reimburse the fares of eighteen passengers and having the bus impounded while investigations were carried out. It had taken several hours to tie the discovery of the body in the bus shelter to the theft of the funeral car and its deceased occupant.

'So, as soon as they get this Mumford thing into court we should be able to bring him home?' said Maureen.

'Sooner I should think, if Mumford's already confessed. Have yer told young Brian?'

'I've sent word, but I don't expect him to come and visit. Maybe when I get Jacky home eh?'

'Aye love.' Charlie smiled and nodded encouragingly – but he wasn't holding his breath.

Brian had got as far as the bus station. He was only doing it for his mother – certainly not for Jacky, who had been a thorn in his side all his life with his clever remarks and even cleverer ways. Finding out that his father was a rapist had been the last straw for him, especially with Jacky's dad, Frank McGovern, becoming more of a folk hero every passing day. Brian hated the skipping song. Paradoxically he also hated Mumford, but he didn't know why. He went to the ticket kiosk and stood in the queue until it was his turn.

'Return to Sheffield, please,' he said.

'That'll be five and sixpence.'

'Eh?' said Brian.

'Cheap day return, five and six.'

'Nowt cheap about that!' Brian said. 'Yer can stuff yer ticket.'

He walked away. There was a limit as to how far he'd go to get on his mother's good side. And spending five and six to go see his half brother lying in hospital was too high a price.

Anyway, by all acounts, the boy was going to be all right, so Brian visiting him wasn't going to help. It wasn't as if Jacky would want him to go.

Mumford was paler than usual as he walked out of the magistrates' court. He had been bailed to appear at the Quarter Sessions in Leeds and by all accounts he'd be better off pleading guilty and taking what was coming to him. If perjury was added to the charges he could be looking at a lengthy custodial sentence. This wasn't fair. Why were these people doing it to him? Frank McGovern had got what he deserved and the boy had without doubt broken into his house. What was wrong with fighting fire with fire? That was all he had been doing – playing the bastards at their own game.

A group of children, waiting outside the court, began skipping when he appeared. Skipping and singing *that song*. Mumford's moustache kept jerking sideways, pulled by a nervous twitch he'd acquired since his arrest. Rodney Tripp was there to take his photograph, with the kids in the background – Ellie had contacted him via the Sunday tabloid that had carried his earlier story about Jacky and Fozzie Symonite. She had also persuaded a few children to come along and do the skipping song. As far as the reporter was concerned the latest story which Ellie had told him was far too libellous for any paper to run with without proof. But there might just be a story about a tortured man whose wife had been murdered by Frank McGovern; and about the growing doubt in people's minds regarding the safety of McGovern's conviction. Rodney could just about get away with writing up the skipping song so long as he made it clear it had been made up by the kids and not by the reporter. Ellie was willing to back him on that. She wasn't worried about being sued for slander.

Consumed with self-pity, Mumford gave Ellie a watery-eyed stare which she returned with a stare of her own; full of loathing. Then he realised where he'd seen her before – she was the brat's sister who'd been with the brat that night they had been singing carols outside his house. All was now clear to him. *She* was behind all this – behind everything. It wouldn't surprise him if she was the one who had broken into his house with her brother. His anger assumed primacy over self-pity as he walked over to her and hissed in her ear, 'You're next.'

'Did you hear that?' screamed Ellie as loud as she could. 'He's just admitted it.'

'Admitted what?' asked Rodney, rushing to her.

'He just admitted killing his wife. And he threatened to kill me.'

'I did no such thing,' said Mumford, still twitching.

Ellie squared up to him as Rodney looked on. 'They're going to lock you up, Mumford. And while you're locked up we're going to prove that you killed your wife. And when we do they'll hang you.'

Mumford turned to the reporter. 'She's quite mad, of course. Madness runs in that family. They've done so much damage to me between them – and now the law's trying to help them.' He took Rodney's arm and allowed his tears to flow unchecked. 'Please don't be fooled by her. I'm not a bad person. I didn't start any of this.'

'Don't believe him,' shouted Ellie. 'He lied about us stealing from his house.'

'*Us*?' said Mumford.

Ellie realised she'd slipped up, but what the hell did it matter now? 'Yes, *us*,' she said, caustically. 'I was with Jacky. He'll be asking for his conviction to be quashed and I'll be a witness if needs be.'

'See what I mean,' whined Mumford to Rodney. 'They're all mad.' He turned his back on the bemused reporter, gave Ellie a chilling smile, and mouthed the words, *You're next*.

She felt a shudder run through her body. The self-pity had gone from his eyes and was replaced by icy insanity. No doubt the same insanity that his wife had seen there, just before she died. And she knew that when someone as unhinged as Mumford threatens you it is wise to take them seriously. Rodney Tripp closed his note-book. He might make something out of it, but this wasn't much of a story, it was a feud. And feuds don't sell newspapers, not until someone gets killed.

Perhaps one of them would oblige.

Chapter Twenty-One

November 1955
Maureen rubbed her eyes and sat back from her work. Despite her constant rejection of Charlie's help he kept buying her things she could hardly refuse, such as this electric Singer sewing machine.

'Yer family, lass.'

'But I'm not really.'

His face fell.

'Sorry, that sounded awful. Of course I regard you as family.'

'Yer me grandson's mother and if that dunt mek yer family, nowt does.'

It was a console model, the best money could buy, with a box of attachments including a hemstitcher, zig-zag stitcher, buttonholer, ruffler, gatherer – in fact enough to broaden her capability and allow her to take on more varied and lucrative work. Ellie was working now, having left school with six O Levels, enough to get her a junior secretarial job with a firm of solicitors, so money wasn't quite as tight. Maureen had refused when Charlie offered to buy them a television set and she had gone down to Freeman Electrics in town and bought a 14" Baird on tick.

All in all their situation had improved, although with Brian not living there any more they were still way down the council house waiting list. The landlord had seen fit to bring them into the twentieth century by converting a box room-cum-airing cupboard into a tiny bathroom with a toilet.

It was over two years since Jacky had been released from the boys' home after having had his conviction for theft quashed. Maureen had discussed claiming some sort of compensation for his time locked away but her solicitor pointed out that her son was still guilty of breaking and entering, and perhaps it was best not to pursue the matter as it might cost her money she couldn't afford.

'They wouldn't let him take his 13-plus exam because of that conviction, you know,' she had told the solicitor. 'No one said as much but there were only a few places available and Jacky's name was nowhere near the top of the list. It'll be a right struggle for him to get any O Levels at the school he's at.'

Charlie knocked on the door and let himself in as a matter of course.

'Only me,' he called out. 'I've brought Jacky's present. Where shall I leave it? I thought it'd be a nice surprise when he gets in from school.'

He'd bought his grandson a present for his fifteenth birthday – another bike. He'd taken the old one back to the bike shop and offered it in part exchange for a new one which would fit Jacky's growing body. The lad was shooting up and looked like ending up over six feet, just like his dad.

'You spoil us, Charlie,' Maureen told him.

'I've nowt else ter spend me brass on,' Charlie pointed out. 'I had my Bessie well backed with t' Prudential, so I've a bit put by.'

'You should spend it on yourself. Take Enid on holiday – how's it going on by the way?'

'How's what going on?'

'This romance of yours. You've been taking her out for what . . . three years? Don't you think it's time you made an honest woman of her?'

'Never mind me. What about that policeman friend o' yours.'

'That's all he is, Charlie. A friend. A friend with a wife who's in a wheelchair.'

'Aye, lass. Sorry, lass,' he said, wheeling the bike across the room and leaning it against the wall. 'Me and Enid . . . we're, er . . . well, we're very friendly, an' that's all I'm gonna say.'

'I see . . . and that's all you're going to tell me,' Maureen said.

'Yer've got that right, lass. A gentleman never reveals the secrets of the boudoir.'

'I didn't think boudoirs were all that thick on the ground in Castlethorpe,' Maureen giggled as she nipped off the end of a cotton thread between her teeth. 'Secrets of the boudoir – you silly old sod.'

Charlie gave her a slow wink and tapped the side of his nose. 'Hey, there's many a good tune,' he said, 'played on an old fiddle.'

'So, you *are* sleeping with her.'

'I never said that, lass, any more than you've told me what you get up to wi' PC 49.'

'Well *we* don't get up to anything.'

Not for the first time she regretted the truth of that. It had been almost five years now since she'd had a man lying beside her in bed. It wasn't so much the death of Bert that had kept her celibate, but the death of Frank McGovern. A man she hadn't made love with in over fifteen years; a man she seemed to miss more desperately with every passing day. Bill could well have replaced him in her affections but for the chairbound wife. The part he played in getting Jacky released weighed heavily in his favour; that and the fact that Maureen enjoyed his company. They went to the pictures now and again and they even went to the Jack Street baths together, where Bill's prowess was very much inferior to that of Maureen's.

'You swim better than Esther Williams,' he had told her. 'You look better as well.'

'Come off it. She's a good few years younger then me.'

'Not that many – and she doesn't look as good as you.'

At Maureen's age it was good to have her ego massaged. They had gone so far as to kiss with a passion, but there it had always stopped – she couldn't bring herself to allow their affection to reach its ultimate conclusion. It would add too much disorder to her life. She was coming up to forty years old and needed to broaden her horizons. Somewhere out there was a man without Bill's complications; a man who was alive and kicking; a man she could love without guilt. A man who would take care of her and replace Frank McGovern in her heart. Or was she living in a dreamworld?

'Penny for 'em?' Charlie said.

She came round from her daydream. 'Oh, just daft thoughts,' she said. 'My baby's taller than me now. They're not babies long are they?'

'He's the makin' of a grand young man. What's he thinking o' doing with hisself? When he lived wi' me all he wanted ter be were a fighter pilot.'

191

'Well, he's staying on at school to take his O Levels. I don't know after that.'

'Mebbe university, eh?'

'I haven't ruled it out. He'd have to swap schools to do his A Levels.'

'Does he know all this?' asked Charlie.

Maureen laughed and shook her head. 'Since he came out of that blasted boy's home all he wants to do is leave school. He looks upon school as just another institution and he hasn't had much luck with institutions. Still, I think I've talked him into staying on for his O Levels. One step at a time, eh?'

'He thinks the world o' you, lass. I reckon yer could talk him him into owt.'

'I've left school, Mam,' said Jacky. 'Hello Granddad.'

Maureen and Jacky turned to see Jacky standing in the doorway with an apprehensive smile on his face. There was a moment of silence as Maureen took in what he'd just said.

'What?'

'I've left school. I'm fifteen today and legally I'm allowed to leave. I don't have to stay on 'til the end of term. Not legally. I told Mr Overend.'

'Oh,' said Maureen. 'And what did Mr Overend say?'

'Well, he said he'd have a word with you, but I told him it wouldn't do any good. I did thank him for all his help.'

'Did you now?' She was lost for words. 'Charlie,' she said. 'Do you think you could leave us on our own?'

'Course I can, lass.' Charlie caught Jacky's eye and inclined his head towards the bicycle leaning against the wall. 'Happy birthday, Jacky boy,' he said.

Jacky looked at the bike and smiled, broadly. 'Aw, thanks, Granddad.' He walked towards the bike but his mother stopped him with an outstretched arm, looking meaningfully at Charlie. He took the hint and left.

'Let's just go over this again, Jacky,' she said. 'After all we've discussed, you've just left school without bothering to mention it to me. What about your O Levels next year?'

'Mam, I'm sorry. I really am. You know I hate school.'

'You used to like school.'

'That was years ago. I'm like a fish out of water at Fartown. Mr Overend's okay – but I don't belong there.'

'I know you're a bright lad and leaving without qualifications is a sin.'

'Mam, if I want qualifications I can get them at night school. Fartown isn't a proper school for taking O Levels. Kids staying on to take O Levels are looked on as freaks. If I'd gone to a grammar school it would have been different.'

'They should have let you take that 13-plus exam. It just wasn't fair that.'

'If it hadn't been for Brian I'd have probably passed my exams when I was eleven,' Jacky pointed out.

His mother acknowledged his argument with a shrug that indicated she didn't want to talk about it. 'I'm not happy about you leaving school, Jacky. It's not what I had in mind for you at all.'

'I'll be okay, Mam. Maybe with me paying board we can go off on holiday next year.'

'Don't change the subject.'

'Has our Brian ever said sorry for what he did to me?'

'I said don't change the subject – and no he hasn't.'

'Mam, I never really understood why he hated me so much. Was it something to do with Bert not being my dad – or his for that matter?'

Maureen got up from her chair and hugged him to her. 'No, Jacky,' she said. 'I think it goes a lot deeper than that.' She walked over to the window and looked out into the street. It was a cheerless day. The November sky threatened rain. A paperboy stuffed the *Yorkshire Evening Post* through the letter box and she glanced down at the headlines. MORE SOVIET TANKS POUR INTO HUNGARY. Men killing people. Things never change. Turning back to her son she said, 'Our Brian thinks he's not as good as the rest of us. He felt comfortable with Bert as his dad because Bert and Brian were sort of equals.'

'I don't understand, Mam.'

'I don't fully understand myself, Jacky. It's just something I've thought a lot about over the years. You see, Brian hasn't got the quick brain you and Ellie have got – and the problem is he knows it. He's not stupid by any means, but when you take the mickey out of him he can't fight back, he doesn't know how to. To you these wisecrack comments come easy, but not to Brian. That's why he lashes out. It's not hate, its frustration that he can't think as quickly as you and he didn't do as well at school as you. And maybe he can see you getting a good job and looking down on him later on in life.'

'You mean he was jealous,' Jacky summed up, but his mother wasn't listening.

'When Bert died,' she went on, 'Brian took it very badly. And when I stupidly told him Bert wasn't his proper dad . . . well . . . it was just about the worst thing I could have done.' She sat down at her sewing machine again and idly picked up a piece of cloth. 'The trouble is I still can't forgive him for what he did to you. I can *understand* him, but I can't forgive him. If he came round and said he was sorry for everything he'd done I'd forgive him then . . . but he isn't sorry. You can't forgive people who aren't sorry for what they've done.'

'Would you have let him come back and live with us if he said he was sorry?' Jacky asked her.

'In a flash, love. In the wink of an eye – but he'd have to mean it. The only times I've seen him over these past two years is when I've been round to his digs to give him his Christmas and birthday presents. We're polite to each other and he kisses me on the cheek and . . .'

'And what?'

Maureen shrugged. 'And nothing, that's just it. He knows what it'll take for me to have him back and it seems it's just too much for him.'

'He's become a Teddy Boy, did you know?'

'I had heard,' said Maureen. 'It's a phase.'

'I saw him last week. He looks a sod.'

'They all do. I hope you're not thinking of—'

'No way.'

'Good.'

'I suppose in a way this trouble's all my fault,' Jacky said. 'It's me you're sticking up for really.'

'No, it's more than that, Jacky. In doing what he did to you he hurt me and he knows it. It's as though he's taking it out on me for being stupid enough to be raped. You see, that's another thing. He doesn't know anything about his own father, except that he was a rapist.'

194

'Actually, I don't think our kid thinks that deeply, Mam. He's just pig-headed.'

She gave a short laugh. 'He probably doesn't know himself why he feels the way he does. He's built a barrier between us and him, and he feels safe behind it.'

'Blimey!' Jacky said. 'You've lost *me* now, never mind our Brian. Anyway, there'll be no need for him to feel inferior to me as from Monday.'

'Why?' she asked, apprehensively.

'On my way home from school I called in the pit yard and asked if there were any jobs going.'

'You didn't . . . Oh, Jacky, no.'

'I start on Monday, working on the screens where our Brian started. Maybe he'll come round once he realises I'm no better than anyone else.'

His mother was about to give him a strong argument about taking a job that was so much beneath his capabilities, but realised she couldn't without belittling her other son. In her opinion Jacky was better than most, but was her opinion swayed because he was the son of Frank McGovern? Jacky was examining the bike Charlie had bought him, spinning the front wheel and running his hand over the racing saddle. Making admiring noises.

'By the way,' she said. 'I'm glad you're not thinking of becoming a Teddy Boy.'

'Why?'

'I've made you a suit for your birthday.'

'A suit?'

He looked uncertain. Up until now his mother had made most of his school clothes, but a suit was a different matter altogether. A suit was a fashion item, and fashion was something Jacky was becoming increasingly conscious of.

'How did you know my measurements?'

'Because I'm your mother. I've been watching you grow inch by inch for the last fifteen years.'

'What colour?'

'Charcoal grey, one button, semi-drape. Done everything myself, including the handstitching. Exactly as seen in a certain shop window in Leeds, only this is bespoke tailoring, made out of Lipscombe's finest worsted. There's royalty walking round in cheaper cloth.'

On her last visit to Lipscombe and Lile there had been more than three yards left over from a bolt of top-grade charcoal-grey worsted, just enough to make the suit. Maureen had mentioned to the manager that there was an odd yard or so left and could she have it. She rarely got turned down. Jacky's eyes brightened at her description of his dream suit, the one he'd talked of having seen in Burton's window in Leeds but his mother couldn't afford it.

'It's in your wardrobe,' she told him. 'Try it on . . . and then tell me you're no better than anyone else. Maybe then we can talk about you going down the pit.'

But Jacky did start work at the pit. The same one where Brian worked, although they rarely saw each other and even then never acknowledged the other's existence. A year previously Brian had had further humiliation heaped upon him when he failed his medical for National Service, something he'd been looking forward to as he thought a career in the Army might well suit him. He'd even been thinking of signing on for three years as a regular. But flat feet put paid to that ambition.

'Unfit ter fight but fit fer the pit, eh?' he told the medical officer who gave him the bad news. 'Christ, man. I'm fitter than ninety per cent of the lads who come through here. Can't yer turn a blind eye? It's only me feet fer Christ's sake!'

'It's the marching, son,' said the officer. 'None of the services will take a man who can't march properly . . . sorry, but we don't bend rules.'

So Brian's future down the pit seemed inescapable. If he'd wanted to get out he should have taken notice of Ced and gone back up in the cage the first day he went down. But the mine had swallowed him up, body and soul, in exchange for a regular pay packet. He was working at the coal face now and the money wasn't bad. Another two years and he'd be on top rate. Man's money. He'd also caught the eye of a barmaid in the Moulder's Arms and had taken her out a few times. She was no oil painting but she admired his Teddy Boy suit and laughed at his jokes, and sympathised with him when he told her his version of how and why his mother had kicked him out. He stopped short of telling her he was the son of a rapist. That was something no one would ever know, unless his prat of a brother told on him.

196

In the meantime Jacky had caught the eye of Sandra Symonite, Fozzie's cousin. All he had to do was to overcome his shyness with girls and ask her out – and evidently Sandra Symonite was a girl well worth asking out. Jacky was unsure about this whole boy/girl thing. Whereas everyone around him seemed to be growing up too quickly, he was far more reluctant to let go of his childhood than most. He had 'gone out' with a girl from the next street but it didn't get beyond two trips to her Methodist Youth Club and a couple of chaste kisses. By and large he preferred the company of his pals.

'She fancies yer like mad,' Roy Barnwell told him. They were on their way to Monkton's Corner, an informal meeting place for their friends, one of whom was Sandra. 'Why don't yer take her to t' pictures?'

'She's goin' out with Kevin.'

'No, she finished wi' Kevin last Tuesday. I reckon she's got her eye on you.'

'What if she says no?'

'I'm tellin' yer, Jacky. She won't say no. Blimey, even *I've* been out with her.'

'*You* ask her for me.'

'If I ask her,' Roy said, 'it'll be ter go out wi' me again, never mind you. Yer do yer own courting.'

'What shall I say?'

'Just say there's a good picture on at t' Rialto and does she fancy going?'

'I don't even know what's on.'

'Blimey Jacky boy! Yer very backward in comin' forward.'

'Okay, I'll ask her.

A group of teenagers were already there, the girls sitting on a wooden bench, with boys hovering around them, chatting, smoking and generally showing off. In response to a nudge from the girl sitting next to her, Sandra turned round and looked at Jacky and Roy. She smiled briefly before turning to chat with her friend.

'Told yer,' said Roy.

'Told me what?'

'Told yer she fancied yer. Did yer see that look she gave yer. That were a "come on" if ever I saw one.'

'Give over. She hardly looked at me.'

'I'm tellin' yer, Jacky boy, she fancies yer like mad. Go fill yer boots.'

'Right.' Jacky squared his shoulders ready for the inevitable rejection from the best-looking girl in the group, by far.

'*Blackboard Jungle*,' whispered Roy in his ear.

Jacky hesitated. 'What?'

'It's on at t' Rialto. *Blackboard Jungle*.'

'It's an A – I can't get in for an A.'

'Give over, yer look sixteen. Anyway she can take yer in. She's seventeen.'

'Is she? Blimey she's a bit old for me. I didn't know she was seventeen.'

Urged on by Roy, Jacky edged towards the bench on which Sandra was sitting.

'Have you seen, er . . . *Washboard Jungle*?' he asked, nervously.

She smiled in anticipation, as did most of the others. Jacky had a reputation as a joker so they assumed he'd said it on purpose, just for a laugh. He hadn't. They were waiting for the punchline. Jacky realised this and racked his brain.

'It's like *Blackboard Jungle* . . . only cleaner,' he said. It wasn't much but it earned him a laugh from Sandra, who laughed easily.

'Do you fancy going to see it then?' he asked with growing confidence.

'Which one?' she asked. 'The clean one or the dirty one?'

'The dirty one,' he said. 'You'll have to take me in, though. I think it's an A.'

'She's good at takin' lads in,' said Sandra's friend, with a wink at Jacky. 'Yer'll have ter be careful she doesn't chew you up and spit you out.'

'Shut yer face, Dawn Backhouse!' admonished Sandra. 'Yer'll give him the wrong impression of me.' She smiled up at Jacky and he noticed a smudge of lipstick on her teeth. 'Yes, I'd like ter go see it,' she said.

It was a cold night and they both wore coats as they met outside the cinema. They stood waiting for the first house to clear before their queue shuffled forward. Jacky had no small-talk for an occasion such as this. He could more than hold his own with boys, but girls were a different matter altogether.

'Are you always this quiet?' she asked.

'What, er, no.'

'I always thought you were a bit of a joker. Good for a laugh. I like a laugh. Tell us a joke.'

For the life of him Jacky couldn't think of one. All the jokes he knew, and just when he needed one, it wasn't there.

'You look very nice,' he said, lamely.

'I hope that's not your idea of a joke.'

'No, you do. You look very nice.'

'Thank you.'

He noticed that she didn't return the compliment. Maybe she would when she saw the sharp suit he was wearing beneath his coat.

'Our Fozzie's not happy that I'm coming out with you,' she said.

'Your Fozzie's only happy when he's miserable.'

'That's true,' she laughed. Jacky laughed as well. The ice had been broken. Fozzie had his uses after all. They arrived at the kiosk and Sandra fumbled in her pocket for her purse.

'It's okay,' Jacky said. 'I'll get these.'

He paid for two tickets in the one and nines – the stalls. It was she who led the way to the back row where they sat in the end seats with Jacky next to the wall. There was a space at the back for his coat. He made to put it there but she stopped him.

'Keep it on yer knee,' she said. 'Yer never know.'

Jacky wondered who could steal his coat from such an isolated spot but nevertheless put his coat across his lap. He took out a packet of State Express, lit two and handed her one, hoping such sophistication would impress her. He had outgrown the meagre legroom afforded by the cinemas of the day and rested his knees against the back of the seat in front. The cinema filled rapidly. The lights went down and with them the murmur of the audience. Cigarette smoke was illuminated as it floated across the projector beam. Someone flicked a tab-end through the beam; it raised a couple of laughs and a curse from the man it landed on, causing more laughs. Usherettes were shining torches to identify odd seats and asking people to move up so that couples could sit together.

There was a documentary about polar bears in Alaska, then the Pathé News, followed by a Popeye cartoon and trailers for Forthcoming Attractions: *The Benny Goodman Story, Davy*

Crockett, Guys and Dolls, and *Doctor at Sea*. Then the house lights lifted from dark to dim, faded curtains swished across the screen and the usherettes became ice-cream sellers, walking down the aisles with their trays of wares to take up station in front of the screen. Queues formed. Jacky asked Sandra if she wanted anything. She declined, then whispered in his ear.

'Before it starts do yer want me ter get it out for yer?'

'Get what out?'

She slid her hand under his coat and laid it on his groin, which she squeezed, gently. 'This,' she whispered, without taking her eyes from the screen curtains. 'It's only right. You paid for us in.'

'Right,' said Jacky, not knowing how else to react. Within seconds he felt himself going hard, which made him both embarrassed and aroused. She took his silence for a 'Yes' and unfastened him with a certain expertise. Jack's breathing quickened. The cinema was packed and he was sure everyone knew what was going on in their corner of the back row. But nevertheless he was enjoying it far too much to protest. The lights went back out and the curtains swished open.

Bill Hayley and his Comets began to play 'Rock Around the Clock' over the title sequence. Some youths in the audience began to sing along with the number that was to prove the advent of Rock and Roll. Jacky's breathing quickened and soon overtook the beat of the song. It seemed that everyone in the cinema was singing along now and he was glad it was loud because it drowned his final, stifled moan of pleasure. Sandra produced a handkerchief and tidied him up to the accompaniment of the final guitar riff. Jacky would always remember the tune with great affection. She kissed him on the lips and whispered, 'Not bad – bigger than Roy Barnwell's.'

'Oh,' said Jacky, 'is it?'

'It's not as big as Kevin's. He's got one like a length of hosepipe. Mind you, it takes some bringin' ter life. You were a bit previous, if yer don't mind me sayin' so.'

She laughed out loud and offered him a Wild Woodbine. Glen Ford came on the screen and someone in front told her to shush. Jacky hoped no one knew what they'd just been up to.

'I always think it's best to get stuff over an' done with before the picture starts,' she whispered to him. 'No point payin' good money and not seein' the picture cos of all that snoggin' an' stuff

200

. . . Mind you,' she added, 'if yer wantin' a bit on the way home I'd better warn yer, I don't go all the way. I'm not like that.'

'Fair enough,' Jacky whispered. At that moment in time he had little inclination to go all, or any part of the way. He puffed on his Woodbine and watched the film.

Growing up, he thought to himself, isn't all bad.

Chapter Twenty-Two

Ellie didn't see Mumford staring at her from across the street. It was March 1956 and he had been out of prison for six months. His insurance agency had been forced to close down when he was jailed for three years for fraud and perjury. He had been released after two years and was now in the process of rebuilding his life and business. He had visited the various insurance companies for which he had been an agent and gave them all the same well-rehearsed sob story. How losing his wife in such a way had left him unbalanced and with a deep grudge against the killer's family. But he had been made to pay a price and it would be unfair for him to lose everything. After all, he had been a good agent, bringing them lots of business.

Most of them agreed, provided he changed the name of the agency; preferably bringing in a partner as a front man whose name could be used. The skipping song was still being sung, although many of the kids singing it knew little of its significance. It was through the windows of Bradfield's Insurance Agency that he watched Ellie. Les Bradfield was young and keen and very much a junior partner. Mumford intended getting rid of him once the company was up and running. He also harboured thoughts of getting rid of Ellie Gaskell, only in her case it would be more permanent.

She had developed into a good-looking young woman who had just celebrated her eighteenth birthday. Mumford conjured up a vision of her lying naked on his bed as he plunged a knife into her. Beads of sweat formed on his forehead. He took a handkerchief from his pocket and wiped his brow.

'Are you all right, Victor?' Les asked.

'Not yet . . . I won't be all right until I've got all my affairs settled.'

'Shouldn't be long now,' said his young partner brightly. 'All this advertising seems to be doing the trick. Do you think we should get another phone line in?'

Mumford nodded but his thoughts were still fixed on Ellie who tossed her long hair from her face and strode down the street with the grace and vulnerability of a young fawn.

Ellie paused before her reflection in a shop window. Maureen had mentioned her to Lipscombe and Lile who were bringing out a catalogue and needed mannequins. The manager at Lipscombe's had been round to see her and fixed an appointment with the agency who were supplying all the models. With his recommendation she knew she'd probably get the job. It was only a one-off but it might lead to better things. In the meantime she had her job at the solicitors. She wasn't aware that she was walking past Mumford's new office and that he was looking at her. His absence hadn't made her heart grow any fonder of him, but her thirst for justice had abated.

She was tall and slim, with much of her mother's beauty – Maureen had no objection to her daughter being a fashion model. As a young woman she'd turned down the opportunity herself, in favour of art college . . . and the likes of Morgan Pettifer.

For Jacky life was running smoothly. Sandra Symonite had dumped him after their one and only date, and gone back to Kevin.

'She reckons he's got a dick like a hosepipe,' Jacky told Roy Barnwell, a few days later.

'That'll be it then,' said Roy. 'Did you pay for her into the flicks?'

'Yes, why?'

'And was she grateful?'

'I suppose so.'

'Grateful enough to get it out for you?'

Jacky hesitated, embarrassed.

'She did, didn't she?' persisted Roy. 'She did it ter me when I paid for her in. She reckons she doesn't like to be beholden to anyone. There's a lot of lads round here she's not beholden to – and I reckon you're the latest.'

Jacky blushed, then countered, 'She said mine's bigger than yours.'

It was Roy's turn to blush.

'You could have told me what she'd do,' said Jacky, reproachfully. 'She took me in the cemetery on the way back.'

'Blimey! Yer got further than I did. How far did yer get?'

'As far as that one-armed angel. I tripped over a gravestone and banged my knee. I didn't feel like doin' owt after that.'

'Chicken. No wonder she dumped yer.'

At the back of Jacky's mind was the unfinished business with Victor Mumford. Neither his mother nor Ellie talked about Mumford much. It was as though they thought they'd done as much as they could and had decided to get on with their lives. His granddad had shaken his head and said, 'Leave it, lad,' when Jacky questioned him about it. 'He'll get his come-uppance one way or another. Fellers like him allus do.' But Jacky wasn't too sure about that. 'It'd be better if you and that brother o' yours could make things up,' Charlie added. 'Yer mam'd be ever so pleased if yer could.'

Jacky was aware of this. His mother didn't mention it much any more. She was aware that Brian was the problem rather than Jacky, who had only ever reacted to his brother. It seemed to her that Brian would hold a grudge all his life and there was nothing she could do about it.

'I know she would, Granddad,' said Jacky. 'I'd make it up like a shot – but he won't.'

'How d'yer know? Have yer tried lately?'

'Granddad, he's four years older than me. I'm still a lad, he's a man. Don't you think it's up to him to make a bit of an effort?'

And so life went on in the Gaskell household. Charlie had become engaged to Enid Wharmby, but a marriage date hadn't been talked about. It was as if a betrothal gave them all the respectability they needed to continue their very close relationship without actually getting married.

Chapter Twenty-Three

The accident which made the brothers realise that blood is thicker than water occurred halfway through the early shift on the first day of spring 1956.

Jacky had graduated to working with the ponies at the pit bottom; his brother had become a face-worker. Because of this they saw each other more often, but still Brian didn't acknowledge his younger brother. The other miners thought it odd at first, but a thousand feet underground is an odd place to work at the best of times, so no one mentioned it to either brother. It was their business and no one else's.

Deep in the mine, half a mile away from where Jacky was urging his four-legged charges to pull the heavy tubs up to the cage, one of the pit props creaked ominously. An older miner, Clem Simson, shushed his three companions, one of whom was Brian.

'Shhh . . . listen ter that.'

The prop creaked again, as did another prop further down the pit face.

'They're talkin' to us,' said Clem.

'Oh, aye,' smirked Brian. 'What're they sayin? . . . Are they sayin' we can knock off early?' The other two miners grinned.

'They're sayin' there's summat wrong,' said Clem, ominously. 'That's what they're sayin'.' His eyes glinted fearfully in the light of his mates' lamps.

'Give over, yer daft owd goat,' grinned Albert, uncertainly.

'Still believes in the bloody tooth fairy does Clem,' said Fred, the fourth member of the gang. 'He's waitin' for that last tooth of his ter drop out so she'll leave him some beer money under his pillow – aren't yer, Clem?'

Clem displayed his lone tooth in a defiant grin. 'Yer laughin' now,' he warned. 'Yer'll be laughin' on t' other side of yer faces afore long.'

The props creaked again and the four men waited and listened until the creaking stopped, then they set to work again, hacking, drilling, shovelling, cursing. It was back-breaking work at the best of times, never mind having to do it in a dirty black hole, deep under the earth.

A hundred feet above them the rock strata whined and shifted like an old dog settling down for the night. A narrow, horizontal fault, just a foot wide, which had been there for several hundred years, suddenly slammed shut when subjected to the shifting pressure around it, and caused another crack to open somewhere else. It was the way of things under the ground. Where one door shuts another door opens – only these were not doors of opportunity, far from it. The shifting and settling gained momentum, caused by cavities being created by the mining. The weight carried by the pit props was momentarily doubled and trebled as the load above kept coming and going, like boys playing on ice.

At the pit bottom Jacky, who had stopped work for a cheese sandwich and a swig of cold tea from his water bottle, wafted away a fall of dust, then looked up at the RSJs supporting the roof above him from whence the fall of dust had come. There were more heavy sprinklings falling in other parts of the pit bottom, illuminated by the fluorescent lights. Jacky took his sandwiches into the onsetter's cubby hole – he didn't fancy eating a mouthful of coal dust – and made up his mind to find himself a cleaner, safer, more healthy job at the earliest opportunity. When the telephone rang, he looked at it, uncertainly. Sid, the onsetter, was busy with one of the cages and shouted across to Jacky, 'Get that, lad.'

It occurred to Jacky that he'd never answered a telephone in his life. He didn't know what to say. Picking up the phone he said, 'Hello?'

'Sid, it's Chas—'

'This isn't Sid.'

'Who is it then?'

'It's Jacky Gaskell.'

There was an uncertain silence. 'Can yer put Sid on?'

Jacky put down the phone and shouted through the door to the onsetter. 'He wants to speak to you.'

'Who does?'

Jacky went back to the phone. 'Who is it?' he asked.

'Is that Sid?' said the voice.

'No, it's still Jacky Gaskell.'

'Bloody hell fire! Look, tell Sid ter send a message for Clem ter come up ter t'manager's office straight away – it's his missis . . . have yer got that?'

'Yes,' said Jacky.

'It's important. Is Sid not there?'

'He's busy but I'll tell him.'

'Just tell him it's important. Tell him it's Clem's missis.'

The phone went dead and Jacky, urged on by the caller's tone, ran out to relay the message on to Sid, who pushed back his helmet and scratched his head. 'You'll have ter go,' he decided. 'Lads are not s'posed ter go to t' face but this is an emergency. Did he say what were wrong wi' Clem's missis?'

'No.'

'No,' said Sid. 'I don't suppose he would. I reckon she's prob'ly pegged it. Clem'll be gutted, poor bugger. It were expected, but yer never ready fer summat like that. Christ, they've been married fer nearly forty years, poor owd bugger.'

Jacky hardly knew Clem so he wasn't in a position to comment.

'Look,' decided Sid. 'There should be a loco where Clem is. You run down there, lad, an' tell him to come back on it. Just tell him he's wanted, no more. Yer might as well ride back with him.' He pointed towards a roadway at one end of the chamber. 'He's workin' on t' Lower Main face. Frame yersen an' yer should be there in ten minutes.'

Jacky set off at a trot, his lamp battery case banged against his waist and the beam of his cap lamp danced across the floor of the roadway as he ran alongside the narrow-gauge rail track. It was the first time he'd ever been to the pit face and his excitement at the prospect was tempered by the sad reason for going. The roadway, like the pit bottom, was illuminated by dirty, fluorescent tubes which cast down a gloomy, barely adequate light. Occasionally the tubes flickered which gave an eerie look to the seemingly endless tunnel.

A loco, pulling a string of tubs filled to the brim with house coal, passed him coming the other way. The driver opened his mouth to ask what he was doing down there but Jacky ran on

207

without stopping. The floor was uneven and littered with the general detritus of the pit, causing him to run with his eyes glued firmly to the ground, across which he skipped and jumped with all the energy of youth.

He knew Brian was working with Clem and wondered what sort of reception he'd get. Not that anything his brother could say would worry him. Poor old Clem. Everyone knew his wife was ill but Clem couldn't afford to take time off to be with her, which was a shame. Unlike a lot of the men down the pit Clem had never been known to say anything but good about his wife. He was a wizened old sod, but he thought the world of his missis.

Jacky stopped in his tracks as the walls and roof around him shuddered; a thick cloud of dust filtered through the steel mesh lining the roof between the arched beams. For a second he was frightened, then he remembered he'd never been this far down the mine before and no doubt it was all perfectly normal. It was a strange world down here, in the bowels of the Earth – a world he didn't plan on inhabiting much longer. He wanted to work in a world where your sandwiches didn't taste of coal and your mouth and nose weren't always clagged up with black grime. It got in your hair, your eyelashes, even into the pores of your skin and would make a permanent home there if you didn't painfully scrub yourself clean after every shift.

The dust cleared and Jacky jogged on. It was important to get the message to Clem as soon as possible. He stopped again when he heard a noise like someone crying in the distance. There it was again. But it wasn't a human sound – more of a creaking groan. Probably perfectly normal. The men who worked down here no doubt wouldn't even notice it. How could anyone want to spend their whole life in a pit? Jacky knew he'd been a bit impulsive getting a job down here on the day he left school. Perhaps he'd been trying to prove something. Attercliffes Joiners and Undertakers were wanting an apprentice; that sounded the very job for Jacky. His mam had promised to make enquiries for him. Spring had come and he wanted to be out in the fresh air, not down here.

On either side of him were the entrances to worked-up faces where the miners had dug out the coal further and further into the seam, before moving on and allowing the roof to fall in behind them; a method of working that would one day result in huge compensation claims for subsidence from property owners high above them. But it was either that or do without coal.

He arrived, breathless, at a place where a line of tubs were being loaded. A conveyor trundled out of the face and deposited coal into a steel hopper on the floor, from where two men shovelled it into the tubs.

'Is Clem Simson working up here?' Jacky asked. 'I've got a meassage for him.'

'Aye lad,' said one of the men. 'Is it his missis?'

'Yeah,' said Jacky.

'He's workin' right up at t' far end.' The man peered at Jacky. 'He's workin' wi' your kid. Right up at t' far end. Happen fifty yards.'

'Right,' said Jacky, crouching to scramble up the face which ran at a right angle to the roadway. He crawled beside the conveyor, at the other side of which, at intervals of ten yards or so, gangs of men hacked away at the coal seam, some with pneumatic drills, some with hand picks. He passed a Davey lamp hanging from a nail in a prop, but apart from that the only light came from the men's cap lamps. Further along he passed a canary, chirping cheerfully in its cage as it watched the men work; it would continue to do so until it got its first whiff of methane.

One gang had stopped for a snap break and were laughing at a dirty joke that Jacky only caught the end of. It was an environment normal to them. But it would never be normal to him.

On the other side of him were the old, collapsed workings. The roof of the road he scrambled along was held up by wooden pit props, six inches in diameter, spaced at five-foot centres and supporting thick wooden planks. The roof was hard rock and varied in height from seven feet down to five and Jacky was glad of his helmet, which suffered more bangs and scrapes in that short journey than in all the time he'd worked down the pit. It was a dark, noisy, dirty, fascinating place, but not fascinating enough to change Jacky's mind about wanting to work as a joiner in the clean air above.

The face traversed from one road to another. One road led to the upcast shaft and the other, the one Jacky had come down, to the downcast shaft. It was the warmest part of the pit. A constant stream of ventilating air was pulled through the mine by a giant fan at the top of the upcast shaft. Jacky was now sweating, as were most of the men he was passing. Some were working in vests, some stripped to the waist; one huge man wore only boots, knee pads, helmet and a grimy jock strap. Jacky was now almost at the other end, about to come out into the parallel roadway. Clem would be in the last gang. Jacky stepped over the conveyor and approached the four-man team – Clem and Albert were wedging a pit prop into position.

Clem looked at Jacky, who wasn't old enough to be down here and would only be allowed down to bring an urgent message. Brian, working a drill, turned to look at his younger brother, who was looking at Clem. He switched it off, as if knowing why Jacky was here.

'Is it the missis?' Clem asked, in a low voice, his eyes averting Jacky's, as if afraid of the answer.

Jacky hesitated, having been told not to mention Clem's wife, just to tell him he was wanted. He shrugged at first, then he gave in and nodded.

'Is she—?'

The boy shook his head vigorously. 'No idea, honest, Clem. All I know is to come and get you. I don't know any more than that – honest. They want you up at the manager's office.'

Clem nodded and put down his lump hammer. 'I should have been with her, not down here in this fuckin' hole.'

It was the first time any of them had heard him swear. Jacky felt unreasonably guilty. It was a cramped and filthy place to be imparting bad news of any sort. Especially news so bad it made a good man swear.

'Er, Sid said to go back on the loco,' mentioned Jacky, lamely. He glanced at Brian, but there was no enmity in his brother's face, not under these circumstances. 'I'll come back with you, if it's okay.'

'I don't suppose owt'll be okay ever again, lad,' said Clem, his voice croaky, but with controlled emotion. He wasn't going to weep or make a scene or look for sympathy. There was all the sympathy he needed in the silence of his workmates. Then the silence was broken by a loud rumble and an obscene, frightened curse from one of the men. The roof they had been propping collapsed with a suddenness that took them all unawares. Clem disappeared under a huge rock, Jacky instinctively hurled himself

210

forward and the other three men flung themselves, face down, on the pit floor.

No one moved or spoke for a good minute afterwards. The air was thick with choking dust. All of them were covered in a layer of grime and coal and rock. Albert's cap lamp was smashed by a lump of rock that would have killed him instantly had it not been for his helmet. Jacky lay very still, fearing another fall that would finish him off. He didn't know who was alive or dead – he didn't even know what condition *he* was in. There was a stabbing pain in his shoulder but he seemed to be able to move his arms and legs. What really worried him was the silence.

'Is everyone okay?' he called out.

'Is that you, Jacky boy?' It was Brian's voice.

'Yeah.' Jacky pushed himself to his knees and squinted through the dust, through which his cap lamp managed to pierce just a short tube of light. There was nothing at the end of the tube, just more dust. 'Are you okay, Brian?'

'I think so . . . Jesus!'

'What?'

'Clem, are you okay, Clem?' The dust was slowly clearing and Brian was just able to make out Clem's legs protruding from the fallen rock. The man's boots were easily recognisable with their myriad segs. 'Jesus! Clem's buried under this bloody thing.'

Jacky counted two lights, one of which presumably would be Brian's. Someone moaned. The dust was filtering away through gaps in the fallen rubble, sucked out by a distant extractor fan.

'Fred, Albert,' called out Brian, 'are you lads okay?'

Another moan. The same man as before – Albert. Fred remained silent, then Albert sat up. He took off his helmet and rubbed his head; blood was pouring from it, all down the side of his face.

'Bloody hell!' he said.

Fred opened his eyes and looked up at Brian. 'What were that?' he said, weakly.

'I think that's us knackered,' Brian told him. 'Unless we can dig oursens out.'

Fred moaned and said, 'Oh shit!' Then he rubbed his leg and moaned even louder.

211

'God knows why this lot didn't come down,' said Albert, looking up at the rock above. 'We could do with proppin' it afore we start doin' owt.'

'Nowt ter prop it with,' said Brian, looking around. 'We ought ter get Clem out from under.' He leaned down towards where Clem's feet were projecting from the fallen rock.

'Clem,' he shouted. 'Can yer hear me?'

No reply.

'We'll never shift that,' said Fred, grimly, shining his cap lamp on the rock that was pinning the silent Clem to the floor. 'There'll be a couple o' ton in that at least.'

'Won't someone come for us?' Jacky asked.

'Eventually,' said Fred. 'Depends how much stuff's come down. It could run fer a hundred feet or more could this fall.'

'Or it could be just a few yards,' said Albert. 'We've no way o' knowin'.'

Brian pulled out a piece of rock from near the roof and handed it to Jacky. 'Here,' he said. 'Throw it over yon.'

Jacky threw the rock a few feet away then took another piece from his brother – an escape tunnel was under way. Albert and Fred watched in silence. Neither seemed physically capable of helping. Albert's face was caked in blood and Fred couldn't move one of his legs.

'Try shoutin' lad,' Fred advised. 'It'll do no harm.'

Brian shouted, 'Hello, is anybody there?' as loud as he could. They all listened for a reply but none came.

The shifting rock had found its weakest level in the Lower Main face and had settled into it – at least most of it had settled. All along the face men were either trapped or dead. Some had managed to get out; others, like Jacky and co., were trapped in pockets that hadn't yet collapsed.

Fred sniffed the air. 'Gas,' he said.

Jacky could smell it now. Methane gas was seeping through the cracks and crevices all around them. It wasn't very strong but it was certainly worrying.

'Well, I'm not waitin' for 'em ter come an' get us,' said Brian, working away faster now. 'Aw shit! We're diggin' blind here. Fred, what d'yer reckon's t' best road out?'

Fred tried to orientate himself. 'No point goin' back down t' face,' he concluded. 'It could be as bad as this. We're right next to a road. The odds are it'll have held . . . try that way.' He indicated the direction with his hand. 'It's only a few yards.'

'Right,' said Brian.

The two brothers worked away feverishly. Brian was now full length in a tunnel he had created, only his boots were in view. His progress slowed as he had to pass each piece of rock behind his body into Jacky's hands. On top of which there was no way of propping this tunnel. At one point it collapsed and Jacky had to pull his brother clear and back into the chamber where the two injured men sat helplessly.

Clem's boots still projected from under the rock like a memorial to the man who must surely be dead. It didn't trouble the others too much as they felt they might well be joining him soon, barring miracles. At least it was all over for him. What would they have to go through before it was over for them? Brian looked shocked and defeated. His face and hands were lacerated with gashes from where he'd been dragged past fallen rock by his brother.

'We can't be too far away,' decided Jacky. 'I think I'll have a go.'

Brian gave him a grim look and Jacky thought he was going to say something nasty, so he had his answer ready. Why break the habit of a lifetime?

'Good lad,' Brian said. 'Yer a lot skinnier than me. Yer'll not tek up as much room. Make a way through an' we'll find a way of proppin' it so we can get Fred and Albert out.'

Fred and Albert both visibly brightened at such a hopeful prospect. The gas smell was getting stronger. It only needed something to spark it off. The pain in Jacky's shoulder seemed to have eased. Maybe it was just one of many aches and pains he was acquiring and took little notice of because of his desperate situation.

'I thought you two lads didn't get on,' said Albert.

'We don't,' Brian said. 'He's a clever little pillock is Jacky boy. Too clever for his own bloody good. But he'll do fer me if he gets us out of here.'

'Sounds fair enough ter me,' said Albert. 'Hear that, Jacky boy? Get us out an' your kid'll give yer a big wet kiss.'

Jacky grinned in the gloom. 'I said I'd give it a try. Don't try an' put me off with yer nasty threats.'

Albert and Fred laughed and Jacky could see Brian's teeth. He was smiling. Jacky couldn't remember his brother ever smiling at him before. He climbed into the partially collapsed tunnel and began passing rocks back to his brother. At various points he pulled out bigger rocks which he made a space for and used as props. Brian saw what he was doing and called out advice and encouragement.

'Yer brains might get us out of here yet, Jacky boy.'

'Promise not to kiss me if we do get out.'

'Can't promise that, Jacky boy. I might let yer off nickin' me bike though. Took me a year ter pay off a bike I never had.'

Maureen was at her sewing machine when the steam hooter at the colliery began to give a continuous series of short blasts – the signal for a mining accident. It was almost half a mile away but it carried through the morning air like the howl of a banshee and was heard by everyone in the town. Charlie froze with horror. Not again. He didn't know which shift the brothers were working on but it was instantly clear when he went to the door and saw Maureen's face as she ran out into the street.

'I'm comin' with yer, lass,' he said, going back inside for his coat.

People were rushing out of houses the length of Gaythorne Street and running up the hill to the pit. Charlie struggled to keep up with Maureen as they turned right into Gaythorne Terrace and past the drawn curtains at number twelve. Clem Simson's house. They didn't know it yet but he and his wife had died on the same day. That would have suited Clem – he wouldn't have managed very well on his own.

There was a crush of people going through the big iron gates and across the pit yard. Four policemen were there already, trying to marshal the crowd into some sort of order. One of them, a sergeant, clambered onto the back of a truck and waved his hand to calm them.

'Please,' he shouted. 'We don't know the full story yet. There's been a roof fall in Lower Main—'

His announcement was interrupted by mixed cries of anguish and relief, the latter from the friends and loved ones of men working on the other seams. The pit manager got up beside him.

'There's also been a fall in one of the roadways so we can only get to the seam from one end . . . pit rescue are down there now. We can hear men shouting so we know there are many men alive. There's gas down there so we're having to take every precaution. We're evacuating the whole pit . . . so when you're reunited with your men please leave the immediate area. Only those belonging to missing men should stay inside the gates. As soon as we have further news we'll let you know.'

The manager's face was drawn with anguish, as if he knew more than he had been prepared to divulge. Which of course he did. From the shouts of the trapped men they knew that some had been killed and badly injured, but until he knew who and how many it was unwise to say anything. The crowd went strangely silent. They didn't speak to each other because they had nothing to say until they knew what they were dealing with. Some would be relieved before the day was out and some would be heartbroken. At that moment in time they didn't know who would be comforting whom.

Jacky had never felt so exhausted in his life. His mouth was bone dry and caked with dust, his skin dripping blood from dozens of cuts and grazes.

'Keep goin' Jacky boy,' urged his brother. 'When we get out me an' you are goin' for a pint of Tetley's. What d'yer think about that?'

A pint of beer sounded fine to Jacky. He'd never been in a pub but he had to start sometime and now was as good a time as any.

'You'll have to pay,' he said, as he heaved another piece of rock past his bruised body to his brother who, in turn, passed it back to Albert. They had been working for over an hour and the tunnel was about five yards long.

'Yer tight little sod,' said Brian.

'I'm too young to go in a pub,' Jacky pointed out. 'So I can't be seen buyin' beer.'

'We'll get Charlie ter buy,' decided Brian. 'He's never short of a bob or two. Bloody hell, have you farted?'

'It's not me,' said Jacky, 'It's gas. It's gettin' stronger.'

'How much further . . . any idea?'

'No . . . hang on . . . yeah.' Jacky pushed at a rock in front of him and it gave way. 'I think I'm through,' he called back,

215

excitedly. He shone his lamp into the empty cavern beyond his slender tunnel. 'Yeah. It's goin' to be okay. We've done it.'

Brian passed the news back to Albert who had already heard and was telling Fred.

'Try shoutin' . . . see if anyone's there,' said Brian.

Jacky shouted as loud as he could and listened for a reply. There was only a muffled sound coming from the collapsed pit face to his right. He pulled himself through and looked back to see where his brother was. Brian shuffled to the end and poked his head out, relishing the dusty, gaseous air as if it were champagne. Their two beams of light picked out the extent of the disaster. The roof of the pit face, right up to the part they had been working, had collapsed. Immediately to their left was an unlit roadway which should provide their escape – so why had no one come down it to help them?

'Shouldn't there be lights in that road?' Jacky asked.

Brian nodded. 'Must've got knocked out. There'll be summat wrong down there, or they'd be swarmin' over here like flies round a jam pot.'

'It's better than bein' trapped in there,' said Jacky, stepping out into the roadway. He directed his light up to the arched steel beams that supported the roof. 'We should be okay here till they come and get us.'

'That's if t' gas dunt get us first,' Brian said, sniffing the air. He made no attempt to climb out and join Jacky. Behind him Albert was asking what was happening and Brian called back that he'd be with him in a minute. 'Anyroad – well played, our kid,' he said to Jacky. 'Make this end safe. I'm goin' back to help Albert get Fred out. See if yer can find a rope or summat. We might have ter pull him through.'

As Brian shuffled backwards, Jacky did his best to prop up the end of the tunnel. It was a precarious exit but beggars can't be choosers. He shone his cap lamp all around but couldn't see any rope, so he went back and shouted down the tunnel to his brother.

'Brian.'

'What?'

'Do you definitely need rope? I can't find any round here.'

'There's bound ter be summat we can use,' called back Brian. 'Hang on, I'll come out an' give yer a hand.'

Jacky recommenced his search and within half a minute was

enveloped in a thick, choking shower of dust that had him retreating up the roadway, coughing as he went. Then came a sudden clump, like someone slamming a massive door, deep inside the mine. But it wasn't a door and it wasn't far away. It was just the mine making its final adjustment; settling itself into position right on top of Albert and Fred. It ended their lives instantaneously. Men still alive and further down the face shuddered with fear. They knew what the sound was and prayed for their own survival. Jacky ran back to the tunnel. Dust was everywhere but he could just make out the glimmer of a cap lamp near the floor.

Brian was lying face up beneath a mountainous rock. The lower half of his body was buried and his face was covered in dusty blood. The roof all around was still held up by props which gave Jacky the confidence to approach and kneel beside his older brother.

'Brian . . . are you all right?'

Brian forced his eyes open. 'Can yer get me out?' he asked. 'It's bloody killin' me is this.'

Jacky shone his lamp on the rock which was pinning his brother to the floor. 'I think's it's too big, Brian.'

'Give it a try, Jacky boy.'

'Okay.'

Jacky went around the side of the rock and managed to get his fingers beneath it. He knew all along that it was hopeless but he didn't want Brian to think he hadn't tried. He heaved until he thought his damaged shoulder was going to snap off.

'I can't budge it, Brian. Hang on, I'll see if I can find something to lever it up with.'

'I'm thirsty,' Brian said. His voice was little more than a croak. 'I could murder a pint.'

'I've got a Spangle,' Jacky said. It sounded so pathetic.

'Okay,' murmured Brian. He opened his mouth to receive the sweet like a man receiving communion. Jacky placed it gently onto his brother's waiting tongue.

'I'll go look for something to make a lever.'

Brian shook his head. 'Don't leave me, Jacky. I can't feel owt now. We'll just wait 'til someone comes, eh?'

'Okay, Brian. Shouldn't be long.'

Brian closed his eyes and sucked on the Spangle, then the sucking stopped and Jacky instinctively knew this could prove

217

dangerous. If his brother fell asleep he might not wake up. He needed to keep Brian alert and thinking.

'It was me who took your bike,' he said.

Brian opened his eyes and croaked, 'I bloody knew it was you!' He spat the sweet out. 'Why did yer nick it?'

'I were that mad that yer'd set me up for wreckin' Boothie's office.'

Brian forced out a smile. 'I didn't mean for yer not ter take yer scholarship. He's a right pillock is Boothie.'

'He's that all right,' Jacky agreed.

Brian stared at him for a long time then said, 'Sorry . . . I've been a bit of a pillock meself.'

'I could never figure out why. It was always you that started stuff.'

Brian lay there, staring up at the rock ceiling, spitting out dust that was clogging up his mouth. 'Have yer got any more spice?' he said. 'I wish I hadn't spit that Spangle out now.'

'That was my last one.'

'Find it for us, will yer?'

Jacky searched around and found the remains of the sweet, caked in dust. He cleaned it off with the cuff of his coat then gave it a quick suck himself before he popped it back in his brother's mouth. 'Don't say I never give you anything,' he said.

Brian sucked away, thinking about Jacky's original question. 'I could never keep up wi' yer, that's why. Neither you nor our Ellie.'

'You never picked on Ellie.'

'She never gave me no backchat, didn't Ellie. It was as though she knew. You allus had a mouth on yer.'

'What? And you didn't? You gave me some right slaggings.'

It seemed an effort for Brian to turn his eyes to Jacky. 'Mebbe I allus wanted a younger brother I could stick up for. One what looked up ter me.'

'I looked up ter yer.' Jacky qualified this by adding, 'Sometimes.'

'Bollocks, Jacky. Yer never looked up ter no one.' He forced out a smile and his teeth shone white against his blackened face. 'Which is good, our kid. I wish I could be like that. Never look up ter no one. That's gonna be my motto from now on. Anyroad, if I've been a pillock to yer, I'm sorry. But it dunt mean ter say I'll stop bein' a pillock once I get out of here.'

'Once a pillock always a pillock,' said Jacky, with as much of a smile as he could muster. 'I wouldn't know what to do if I didn't have a pillock for a brother. By the way, what you just did for Fred and Albert, I'll always look up to you for that.'

'Didn't do much good, though. Do yer think they're dead?'

Jacky shrugged. 'I can't get to them, that's for sure.'

Brian coughed and a trickle of blood came from the corner of his mouth. Jacky saw it but chose not to mention it. He'd heard that blood coming someone's mouth was never a good sign. Brian's hand reached upwards. Jacky took hold of it.

'Am *I* goin' ter die, Jacky? I feel like shit.' Brian coughed again. More blood.

'Don't talk so soft, our kid. You don't die just because you feel like shit. You'll be okay. No worries about that.' The light was leaving his brother's eyes and Jacky knew these were empty words.

'Don't leave me, Jacky boy. Stay with me. I don't want to die on me own.'

'I won't. It shouldn't be long.' He heard digging sounds coming from down the roadway. 'I can hear them,' Jacky shouted. 'They're here, Brian. We're gonna be okay.'

But his brother's mind was elsewhere, 'Get that . . . bastard Mumford,' he words were punctuated by the weakest of coughs. His voice was scarcely audible.

'What?' Brian's words suddenly registered in Jacky's brain. 'Mumford? Oh, right. Don't worry, we'll get him.'

He wanted to say, Please don't die, Brian. Not now we're friends. But that might scare his brother. Scare him to death, maybe. The digging sounds seemed louder, more determined. Determined to save Brian's life.

'Are we . . . are we all right then . . . me an' you, Jacky boy?' It was a monumental effort for Brian to talk.

'Yeah, right as rain, our kid,' Jacky assured him. 'You'll be buyin' me that pint before you know it.' *Don't you dare die on me now.*

'That's all right, then . . . Oh, before I forget . . .'

'What?' asked Jacky, his mouth was now inches from Brian's face as his brother coughed out his words. The remains of the Spangle appeared between his now bloodied teeth and Jacky removed it, gently.

'Yer'd best tell me mam I love her . . . I reckon she'll want to hear that . . . Yer know what she's like. Tell our Ellie the same.' As the light died from his eyes he mouthed the words, 'You an' all.'

A silent declaration that Jacky would always remember.

'I love you as well, our kid,' he said.

But Brian didn't hear. He had died with his eyes open and holding his younger brother's hand. Jacky's tears, lit only by his cap lamp, dripped onto Brian's dirty, bloodied face. It was the saddest he'd felt in his life. He was still there twenty minutes later when the pit rescue men arrived.

Jacky was the last to come out alive. Twelve men, three of them badly injured, had already been brought to the surface by rescue teams working from the other end of the face. Nine men were still down there, including Brian, Albert, Fred and Clem. All nine were dead. The road Jacky had escaped into was blocked and it had taken the rescuers almost two hours to break through. By this time Maureen had given up all hope.

At first she couldn't understand why Jacky should be numbered among the missing. On the way there Charlie had assured her that Jacky would be working well away from any danger and would be waiting for her when she got there. Sid, the onsetter, saw her and told her otherwise.

'It were my fault,' he told her. 'I had a message needed sendin' ter Clem Simson about his wife and I sent young Jacky. Christ! I hope the lad's okay.'

'Yer'd no bloody right!' Charlie roared. 'He's a lad . . . lads have no business bein' at pit bloody face!'

'Charlie, it's okay,' said Maureen. 'He meant no harm. Let's wait and find out what's happened.'

Shortly afterwards Ellie joined them, and they stood together in a shocked little group waiting to hear. Most of the rescued and safe men had left the pit yard with their friends and loved ones.

The first two dead men came up in the cage. The gates were opened by the manager. A short discussion took place and he turned and went across to one of the waiting groups. A young woman collapsed and had to be supported. Then the manager looked towards another group which included a middle-aged woman.

'Not my Barry?' said the woman.

'I'm sorry, lass.'

She nodded her acceptance of her fate with a quiet dignity and went over to see her son. Kneeling down beside him she buried her head in his chest and sobbed gently as the men stood by, quiet and helpless. She had lost her husband in the war and now this. The bereaved young woman was helped to her husband's side, where she flung herself on him and cried, loudly and pitifully.

These sad cameos were repeated twice more. It was becoming unbearable for the waiting friends and loved ones to see the cage arrive, only to find it wasn't bringing up their man.

Then a shout came from the winding engine house which was linked by phone to the pit bottom.

'They've found another live one!'

An odd sound came from the waiting people. Speaking in a strange, wordless voice. Not happy, not sad. The voice of hope. Joe, the engineman, went back into the engine house and picked up the phone; then he put it back down and came out again. He looked at Maureen and imparted his news without the hint of a smile.

'It's your Jacky. He's okay.'

Maureen felt a rush of relief, then she ran past disappointed faces to confront Joe. 'Did they say anything about Brian?' she asked. 'I'm told Jacky must have been with him. Are they both all right?'

Jacky had told his rescuers about Brian, Albert, Fred and Clem. Joe knew this. He looked, sorrowfully, at Maureen.

'From what I hear, I don't think there's anyone else left alive down there, love. It's a right bloody mess. Jacky's on his way up in t' upcast shaft over yon.'

He pointed to an adjacent shaft identified by its winding wheel which had just started turning, bringing one of her lost sons back to her. Maureen, Ellie and Charlie walked towards it. The only thing going through Maureen's mind was whether or not the boys had managed to make up their differences in time. And she felt ashamed and guilty at the relief she had got when she heard Jacky was alive. It more than outweighed Brian's death. That wasn't right. Christ! What sort of mother was she?

Chapter Twenty-Four

They sat around the dining table, the survivors of the Gaskell family. The funeral guests had left and Maureen's gaze went from one to the other. 'It's been a bad five years for you two kids. You've lost a father each and now a brother.'

'I've lost two dads and a brother.'

'Sorry . . . I know you have, Jacky.'

'Frank McGovern's special to me as well,' Ellie reminded her mother. 'Even though I never met him. I never thought we'd lose our Brian, though.'

'He died a hero,' said Jacky. 'He'd have liked that would our kid.'

'They were all heroes in their own way,' agreed Maureen. 'Bert was an unlikely hero, but maybe he was the bravest of the three.'

She got no argument from Jacky or Ellie. Brian was buried at the side of Bert, the man he'd regarded as his father for most of his life. Maureen had drawn enormous comfort from the story Jacky had told her of the last hour of that life. How brave he had been, going back to help Fred and Albert; how he and Jacky had become friends at last, and how Brian had said to tell Mam and Ellie that he loved them. Jacky had quoted Brian's words verbatim so that Maureen would know he wasn't just making it up for her benefit.

'Do you remember what his last words were?' Maureen suddenly asked. She was wearing the same outfit she had for Bert's funeral and she looked no less beautiful.

Jacky was sure his brother had meant these words to be personal and had resolved to keep it that way. A part of his brother that was his and his alone; no one else's not even his mother. He looked into her eyes and immediately lost his resolve.

'After he told me to tell you he loved you and Ellie . . . he sort of told me he loved me as well.' He wrinkled his nose as he said it, mildly embarrassed. This left his mother and sister in floods. Jacky wasn't sure he'd done the right thing.

'Sorry,' he said.

Ellie took his hand. 'Don't be,' she told him. 'It's the most beautiful thing I've ever heard.'

'Aw, give over.'

This meant it would be repeated time and again and Jacky wished he'd kept it to himself. 'Mind you, it's something I'll never forget,' he admitted, tearful himself now. 'I told him I loved him as well . . . but it was too late.'

'No it wasn't,' Ellie assured him. 'He'll have known.'

'Deep down, Brian was a good boy,' said Maureen, drying her eyes. 'I never stopped loving him, even when he did the stuff he did.'

'He never said a wrong word to me,' Ellie told her mother.

'He thought the sun shone out of your backside,' said Jacky. 'He'd have run through a brick wall for you, our Ellie.'

'He once thumped Terry Connolly for saying mucky things about me,' she remembered. 'I was only thirteen.'

'Mucky things about you!' said Maureen. 'I'd have thumped him myself if I'd known?'

'It was harmless,' laughed Ellie. 'My bust was beginning to show and Terry made some rude remark. I've forgotten what it was now. Our Brian wasn't having any of it, though.'

Jacky looked out through the window at the bright, spring sky. 'I wonder what he'll be thinking? All of us down here saying nice things about him.' He walked around the table to his mother and placed a comforting arm around her shoulder. 'He died a hero's death, did our kid. And I'm gonna have his name inscribed on my watch alongside Frank's.' He sat down again and, as if to mark this decision with a celebration, he fished out a packet of State Express from his pocket and took one out without looking up at his mother for her approval. It was the first time he'd attempted to smoke in her presence.

'Er . . . excuse me, young man. How long have you been smoking?'

He gave her a defiant grin. 'Six months, maybe. All I wanted to do when I was stuck down that pit was have a fag. All our kid wanted was a pint of Tetley's. Anyway, I thought you knew I smoked.'

'I did know. I just thought I'd ask, that's all. It's bad for you, you know that.'

'Is it?'

'Yes, it is. And I'll tell you something that's even worse.'

'What?'

'Smoking a cig without offering them round.'

'Eh?'

'Offer them round. It's called manners.'

'Mam, you hardly ever smoke.'

'I do in times of stress.'

Jacky offered the packet to her. She took one, so did Ellie.

'Hey!' Jacky grumbled to his sister. 'I know for a fact you don't smoke. I only had three left.'

'Times of stress,' said Ellie, taking a light from Maureen and coughing out the smoke. She looked at Jacky and smiled, mischievously. 'I'll get used to them. You keep buying, I'll keep smoking.'

'I think I'll give up,' he said. 'I can't afford it.'

The three of them smoked in silence. It was a rare, contented moment in Maureen's life. A moment she'd needed after the week of trauma she'd had. Only a week? A lifetime more like. Maybe one day her life would hit smooth waters. Then her thoughts turned to Bill and her moment of contentment was gone. Bill was another trauma in the making if ever there was one, but she couldn't get him out of her thoughts. If only he wasn't married. The wisest course of action would be to steer clear of PC Bill Scanlon and let her life settle down; do that and all her problems would be behind her. No point looking for trouble. Jacky's voice interrupted her thoughts.

'Do you know what else Brian said just before he died?'

His mind was a thousand feet below ground, watching the life drain out of his brother.

Maureen and Ellie looked at him, waiting for him to answer his own question. He glanced up at them and hesitated, wondering if he was stirring up a hornets' nest once again. He could still hear Brian's voice and the fading light in his eyes as he coughed out his last few words. Jacky felt he had no right to keep any of these words from his mother and sister.

'He said, "Get Mumford".'

'Get Mumford?' repeated Ellie.

'In fact, if you want me to quote him,' Jacky added, 'he said, "Get that bastard Mumford" – and I'll tell you what, he's right. I've been thinking about it a lot. That two years he did for fraud an' stuff wasn't enough for takin' Frank's life.'

The two women went quiet, for different reasons. Maureen's heart sank when she looked from one face to another. Then she closed her eyes as she realised the implications. Jacky was of course right. Mumford held the key to all the unhappiness her family had suffered over the last few years. But she was older and wiser and she knew that life wasn't just or perfect and the best thing would be to forget about Mumford or he'd haunt them forever.

'How do we get him, though?' Ellie asked. 'What we tried last time was stupid.'

'That was your idea,' Jacky pointed out.

'Thanks for reminding me. I'm sorry you got caught and locked up.'

'Hey, I'm not blaming you for that, Ellie. If Mumford hadn't farted we'd have got away with it.'

Maureen hadn't heard this part of the story. Jacky filled her in on the details – telling the story as only he could, and having her laughing.

'I gave birth to a right trio,' she chuckled. 'A hero and two comedians.'

Her face straightened as she faced up to the reality of a situation that needed resolving once and for all before they could get on with their lives. Mumford had done the family so much harm. While he was in jail he'd been out of sight, out of mind. However, he was a free man now, a man absolved of his known crimes. But only in the eyes of the law. Not in the eyes of God and the Gaskell family. The truth of the matter was that they either lived with the injustice or they let it continue to ruin their lives.

'One thing that always puzzled me,' said Jacky, 'was what happened to the knife he stabbed his wife with?'

Maureen sighed. How many times had she heard this? 'We don't know,' she said, patiently. 'The police don't know, only Mumford knows. The truth is we'll never know. And if we don't accept that, it'll drive us mad. We need to forget it and get on with our lives.'

'Well, he obviously got rid of it before the police came,' said Ellie to Jacky. Maureen sighed again and shook her head.

'I suppose he must,' Jacky agreed. 'But we know he probably didn't leave his house – or at least his garden – between stabbing her and the cops coming. It's always puzzled me.'

'It puzzled Bill as well,' Maureen said. 'It's a puzzle he spent a lot of time trying to solve, and remember, he was at the crime scene.'

'But *we* know Frank didn't do it,' Jacky said. 'So what happened to it?'

'For God's sake!' said Maureen, stubbing out her cigarette. 'We've got to let this thing go.'

Ellie gave her mother a benign smile and suggested to Jacky, 'Maybe with the police thinking Frank had taken it they didn't search Mumford's property as thoroughly as they should. And as soon as they left, he got rid of it.'

'Maybe,' Jacky agreed. 'That'd be the sensible thing to do. The thing that someone who isn't a nutter would do.'

'You mean the sort of nutter who claims on insurance for a watch, then carries on wearing it?' said Ellie.

'Exactly that sort of nutter,' Jacky said, happy to have an accomplice in his theory. 'Someone who thinks he can get away with murder.'

Maureen could see where this was going. She held up her hands to stop them taking this any further.

'Whoa! Hold it right there. You are *not* breaking into his house again to look for a knife. Anyway, even if you find a knife how are you going to link it to the murder after all these years? The woman's been cremated. It could be any old knife you find.'

'Blood, fingerprints?' surmised Jacky. 'I don't know. It was just a thought, that's all.'

'He'd have wiped it clean,' his mother pointed out, wearily.

'Maybe not,' Jacky said. 'Who knows how nutters think?'

'I think we should ask Bill,' decided Ellie, looking at her mother. 'What do you think, Mam? It'd do no harm.'

'Bill?' said Maureen. 'Well, I don't suppose it would do any harm.' She wasn't entirely against this idea, but perhaps not for the same reasons as her children. Whatever the future held in store for her it wasn't going to be plain sailing. She wouldn't know what to do with it if it was.

'Oh, by the way, I spoke to Herbert Attercliffe at the funeral,' Jacky told her. 'He said I can have the job if I want it.'

'And . . .?'

'I start Monday. My sick leave's up at the pit. I'm going to tell them I'm not going back.'

'I think they'll understand,' said Maureen. 'Does Mr Attercliffe know about your little escapade with the dead body?'

Jacky smiled, mainly at the memory of Aaron. 'He mentioned it. He reckoned if I could take a dead body for a drive in the country and sit her in a bus shelter I was cut out for the job.'

The following day Mumford watched Ellie stride down the street once again and the germ of an idea formed in his mind. It was over four years since he'd murdered Marion – five since he'd killed his wife – and he needed to quench his raging thirst for more of the same. His memories of the killings had kept him going during his time in prison. Now he was more than ready to do it again. Killing women was easy – he'd proved that twice. Fraud was a crime he'd stay clear of in future. He wasn't cut out for fraud – too honest a person deep down. But killing naked women – that was something he had a real flare for.

Chapter Twenty-Five

'This thing with Mumford – the kids can't let it go. They want you to help them find the murder knife.'

Maureen was walking back from the pictures with Bill. It slightly worried her that he didn't seem to care who saw them together. As it happened, the people who knew Maureen didn't know who Bill was, and vice versa, so no one made a connection and it hadn't been a problem. But even if it had, Bill didn't seem to care. Maureen knew his wife was in a wheelchair, but that was all she knew. She never asked about Pam, assuming Bill would broach the subject when he was good and ready. He never had.

'Find the murder knife after five years? Bit of a tall order.'

'You might have to humour them. Then tell them how impossible it all is, and how they must learn to let go.'

'Maybe it's too much for them to let go,' Bill said. 'Especially for Jacky.'

'My Jacky only knew him for ten minutes.'

'I suspect it was the longest ten minutes of his life.'

She couldn't argue with this so she just nodded and went on, 'Jacky has this half-baked theory that the murder weapon's still around somewhere. And if we can find it we can prove Mumford did the murder.'

Bill nodded and chewed Jacky's theory over in his mind. Maureen's arm was linked in his, and to the world they looked just like a husband and wife out for a stroll, chatting amiably about family affairs.

'Maybe the first part of his theory's not so half-baked – the bit about the missing knife,' he mused.

'Oh heck, not you as well. I was hoping you'd tell him to forget it.'

'Well, I will if you want.'

Maureen shook her head. 'What I want is for it all to go away. But it seems to me it won't – not while Mumford's still around.'

Bill continued with his musing. 'That blasted knife seemed to vanish off the face of the earth. Trouble is, I'm not sure what could be done now, even if it did turn up. God, I wish there was something I could do to make your life easier.' He put his arm around her and squeezed her to him. The pleasure she got from this was tinged with guilt. She needed a man like Bill in her life. In her life and in her bed.

Across the road was a man in a wheelchair being pushed along by a woman, probably his wife. His head was slumped and one of his trouser legs was tucked underneath him – legless and empty. The crippled man had a grey, gaunt face that looked to have aged quickly. He could have been sixty but Maureen guessed he was more likely to be in his thirties, possibly a casualty of war. In fact on closer inspection he was wearing a short row of medals on his jacket. Maybe his wife had stuck them there to show what the war had cost them and to make able-bodied people feel guilty. The woman appeared long-suffering but had no doubt accepted her burden as part of her wedding vows. *For better or for worse.* Maureen looked at the couple and then back at Bill to see if he looked guilty – but he hadn't noticed them. He was too engrossed in his thoughts.

'He's a creepy little bugger is Mumford,' he said. 'I was in court when he got sent down. He started crying when they took him away. I've never seen a man look so sorry for himself. I reckon he did his wife in without a second thought.'

'I bet he laughed when they hanged Frank,' said Maureen, bitterly. 'That's what I can't handle. The thought of him laughing at Frank being hanged.'

'Did you love Frank?' Bill asked, suddenly.

Maureen answered without hesitation.

'Yes.'

He gave her another squeeze and she was tempted to add that she loved Bill as well. But this would complicate her life just a bit too much.

'I reckon if Mumford did do it he's the type to kill again,' Bill

229

remarked. 'Weirdos like that have no conscience. They do it to make up for being so inadequate. If he does kill again he might slip up. That could be the time to nail him.'

'Maybe he already has killed again.'

'Could have. There's a missing person's list as long as your arm. Most of them turn up. Not all of them though.'

'What do you think happens to those who don't turn up?' Maureen asked.

'Who knows? It's not as difficult as you think to vanish into the woodwork without anyone knowing, or even caring where you are. Some of them have good reason to take off – family problems, debt, fed up with their old life – all sorts of things. Some of them might be dead for one reason or another.'

'Including murder?'

'Including murder.'

'Better not tell Jacky,' said Maureen, 'or he'll be digging Mumford's garden up, looking for a body.'

Bill laughed. 'He's a lad is that. If I had a lad I'd like him to be like young Jacky.'

It could be arranged, Maureen thought. She looked at him and wondered, not for the first time, where their relationship was headed. Suddenly she wanted him more than she'd ever allowed herself to realise. They had been going out together for almost three years now and yet she scarcely knew him at all.

'Bill, I know we don't talk about your private life, but I've often wondered . . . why didn't you have children?'

He'd never mentioned his wife, except that she'd broken her back in an accident at a dance hall, but he hadn't elaborated, which was okay by Maureen; it was a road she didn't want to travel down. They were friends, not lovers – kissing cousins, Bill said. Both wanted more but Maureen wasn't prepared to allow their friendship to go inside the bedroom door; she didn't want to share his body with his wife. For a decent man considering leaving an empty marriage, a wife in a wheelchair is an insurmountable obstacle. And Maureen knew it.

He didn't answer at first. She was ready for him to ask what business it was of hers.

'It was Pam's decision,' he said, after some thought. 'She said she wouldn't be able to cope. I always thought it might be something to do with her not wanting to be left with the kids if our

230

marriage went wrong – there's some sense in that when you come to think of it.'

'So she was never sure of you?'

Bill smiled and shook his head. 'Are we wise, talking about Pam after all this time?'

'Maybe not.'

'But you'd like to?'

'Yes, I think I would,' she admitted. 'You're probably the best friend I've got in the world, but I know so little about you.'

'Don't you have any friends at Lipscombe and Lile?'

'Oh, I've been out with some of the girls, but . . .' She pulled a face.

'But they're not your type?'

'Not really.'

'Not many women are your type, Maureen. Certainly not many round here.'

'Hey, we were talking about you,' she reminded him. 'Don't change the subject.'

'Right,' he grinned. They rounded a corner and the lights of a pub came into view. 'Buy me a drink and loosen my tongue. I think I'll have a glass of whatever that lad on the back row was on.'

It was a Monday night and they'd been to the first house at the Rialto to see *Bus Stop* with Marilyn Monroe. They had sat just two rows in front of where Sandra Symonite was treating her latest boyfriend to one of her covert manipulations, only the boyfriend had lacked self-control and, as the big moment approached, he had let out a mounting howl of ecstasy that had Sandra hurrying from the cinema, leaving her erstwhile beau to face his embarrassment on his own. Maureen smiled at the recent memory.

'I don't think you get that out of bottles,' she said.

'Pity.'

'Won't Pam be expecting you home?'

'I'm a copper. She'll think I'm working overtime.'

'What will she be doing right now?'

Bill looked at his watch. 'Well, she'll be home from the stamp club, so I guess she'll be faffing around with her albums.'

'Stamp club?'

'She's a stamp collector,' Bill explained. 'Her choice of hobby's a bit limited. She plays the piano a bit and reads a lot.'

231

'I see.'

They sat in a booth, opposite one another. Bill was smoking and Maureen was resisting the temptation – not the the only temptation she was resisting. He was an attractive man and his scarred forehead was a part of that attraction; an heroic scar. A scar earned in combat.

'It's my fault she's crippled,' Bill said, almost as soon as they had sat down. It was as though he wanted to get that out of the way. Maureen just said, 'Oh.'

'I didn't do it on purpose.'

'I don't expect you did.'

'We were drunk and fooling around in a dance hall and I managed to drop her on the floor. Broke her back.'

'Oh no!'

'Oh yes, I'm afraid.'

This seemed to explain some unasked questions, one of which was 'Is that why you married her?'

'Everybody *expected* us to get married,' he said. 'We'd been going out together for four years. Never had another girlfriend before I met Pam. If I hadn't married her after doing that to her—'

'Before that happened you weren't *planning* on marrying her, were you?' she guessed. Her eyes searched his for the truth. Bill held her gaze for a second, then smiled and looked down.

'As a matter of fact I was planning on packing her in that very night. Only I'd drunk a bit too much and instead of getting on with it, I started to act the goat with her.'

'Typical man. Too ready to take the easy way out when it comes to relationships. Why were you packing her in?'

'I'd met Kathy McAlister.'

'Kathy McAlister?'

'The girl I should have married.'

Maureen took his hand and squeezed it. 'Poor Bill. Trust you to do the noble thing.'

'Yeah,' he sighed. 'Trust me . . . Pam's not a bad woman. You'd probably like her.'

I doubt that, Maureen thought.

He took a deep drink and placed his glass back down on the table. 'She knew all along, of course,' he said.

'Knew . . . knew what?'

232

'She knew I was going to pack her in. She knew about Kathy McAlister. I only found out a few years ago. Round about the time I first met you, as it happens.'

'You're not saying she broke her back on purpose, just to trap you into marriage?'

Bill gave a short laugh. 'Hardly. In a way I don't even blame her. You see, I know she loved me. Still does . . . I think.'

'If she really loved you, wouldn't she have let you go?'

He shook his head. 'Think about it, Maureen. Pam had not only just lost the use of her legs but she was also in danger of losing the man she loved. She's only human, for God's sake. All she did was salvage what she could – which was me.'

'Sounds to me like you're making excuses for her.'

There was a bitterness in Maureen's voice. There was obviously no way forward. She definitely wanted more from Bill, but Pam's disabilty was just too big an obstacle. She couldn't ask Bill to leave his wife. Maybe she should just cut her losses and stop seeing him.

He took her hand and said, 'Without me, Pam hasn't got a life.'

'Does she know you're seeing me?'

'Possibly. She wouldn't say, even if she did. She doesn't want to rock the boat, you see.'

'I think she's being selfish!'

'Maybe she is. Maybe she's got reason to be selfish.'

'Bill, all this guilt's ruining your life. Under the same circumstances I wouldn't have married you, not if I loved you. She had an accident. If you hadn't been involved in it, would you have married her?'

'No, I don't suppose I would. Look, I've been through all this a million times. If you want to end what little we've got I won't blame you. Or we can go on as we are and if someone else comes along for you I won't stand in your way.'

She sipped her drink and mulled over his words, looking at him, steadily, over her glass. 'There isn't anyone,' she said, eventually. 'Not at the moment, anyway'

'Good.'

'What happened to Kathy McAlister?'

'Kathy McAlister.' He spoke her name with fondness. 'She took it very badly. It was one of those instant attraction things.'

'You mean love at first sight?'

233

'Something like that. I'd taken her out a couple of times and I just knew she was the one – at least I thought she was. Maureen, I was nineteen, what the hell do you know when you're nineteen?'

'I'll tell you what you know. You know who you love when it comes along – it doesn't happen all that often.'

'Doesn't it?'

'Once, maybe twice in a lifetime.'

Their eyes met and Bill said, quietly, 'All right. I suppose I kid myself that I can't have known an emotion as deep as that at nineteen. But you're right. I definitely loved Kathy McAlister.'

'And you broke her heart for Pam. Wow!'

'I broke my own heart, I know that.'

'I can't believe I'm hearing this. Bill, how could you do it?'

'Well, it wasn't easy.'

'It wasn't sensible either.'

'Maureen, I had no option. It was the hardest thing I've ever done in my life. When I told Kathy what I'd decided she just started crying. She didn't say anything, she just backed away from me as though I was carrying some sort of plague. Next thing I knew she was engaged to a lad from Ferrybridge. They got married and moved away. To be honest I was sick when I heard.'

'Sounds like a rebound job. She'll still be carrying a torch for you.'

'I hope she's not. I really wouldn't like her to be unhappy.'

'Believe me, Bill, she'll still be unhappy about losing you. Basically, you got your sums wrong.'

'What?'

'You made two people unhappy and just one person happy. That's bad arithmetic. And I'm not convinced that you're the love of Pam's life.'

She took one of his cigarettes from the packet lying on the table between them and put it between her lips for Bill to light. He frowned slightly.

'I thought you didn't smoke.'

'I don't, normally.'

She took a drag, coughed slightly and said, 'Did I ever tell you I hate moustaches?'

'What? Not that I can remember. I happen to like my moustache. Kathy hated it, that was the only good thing that came out

234

of me packing her in. She'd have persuaded me to shave it off. Pam says it suits me.'

'Whatever Pamela wants, eh?'

'Ah, sorry.'

'What for? If you'd chosen Kathy McAlister I wouldn't be here with you now.'

Maureen said it with a short smile, which Bill returned when he recognised the irony of the situation. Or was there more to this situation than just irony? He needed to get something absolutely clear in his head.

'No,' he agreed. 'You wouldn't be here. But you are. And the situation's not ideal for you. But, despite that, you're still here.'

'You're not a policeman for nothing.'

'Maureen,' he said, gravely. 'Can I ask you a very important question?'

'Do I have to give a very important answer?'

'I'd like you to.'

'Fire away.'

'Maureen . . .' He was nervous. She was curious.

'That's me,' she said.

'Maureen. Just so I know exactly where we stand. Am I . . . am I right in thinking that you're prepared to give me a second chance at which choice to make – the happiness choice or the noble choice?'

She unravelled his thoughts and put them back to him in plain English. 'You mean, will I have you if you ever decide to leave Pam?'

'Something like that.'

From the look in his eyes she knew if she said 'Yes' the noble choice might well fly straight out of the window, thus condemning his chairbound wife to a life of bitterness. She would get her man, but at the cost of a lifetime of unwarranted guilt, and she'd spent enough time living with guilt. If ever that happened the responsibility had to be all his. He must first leave Pam for all the right reasons and then take his chance with her. Even then it could be too much of a burden. The recent image of the man in the wheelchair came to her mind.

'Sorry, Bill,' she said. 'I don't want to be responsible for you leaving your wife.'

235

Chapter Twenty-Six

Fozzie Symonite was working a pneumatic drill, digging up the tarmac outside Mumford's office. He was the most junior member of the four-man council gang doing road repairs. Two of the others were shovelling the flaked-off tarmac into a dumper which was being driven by a fourth man. The hardest job had been left to Fozzie, the youngest, the biggest and the thickest. The noise brought Mumford to his shop door where he stood, glaring at Fozzie.

The youth yanked the jack-hammer out of the road and wiped his forehead with the back of his hand. It was late summer 1956.

'Will you be making that noise for long?' Mumford called out. 'We can't hear ourselves think in here.'

'Long as it teks, pal,' retorted Fozzie. Then he recognised Mumford. 'Hey! I know you.' His voice was unnecessarily loud. The other workers stopped shovelling to see who the lad was shouting at.

Mumford sniffed. 'I hardly think so.'

'I bloody do – I know yer. You're the feller what got locked up cos o' Jacky Gaskell.'

Mumford spun on his heel and disappeared into the shop. He didn't want his past life discussed in the street by roadmenders and the like. What he didn't know was that he and Fozzie had something, or someone, in common.

Jacky Gaskell had once again come into Fozzie's life, insofar as he'd got that joinery job that Fozzie had wanted. A job that would have given him a proper trade, not just being a labourer.

After a while the gang stopped for a tea break and Fozzie made his way into the shop. Mumford was sitting at a corner desk, poring over a ledger and running a pencil up a column of figures, adding them up as he went. The hair at the back of head was thinning and his suit, which he'd bought prior to going to jail, looked too big for him. The youth leaned on the counter and spoke through a mouthful of cheese and egg sandwich.

'He's a pillock, that Jacky Gaskell.'

'Can I help you?' inquired the girl on the counter.

Fozzie shook his head at her, spraying crumbs from his mouth. 'I'm talkin' to '*im*, love,' he said, nodding at Mumford, who turned and looked at him, bleakly.

The girl regarded Fozzie with distaste, then she addressed Mumford. 'Is it all right if I nip out to the Post Office? We need stamps.'

She left without waiting for a reply, so eager was she to remove herself from Fozzie's unwholesome presence. The youth watched her leave before returning his attention to Mumford. 'It were Gaskell's sister what made up that song about yer. I bet yer didn't know that, did yer?'

'Look, would you mind leaving?' snapped Mumford, irritably. 'It's bad enough trying to work with all that racket going on outside without being disturbed by the likes of you.'

Fozzie seemed impervious to Mumford's insult. 'Yer all right, mister. I know that song's a load o' bollocks. They're a family of bloody liars are them Gaskells – liars an' murderers. He were Jacky's dad were that McGovern. Him what topped your missis. Yer know that, don't yer? That meks Jacky a proper bastard.'

'Yes, I do know that. Now would you mind leav—?'

'We stuffed him well an' truly once,' chortled Fozzie, spraying more crumbs. 'Me an' that newspaper geezer. Stuffed 'im like a Christmas turkey.'

'Look, if you don't leave I shall have to ring—' Mumford choked back his threat and studied the masticating youth. 'Weren't you the boy with his picture in the paper, some years ago? The one assaulted by young Gaskell?'

Fozzie grinned, displaying an array of brown and broken teeth. 'Black eye, busted lip – that were me. We set 'im up, me an' that newspaper geezer.'

'Set him up? I thought young Gaskell beat you up?'

'Give over. D'yer honestly think a scrawny little pillock like that could beat me up? Nah, we set him up. I'm surprised yer let a

237

little pillock like that get yer sent down. If it'd been me I'd have stuffed him up again.'

'Oh, and how would you have done that?' There was both scorn and curiosity in Mumford's question. He didn't think such a lout would have the brain power to 'stuff up' the Gaskell boy. But you never know.

Fozzie shrugged and pushed a piece of escaping cheese back into his mouth with a grimy finger. There was a hair growing out of the mole above his lip, which added to his general unsavouriness. 'Mebbe I'd ring that newspaper geezer up. Him what's allus writin' about Gaskell. He wrote about you once, if I remember rightly. When yer got banged up 'cos o' Gaskell.'

'Oh, him. Did more harm than good. Ninety per cent fiction, ten per cent fact.'

Fozzie didn't understand percentages but he grasped Mumford's meaning. 'They don't give a sod what they write just as long as they make a few quid. I reckon you an' him could cook up a right story about them bloody Gaskells. That's what they do, yer know, these newspaper geezers. They mek stories outa nowt. I tell yer what, if *I'd* done time for Gaskell I know I'd like ter stuff 'im.'

Mumford studied Fozzie intently; his brain was ticking over with the kernel of an idea. 'This newspaper fellow . . . I don't suppose you remember his name, do you?'

'I might,' grinned Fozzie, rubbing his thumb across his fingers in the time-honoured way.

Mumford took a note out of his wallet and held it just out of Fozzie's grasp. The youth eyed it disparagingly.

'Ten bob? It's gorra be worth a quid. I've still got t' paper wi' me picture in it. It's got this geezer's name in it. Give us a quid an' I'll nip 'ome at dinner time and fetch it. Yer can only look at it, though. It's th' only one I've got. Never 'ad me picture in t' paper before.'

'Okay, a pound . . . and please . . .'

'What?'

'Try not to make as much noise out there.'

Fozzie wiped his mouth with the back of his hand, leaving a smear of grime. 'Give us half a dollar and yer on.'

Mumford hesitated, then handed over half a crown. 'Word of honour?' he said.

238

'Word of honour,' grinned Fozzie. 'I've finished on t' jack-hammer. It's all shovellin' an' diggin' now.'

Mumford scowled at being duped so easily by someone of, seemingly, a lesser species. 'In that case you only get seventeen and six this afternoon.'

Fozzie opened his mouth to protest.

'Or nothing,' said Mumford.

Mumford's plan was already in place by the time Fozzie turned up with the old newspaper. He led the youth through to the back office, away from the disapproving stare of his counter clerk. Then he nodded his approval as he read the story of how Fozzie had been beaten up by the son of Frank McGovern.

'So, this Rodney Tripp put you up to it, did he?'

'Yeah. I don't know where he got me name from. I had ter make it look as if Gaskell had beaten me up, so he could take a photo of me.'

'How much did he pay you?'

Fozzie worked out the maths laboriously. 'Half a crown,' he said, 'then two bob.'

'Four and six to take a beating like that? And I'm giving you a pound just to bring me a newspaper. I must be going soft.'

Fozzie's face turned uglier than usual. He pushed it into Mumford's, who recoiled. 'Hey, yer greasy little bastard! We've gorra deal.'

'All right, all right. I didn't say we hadn't,' placated Mumford. He took a ten-shilling note and a handful of change from his pocket and counted it out. 'There, seventeen and six, paid in full.' He wrote down a few details from the article and gave Fozzie the newspaper back. The youth took the money and went outside. A minute later he started up the pneumatic drill once again. He did it purely to annoy Mumford to whom he had taken a dislike. But Mumford was oblivious to the noise. He had a plan which would damn the Gaskell family and earn him a lot of public sympathy; and public sympathy would help his business. It would be tricky, dangerous even, if he didn't take every precaution, but there was a way. A way which included the slapdash but punctual Mrs Fisk and the amoral Rodney Tripp.

Clarice Fisk, Mumford's daily help, was nothing if not punctual. She came in at nine a.m. precisely, three times a week, gave

239

the house a light dusting, washed his dishes, put out the empty milk bottles and helped herself to food from his fridge. He'd thought about sacking her but he couldn't face the task of finding a replacement – and she was better than nothing, just. As the plan unfolded in his mind a thin smile leaked across his face. It spread further when he found Rodney Tripp's number in the phone book under Tripp R., Investigative Journalist.

A short while later Les Bradfield walked in and asked what sort of a day Victor had had. Mumford assumed a confused expression and said, mysteriously, 'Hard, Les . . . maybe too hard. I think I'll go home. I can't take much more of this.'

'Are you all right, Victor?'

Mumford was already leaving. 'I just need time to think, that's all. All the best, Les.'

At five to nine the following morning Mumford sat in his car wondering about switching the engine on. How long did this thing normally take? He had no real idea but he was fairly certain it would be a lot more than five minutes.

His car was in the garage and there was a garden hose running from the exhaust and in through the car window. He turned on the engine and was surprised that he didn't break down with a fit of coughing. No problem. He could take this for five minutes without passing out. As a precaution he kept his fingers on the ignition switch. If he felt drowsy he would switch off, but not until the last minute. He had to make it look as realistic as possible, but he was not going to gamble his life on Clarice Fisk's punctuality.

In the event, the carbon monoxide fumes quickly sabotaged his senses and Clarice Fisk did indeed save his life. She was a big woman. Big enough to drag him out of the car and into his driveway where she left him, gasping and coughing, as she ran into his house to ring for an ambulance.

Two policemen came to interview him in his hospital bed and he told them he was very sorry to have been so much trouble but he'd had personal problems dating right back to the time his wife had been murdered by Frank McGovern. Then he said he was tired, closed his eyes and feigned sleep as he listened for their reaction. The two officers stood a few feet away from his bed and, after a few minutes began to speak in low voices.

'I wonder if there's any truth in that song the kids sing?'

Mumford could feel their eyes on him. He gave a light snore; they continued with their conversation.

'According ter Billy them Gaskells reckon he's still got that knife in his house somewhere.'

'Hey! Wasn't it Billy Scanlon who felt this feller's collar?'

'I reckon he's having it off with the mother.'

'Can't say I blame him – have yer seen her? She's a bit of all right.'

'I know – I wouldn't climb over her ter get ter my missis.'

There was mutual sniggering and the conversation dwindled away down the ward and into the corridor. Mumford waited until he was sure they'd gone for good then he went to the phone and rang Rodney Tripp.

'My name is Victor Mumford,' he said, 'and I have a story which might interest you.'

Jacky had taken the job with Attercliffe's, Joiners and Undertakers. Half a dozen lads had applied for the job, including Fozzie, but Herbert Attercliffe knew a good prospect when he saw one.

'Yer need a good head on yer shoulders ter be a joiner, lad. It's the only trade worth learnin' nowadays. They'll not need brickies much longer, not with all this crappy concrete stuff they're puttin' up. There'll come a day soon when if yer need a good brickie yer'll have ter tek a shovel ter t' cemetery an' dig one up.'

Jacky spent that summer helping a joiner to fix roof trusses on a new council housing estate, one that Maureen had her eye on. The weather was warm and Jacky was happy and felt he had found his niche in life. None of the family had spoken about Mumford since the day of Brian's funeral. Jacky had no bright ideas about how to prove his dad's innocence and, as one good day turned into another, the thought of exacting impossible justice went further and further from his thoughts.

On occasions he was sent to help pick up bodies and take them to the funeral parlour, but this was a branch of the business he wished to avoid, despite it being lucrative and a never-ending source of income; his day 'on the run' with Aaron had put him off dead bodies for life. It was on one of these trips, late in the summer, that his contented life took yet another jolt. He was with Herbert Attercliffe when he went to collect the body of a

241

man well into his eighties who had died on the toilet during the night.

'He'll not cost us much in wood,' winked Herbert, as they got out of the hearse and knocked on the door. 'Poor owd Alfie's not t' size o' two penn'orth o' copper. It's t' biggest wonder he didn't fall down t' pot. I've seen more meat on a butcher's pencil.'

His knock started a dog barking inside. Herbert swept off his hat when an old woman came to the door. Relief flooded over her face when she saw him.

'Ee, Mr Attercliffe. Thank God yer've come – I were gettin' past meself. T' bloody dog's had him out on t' landin' three times.'

'It happens, Mrs Stebbins,' said Herbert, soothingly. 'Did he kick the animal at all when he was alive? Animals can harbour revenge. There are some vengeful creatures in the animal kingdom, Mrs Stebbins.'

'They never saw eye to eye,' she admitted. 'Alfie used ter grumble that t' dog got fed better than him.'

When they went upstairs to see the body it seemed to Jacky that Alfie might have a point, but he was a lad and it wasn't his place to argue. It was by now the tenth dead body he'd seen in his life and, despite Alfie's age and gaunt appearance, he looked by far the most serene; happy to have left his troubles behind. He lay on a bed, wearing a torn nightshirt which was untidily hitched up to reveal his scrawny legs. This drew an unwarranted comment from Herbert.

'By the heck! Last time I saw a pair o' legs like that, Mrs Stebbins, one of 'em had a message tied to it.'

The old woman frowned as Herbert hurriedly added, 'We have ter keep our sense of humour in this trade, love, else we'd be roarin' us eyes out every day. It's bein' so cheerful as keeps me goin'.'

'Happen yer right,' she said, covering up her husband's legs. 'He were never very robust – and I haven't a clue where his dentures are.' She looked, accusingly, at the abnormally large mongrel happily wagging its tail, with a piece of Alfie's nightshirt caught in its teeth.

'Not ter worry, Mrs Stebbins. We've a box o' spares back at the shop. We'll have him laid out an' grinnin' like Errol Flynn.'

'Mek a nice change,' she said. 'He never did much grinnin' when he were alive.' Then she looked over Herbert's shoulder at Jacky and said sharply, 'Hey! That's not *him*, is it?'

242

'It's my new apprentice, if that's who yer mean,' said Herbert, genially.

The old woman screwed up her eyes, then brought a pair of round spectacles from her apron pocket. She put them on and peered at Jacky again. 'Happen, not,' she decided, taking them off. 'It were only a young 'un what had his picture in t' papers – but they said he were workin' fer a Castlethorpe undertaker. What's yer name, lad?'

'Jacky Gaskell.'

'Well I'll be buggered. It *is* you.'

'What's him?' Herbert asked.

'Come downstairs an' I'll show yer. Don't yer read t' bloody papers?'

'We're up with the larks, Mrs Stebbins. We don't have time fer papers.'

'Well, yer'll have time fer this.' She handed Herbert the *Daily Herald*. A photo of a youthful Jacky occupied much of the front page beneath the banner headline: THE INNOCENT FACE OF EVIL.

Underneath were the words: *Rodney Tripp exclusive.* The article began on the front page and was continued on pages two and three.

This is the face of ten-year-old Jacky Gaskell, the illegitimate son of murderer Frank McGovern, taken five years ago on the day McGovern was hanged for the brutal murder of his mistress, the wife of insurance agent Victor Mumford. McGovern, who didn't fight in the War, had an adulterous affair with Maureen Gaskell while her honourable husband was in France with the British Expeditionary Force. The result of this seedy affair was Jacky Gaskell.

Victor Mumford was rescued from a suicide attempt on Tuesday by the brave intervention of his housekeeper, Clarice Fisk.

Since his wife's murder Mr Mumford has been subjected to constant harrassment by the Gaskell family. Just after the execution of McGovern, Eleanor Gaskell, Jacky's sister, wrote a slanderous skipping song which is still being sung by the children of Castlethorpe and many other towns in the West Riding of Yorkshire. This song accuses Mr Mumford of killing his own wife, to whom he was a devoted husband.

In 1953 the brother and sister burgled Mr Mumford's home. Only Jacky was caught and arrested. The boy was sent to a

243

reform school but was released on a legal technicality when one of the items listed as stolen – a watch – was found to be still in Mr Mumford's possession. Astonishingly, Victor Mumford was imprisoned for fraud and perjury. His state of mind after losing his wife in such a fashion, and being constantly persecuted by the Gaskell family, was not taken into consideration by the court.

While at reform school Jacky Gaskell attempted to escape, along with another boy, who was subsequently killed in the car they had stolen. In the back of the car was the body of an old lady. The ghoulish Gaskell left her body in a bus shelter as they continued their flight from the law.

Gaskell was expelled from his school in 1952 for wrecking the headmaster's study in a wild act of vandalism and the photograph we publish on this page is of Foster Symonite, a fellow pupil, after he had been viciously assaulted by Jacky Gaskell in that same year.

Earlier this year, Brian Gaskell, Jacky's elder brother, who Jacky was known to have disliked, was killed in a mining accident. He was with Jacky when he died. We make no accusations regarding the brother's death but, in the light of Gaskell's past record, we leave the readers to draw their own conclusions.

When asked why he wanted to kill himself Victor Mumford made the following statement: All I wanted was to be left alone. I've been persecuted by Frank McGovern, by his son's family, by the children who sing that awful song and by the law. I just wanted it all to end. I'm sorry for all the trouble I've caused.

'Bloody hell!' said Herbert passing the paper to Jacky. 'This dunt sound like the lad I know.'

Herbert and the old woman watched Jacky read it, with his face going ever redder. He handed the paper to the old woman and looked up at Herbert.

'They twisted everything,' he muttered. 'I didn't do any of this stuff.'

Herbert sighed. 'Trouble is, lad – yer did.'

'I didn't, honest.'

'What I mean, lad, is yer probab'ly didn't do it like it says here, but they only have ter twist the truth a bit ter turn it right on its head.' He turned to the old woman for her support. 'Isn't that right, love?'

'All I know,' she said, sharply, 'is that I don't want him anywhere near my Alfie.'

Herbert sighed. 'Aye, lass. Happen yer right.' He turned to Jacky. 'Get yersen back ter t' yard lad. We'll try an' sort summat out.'

'Do you know, I'd actually given up on trying to get Mumford,' Maureen said. 'Not now, though. Oh no. Now we've got to get him. This isn't revenge, this is a crusade.'

She, Bill and Charlie were sitting in Charlie's house due to unwanted attention from reporters who were trying to do follow-ups from the family's point of view.

'Now's not the time,' Bill had advised. He had called in to see Maureen as soon as he read the story. 'It puts the police in a bad light as well, with us arresting Mumford – especially me, with me being the arresting officer. We've been told not to say anything. Let the flak die down . . . *then* make a statement.'

'How long?' inquired Maureen.

'Wait 'til people are eating their fish and chips out of the paper.'

'Will it do any good?' Charlie asked.

'It's called damage limitation, Charlie.'

'I see,' said Maureen, dismally. 'Limit the damage . . . is that all we can do?'

Bill gave a reluctant nod. 'That suicide bid was his master stroke,' he said. 'I can't believe he meant to do that. Trouble is, everybody else is going to believe it. He's got them feeling sorry for him.'

'He's an absolute weirdo,' Maureen said. 'It gives me the creeps just to think about him.'

'Mumford's a very dangerous man, Maureen. I suggest you stay clear of him. He'll slip up one day. He might have the public fooled but there's plenty down at the station who aren't convinced.'

'You mean they think my Frank was innocent?' said Charlie.

Bill looked at him. '*Your* Frank?' he said, bemused. 'What's Frank McGovern got to do with you?'

Charlie gave a slight wince and looked at Maureen, who shrugged.

'It's sort of a family secret,' she said. 'We just don't broadcast it, that's all. I'm amazed the papers didn't pick it up. Charlie's Jacky's granddad.'

'So,' deduced Bill, 'You're Frank McGovern's father?'

'You should be a detective, lad. You're wasted in that uniform.'

'Why didn't you tell me?' Bill directed his question at Maureen.

'Like I said, it's a family secret.'

'Pity I'm not part of your family,' Bill said, almost petulantly.

Maureen raised her eyebrows and gave him a look that said, You know what you have to do.

'Anyway, yer know now,' Charlie said, sensing discord between the two of them. 'And it's not summat we want broadcast.'

'No . . . it's not something I'll be broadcasting.' Bill returned his attention to Charlie and a sudden realisation struck him. 'Good God, Charlie! You must hate Mumford as much – or more than any of us.'

'It does me no good ter be breathin' the same air as him, that's fer sure, lad. But what can I do about it?'

'I don't know, Charlie,' admitted Bill. 'I honestly do not know.'

'Let's just hope he slips up,' said Maureen.

Chapter Twenty-Seven

Summer turned to winter but Mumford still hadn't slipped up. He was glorying in his new-found popularity, although, like tens of thousands of others he'd been struck down with Asian flu which had set back the rebuilding of his business a few weeks. But he could live with that. Life moved on. The world was changing. The Russians had just put a dog called Laika into space, Elvis was singing 'Heartbreak Hotel', girls wanted to look like Sandra Dee, Leeds United were back in the First Division, people in the street were smiling at Mumford and saying things like 'Hello' and, 'Don't let the bastards grind you down, Victor.' He was in seventh heaven – to have his way with the Gaskell girl would be the icing on the cake. She needed to be taught not to make up slanderous songs about him. He had fantasised about her ever since he'd seen her walking down the street that spring day. It excited him that he knew he could make his fantasy come true with a little planning and cunning. He'd got away with two murders and fake suicide attempt and the public all loved him and thought him badly treated. Raping and murdering Ellie Gaskell would be oh so sweet. And he had a simple plan. The seed of which had been sown in his mind by two policemen talking by his bed.

Ellie was still working at the solicitors; her fashion-modelling career had started and finished with the Lipscombe and Lile catalogue. There had been a promise of more to come but she suspected that her sudden notoriety hadn't helped; she was just grateful that the solicitors for whom she worked had accepted her explanation and had kept her on. Maureen had put the Gaskell family side of the story to several reporters who had all gone away

247

and written lurid versions that sold newspapers but didn't help the family one bit. On balance she felt she'd have been better off saying nothing. For some reason her workload had suddenly halved and she relied heavily on the meagre wages of her children. Ellie answered the call herself when Mumford rang her up at work.

'I'd like to speak to Miss Eleanor Gaskell, please.'

He spoke in a gruff, pseudo-posh voice which Ellie didn't recognise.

'Er . . . speaking.'

'Ah, Miss Gaskell. You don't know me, but I can assure you I'm a friend. You may be interested to learn that the knife that killed Victor Mumford's wife is hidden somewhere in his cellar – still with her blood on it probably – not to mention his finger-prints.'

Ellie tried to interrupt but he cut her off.

'Please don't ask me any questions, Miss Gaskell. Just be assured that what I say is the truth. I know if I told my mate Billy Scanlon he'd do something stupid and lose his job. Trust me when I say I know a lot about this case and I'm convinced the verdict was wrong, only I'm not in a position to do anything about it. If you wish to take a look for yourself, tonight would be a good time. Mumford will be out all evening. If your brother comes with you make sure he's not caught. In view of the newspaper article the courts will not wish to be seen as soft.'

Mumford put the phone down and smiled to himself. His plan was coming together. Of course he had a contingency plan. You must always have one of those. If Ellie's brother came with her he'd ring the police and have them locked up. But if she came at all she was much more likely to come on her own – which would mean she hadn't told anyone. No one with any sense would allow her to come to his house on her own. He looked through the window at the patch of ground covering Marion's body.

'You'll probably be having company tonight, Marion dear,' he said. 'That'll be nice for you.'

Ellie had been acting strangely all evening – as if she had some-thing to do that scared her. Jacky knew that feeling himself and he'd seen it before in his sister – the night they broke into Mumford's house. They had the wireless tuned in to Radio

Luxembourg and Dickie Valentine came on, singing 'The Finger of Suspicion' – one of Ellie's favourites, but she didn't seem to be listening.

'Ellie, are you okay?' Jacky had asked. 'It's Dickie Valentine.'

Their mother glanced up from her book and looked first at her son, then at Ellie, who shrugged and left the room saying she felt fine.

'Leave her,' advised Maureen. 'Us women have funny moods at times. Could be Gavin trouble.'

Jacky nodded, but this was a funny mood he seemed to recognise. When Ellie went out at around nine o'clock, and said she was going to see Gavin, her boyfriend, Jacky knew something was amiss. Gavin was in the Clugston Arms darts team and that night they had a match against the Dog and Gun. Ellie hated sitting watching him play darts; it had become a bone of contention between them. He put his coat on and followed her out saying, 'I'm going round to see Roy.'

'Don't be late,' his mother said.

Jacky noticed she hadn't said that to Ellie and he wondered at what age he'd be allowed to grow up.

'I won't.'

By the time he got to the gate Ellie was out of sight, having vanished into the first dense fog of the winter. He listened for her footsteps but couldn't hear them above the sound of a wagon crawling past. The driver called out to him, 'Is this Gascoigne Road?'

'No, it's Gaythorne Street.'

'Gaythorne Street? Where the bloody hell's Gaythorne Street?'

'It's here,' said Jacky hurrying off into the fog. Ellie couldn't have been no more than 50 yards away, but she might just as well have been a mile. He hadn't a clue where she was.

Ellie put up the hood of her duffel coat as she headed through the streets towards Mumford's house. She planned on breaking in through the same window as before, only this time without the finesse. Break the glass as quietly as she could and undo the latch. The old street lamps had been recently converted from gas to electricity but still they failed to penetrate this fog, a real pea-souper. In her pocket she carried a bicycle lamp with new batteries, bought that day for this very purpose, and a small carrier bag in which to place the knife. She would pick it up in her gloved hand and drop it into the bag so as not to smudge any prints. Her heart was pounding so hard she thought it would burst, but she knew she had to do this. She'd have felt better if Jacky had been with her but the mystery caller was right, it was too much of a risk for Jacky. Her biggest doubt was the authenticity of the caller. He sounded as though he was a policeman with information he himself daren't act on 'I know a lot about this case' – that was copper's talk, definitely. He said he was a mate of Bill Scanlon as well – that had given her confidence. She'd thought about asking Bill, but then he'd be compromised if anything went wrong. Her mother *might* have helped but she'd have been more likely to involve Bill. Charlie would have come like a shot but he'd have been too much of a liability. She had even thought of involving Gavin, but he'd be playing his precious darts, which would no doubt be much more important than helping her. After tonight she'd dump him.

No, she had to do this on her own. She just hoped the knife wouldn't take much finding when she got there.

What little traffic there was crawled along not much faster than she was walking, their headlights reflected off the fog into the driver's eyes, limiting their vision even further. One wise driver even had a woman running a few yards in front of his car, shouting directions back to him as his headlamps illuminated her jogging backside. Presumably, thought Ellie, she'd be the first to catch it if they unexpectedly came across another car. The man was probably a darts player. Men.

Maybe Mumford wouldn't venture out on a night like this. Part of her hoped he wouldn't, the cowardly part – or was it the more sensible part? The lights in his house would give her the answer. But what if he was one one of those people who left lights on even when they were out, to deter burglars? That would be just hard luck, she decided. Just one light on, anywhere in the house, and she'd go home and tell everyone about the mystery caller. Let them decide what to do.

When she reached Mumford's street her courage was failing her. It wouldn't have been so bad on a nice night. A night with stars and a cheerful moon, instead of freezing fog of a density that she could almost taste. Her nose was bunged up and she took out her handkerchief to give it a good blow. As she did so she realised

250

the stupidity of what she was doing. Who the hell did she think she was – Dick Barton, Special Agent? She was a solicitor's clerk, for God's sake, a mere girl. Face it, Ellie, Mumford's won.

She turned to retrace her steps when she heard a girl's voice not far away; a voice as ethereal as the fog that shielded its owner from Ellie's sight. There was the rythmic lash of a rope against stone flags – a skipping rope. The girl's delicate voice floated through the gloom, singing the song that Mumford hated most in the world and Ellie realised he hadn't completely won. Some kids hadn't been taken in by the newspaper article – the odds were that they hadn't even read it. Newspaper articles come and go, but skipping songs have real endurance.

Mumford stood in the dark of his bedroom with his eyes fixed on the gate. Lit by a street lamp he could just make it out. As soon as she appeared he would go downstairs and wait for her. He'd know within a second which window she'd chosen – she'd probably have to break the glass. In one hand was a hammer and in his belt was a knife – a large kitchen knife. He'd kill her in the kitchen, where the blood would wipe up easily from the linoleum floor. But she wouldn't die easily. And she wouldn't die a virgin – if she still was one.

A figure appeared at the gate and stopped. The fog was too thick to make out who it was, but there was only one. So that was good. If it was her it meant she'd come alone – and the game was on. His heart quickened and he felt a stirring in his loins when he pictured what he was about to do to her. Yes, the figure was moving down his drive. It was hooded and hard to make out, but he knew it was Ellie.

He hurried down the stairs and stood in the hallway, listening for the sound of someone forcing an entry. There was a crash in the kitchen. His grip tightened on the shaft of the hammer and he eased open the kitchen door. It creaked just as it had when Jacky opened it that time. Then he closed it quickly when he saw a light outside the window. Had she heard the creak?

Ellie was too busy struggling with the latch to hear creaking doors. She switched on the lamp so that she could see what she was doing and managed to push the locking lever to the open position. The sliding sash window, counterbalanced by iron weights, moved up easily. She shone the torch inside so that she could get her bearings, and climbed in. As soon as her feet touched the linoleum Mumford burst through the door, with the hammer held high.

Ellie threw herself to one side as it came down. It struck her on her left shoulder and she heard her own bones break just before she collapsed to the floor. The lamp was still in her right hand and shining directly in Mumford's face. Instinctively she held it there as he knelt over her and took the knife from his belt. The pain in her shoulder was almost unbearable and she felt herself losing consciousness. Mumford was tearing savagely at the toggles on her duffel coat, swearing at them, slashing them with his knife. He pulled the coat open then held the knife at her throat.

'Is this what you're looking for?' he taunted, 'A murderer's knife?'

There was drool coming from his mouth and Ellie began retching. Her back arched as she turned her head away from him and vomited with fear, pain and disgust.

'It's not here, girl,' he sneered. 'Never was. Not after that night anyway. Threw the bugger away. Some kids in the school yard probably took it.'

He tugged at the buttons of her cardigan, ripping it open. 'So I'll have to kill you with this.'

Ellie was terrified now. Totally convinced she was going to die. 'Please, Mr Mumford,' she pleaded. 'Don't kill me, please. I'll do anything you say.'

A thought came into his head. Raping a compliant victim had to be easier than a struggling one. 'What's it worth, then?' he said. 'For me not to kill you.'

'Please, I'll do anything . . .'

'Anything?' he snarled.

'Please don't kill me.'

He fully intended killing her. Having her here like this was his dream. He snatched the lamp from her hand and sat back on his haunches.

'Take all your clothes off.'

'Please, don't, Mr Mumford.' Tears were streaming down her cheeks.

'Now!'

The savagery in his voice made her jump and wince with pain.

With her right hand she tried to undo the fastener on her skirt, but the pain in her shoulder made this just impossible. She began to cry.

'I can't,' she whimpered. 'Oh please, Mr Mumford.'

'Here,' he said, harshly. 'I'll bloody do it then.'

Mumford put down the knife and undid her skirt. He had just pulled it down around her ankles and was tugging at her knickers when a blow to his head knocked him senseless. A large stone had come through the window, hurled with some force. He slumped over her.

'Ellie?'

She heard Jacky calling out as he scrambled into the room.

'Are you okay?'

But she was far too shocked to answer him. Jacky rolled Mumford's unconscious body off her and realised with disgust what this man had been about to do to his sister. He could see the hammer in the lamplight and snatched it up in a rage, about to hit Mumford with it.

'No, Jacky!' screamed Ellie. 'Don't.'

For a fleeting moment Jacky's mind went back to the time he'd been about to hit Brian with a chair and his sister had shouted at him. She had stopped him that time, but Brian had only been a pain in the arse. This man was evil. This man deserved all he got.

'Honest, Jacky. It's not worth it.'

Her brother allowed his anger to subside. Blood was pouring from a wound in Mumford's head. With a bit of luck the bastard might be dead anyway.

'Just get me out of here, Jacky.'

'What are you doing here anyway?' he asked her.

'I'll tell you later. My shoulder's broken; I need to get to a hospital.'

'Okay.'

She tried pulling her skirt up. 'Blast! It's no good. I can't do it.'

Jacky ended up doing it for her, then he lifted her gently to her feet. 'Can you walk?'

'Yes, I think so. Oh Jacky, thank God you came. He was going to—'

'I know,' he said, not wanting her to go into details. 'Come on. We'll use the front door.' He picked up the lamp and kicked Mumford, hard, in the teeth as he passed. The man gave a moan,

253

which indicated he was alive. Jacky didn't know whether to be relieved or disappointed. Then he thought of what had nearly befallen his sister and, on balance, he was disappointed.

It took them three-quarters of an hour to make their way through the freezing fog to Castlethorpe Hospital. During this time they got their story straight. If Mumford reported her to the police she'd simply tell them the truth. How he had enticed her there and had attempted to rape her. But Ellie doubted very much if he'd risk a charge of rape and attempted murder. She groaned about her shoulder a lot but she was surprisingly composed considering her ordeal. The sight of Mumford lying there unconscious had helped relieve some of the shock. The foul man had been beaten at his own game.

'He set the whole thing up and it went wrong for him,' she said. 'He'll be more worried than we are. I don't think he'll dare say anything. God, Jacky, I was frightened. I was begging him not to kill me. Do you think you killed him?'

Her question was posed with a note of hope. Her terrifying and degrading ordeal had had a mind-altering effect on her.

'I don't know. If I did we could be in a spot of bother,' Jacky pointed out. 'Maybe we should just tell the cops what happened.'

'No! We mustn't do that.' Ellie sounded panicky. 'If he's dead they could do us for murder.'

'Okay, okay! Don't worry. Take it easy. I'm on your side.'

'It's just too much of a risk,' she explained, rational again now. 'The police got hold of the wrong end of the stick last time and you ended up in reform school. And that newspaper article left a nasty taste in everyone's mouth. We're not flavour of the month, us Gaskells. I'm just thankful it's a cold night.'

'Why?'

'It meant we were both wearing gloves. No fingerprints. How would they know it was us, if Mumford's not alive to tell them?'

'Good thinking. Best not to say anything then,' Jacky agreed. 'Tell the hospital you fell down some steps.'

'Hey! How come you knew where I was?' she asked, suddenly curious.

'I knew you had something on your mind, so I followed you when you went out. Mind you, I couldn't see you. Going to Mumford's was just a shot in the dark.'

'Or in the fog,' said Ellie, squeezing her brother with her good arm. 'Thanks, Jacky . . . Jesus Christ! This really bloody hurts.'

'Language, Eleanor.'

Mumford regained consciousness just as Ellie and Jacky were going through the hospital door. For a long time the crippling pain in his head was all he could think about. He hadn't a clue what had happened, but as the pounding in his head eased, some of the events of that evening came back to him. His memory remained very sketchy, although they were enough to worry him. How the hell had she got away from him? Had she gone to the police? How long had he been unconscious? And why had he lost so many teeth? Had she hit him in the mouth? Getting up was an effort so he stayed where he was and slept until cramp and the pain in his mouth woke him up. It took him ten minutes to get upstairs to bed. Jesus! She wouldn't get away with this.

Maureen was beside herself when she heard what had happened and was all for going to the police. Ellie had been kept in hospital.

'I left Mumford in a bit of a state, Mam,' Jacky told her. 'I'm not sure what will happen to me if the police get involved.'

'In a state, what sort of state?'

Jacky lowered his eyes. Maureen pressed her hands to her mouth and said, 'Oh my God!'

'He was alive when we left him, but I gave him a real good kick in his teeth when I passed. I couldn't help it, Mam. You should have seen our Ellie.'

'So he could be dead?'

'Doubt it, but he could be,' Jacky said. There was no guilt or remorse in his voice; he could have been talking about a dead rat. 'Ellie said to keep quiet about it. We were both wearing gloves, so there won't be any fingerprints. Nothing to connect us to it.' He looked at his mother. 'Mam,' he said. 'To be honest, I hope he *is* dead . . . is that bad?'

His mother pulled him to her. He was taller then her now. 'If it's bad, Jacky boy,' she said, 'then I'm as bad as you. But it'll put paid to any hopes of getting Frank's name cleared.'

Jacky had a thought. 'Unless . . .' he said.

'Unless what?'

'Unless the murder knife actually *is* in the house, with all the

255

evidence still on it. He's such a weirdo I wouldn't put anything past him.'

Maureen gave this some thought then shook her head. 'No,' she said. 'No one's *that* weird.'

But the possibility remained in both of their minds until Jacky put it to Ellie when they visited her in hospital the next evening, after an operation to put her shoulder back together.

'He told me he threw it away,' she remembered. 'I think he said he threw it over the wall into the playground.' She looked at her mother. 'By the way, Mam, I dumped Gavin. He came here before he went to work. All he could talk about was winning his darts match last night.'

'Ah! I rang him to tell him you'd hurt your shoulder,' her mother explained. 'I didn't say how. He said the hospital's on his way to work. I suggested you might like some flowers to cheer you up. Sounds like I put my foot in it.'

'Doesn't matter,' Ellie said. 'It had to be done. He seemed more surprised than hurt. Took his flowers away with him. That must be a first – the nurses couldn't believe it. Can you imagine it? Someone brings you flowers and takes them away just because you've dumped them.'

'Wouldn't the police have found it?' said Jacky, unhappy with all this irrelevant talk of Gavin and flowers.

'Found what?' inquired Ellie.

'The knife that Mumford said he threw into the playground. The one you went looking for last night and nearly got yourself killed for. That's what.'

'Keep your hair on,' said his sister. 'Kids could have taken it. That's what Mumford thinks happened to it.' She looked at her mother. 'He told me that because he didn't think I'd be around to repeat it. Oh, Mam. I was so scared.'

Maureen took her daughter in her arms and held her. She missed Brian so much, despite the trouble he'd caused her. He was her boy. She couldn't have coped had she lost Ellie as well. The very thought of it frightened her.

'I know, my darling. I don't know what to say to you. The truth is you shouldn't have been there. But I'm so proud of you.' She held out a hand for Jacky to hold. 'Proud of both of you.'

'Funny I never heard anything about that,' said Jacky, who was deaf to any conversation that wasn't about the knife. 'I'm sure I'd have found out if a kid had taken it. I mean, the cops were offering a five-pound reward for anyone who found it. *Five pounds* – that's a lot of dosh. If it was a kid he'd have handed it in.'

'I gather Mumford hasn't reported this to the police,' Ellie said.

'Well, not so far.' said Jacky. He looked at Frank's watch, to which he had added Brian's name. 'I s'pose there's time,' he added gloomily. Then he lowered his voice. 'That's if he's alive. He could still be lying there for all we know.'

'Doesn't he have a daily help who goes in and cleans for him?' Ellie asked.

Jacky perked up. 'That's right,' he remembered. 'If he was dead she'd have rung the cops. I walked past the end of his street this afternoon but there weren't any coppers there. Let's hope he keeps his trap shut.'

'He will,' said Maureen, confidently. 'Guilt's keeping his mouth shut. If he opens his mouth he could be in a lot more trouble than you two. You accuse him of attemped rape and he can say bye-bye to his business, even if he's found not guilty. Mud like that sticks for a long time. I often wonder if I did the right thing not going after Morgan Pettifer.'

Chapter Twenty-Eight

Victor Mumford examined his teeth in the bathroom mirror. The new plate hadn't been right ever since he'd had it fitted to replace the five teeth he'd lost six months ago earlier. The dentures were too big and he had shaved off his moustache. Those few people who were kindly disposed to him said he had a vague look of the old king, although most thought he looked like a cross between George Formby and last year's Grand National winner. For the hundredth time he ran through the events of that night.

Surely *she* hadn't done this to him. A few days later he'd seen her walking around with her arm in a sling, so he hadn't imagined her being there. He'd been on that kitchen floor for hours. Unconscious, waking up in pain, trying to get to his feet, trying to figure out what had happened. He'd remembered enough not to report it to the police. That would have been a very unwise move. All the next day he'd stayed home, licking his wounds like a beaten dog and watching through the window for the police to come and arrest him. But he wasn't sure what for. Rape, perhaps?

How far had he got with her? One minute she was underneath him, screaming for mercy and then ...? Blast! He couldn't remember. He'd never remember, not after all this time.

The odds were that someone else had been there. Probably her brother. The brat who had been the bane of his life. He'd have been the one who defaced his shop window. It was high time he dealt with that lad once and for all. Then he'd take the sister – and the mother after that. She was a real looker, the mother. He'd enjoy taking mother and daughter. Both at once would be good. How could he do that? Planning, that's how. Better planning than last time.

Business was booming. The newspaper article had done him the world of good. Time to get rid of Les Bradfield, which was easy the way Mumford had set the partnership up. All he had to do was pay him off and say goodbye. Simple as that. Mumford would keep Bradfield's respectable name above the door, of course – nothing illegal about that. He'd sack him today and take on a salaried employee to do Les's work. Preferably a good-looking woman who was eager to better herself.

Chapter Twenty-Nine

Monica Nuttall, who once promised that she'd go out with Jacky when he was at least eleven, was at Alfreton Girls' High School. It was 1957 and now he was sixteen and earning a bit of money she'd kept her word, but had made him promise that he'd go to night school to get some qualifications. He didn't need telling: He had already enrolled, even though the classes didn't start until September.

Jacky liked the building trade. There was always something to show for your day's work, unlike mining where all you saw was a slightly bigger hole in the ground. He liked the physical lifestyle, the fresh air and the crack with the men, especially the Irish lads who did the ground work. He already knew that one day he'd start up on his own, just as soon as he had learned enough about the job. There was an engine inside him driving him on; an engine called Mumford. Frank being wrongly hanged was bad enough, but what Mumford had tried to do to Ellie was a whole lot worse. One day he'd make himself big enough and powerful enough to destroy that man.

Unless there was a quicker way.

Short of breaking into Mumford's house again he had done everything humanly possible to find the knife. Jacky had asked everyone he knew who was around at the time. Why hadn't it been handed in when there was reward of five quid? Someone had told him about a couple of kids from St Joseph's Catholic school who used to play in the yard because they were banned from playing in their own school yard, but Jacky couldn't track them down.

One day, while Mumford was at work and after the daily help had gone home, he had walked boldly into Mumford's garden posing as a gardener and spent several hours searching every inch of ground, before leaving the place exactly as he found it. If Mumford ever heard about it nothing was done.

'You're really obsessive about this,' Monica told him. 'I mean, even if you find it, do you really think there'll still be fingerprints and blood on it?'

'I don't know what to think. Even if it hasn't got fingerprints on it we can prove it *could* have been Mumford who did the murder – if it was found within throwing distance of his garden.'

'It sounds like a long shot,' Monica said.

'So's doing the pools. It doesn't stop people filling their coupons in every week though, does it? Mon, you don't know what it's like. It's something that won't go away. My mam and Ellie are the same, so is Granddad. It really eats into me.'

'But you only saw your dad once.'

'I know. Ellie never met him at all.'

'Is there more to this than I know about?' Monica asked, shrewdly.

Jacky hadn't told her about Mumford trying to rape and murder Ellie. No one but the family and Bill Scanlon knew about that.

'Was it you who painted "Murderer" on his shop window?' she said, challengingly.

Jacky looked at her.

'You can trust me,' she assured him. 'Go on. I know it was you.'

'It wasn't actually,' he said, truthfully. 'No idea who it was. Mumford thinks it was me, so that's all right.'

It would have amused him to learn that the real culprit was his granddad, doing his bit for the cause.

Jacky and Monica spent their Wednesday evenings at the Linley Street Methodist Youth Club. Few of the kids who went were Methodists but that didn't seem to bother Sister Evelyn and Mr Collier who ran it. It kept the kids off the streets and the sister extracted a prayer out of them once a week. Some of the lads had joined the Boys' Brigade which was run from the club but Jacky didn't fancy the idea of marching through the streets behind a big drum, which was the only instrument offered to him. He had quite fancied a cornet or even a euphonium but it was the big drum or nothing. So Jacky had chosen nothing.

Monica was a bright, pretty brunette and the only girl he'd

taken out since Sandra Symonite. Monica knew he'd been to the pictures with Sandra.

'Did you pay,' she asked, innocently, 'into the pictures?'

'Yes,' Jacky said, unaware of the trap she was setting.

'So she'll have got it out for you, then.'

'What?'

'Your willy. She always gets boys' willies out if they pay for her in the pictures. She reckons she doesn't like to be beholden to them.'

'Well, she didn't get mine out.'

Lonnie Donegan's 'Cumberland Gap' came on. Jacky and Monica went into action. Jacky fancied himself as the best bopper in the youth club, except maybe Roy Barnwell. Every time their faces came together Monica continued the conversation.

'She gets everyone's out.'

Jacky spun her round, but she came back with.

'It's her hobby.'

Lonnie and his skiffle group gave of their best. It was his first UK number one. Monica twirled under Jacky's arms and called out, 'She'd get mine out if I had one.'

'Well, she didn't get mine out.'

'Liar.'

The music stopped and someone called out to Jacky that it was his turn on the table tennis table. He'd be playing the winner of the last game – probably Roy Barnwell, who rarely lost a game and would no doubt beat Jacky. He passed Sandra Symonite on the way and remembered that he could beat Roy at *something*, which made him smile. Elvis began singing 'All Shook Up' as a scuffle started up in the entrance hall, probably about a girl. Mr Collier broke it up with a threatening word. Everything was back to normal. Jacky thought of Mumford as he picked up the bat. His world would never be normal while that man was around.

He duly lost 21–12, which was quite respectable for him. Monica arrived with an orange juice in anticipation of him only playing one game.

'Beaten you again, has he?'

'Just.'

'You can have another game if you like,' Roy said. 'I've had enough. Fancy a dance, Mon?'

Monica and Roy disappeared into the main hall as Jacky

knocked the ball across the net to the next player. He didn't look upon Roy as a rival for Monica's affection. In fact he didn't look upon anyone as a rival, such was his self-confidence. Brian's words came back to him. 'Yer never looked up ter no one.'

Jacky won the next game by a single point and stayed on the table for a third, a record for him. It was Fozzie's turn next, the worst player in the club. Mr Collier came into the room, warned by some of the members – Fozzie versus Jacky was an explosive combination.

Sandra's brother was large, lumbering and uncoordinated and only won points when Jacky made errors. He didn't make many of them because he wanted to humiliate Fozzie, which he did – to the bigger youth's anger. Fozzie hurled his bat, viciously, across the table and caught Jacky just above his left eye, cutting him. As Mr Collier escorted the smirking youth out of the club with a warning not to come back, Monica rushed in, concerned.

'It's nothing,' Jacky said. Blood was running down the side of his face.

'It probably needs a stitch or two, lad,' said Mr Collier.

'It's only a nick,' Jacky assured him. 'Once the bleeding's stopped it'll be all right. Have you got any plasters?'

'I'm taking you home,' insisted Monica.

'I don't want to go home.'

'Well, you're coming with me. You need a bit of looking after.'

Shouts of 'Ooooh' came from the watching crowd. 'I should take her up on that, Jacky boy.'

It was a warm evening. There was a small wood on the way home, leading down to the canal. Jacky took her hand and led her down there. He felt an urge he'd never felt with Sandra. With her he'd been more or less ambushed. Monica turned to face him and put her arms around him.

'How is it?' she asked.

Jacky touched his plastered eyebrow. 'It hurts.'

He kissed her. They had been going out for two weeks and things hadn't got any further than that, although Jacky sensed his luck might be in now. Her affection for him had been reinforced by sympathy for the wounded soldier. His eye didn't hurt much but there was no advantage in telling her that.

'I don't want to go all the way with you, Jacky,' she told him.

263

'I've never done that before.' Then she kissed him and pulled him onto the grass. They rolled away from the path until they were hidden from the world. She unfastened his belt and soon had her hand where only Sandra Symonite had ventured before.

'Hmmm,' she said. 'What did Sandra think of it?'

Jacky wasn't thinking clearly. 'She said it was bigger than Roy Barnwell's.'

'Ha!' she exclaimed, triumphantly. 'She *did* get it out.'

'Ow!'

Monica was squeezing him, as if to punish him for his lie.

'Ow! All right, all right – she did,' he admitted. 'There wasn't much I could do about it.'

She eased her grip and massaged him gently as she wriggled, with Jacky's help, out of her skirt.

'Bigger than Roy Barnwell's, eh?' she commented. 'I wouldn't say that.'

'Eh?'

They kissed and undressed and caressed with the clumsy passion of youth until Jacky came to the inevitable climax and collapsed on the grass beside her, with Monica stroking his hair and unable to interest him in further activity.

'I was lying,' she said.

'What? About Roy Barnwell?'

'About not wanting to go all the way. I do. I'm scared, that's all.'

'And me.'

'You'd have to use something.'

'Use what? Oh, sorry, yeah.' Jacky was still in sexual recovery and not thinking straight.

'My mum and dad are going out on Friday night. You could come round. They won't be back 'til midnight.'

'Okay.'

'Can you get something before then?'

'Yeah, sure. Course I can.'

'They sell them in threes, so I'm told.'

'Yeah, so I understand.'

Monica kissed him and said, 'I was kidding about Roy Barnwell.'

'In what way?'

She gave him a non-committal, coquettish wink and fastened

her skirt. Jacky sat up and stared down at the canal, wondering how he was going to get a packet of three before Friday.

Earlier that evening Bill had knocked on Maureen's door. Maureen herself answered.

'Are the kids in?' he asked. 'I, er . . . I need a word in private.'

'Ellie's at the pictures, Jacky's gone to a youth club. Judging by the time he took getting ready I think he's got a girlfriend.'

'Lucky lad. I hope he's got more sense than I had at his age.' He sat down and lit up, a combination that brought a smile to Maureen's face. Her smile turned to a look of curiosity when it became obvious he had something serious to say to her.

'I'm ready for our private word,' she said.

He shook his head. 'Maureen, I wish I knew where to start.'

'At the beginning?'

'I know. The beginning. It began with me dropping Pam on her back. And it's ended with me not knowing which way to turn.'

'You could always turn to me. What is it? Bill?'

'Look, after what happened with Mumford last year you need to stay vigilant.'

'I know that. We all know that. Is that what you came to tell me?'

'It's just that I can't be around to keep an eye on you all the time. Maybe Ellie should have reported it.'

'You know why she didn't. You agreed . . . Bill, what is it? Is this the private word you wanted?'

'No. I just want you to be safe, that's all.' His head was down but she could see tears in his eyes. Something she'd never seen before. 'I love you,' he said. 'That's what it is.'

'Oh.'

Her heart took a leap in the right direction. They had always stopped short of declaring their love for each other – because of Pam. But it had seemed to her that Pam was an obstacle they would soon overcome. Had that time now arrived?

'Don't say anything, Maureen. Don't say anything daft like you love me. Because I don't want to hear it. I couldn't stand to hear it.'

'Okay, I won't say it. Bill, will you tell me what all this is about?'

'It's about me being an idiot again.'

'An idiot?'

He nodded. 'We never do it, you see. Have sex. Rarely, anyway. I've learned to cope. But we did it last month. First time for God knows how long.'

'Bill, I assumed you would. You're married to her.'

'I'm not married to *her*.' He sounded unusually bitter. 'I'm married to a bloody wheelchair.'

'That's cruel, Bill.'

'I *am* cruel, that's just it. She definitely knows about you, you know.'

'Ah . . . well, I thought she might. We haven't exactly kept it a state secret. Does she think we've slept together?'

'Yes. And for reasons I can't explain I didn't tell her any different.'

'And?'

'And what?'

'And . . . did she go mad? Did she throw things at you? Did she break down in tears. Did she do any of the things a wife does when she finds out the husband she loves has been unfaithful?'

Bill shook his head. 'No, she didn't do any of those things. She just sat there and looked . . . sort of forlorn.'

'Forlorn?'

'Sort of.'

'Bill, sort of forlorn doesn't sound like a woman in love. It sounds more like a woman who's feeling sorry for herself.'

'I could have put her out of her misery and told her that you and I hadn't slept together . . . but I didn't.' He looked at Maureen. The tears were still there. 'Maybe it was just wishful thinking, eh?' He shook his head and gave a sad smile. 'I knew there'd never be a *me and you* until I settled things with her, once and for all. You made that plain enough. And, to be honest, I had it all planned.'

'Had what planned?'

'I had it planned on how I would leave her. Just like I had it planned when I met Kathy McAlister. What the hell is it with me? Why can't I get things right?'

Maureen was perplexed. 'Bill, what are you getting at? What's this all about?'

He took a deep drag on his cigarette and held the smoke in until he thought of his reply. Then he exhaled and looked at her, with enormous sadness in his eyes. 'Maureen, it's all about me being stupid. It's all about bad timing, which has been the story of my life. I think I'm destined to miss out on the main chance by a whisker every time it comes within my grasp. Maybe I should just accept what I am. One of those blokes who just miss out on things.'

'Bill, if you don't tell me what this is about I'm going to hit you.'

He blurted it out in one breath. It was the only way he knew. 'It's about the fact that she's pregnant and I've just promised her that I'll stand by her and never leave her . . . until death us do bloody part.'

There was a long silence.

'Oh,' said Maureen. 'I see.'

Her heart had by now lurched in the wrong direction. She felt tears of her own arriving. She'd be forty-one next week. Bill had been her Last Chance Saloon. Trying to talk him out of it was an option that came immediately to her mind. But the decision was his. She knew that. She had always known that.

'Has she had it confirmed?'

It seemed a petty thing to ask. Maybe she just wanted to eliminate every chance of their ever being together. Every chance of happiness.

'She's definitely pregnant,' he said. 'I wouldn't be telling you otherwise.'

'Because being late's no guarantee—'

The look in his eyes cut her off. 'The doctor confirmed it today. Pam didn't tell me until she knew for sure.'

Maureen couldn't think of anything else. 'So,' she shrugged, resignedly. 'Is this it, then?' She nudged away a tear with her knuckle.

He gave a long sigh. 'Maureen, I've got no choice.' He looked up at her, as if asking her to tell him otherwise, to suggest a way out. 'Have I?'

'No, Bill. I don't suppose you have,' she said. 'I'm struggling to compete with a wife and a wheelchair. But a wife, a wheelchair and a baby . . .'

'I wouldn't just be leaving her, I'd be leaving my child.'

'Bill, I've never asked you to to leave anyone. It was never on the cards, remember?'

267

'I was planning to leave her.'

'You said.'

'Would you have had me?'

Maureen didn't answer. She thought it was an unfair question under the circumstances.

'Sorry,' he said, understanding her silence.

She gave a wry smile. 'I don't know – she finds out about Kathy McAlister and she breaks her back, she finds out about me and she gets herself pregnant. She's determined to hold on to you, one way or the other.'

'Now *that* was cruel.'

'It's also rubbish,' Maureen admitted. 'But I'm sorry. I'm just not up to talking sensibly about this.'

Bill got to his feet, wanting to hold her and crush her to him but he didn't trust himself.

'Do you want to hear something daft?' she said, as he stood at the door.

He stopped with his back to her and said, in a despondent voice, 'Probably not, but go on.'

'I love you.'

He shook his head and his shoulders sagged as if it was the last thing he wanted to hear, then, without turning round, he stepped out of the door and out of her life.

The following morning Jacky was standing on the scaffolding, drinking a mug of tea. Down below in the spring sunshine a group of boys, all around his age, made their way home from school. Their blue blazers identified them as Castlethorpe Grammar School boys and Jacky was envious because he should have been one of them, and wasn't, through no fault of his own. One of the boys had been in his class at Barr Road School. He was nowhere near as bright as Jacky, but he wore the blazer and Jacky wore the overalls. Soon they'd be taking their O Levels; lies and general misfortune had robbed Jacky of that chance.

'I've marked all the ends of them roof spars,' said the joiner. 'When yer've finished yer tea, start cutting 'em, Jacky boy, while I bed this wallplate on.'

The weather was still fine which was more than could be said for Jacky. He was thinking about Monica Nuttall who had lain more or less naked beside him just twelve hours ago.

268

'What?'

'That bang on yer head must have done more damage than yer think. Yer don't know whether yer on this earth or flamin' Fuller's. Frame yersen lad.'

'Sorry.'

Jacky could of course enlist his workmates' help in buying the necessary but would have to suffer the consequences. He'd never hear the end of it. There was a chemist just a couple of streets away. He'd call in at dinner time.

There were other people in the shop. He had hung around outside for ten minutes hoping for it to empty so he could dash in and out, but for every person who left another went in. He'd have to bite the bullet and go for it. Nothing ventured nothing gained – and there was a lot to gain here. He went in. Perhaps if he camouflaged his purchase amongst other less embarrassing items it might help. The chemist had white hair, a white coat and half-moon spectacles and would have looked out of place in any other job. Jacky scanned the fascinating labels on the rows of oak drawers behind where the man was serving an old woman. Tincture of myrhh, oil of cinnamon, charcoal, ipecacuanha, chloroform.

'Yes, young man?' said the chemist, resting his hands on the counter in the time-honoured fashion of all shopkeepers. The old woman was leaving the shop and someone else was coming in. Jacky tried to get his order out before that someone arrived at the counter

'Erm . . . a bottle of Aspros, some cough linctus and . . .' he lowered his voice, '. . . a packet of Durex please.'

The chemist looked at Jacky, unnervingly. First at his plastered eyebrow, then at him and asked, 'What sort of, er . . .?' He paused; Jacky panicked. 'What sort of cough have you got?'

'Oh, it's er, it's not for me it's for my mam. All for my mam. Everything.'

'Everything's for your mother?'

'Yes. It's sort of a throaty cough.'

The chemist placed the first two items on the counter then turned back to his shelves. 'And would your mother like the large or the . . . or the usual?'

'Oh . . . erm,' Jacky remembered Sandra Symonite's assessment of him. 'Large, please.'

'Large it is.' The chemist placed a packet of twenty-four contraceptives on the counter. 'These are ten shillings,' he said. 'Works out cheaper, tell your mother. Twenty-four for ten shillings; very good value, that.'

Jacky sensed that the person behind had taken an interest in his purchase. Getting out quickly would be ideal. But he didn't have enough money.

'Oh, I er, I thought they were only one and nine,' he said, lamely.

'One and nine for three, young man. I thought you asked for the large ... ah!' He looked at Jacky over the top of his glasses. 'Perhaps you misunderstood me.'

His eyes momentarily flickered down to Jacky's crotch, which Jacky instinctively covered with a hand. There was a snigger from behind. A man.

'I'll, er, I'll just take the three,' said Jacky. Pink-faced now.

The chemist sighed and swapped the packets over. 'That'll be four and a penny altogether.'

Jacky handed the money over and hurried to the door. The chemist called after him. 'If your mother wants the large contraceptives I'll change them for her.'

'Right,' said Jacky.

As he went out of the door he heard the customer say to the chemist, 'It'd be a shame to spoil her weekend.'

Jacky spun round, suddenly annoyed because the customer had made a dirty joke about his mother. But he didn't know what to say because the joke had been prompted by his own lies, so he hesitated a second and turned to leave. Just at that moment another customer came in and the door banged against Jacky's head. The same place as before. Although he was in pain he hurried out.

His eye wound had opened up again and blood was pouring down the side of his face, faster than before. He tried to stem it with his shirt sleeve and he knew the sensible thing would be to go back to the chemist and ask for help. But his embarrassment overcame his pain and he made his way back to the site where the joiner patched him up from the first-aid box and sent him to the hospital.

'It needs stitching, lad. Fer God's sake try not ter bang into owt else on the way there.'

*

270

Maureen was staring out of the window. Work forgotten. Wondering how her life had come to this. Whatever ill-fortune had befallen her, none of it had been of her doing. Raped and made pregnant; marriage of convenience, albeit to a lovely man; sent a telegram saying her lovely husband was dead; found a new man whom she really loved; resulting pregnancy; dead husband turns up; the man she really loved hanged for a murder he didn't commit; real murderer doing his damnedest to destroy her family – and almost succeeding; her eldest boy killed down the mine; and her one hope of love and happiness now lost to her. Life had thrown a lot of rocks at her. Then she allowed herself a smile and told herself not to grumble because, apart from that, things had been running smoothly.

Jacky came into view with his head swathed in bandages. It didn't surprise Maureen. People coming home in one piece would surprise her. He came through the door and offered no explanation for his injury, but said, 'I think I might have an idea what happened to the knife.'

His wounded eyebrow had needed four stitches – the bandage was mainly for protection after Jacky told the doctor he had bumped it twice in twelve hours.

'Short of supplying you with a crash helmet young man, this is the best we can do,' said a nurse.

Some of the hospital staff were kicking a ball around the hospital yard as he came out. It came towards him and he, without thinking, volleyed it back. But his aim was awry and it headed for a window, the top half of which was open. The ball went straight through without touching the sides. Some of the players laughed. One said, 'I should make yourself scarce, son. If the matron catches you, you'll have more than your head bandaged up. That's her office you've just kicked the ball into.'

Jacky hurried away, grateful that the window had been open. The usual football-through-the-window policy was 'Pay for your own china', and Jacky had paid for a fair bit of china in his career as a street footballer. As the ball went through the open window he'd had a flash of déjà vu. It was a replay of an evening when he and Roy and a few others had been playing football in the school-yard. Although it had been the middle of winter the caretaker, Mr Hepton, often left the boiler-room window open – to let out steam,

271

so he said. The kids reckoned it was to let out the smell of his farts. Sometimes he'd forget and leave it open all night. He wasn't the most conscientious of caretakers, wasn't Mr Hepton. That night Jacky had slammed the ball straight at the window, just like he had today. And it went straight through the open top half without touching the sides. Just like today.

Then a thought struck him. The boiler-room window was bang opposite Mumford's garden. A knife thrown with some force could have sailed clean across the playground and through the open window. That's if the window had been left open that night, which was quite possible knowing Mr Hepton's slackness. Mystery solved. Simple. Mumford's knife had ended up in the boiler room. So why hadn't Mr Hepton handed it in at some stage? If it had been covered in blood surely even Mr Hepton could have put two and two together.

Jacky found the answer with no difficulty. When he climbed through the window that night to retrieve the ball he had seen all sorts of boilers and pipes and junk and paraphernalia in there. It had taken him a while to find something as large as his football which had ended up underneath a big meter cupboard. A knife could be easily lost – especially if no one was looking for it. It could stay lost for years, still covered in blood and fingerprints. Mumford's fingerprints.

Jacky couldn't get home fast enough.

Chapter Thirty

'We can't involve Bill,' said Maureen, firmly.

'Why not?'

Ellie gave her brother a look. Jacky shrugged, not understanding. Maureen smiled at her son's naivety.

'Bill's wife's having a baby. He doesn't need me in the background.'

'But—'

'Jacky!' warned his sister. She tapped her temple with her fore-
finger. Ellie knew about the baby.

'I just don't see why Bill's wife having a baby should stop him
from helping us catch Mumford,' argued Jacky, reasonably.

'Whatever we do,' his mother told him, resolutely, 'we'll have
to do it without Bill's help.'

'So, we go to the police and ask them to search the school boiler
room for the murder knife,' suggested Jacky. 'It's dead simple.'

'There are one or two problems,' Ellie pointed out. 'Such as
why would the police want to spend valuable time trying to solve
a crime that they've already solved?'

'And how are we supposed to know Mumford threw the knife
over the wall?' added Maureen. 'Mumford told Ellie on the night
he attacked her. At the time she reported neither the attack nor him
telling her about the knife. What do you think the police will make
of that? Whatever we tell the police we'll have to get our story
straight. They might even need a warrant to search the boiler
room.'

'*I* wouldn't need a warrant,' Jacky said.

His mother and sister looked at him. Ordinarily Maureen would
have jumped down his throat, but he had a point. It was an avenue

273

worth exploring. 'So, you go into the boiler room and you find the knife,' she said, 'What then?'

Jacky shrugged, as if the answer was obvious. 'Then we report it to the police.'

Maureen shook her head. 'Report what? That you've found a knife in the school boiler room. Why should they be interested?'

'Supposing *I* found it,' Ellie suggested to her mother. 'I'm a bit more credible than our Jacky.'

'Eh?' Jacky protested.

'I haven't got a criminal record,' Ellie pointed out. 'If I find it, Mam goes to the police and tells them the whole story of Mumford trying to rape me, and why I didn't report it at the time. I'll wait in the boiler room. They'll have to come for me if only to do me for breaking and entering. Then I can show them the knife, tell them I heard him confess to his wife's murder and that I think they'll find his fingerprints and her blood all over it.'

The two of them looked at their mother. 'It's got to be worth a try, Mam,' Jacky said.

'We'll all go,' Maureen decided. 'If we find it, you two stay there and I'll go to the police. I might ring that awful reporter up and tell him to get his scrawny backside down there and do something useful for a change. If a reporter's there the cops will have to take us seriously.'

Jacky was beaming all over his face. This was the stuff. All three of them in it together. How could they lose?

'Shall we tell granddad?' he said.

'Why?' Ellie asked.

Jacky couldn't think of a reason. 'I just thought I'd ask,' he said.

'Best keep it between the three of us,' said Maureen. 'I think Charlie's got enough on with Enid wanting to get married.'

'What?' exclaimed Ellie and Jacky in unison.

'He seems a bit reluctant,' said Maureen. 'Personally I think it'll do him no harm.'

'I hope he hasn't got her into trouble.' Jacky said it with a straight face. 'After all I've told him about women.'

Maureen kept a straight face as well. 'I think *you* might be in trouble if he hears you talking like that.'

'She seems good fun,' Jacky remembered. 'We once saw them at a bowls match, me and Roy. They seemed to be getting on all right. They laughed a lot.'

'That's what Charlie needs,' Maureen said. 'That's what we all need from time to time. A good laugh.'

'Maybe we will when we've got Mumford,' said Jacky. 'Maybe we'll have a real good laugh. When shall we do it?'

'No time like the present.'

Maureen knew that if she gave herself time to think she'd see the sense in not doing it, and she didn't want that. Both her children had made an effort to clear Frank's name. It was about time she joined in. No matter what the consequences. The odds were heavily stacked against the knife being there but at least she'd have done something instead of sitting round waiting for life to throw yet another rock at her. And deep down she knew they'd find the knife. What Jacky said solved a mystifying puzzle.

Her heart was lifted. Bill was temporarily forgotten. She was taking charge of things, even if they went wrong. Jacky gave her a wide smile that told her he was proud of her. That he loved her. Perhaps in the balance of things it was enough. The love of two children weighed against all that life had thrown at her. Yes. Things were in her favour. More good than bad.

But she wouldn't object if a little more of the good stuff came her way.

It was nine-thirty in the evening and there was just enough light left in the day for the Gaskell family to see by. Some boys playing football in the school playground had been scared off by Jacky who had gone on ahead and told them the police were patrolling every so often because some kids had been trespassing on school property and vandalising the school. The coast was clear when his mother and Ellie arrived. Jacky had the boiler-room window open already, although he'd had to break the glass to do it.

'No one heard me,' he assured them. But he was wrong.

Mumford was in his back bedroom when he heard a faint tinkle of glass. He looked out of the window and saw Jacky leaning in through the boiler-broom window, trying to open it.

Mumford stared at the familiar figure for a second, then he recognised who was under the bandages. He immediately picked up the telephone to dial 999. It was only the second time in his life he had ever done this and it brought back a memory. His finger began to shake as it had that last time. He took it out of the dial and stared at it, amazed that a simple thing like a memory could have

275

such an effect. Then he smiled to himself. Of course it could. He'd been feasting off his memories for five years. His finger was steady by the time he tried again. This time he wasn't panicking.

'Emergency, which service please?'

'Police, please.'

Seconds after he'd reported the break-in, Ellie and Maureen arrived. Mumford was delighted. The police would get all three of them.

The two women fascinated him. Both of them beautiful. Both of them well worthy of all the trouble he intended taking with them. A vision of it flashed across his mind as he watched Ellie climb through the window, followed by Jacky.

What the hell were they doing? Was he being paranoid in thinking it was something to do with him – so near to his house? What connection did the school have with him? With the night he killed his wife?

'Oh, Jesus . . . no!'

Mumford's delight turned to horror as he realised what they were after. And they could well be on the right track. He had noticed the open boiler-room window on many occasions, mainly in winter, presumably to let the steam out. And it had been winter when he had thrown the knife over the wall. Thrown with plenty of force for it to have reached the window through which Ellie and Jacky had just disappeared. What if the knife was there? Covered in dried blood and his fingerprints. No, that would be ridiculous after all these years. It would have been found. But would it? What if it hadn't been found and was still lying there, waiting to hang him? The Gaskells obviously thought it was still there. Why? What the hell did they know about this?

Sweating from every pore he ran downstairs and into the garden. He must stop them. This was wrong. They were trespassing. Doing criminal damage to school property. Where were the police? He'd told them what was happening and who was doing it. What more did they need? They should be here by now. Arresting that bloody family who had caused him so much grief over the years. He shouted over the wall, although he couldn't see them from where he was, nor they him.

'Oi! Stop that. I know what you're doing.'

Maureen leaned in through the window. 'Someone's shouting at us. We'll have to ignore them. Any luck?'

'Not yet,' said Ellie. 'God! It's a right tip in here. That caretaker wants sacking. It stinks as well.'

'Fish,' observed Jacky. 'It stinks of fish. No wonder old Hepton kept the window open. Can I borrow the lamp, Ellie? I want to have a look around the back of the boiler.'

Ellie handed him the bike lamp, the one she'd used when she broke into Mumford's house. He found several empty beer bottles mixed in with old rags that had probably got knocked off the top of the boiler where Mr Hepton had put them after using one to open the hot boiler door. Jacky rummaged around among the crusty pile with some distaste, then he felt something hard. Very carefully he picked the rags away one by one until he revealed a knife. He tried to contain his excitement.

'I've found a knife,' he called back, as calmly as he could.

'What did he say?' Maureen asked, her head poking in through the window.

'He's found a knife,' Ellie told her. 'Don't touch it, Jacky.'

'I know. I'm not stupid.' He examined it very closely, and very delicately peeled away the remaining rags. 'It looks as if it's got dried blood on it. I reckon it's been here for years.'

'Let me have a look,' Ellie said. She took her brother's place and inspected the knife at close quarters. 'It definitely looks like dried blood,' she confirmed. 'It's covered in it.'

'It's got to be Mumford's knife,' Jacky said.

'Are you sure,' his mother asked, cautiously. 'We need to be sure.'

'Sure as we can be,' Ellie said, coming out from behind the boiler. 'I think you should ring the police, Mam.'

'Well, that's what we came for. I'll come straight back after I've rung them,' Maureen said. 'Take care, you two.'

She ran out of the school yard towards the telephone box which was about 300 yards away. It took her less than a minute to get there – a combination of fitness, elation and desperation. She was ringing the police as Mumford was clambering over the wall with the help of a water-butt he'd had to climb on to get over. Then she made a quick, cryptic call to Rodney Tripp.

'Mr Tripp, you want a story? Get your pathetic self down to Barr Road School. We've found the murder knife!' She didn't wait for an answer. If he didn't come, he didn't come. She had more important things to worry about.

277

Jacky had by now climbed out of the window, leaving his sister examining the knife. Mumford had armed himself with a rock from his garden and approached the boy from behind. His arm was raised as Ellie glanced up.

'Jacky!' she yelled.

Jacky turned to look at his sister, enough to turn a direct hit into a glancing blow, just above his ear. He fell to the ground with Mumford standing over him, madness in his eyes, ready to finish him off.

'We've found the knife. You're a dead man, Mumford!' Ellie was shouting, frantically, to distract him. She knew what he was capable of.

Mumford turned to look at her, but she was standing in the dark, out of his vision. Still dazed, Jacky made a grab for the man's legs and tried, unsuccessfully, to bring him to the ground. Ellie climbed out of the window and went to help her brother. Jacky was pushing himself to his knees with one arm and warding off Mumford's blows with the other as he hit him with the rock again and again. Ellie aimed a fierce kick at Mumford's groin. He gasped in pain and sank to his knees, yelping like an injured dog.

Jacky was covered in blood by now, most of it from the re-opened wound, and was the cause of much consternation to Ellie. Mumford was alternately moaning and screaming irrationally.

'What are you doing here? Trespassing. Criminal damage, that's what you're doing. Assault as well. Well, I've called the police, mister, and they'll have you this time. No mistake this time. What do you think of that?'

Jacky was in pain but he knew he'd won. He stood over his cowering, defeated adversary.

'We've found the knife, you bastard,' he said, with loathing in his voice. 'It's still covered in blood. Caked in the stuff. Your wife's blood. You threw it over your wall and it went straight through the boiler-room window. That's why no one ever found it. It'll be covered with your fingerprints. You're going to hang, Mumford. Hang by the neck until dead.'

'They can't hang two men for the same crime,' Mumford whined, miserably.

'They can – we've checked,' said Ellie, who hadn't. 'You'll be swinging from the end of a rope before Christmas.'

'It was a crime of passion!' wailed Mumford. 'He was in bed

with my wife. The court will understand.' He was weeping pathetically now.

'You're a murderer,' Ellie said, with absolute loathing for the man. 'You killed two people. Your wife and Frank McGovern.'

'They deserved to die,' he snivelled. 'I didn't mean to kill my wife. She shouldn't have been doing it with him.' Then his mood changed again, to a pathetic rage. Madness lit up his eyes. 'I had to kill her, don't you see. She deserved it, the dirty bitch!' He clenched his fist and jabbed his arm up and down in a stabbing motion, re-enacting the murder. 'Naked and with him. Naked. You dirty bloody bitch!'

Jacky and Ellie stared at him in amazement. His moods were swinging by the second, reliving the moment of his wife's violent death, and if they didn't know better they'd say he was enjoying the experience. There was a wild grin on his face as he stabbed away at his invisible victim.

'You as well, Mrs bloody high and mighty Halliwell. You're no bloody better.'

Jacky took a step backwards, away from this man who was clearly deranged. He put his arm around Ellie's shoulder as they watched Mumford raving on the ground. 'Who's he on about,' he asked. 'Who's this Mrs Halliwell?'

'No idea,' said Ellie.

'I think we might know.' The voice came from behind.

Jacky and Ellie spun round to see two policemen standing there, and Maureen just arriving.

'You were quick,' she said to the two constables, neither of whom was Bill, to her disappointment. 'I've only just got back from the phone box.'

'We were responding to a 999, madam. In fact I believe this is the very man who called us.' He nodded down to Mumford, who was sitting on the ground staring blankly into space with tears streaming down his face. 'Good job he did, really. We might have missed all that.'

'He's confessed to murdering his wife,' Jacky told them.

'I know, lad,' replied one of them. 'We heard him. You're young Gaskell, aren't you? Pity Mr Mumford didn't ring for an ambulance as well. Strikes me one would come in handy right now.'

Maureen saw the state of her son. What she first took to be dirt

279

in the dim light was blood. 'Oh my God, Jacky. Did he do this to you?'

Before Jacky could reply she hurled herself at Mumford, who curled up under her barrage of blows. It took both policemen to pull her off.

'I'm okay, Mam,' Jacky assured her. 'Most of this blood's from my old cut eye. It might need stitching up again.'

Maureen hugged both of her children to her and apologised to the policemen. 'I'm sorry about that, but this man's done so much harm to us all.'

'When you rang, Mrs Gaskell, you said something about a knife?'

'That's right, constable. The knife he killed his wife with. I believe it's still in that boiler room where my children found it. It's a pity the police didn't think to look there. It cost Jacky's dad his life.'

The two officers looked suitably guilty just as Rodney Tripp turned up at speed, his camera bouncing around his neck.

'Who are you, sir?' asked one of the policemen.

'He's Mumford's mate,' Jacky said.

'I'm a reporter,' said Tripp. He looked at Maureen. 'She rang me. Something about finding a murder knife?'

'You're quick on your feet, I'll say that for you,' Maureen said.

'I just live around the corner.'

Jacky confronted him. Tripp was already taking a photo of him as Jacky said, accusingly, 'Your mate's just confessed to murdering his wife. So all that stuff you wrote about my dad and about us was lies and rubbish.'

'Good, that's all good stuff,' said Tripp. He looked at the blood on Jacky's face. 'Did he do that to you, lad?'

'Some of it. The stuff under the bandage comes from a table tennis bat and a door.'

One of the policemen laughed at Jacky as the other pulled Mumford roughly to his feet. 'I believe your name is Victor Mumford is it not?'

Mumford nodded, sullenly.

'Victor Mumford. I am arresting you for the murder of your wife. You do not have to say anything but anything you do say will be taken down and may be used in evidence against you.'

'That'll do for starters,' said the other policeman. 'You can tell us all about Mrs Halliwell when we get down to the station. Hello, what have we here?'

He bent down and picked up the packet of Durex that had cost Jacky so dearly the previous day, as Rodney Tripp clicked away with his camera. Jacky was aghast. The policeman looked at Mumford. 'You won't be needing these, sir,' he said. 'Not where you're going.'

Mumford hadn't a clue what the policeman was talking about, but recovered just enough presence of mind to glare at Jacky, who was still considering the implications of losing what the policeman had just found. He'd have to go through all that again. Which was harder than catching murderers.

'Trust him to have something like that on him,' said a disgusted Ellie as Mumford was led away. 'Dirty old man.'

'It must have fallen out when we were fighting,' said Jacky, innocently – and truthfully.

A suspicion crossed Maureen's mind as she looked at him. Then she shook the thought from her head. Not her son. Not her Jacky boy. She took hold of Rodney Tripp's lapel.

'This time, for once in your life, tell the truth, Mr Tripp. You've played your part in the misery inflicted on my family. Now you can make amends.'

'You can be sure of that, Mrs Gaskell,' Tripp assured her. He couldn't believe his luck. This was the scoop of his life and these people, who had just cause to hate him, had given it to him on a plate. Let them down? He wouldn't need to. 'I'll tell the truth, the whole truth and nothing but the truth. I can't say fairer than that, can I?'

'Just so long as you do.'

It was Ellie who started it. She'd been waiting to sing the skipping song under these circumstances for years. Jacky joined in, instantly. Maureen had never sung it before but she did now and nudged Tripp into song as they all marched in step behind the two constables as they took Mumford to the police car. There was a smile on Maureen's face. This was a good time. She thought about Bill and wished he could have been there to share it. He would have enjoyed this moment.

Chapter Thirty-One

Mumford handed the pen back to the inspector and sank his head, despairingly, into his hands. The officer examined the signature and passed the signed confession sideways to his sergeant who nodded his approval.

'At least I won't be hanged,' Mumford muttered to himself. 'I couldn't handle the thought of that.' He looked up at the inspector. 'You did say they wouldn't hang me if I confessed to everything?'

Mumford's solicitor raised a surprised eyebrow and glanced at the inspector, who said, 'I don't think I said exactly that, Mr Mumford. All I said was that a full confession *might* go in your favour when it comes to sentencing. But you must remember you're responsible for three deaths. Two murders and a man wrongly hanged for one of them. The courts would need a good reason not to pass the same sentence on you. They may well view your case in a less than favourable light; allowing a man to be hanged for something you did. You've made us look bad, you see. The police, the judiciary, right up to the Home Secretary. And apart from anything else it's going to cost a fortune in compensation.'

'Compensation?' frowned Mumford. 'Who gets compensation?'

'A son has been deprived of his father. The circumstances are not straightforward but it doesn't alter the fact.'

'You mean the Gaskell brat?'

'The young man will be entitled to thousands, I shouldn't wonder, and all out of the public purse.'

'Jesus,' whined Mumford. 'I can't stand this. And all because I was stupid enough to throw the bloody knife away. I should have known it'd come back to haunt me. How could I have been so stupid?'

'Oh, I shouldn't trouble yourself about that, Mr Mumford,' said the inspector, briskly. The sergeant sitting next to him tried to suppress a grin, as did a constable standing by the door. 'You see, as it turned out, the knife young Gaskell found in the boiler room wasn't the murder weapon.'

'What?' Mumford's jaw dropped open, in disbelief. 'Not the murder weapon?'

'Nothing like it as a matter of fact.'

'How do you mean?'

There was a short burst of laughter from the back of the room. The sergeant spun round in his chair and glared at the constable. 'Constable, if you must snigger, do it in the corridor.'

The inspector turned to look at the chastened young policeman. 'I appreciate there is an irony here, constable, but we have to be professional. This is a very serious matter.'

'Yes, sir. Sorry, sir.'

The inspector returned his attention to Mumford. 'Sorry about that, Mr Mumford. He's very young, but when you hear this, perhaps you'll appreciate the constable's mirth. You see, it was a fish-gutting knife that young Gaskell found, nothing like the murder weapon, which we believe was probably a jack-knife. The knife the boy found was covered in dried blood all right, but it was fish blood. The school caretaker apparently lost it years ago. He's a bit of a fisherman and he used to gut his fish in the boiler room – which is the main reason he often left the window open. People thought it was to let the steam out, but it was more to do with the smell. The man needs a bit of a talking to, if you ask me.'

Mumford seemed to sink within himself, gibbering. 'What? Not the knife. So, I'd no need to . . . Oh my God, it wasn't even my knife.' He suddenly uncoiled and sprang to his feet, spitting bile at the inspector, who sat back in his chair. 'You tricked me, you bastard! You tricked me into signing a confession. You told me you'd got the murder weapon and you hadn't. My confession was obtained under . . . I don't know, something or other . . . false pretences . . . whatever it is. It doesn't count!'

He was banging his fists on the table to the dismay of his solicitor. The young constable came forward and, very forcefully, sat Mumford back in his chair.

'Thank you, constable,' said the sergeant. 'You see, it's not all fun and games.'

'No, sarge.' The constable was pleased to be back in the sergeant's good books.

The inspector leaned forward. 'Mr Mumford. I think you'll find your confession *does* count. It counts very much.' He looked at Mumford's solicitor, who gave the briefest nod.

'As far as I know,' continued the inspector, 'the only person who claimed the knife in the boiler room was the actual murder weapon was young Jacky Gaskell. Kids eh? Apparently he has a bit of a bee in his bonnet about you. We certainly made no such claim. Never mentioned the knife as I recall.' He looked at the sergeant for his confirmation.

'Never a mention, sir.'

'Thank you, sergeant. Personally I had my doubts about that knife from the start. Still, all's well that ends well. Now that you've very kindly told us the truth, we can take it from there. Constable, show Mr Mumford to his cell. Better remove his belt and shoelaces. The balance of his mind looks to be a bit disturbed and we wouldn't want him to come to any harm.'

Chapter Thirty-Two

Monica opened the door to Jacky's knock.

'Hello Jacky. Glad you could make it. Thought you might be too busy with everything that's been going on. It was in the paper, you know.'

'Yeah, I read it.'

'Why's your head bandaged up? Has it got worse?'

He stepped forward, into the light, his face a mass of cuts and bruises.

'Good grief! Look at you. What happened?'

'I banged my head again.'

'I suppose that'll have been Mumford.'

Jacky nodded. It was mostly the truth. She looked good. Her breasts pushed against her pale-blue silk blouse which was unbuttoned far enough down to display more than a hint of cleavage. She obviously hadn't changed her mind. Jacky wondered how she'd take it when he told her he didn't have any contraceptives.

He'd been at the hospital for ages; as bad luck would have it, being stitched up by the same doctor as before.

'Usual, young man?' the doctor said. Then he examined Jacky's latest wounds. 'No. I don't think four stitches is going to be enough. I think we might need a sewing machine to get you back to fighting fitness.'

'Does it cost extra for the jokes?' Jacky said to the nurse. 'Because if it does I want proper ones.'

From the hospital he went home to bed. Most of the next morning he spent at the police station and after that, Rodney Tripp had kept him all afternoon as Jacky told his side of the story.

285

It was a cathartic few hours with the reporter. Jacky told of Booth's cruelty and the deliberate lies that had robbed him of a chance to get to grammar school and how Booth's lies in court had got Jacky sent to reform school.

'I'll have to do some checking before I put this in,' Tripp said, half to himself. 'If it's right it'll cost Booth his job – and his pension, I should think.'

'I want you to put it all in.'

'If it's right, I will, lad, I promise.'

'It's right.'

'Then it goes in.'

He told of Miss Evershed's unjust caning and the lies of the woman in York which had ended up in Aaron being killed.

'I read about the dead woman in the car,' Tripp said. 'I knew nothing about the woman who fitted you up.'

'You can check with the governor of the school.'

'I will, lad. If it's right, it goes in. You've led a full life for a lad of sixteen. Somebody should write a book about you.'

'Maybe they will, one day.'

'And what would they call it?'

Jacky thought for a while, then smiled at a memory of his pal Aaron. 'Last Tram To Hollywood,' he said.

'What?'

'You wouldn't understand.'

Rodney scribbled on as Jacky related how Mumford had farted and caused him to fall off Ellie's back and how, on another occasion, he'd only just stopped Mumford raping her. He showed Tripp the watch his dad had been given for his bravery and the additional inscription to commemorate how his brother had been equally brave, giving up his life trying save his pals down the pit. Tripp kept saying 'Wow!' and 'Marvellous stuff!' as Jacky unfolded his story. He kept the fact that Charlie was Frank's dad to himself; that was his granddad's business, and he had enough on marrying Enid. Apparently he was so delighted with the news that he'd set a date. Jacky hoped he wouldn't live to regret it.

'I'll have this in one of the top nationals,' Tripp said. 'You'll be famous next week, Jacky boy.'

'Will you be putting everything in?'

'Everything that's right. Everything that's not *subjudice* – and a fair bit that might be. If he's confessed we're on safe ground. He's for the high jump is Mumford. Dead men don't sue.'

Tripp was careful to stay clear of Maureen, who might well have had the presence of mind to ask him to split his payment with her family.

'*You* owe me some money,' Jacky said.

Tripp's heart sank. He rubbed his long chin and asked, innocently, 'What money?'

'Half a crown from when you took my photo for the paper when Frank was hanged.'

Tripp gave him a relieved smile and a ten-shilling note.

Jacky looked at it and said, 'I've got no change.'

'Keep it. It's nothing compared to the compensation you'll get.'

'Thanks,' Jacky said. 'What compensation?'

'For your dad being wrongly hanged. Innocent man's life. It should be worth a nice few quid. Thousands I shouldn't wonder. Frank would have wanted you to have it.'

'Frank? Did you know him?'

'Well, not to talk to. But I know he'd have wanted proper compensation for his lad. Any father would.'

'I suppose so. Never thought of it.'

'You've had a lot on your mind, lad. But you've got mental resources. I can see that, just by talking to you. Very strong mental resources for a lad of your age.'

Unfortunately Jacky hadn't had the mental resources to go through another ordeal in the chemist's. Monica led him through to the living room then took him in her arms and held him to her.

'I think you're a hero . . . and a better detective than all those who reckoned your dad did it. I hope they all get what's coming to them.'

'Well, I got it all wrong about the knife, but the end result was good.'

They sat down on the settee without taking their arms from around each other. 'By the way,' she said. 'Those things I asked you to get. It doesn't matter if you couldn't manage it.'

She *had* changed her mind. Pity he hadn't known about it sooner. 'Actually, I did get some but—'

'Really? I hope you didn't go to any trouble.'

'Trouble – how do you mean?'

'It's just that I've heard some boys find it very embarrassing to ask for them.'

'Do they really?'

'So, you got some then?'

'I did, but I lost them when the thing with me and Mumford kicked off. So, it's as well you don't want to. We can just watch the telly or something.'

She smiled and kissed him. 'Who says I don't want to?'

'I thought you s—'

Monica pressed a finger to his lips. 'What I meant was, you'd no need to get them because I've got some. I nicked them from Mum and Dad's bedroom when I got back from the youth club. They haven't said anything. I mean, they can hardly ask their dear, sweet, butter-wouldn't-melt-in-her-mouth daughter if she's nicked a packet of frenchies from their room.'

In the fading, evening light of the room she looked so beautiful. There was a softness about her and a fragrance that quickened Jacky's pulse and he knew the excitement of the last couple of days wasn't over yet. 'So, I didn't need to get any?' he said.

'Not really. Anyway, I'm glad I didn't put you to any trouble.'

'No, none at all.'

Bill had been there an hour, taking over from a constable on the late shift. It was three o'clock in the morning and the thief hadn't turned up at the council yard yet. At least they'd given Bill a radio car to sit in, so he could call for help if need be. Whoever was taking the scrap metal was a thief of regular habits. Every second Tuesday in the month. He was a very tidy thief as well – always locked up after himself. That's why it had gone un-noticed. All the council workers had suspected each other. It could have been going on for years but a new checking system had been put in place and it became fairly clear it was an outside job. But Bill was only vaguely interested in the job. He had other problems.

There were pros and cons to Pam's being pregnant and, having now resigned himself to losing Maureen, he had been very much looking forward to becoming a dad. So much so, that the events earlier that evening had been a kick in the teeth and he didn't know whether he was coming or going.

Being on early turns meant he usually slept until the evening, but the sound of next door's radio coming through the wall of their bungalow had woken him early. It would be his neighbour's son, home from school – he'd have to have another word with them about this. Then he stared at the ceiling and found a smile from somewhere. A son or daughter would give meaning to his marriage. The clock said four-fifteen which meant he'd only had five hours sleep, but rather than catch another couple of hours he decided to get up.

There was a mixture of consternation and guilt on Pam's face when he walked into the lounge, still in his pyjamas, yawning and rubbing the sleep from his eyes.

'I'll have to have another word about that damned lad next d—' His eyes alighted on a suitcase, then on his wife, who was sitting in her wheelchair, all dressed up. 'What's happening? Where are you going?'

It took Pam some time to marshal her thoughts. 'I was hoping to be gone by the time you got up,' she said, quietly.

'Gone . . . gone where?'

'Bill, it's for the best.'

'For the best? What's for the best?'

'I'm leaving you. We don't love each other.'

'Leaving me? You can't leave me.'

'We've been living a lie, Bill. I don't want to spend my life living a lie.'

'Pam, what the hell are you talking about? We're having a baby. It's a fine time to suddenly discover we've been living a lie. You can't just leave and take my baby with you.'

'Bill,' she said, with an edge to her voice now. 'I don't want to live with you any more. I've found someone else.'

Bill shook his head and sat down on the settee. 'This is ridiculous,' he said.

'What's ridiculous . . . another man finding me attractive?'

'I didn't mean that? Another man? Where the hell have you got another man from?'

'I can get out of the house on my own, you know. I get to all sorts of places while you're out playing cops and robbers.'

'I know you do but—'

'But who would want a cripple? I've still got my looks – and everything that matters is in full working order. I still have my needs, Bill – which you were never keen to satisfy.'

'What are you telling me, Pam – that someone else has been satisfying these needs?'

She looked up at him. The guilt had gone from her eyes and was replaced by a look of defiance. 'Yes,' she told him. 'Someone else has been doing just that. Someone able-bodied, who can see beyond these wheels. Someone who's told me he loves me – which is something you never have.'

'What about our baby?'

She shook her head at his naivety. 'Bill, when I persuaded you to have sex with me a few weeks ago it was to cover myself in case things didn't work out for me. You see, I hadn't told him I was pregnant, and I didn't know what his reaction would be.'

'Told who what?'

'Told the father of my baby that I was pregnant.'

'Father of . . . you mean I'm not the father?'

'No.'

'Oh.'

The disappointment he felt took him by surprise. He was suddenly freed from an obligation that had stifled his life for nineteen years, but at the cost of a child he had thought was to be his.

'Could it be mine?'

'I'm three months pregnant, Bill. Work it out for yourself.'

'I'm no good at working stuff like that out, as well you know. I suppose that's why you thought you'd get away with pretending it's mine if the worst came to the worst.'

'I certainly didn't think you'd be suspicious of a wife in a wheelchair. You wouldn't even have bothered working out the dates.'

'I don't suppose I would.'

'And I don't suppose you're bothered that I've been with another man.'

Bill didn't answer, he didn't need to. Pam's infidelity didn't trouble him a bit, but the news that the child wasn't his troubled him. His thoughts turned to Maureen and how she would react to all this. Would she have him back after he'd ditched her in favour of an unborn child? His emotions were in such a turmoil he didn't know what to think.

'So, this . . . this man . . . do I know him by the way?'

'His name's Vernon. You might have seen him. He runs the philately society.'

'Ah, Vernon.' Bill had seen the man on a couple of occasions when he had dropped Pam off at the stamp-collectors' club in Forster Street Methodist Hall, but he wasn't a man who commanded much attention and Bill couldn't bring up much of an image of him, except that he had a beard.

'He works at the hospital,' she told him. 'He's a very nice man. Plays the cello as well. There's all sorts of things we can do together.'

'I'm glad.' Bill meant it. 'So, this Vernon's okay about the baby, is he?'

'Yes, he is. I didn't think he would be, but he is. In fact I wasn't going to tell him. I thought he might run a mile.'

'And if he did, you always had me to fall back on.'

'Something like that,' she admitted without a hint of shame. 'I was hardly going to risk having to cope on my own. Anyway, you'd have loved being a father.'

'Jesus, Pam – have you heard yourself? Nothing matters in this world but you.'

'In my condition I have to look after number one at all times. I learned that the night you broke my back.'

She said it so casually, as though it were a matter of in-disputable fact that Bill was the sole cause of her paralysis. He didn't bother to protest. It was by no means the first time she'd laid the guilt card on him.

'When did you tell him?' he enquired.

'A few days ago. He was really happy about it. He wants me to go and live with him. I left a note for you on the table explaining everything.'

Bill glanced at the note but made no move to pick it up – there was too much going on inside his head. Surely this left the way clear for him to get together with Maureen. Or was it too late? She was a proud woman, not one to be messed around. Perhaps he should have been as decisive as Pam and put himself first. Maybe the word wasn't *decisive*, maybe the word was *selfish*.

'You used this baby to get me to pack Maureen in,' he said, 'knowing full well the baby wasn't mine. I probably won't get her back now.' He gave her a look of admonishment, but saw no remorse in her eyes. 'You're not bothered, are you?'

'Nope. Why should I be bothered about stopping my husband sleeping with another woman?'

'That's just it,' Bill said. 'I wasn't sleeping with her.'

'And you expect me to believe that?'

'Believe what you like. You made sure Kathy McAllister couldn't have me, and now Maureen. Is it your life's ambition to stop me from being happy? You could have sorted this out without splitting me and Maureen up.'

Pam shrugged her disinterest and examined her freshly painted fingernails. Bill's eyes went to the suitcase.

'How are you going to carry that?'

'*I'm* not going to carry it.'

'Who's . . .? Oh, I see.'

'He's due here any minute.'

A car pulled up outside.

'Would you mind?' Pam indicated with her head that he should leave the room. It would be better if he weren't there when Vernon arrived.

'Oh, right. I'll, er . . . I'll leave you to it, then.' He thought for a minute then added, 'There's something I'd like you to tell this Vernon of yours.'

'What's that?'

'Tell him . . . tell him thanks.'

Bill went back into the bedroom and sat on the bed until the quiet movements in the lounge ended with the front door being closed and Pamela leaving his life for good. If only her timing had been better, he could have been with Maureen to share her good day with her. Trust him to bail out just before their big moment arrived. He knew Jacky would come through somehow. He was that sort of kid.

A clip-clopping of hooves disturbed his thoughts and a horse and cart pulled up outside the council yard gate. Bill shook his head and smiled to himself. They should have known. He radioed through to the station: 'Hello, it's Bill . . . sorry sarge . . . Bravo six three. Our villain's arrived. I'll need some help. Preferably someone who can drive a horse and cart . . .'

The ramshackle old thief climbed, laboriously, off his cart, followed by a large, slow dog that stepped on to the pavement and flopped into a recumbent heap.

As he watched the crime being committed, Bill's mind was miles away. He knew exactly what he was going to do. He came off his shift at ten. Straight round to Maureen's. Grovel. Down on bended knee if necessary. Some self-sacrifice might sway things. Shave off his beloved moustache.

Willie O'Keefe lifted up his eye patch so that he could see what he was doing. Two dimensional vision was no good for this job. Over the years the thing for getting stones out of horses' hooves had proved ideal for picking the old, iron padlock on the gate to the council yard where scrap metal was stored by council workers. He never took enough to raise suspicion. Greed caught everyone out in the end – everyone except Willie. He'd been picking that lock with that same jack-knife for umpteen years. He thought back to the night he found it. The night he'd gone to strip the lead flashing off the school roof. It had been bad enough having to hang around up there, freezing, waiting for them two kids to finish playing their football. 'Aha!' Willie cackled to himself as the padlock clicked open. Then there was all this shouting going on over the wall and something metallic had clattered on to the tarmac. What the hell was that? It was curiosity that caused him to shout at the boys and scare them off.

In the dim light it had looked like a mucky old jack-knife, not worth climbing down for. He had picked it up and was back on the roof, still giving the knife a good rub with a rag, when he heard cop cars and doors banging and people shouting. Christ! He'd slid down the drainpipe and whipped the old nag near to death racing her through the streets. He took a good scare that night. You never know who they're after. That's why he went over to Dublin the very next day for a couple of weeks. Stayed a couple of months, just in case.

He didn't get any lead that night, just the old knife that someone had thrown away. At first, in the dim light, it had looked such a dirty, crappy old gadget that he'd half a mind to leave it, but he was glad he hadn't. It had earned its keep had that knife. Good job he'd picked it up.

No one else would have wanted it.